A
FEARLESS
HEART

A FEARLESS HEART

ELIZABETH COLE

SKYSPARK BOOKS

PHILADELPHIA, PENNSYLVANIA

SkySpark Books
Philadelphia, Pennsylvania
skysparkbooks.com
inquiry@skysparkbooks.com

Publisher's Note: This is a work of fiction. Names, characters, places, and incidents are a product of the author's imagination. Locales and public names are sometimes used for atmospheric purposes. Any resemblance to actual people, living or dead, or to businesses, companies, events, institutions, or locales is completely coincidental.

Ordering Information:
Quantity sales. Special discounts are available on quantity purchases by corporations, associations, and others. For details, contact the "Special Sales Department" at the address above.

A FEARLESS HEART / Cole, Elizabeth. – 1st ed.
ISBN-13: 978-1-942316-57-2

♑

1812

A raw wind whipped over the bare meadows and gardens, chilling the woman who walked through them. Her gloved fist clutched the top of her black cape to keep the wind from ripping the garment open. Even so, the gust pushed her hood off, revealing dark curls that instantly tangled in the rough air. She pulled the hood back up and knelt on the garden path, reaching out to press her hand into the frost-rimed soil of a garden bed.

Despite the dour, cloudy sky and the cruel weather, Arcadia Osbourne smiled to herself. Though winter seemed to have a deadly grasp on the land, spring lurked underneath, ready to surge forth. She could feel the soil's softness, and almost hear the awakening of the still-subterranean seeds. One warm, gentle sunny day should do it.

Then she lost her smile. This spring would be different from all the rest. She was alone now, and there were precious few hands to tend the extensive grounds and give her the necessary time to care for the truly rare specimens that were her responsibility to maintain.

No, she wasn't alone, she quickly reminded herself. Though her brother lived in London, Cady knew that she could reach out to him at any time. Their relationship was the sort that didn't require constant attention. A quiet yet bone-deep love had grown up amid some harsh times and intense scrutiny from their very demanding father. If Cady ever needed Trevor, he'd be there in a twinkling.

She noticed a spot of color against the dark soil. A plant was just pushing through the earth—a mere speck with two minuscule leaves. She put her finger under one leaf, though she knew that these first leaves, called cotyledons, did not resemble the identifying shape that all future leaves on this planet would share.

"What are you?" she asked the seedling. "A violet? A moonflower? Or something a little different? I'll just have to keep an eye on you and see, hmm?"

As she regarded the tiny sprout, she was startled by an unexpected movement. A gray spider jumped from the mound of earth to the back of her gloved hand. She shook it off, standing up so quickly that she nearly overbalanced. The pleasure of seeing the new plant evaporated in the aftermath of the spider's arrival.

Did it bite her? No, it couldn't have. She was wearing thick cotton gloves. But what if it had bitten through the fabric? No, she'd have felt it. She would have *had* to have felt it, wouldn't she?

She looked back at the house, feeling that it was too far away now. How had she been so silly as to walk so far from the safety of the buildings? She'd been blithely confident earlier, sure that nothing could happen on a simple walk.

"I'll go back and wash my hands and apply alcohol to the spot," she muttered to herself. "No, take the gloves off first, and check for a hole in the fabric on the right hand. No need to fret over nothing. It's nothing."

Walking briskly back toward the house, she shook her head in disgust. She told herself *it's nothing* a hundred times a day, and the words always failed to reassure her. She knew exactly where the spider had landed, and she focused on the sensations there. Did her skin feel warmer? Was there pain?

No, but there might be soon. She had to stay alert, examine her skin for changes, be very, very careful to not get herself into a situation like this again, and also careful to not worry the servants or let her concern show, because there was very likely nothing to worry about. And she could hardly maintain order over the house and the estate if she were considered touched in the head, could she? The worries piled upon themselves, making it hard to breathe.

Inside the house, the footman Vernon greeted her. "Ah, back already, Lady Arcadia? You must be chilled to the bone." Vernon had served her family for decades, starting out as a scullery lad. He was really too old to serve as a footman now, but who else was available?

"It was brisk," Cady admitted, unclasping her long cape.

Vernon took the proffered cape and stood uncertainly for a moment, until she realized he was also waiting for the gloves.

"Oh, I'll just keep these," she said quickly. "I wanted to look at the stitching before I forget."

"Yes, my lady." The slight crease of his forehead betrayed that he wanted to ask *why*, but he was far too well trained to do so. Still, his gaze was a little reproving, as if Cady had been found wanting in some way. It was a look rather like her father's…and considering that Vernon had worked in the house under her father's rule, the similarity in expression made sense. This whole house was a reflection of her father's ideals.

"I'm going to my room," she said. "Will you tell Cook to have some hot tea and some of those scones sent up?"

She ascended the stone staircase to the upper floor,

conscious of how odd it was to wear the long, heavy, outdoor gloves while parading down the hall. Once in her room, she sagged against the door. Here she was safe. No one to watch her peel off the gloves and stare intently at the right-hand one, stretching and pulling the fabric to ascertain if a spider had nibbled through the layer. Nothing.

"There's nothing. It's a spider, not a pair of scissors." Annoyed at herself, she flung the gloves onto the back of a chair, then raised her hand to the light from the window, tilting it to see if any bump was rising, or the skin was reddening, or she was showing imminent signs of falling prey to the first arachnid of the season.

Nothing.

"Of course there's nothing, Cady. It's *always* nothing."

Bold talk, but her heart was still beating a pattern of *what-if, what-if, what-if* inside her rib cage.

A meow interrupted her worries, and a circle of tabby stretched and stood up on the cushion of a chair near the fireplace. The cat blinked slowly, meowing again.

"Oscar, you have a cat bed of your very own not five steps away. Why must you insist on sleeping on people's furniture?"

She moved to the fireplace and bent to pet the cat. Oscar started purring immediately and pushed his head up to receive firmer pettings and scratches. Cady always admired the cat for his ability to not worry about anything. He'd been discovered years ago as a stray, hiding in one of the sheds. A groundskeeper had been about to drown him, the common practice for stray kittens. But Cady and Trevor had come upon the scene just in time and begged and pleaded for the cat's life to be spared.

In repayment for this mercy, Oscar did practically nothing. He slept all day and most of the night, and he tended to meow loudly at shadows for no particular reason. He sometimes decided to curl up on Cady's own pillow, shoving her to the side in the middle of the night. He occasionally left dead mice inside her slippers.

But Cady loved him all the same. Love is a gift to given, not a prize to be earned.

There was a knock on the door, and Cady stood up straighter. "Yes, bring the tray in!" she called, forcing her tone to be light and cheerful.

"Tea for you," her maid, Martha, announced, carrying a huge tray to the low table by the fireplace. "We'll have snow tonight, I shouldn't wonder. Those clouds look nasty."

"If we do, it will be the last snow of the season," Cady said. "The wild onions are up, and even the garden plants are waking. I don't suppose there have been any takers for those positions I asked Mr Rundle to post? I need a groundskeeper, or we'll all be living in a tanglewood come June."

"He's not mentioned it, but I'm sure we'll have new faces here soon." Martha's optimism was brittle, and Cady knew why. Despite offering greater than usual wages, she still couldn't convince locals to come to the estate. Not with the rumors that began to fly the moment her father, the Earl of Calderwood, passed away.

"Some men to help out would be best, I think. The dogs want exercise, not to mention the horses."

"Perhaps I could walk them…" Cady began to say, though she already doubted herself.

Martha must have been having her own doubts. "Nonsense, my lady. You couldn't possibly manage them on your own."

Her father's wolfhounds were massive creatures able to take down a full-grown deer. Cady lacked the physical strength to hold their leashes should they spot prey. However, the other reason that she refused to walk them (or spend any time with them now) was that she was afraid of them. She hadn't always been. As a little girl, she remembered curling up against the dogs and drowsing before a fire on a winter's day. But now that her father wasn't around, she was always worried that the dogs would turn on her, decide she was the prey, and then tear her to pieces.

Sighing, Cady turned her attention to the tea tray. "Is this all for me, or did I invite ten guests and just forgot about it?" Another poor joke. There hadn't been ten guests at the house for months. She dipped her finger in the dish of cream and then held her finger toward Oscar, who leaned over to lick it off. His yellow eyes gleamed with satisfaction.

"All for you, miss—*not* that cat—and I do hope you'll partake of some of it. You're wasting away. Cook made her onion soup and there's fresh bread and that good white cheese from over the hill. Will you want supper downstairs?" she asked.

Cady shook her head, wearied by the maid's questions. Her own servants ordered her around all the time! "No. Just a tray up here again. About six, and then I'll go to my lab."

"And stay up all night working on your experiments. You'll work yourself sick."

"It's not work, it's just a way to pass the time." Cady couldn't explain the intricacies of botany to Martha, who regarded plants as either useful in a salad, or weeds to be yanked out of the pathway to the dairy. And she certainly couldn't confide the more esoteric hopes she had in her chemical experiments, which utilized the exotic specimens growing in a special glasshouse next to her laboratory. The servants did not like her laboratory, and it was the one place where Cady could count on being alone.

A dark spot moving on the china caused her to jump, and she tipped the plate as she grabbed for it. The darkness fell to the floor.

"Was that a spider?" she gasped.

The maid leaned over with a frown and plucked up the dark spot. "Goodness no. Just a currant that escaped the scone. Besides, it's too early in the year for spiders."

"Of course. My mistake." Cady tried to look calm. How she wished she had someone to talk to, someone she could trust to listen and not laugh in her face when she recited her litany of fears. To hope for someone to *solve* her problems did not even occur to her…and if it had, she would have instantly dismissed the hope as too ambitious. No, the mere presence of a friend would be miracle enough.

There was her brother…but no. She could not add to his complications by piling on her own amorphous, probably entirely fanciful fears.

"Enjoy your tea, my lady," Martha said on her way out.

Cady maintained the proper posture and the light smile until the door closed and the footsteps faded down the hall. Only then did she carefully set the teacup down and curl up into a tight ball on the armchair, folding herself into a tiny, compressed seed. Oscar saw his opportunity and pounced upon the forgotten dish of cream.

Had she also imagined the spider outside in the garden? Was she prodding at her hand, looking for a bite from a creature that was not just harmless, but maybe never even existed?

"I am losing my mind," she whispered. "God help me, I am completely losing my mind."

♑

THAT SAME EVENING, MILES AWAY in London, a large and utterly boring building stood on one corner where Powell and Gate Streets met. A painted placard on one brick wall announced it as a prime location for commerce and progress…which in practice meant that offices were available to let.

A number of firms had their offices in the building, from a tiny one-desk affair rented out by an elderly gentleman offering Russian, German, and French translation services, to a publisher of cheap novels that occupied an entire floor of the building. Nearly all of these businesses were exactly what they purported to be.

One was not.

Despite the hour, a man walked up the steps and opened the far left door. An observer would first notice that he looked dead tired. His eyes were accented by dark circles, and his blond hair hadn't seen the benefit of a comb for several days. His outfit was unremarkable for a laborer, though few laborers came to this building. A shabby greatcoat, perhaps a castoff from an employer, kept off the chill of the night air. His footwear was difficult to discern in the slowly rising mist.

Gabriel Courtenay went inside and proceeded to pass by every door of every business—which was just as well, considering that all the businesses were long closed at this hour. Not that most people would look upon him as a good prospect, with his rough clothing, his unshaven face, and the general air of weariness he exuded.

When he reached the fifth floor, Gabe shuffled down the long hallway and knocked at a door with a sign declaring it to be the offices of Circle Imports. He knocked in a very particular rhythm, showing more energy than his appearance would suggest.

A moment later, the door opened.

A young woman stood there, with ash-blonde hair pulled up in a careless bun. Rather than a high-waisted gown popular at the time, she wore a white shirtwaist and a black wool skirt that was so long it brushed the wooden floors. She regarded him with a critical eye, then said, "Well. If we'd known you had to dig your way out of a grave to get here, we could have delayed the meeting."

"Do I look that terrible, Miss Chattan?"

"Frankly, yes." She stepped aside and gestured for him to enter, then locked the door behind him. This business did not care for uninvited guests. "Aries is in his office. Go on in."

Gabe nodded. As far as he could tell, Aries was always in his office, for Circle Imports was the front for an organization of spies known as the Zodiac. The group was under the jurisdiction of the British government (an obscure branch, to be sure—so obscure that Gabe didn't know which branch it was, or whether the other people working there even knew that the Zodiac existed).

At any one time, there were twelve active agents, headed by Aries—Aries being the first sign of the Zodiac. Aries reported to the Astronomer, who was the true head of the organization. What he or she did with all the information the agents gathered Gabe could only guess. He'd never met the Astronomer, and he never would. Clandestine agencies thrived on mystery. In fact, Gabe had only met three other Signs in the course of his whole career.

One of those Signs was Julian Neville, the man code-named Aries. He worked at all hours, like a spider at the center of a web, pulling this string and that string, gathering signals and weaving a complex pattern to discern what the spies of Europe were plotting next.

When Gabe pulled out a chair and sat down with a little huff of relief, Aries smiled at him briefly. "Capricorn, you're alive. Well, that's something."

"That last assignment was a little difficult," Gabe admitted. "I'd hoped for a bit of a breather."

"I wish I could oblige you. However." Julian slid a sheet of paper across the desk.

Gabe picked it up, reading a list of names:

Sir Michael Montgomery

John Worthham

Wilfred Cawson, Baron Murol

Charles Tompsett

Lewelleyn Parrish

He frowned, matching the names to vague memories of reading news reports over the last few months. "Some of these men are dead."

"All of them are dead," Julian clarified. "The most recent died this week, which is why you probably didn't hear about it. News takes a while to get over to the Continent. And you have been busy."

"What's the connection?" Gabe asked, still processing the names.

"That is what I'd kill to find out. They're all men in positions of importance, whether in government or business or merely by the fact of their lineage. All believed to be very healthy, and with no hint of any physical problems that might turn serious. Yet they have all died. And not by accident or misadventure. They go to sleep…and they never wake up."

Gabe shook his head. "Impossible."

"Precisely. This isn't a coincidence. They were killed."

At that moment, Chattan stepped up to the desk, placing a cup of strong, hot tea at Gabe's right hand.

"Bless you," he murmured, taking the cup and immediately drinking it down. Chattan nodded and sat down on a chair at the side of the desk, halfway between the men.

When he finished (Chattan made excellent tea), Gabe tapped the paper on the desk, picking up his line of thought. "There must have been inquests to determine the cause of death, especially if the men were important figures, and the deaths so unexpected."

"Naturally, there were inquests, and in most cases a doctor examined the body. Not all, of course. Sometimes the families wouldn't permit it, and these are not families you'd want to cross."

"Of the bodies that were examined, what were the conclusions?"

"In each case, death was swift. No signs of struggle, and no one who was nearby the victims recalls a cry for help. As far as the doctors could tell, the victim's heart just…stopped."

"Poison?" Gabe asked.

"It would seem," Julian agreed. "However, most poisons leave traces. Doctors can perform tests to detect chemicals left behind in a drinking glass, or find out what food was eaten. The bodies usually reveal the presence of poison by a peculiar smell, or discoloration in the skin. But in these cases, there's been nothing. We have a doctor working to develop another test, but it will take time."

Gabe frowned. "If there's nothing to find, then how do we know they're all connected?"

Aries glanced at Chattan, who said, "The killer left a sign. At each location one of these was found."

Julian tossed several calling cards on the table. Gabe picked one up and examined the image on the top: a black-ink engraving of multiple flowers.

"What are these pictures of?"

Chattan read off from a paper, "Belladonna, foxglove, and oleander." She looked up. "All famous for being deadly."

"Read the back," Julian suggested.

He flipped over one card and read aloud, "*Et in Arcadia ego*. My Latin is rusty… *And in Arcadia I am*?"

"It's usually translated as 'Even in Arcadia, I am here,'" Julian said. "The *I* is understood to refer to Death. The meaning is that even in Paradise, Death is inevitable."

"So it's a memento mori. I guess that's fitting to put by a dead body. Though no one would mistake London for any kind of paradise."

Chattan gathered the cards again. "I get the impression that the killer has a personal stake in this."

Julian lifted a warning hand, saying, "Whereas I suspect it's just nonsense designed to make us *think* there's a personal reason. The victims are all involved in politics. These killings must be politically motivated, just more violent than the usual methods."

"Why not both?" Gabe asked, thinking as he spoke. "It could be someone's own vendetta against some politicians who have done something they dislike. The victims…are they of the same party? Or have they all voted the same way on a particular issue?"

Chattan was already shaking her head. "It's a good thought, but we've analyzed those possibilities already. Whigs, Tories… The politics of the victims don't align very well, and in fact a couple of the victims weren't exactly what you'd call active on any issue."

She picked up a slim leather portfolio. "There's not much evidence so far, but we have one lead: Calderwood."

"Doesn't ring any bells," Gabe admitted. "What is that?"

"A name," Julian said. "Scrawled on a scrap of paper by the last victim, apparently just before he died. Chattan has compiled a list of possibilities."

The woman handed the portfolio over to Gabe. "There's an estate called Calderwood in Kent, the seat of the Earls of Calder—the Osbourne family. Very famous for its gardens, and in Kent, that's saying something. The last Lord Calder passed away in the autumn of last year, but apparently it's the daughter who's most involved with the gardens and such." Chattan took a breath, then added, "Her name is Lady Arcadia Beatrice Osbourne."

Gabe picked up the card again, reading the memento mori with more gravity this time: *Et in Arcadia ego.* "Interesting," he said softly.

"Yes, exactly," Julian agreed. "Personally, I'd start there. Our research shows that previous generations developed extensive gardens, and imported a large number of plants. In your portfolio, there are some journal articles Lady Arcadia has written, usually under the name of A. B. Osbourne. She is apparently something of an amateur genius in the field of chemistry. Could be that not all the plants at Calderwood are beneficial to mankind. Oh, and by the way, there are rumors that the late Lord Calder died rather unexpectedly—make of that what you will. All the information I could gather about the poisonings, that estate, and the people who live on it is in here. Read it, memorize it, then destroy it."

Gabe nodded. He'd never leave evidence lying around. He prided himself on being efficient and reliable. A good agent was a ghost. Once done with an assignment, he left nothing behind.

Julian leaned forward, suddenly looking deadly serious and very much the spymaster of the Zodiac. "Your assignment is to identify the poison used, track down who makes it, and find out if they are merely selling the poison to someone else, or if they are the culprit behind all these deaths."

"Yes, sir."

"Because of the number of deaths already, you have no restrictions," Julian said. "However you choose to infiltrate the place, whatever you decide as to procuring the information, do as you see fit. I want regular reports sent here—even if you've nothing to report. And don't hesitate to request assistance if you need it. Money or manpower…we'll see that you get it."

"I'll start tomorrow," Gabe promised, then added, "If I may say, sir, I'm surprised you haven't already assigned an agent to this case. I know that there's always more work than people to do it, but still…this has been going on for months."

"You're not the first agent," Julian said quietly, and that was when Gabe noticed the unusual tightness about his superior's eyes.

Gabe went still. "No?"

"The last victim on the list, Lewelleyn Parrish, used the sign of Pisces. He's the one responsible for discovering all that we do know, and that effort took him weeks. But just when he thought he'd made a breakthrough, he stopped reporting in. Two days later his body was found, with only that one word to direct us to the next step."

"The killer knows about the Zodiac?" Gabe asked.

Chattan shook her head. "We have no evidence of that. Pisces was a very careful, even paranoid man. He'd never have mentioned it. But I do believe that he was getting close to the killer, and that's why he was poisoned, even though he didn't fit the previous pattern of the victims being influential men. But the important fact remains: whoever is behind this…they are attacking *us*."

Something deep inside Gabe stirred. He'd been a soldier, he'd known what it was like to lose comrades in the heat of battle. This was different. Worse. So he said, "Well, can't have that, sir. I'll take care of it. Whoever is at the root of this will very much regret it."

♑

JUST OVER A WEEK AFTER Lady Arcadia Osbourne had *not* been bitten by a spider, she did *not* suffer any ill effects, and she continued to live on just as expected. At the moment, however, she would have considered death as an alternative to the absolutely dire experience of receiving visitors at Calderwood on a Wednesday afternoon. Cady did not like receiving guests, but she also did not like *refusing* to receive guests, since it could provide yet more fodder for the gossips. Martha and the others wished her to behave as normally as possible, and Cady was incapable of refusing them when they banded together.

So she had to endure the chattering of the vicar's wife, the weird, stilted conversation of her distant neighbor Mrs Mitchell, the boorish attentions of Mr Pollack, and the usual tedium of Mr Heath, who lived a few miles west.

Though she had been hesitant to leave the safety of her house and gardens in the aftermath of her father's passing, the house didn't feel safe at all at the moment, having been invaded by this cadre of local busybodies.

"More tea, Mr Pollack?" she asked, a smile on her face but her gaze on the grandfather clock behind him. Quarter to two? Hadn't it been quarter to two the last time she looked?

"Why, yes, my lady." Pollack then chuckled. "That reminds me. Perhaps you have heard from the Crown Office about the matter of the, er, shift in succession?"

This question has been posed by Mr Pollack every week since the funeral of her father. To wit: was she Lady Arcadia Osbourne, merely the daughter of a lord…or was she Lady Calder, the heiress? The matter depended on whether her late father's attempt to amend the letters patent would be approved, an effort Cady thought highly unlikely. In any case, this was a distinction of much importance to any suitor, it being in general more attractive to marry a lady with a title and property.

What also hovered in the air was the unasked second issue of concern to Mr Pollack—and half the county: did Arcadia murder her father? An answer in the affirmative would muddy the whole matter of her inheritance, of course, and why marry a lady who might lose everything before it could be adequately disposed of by the lucky husband?

As far as Cady could tell, Mr Pollack did not worry that he himself might be murdered. She found that fact interesting, though not interesting enough to chat about it over tea. Despite her lack of encouragement, he continued to pay compliments and attention to Cady, without actually proposing. He would continue in this way until certain facts about Cady's title and inheritance became settled.

"I remain as I have always been," Cady informed him, noting the flicker of disappointment in his eyes. "To the best of my knowledge, my brother is Lord Calder, as I have always expected."

"And when might we hope to see Lord Calder return to Calderwood?" Mrs Bowcott asked, her voice ringing through the drawing room.

"Yes, when?" echoed Mrs Mitchell, a woman with all the backbone of a wet dishcloth, who'd come along with the vicar's wife and looked very much as if she regretted it.

"He is much committed to life in London," Cady replied evenly. "We do write each other regularly, of course, and I keep him apprised of everything happening here." Not that anything ever happened in such an isolated and rural place.

"A vivacious young lad, as I remember him. It has been *such* a long time," Mrs Bowcott said. "What a shame that he remains in London even now. Why, I'd expect a young gentleman newly come into his title to be at his seat within a fortnight. And yet it has been months. He didn't even attend the funeral, did he?"

"He was on the Continent. Rome, if I recall," Cady said quickly. "It would have been quite impossible to return in time. I told him as much when I wrote with the news of Papa's passing." She did not add that father and son hadn't spoken for years beforehand, and that Trevor very likely commemorated his father's death with a grand party instead of a black armband.

"I do hope he decides to revisit Calderwood soon," Mr Heath said from the sofa where he'd perched the moment he arrived, like a little brown bird on a branch. "Surely, after spending so much time in London, the young Lord Calder will add color to our less glamorous society."

Cady nodded at the words, and actually had to muffle a wild laugh. Trevor would add *something* to this society, but she doubted anyone around here would appreciate it. There was a reason Trevor had chosen to remain far, far away from home.

She wasn't laughing at Mr Heath, though. In fact, he represented a welcome change from Mr Pollack. He was a gardener, and a long-time comrade of her mother's. He had a passion for Italian gardens, and in particular waterworks. His dream was to create the most elaborate fountains and artificial waterfalls and ponds in the whole of

Britain. Cady admired his single-mindedness of purpose, though she wished he cared a little bit more about the actual plants he distributed about his endless water features. Still, he was a true gentleman, and he never put any stock in the rumors rising up after her father's death. She privately guessed that he would offer to marry her if she showed the slightest inclination toward him.

The only good thing about knowing the result of her father's efforts to change her into his legal heir was that it would let Cady know what sort of income she could expect in the coming years. Running Calderwood was a challenge when her father was alive. Now it was even more difficult…never mind the skeletal staff. She looked at the tea things spread out on the little tables in the drawing room. Only a pot of black on offer, and a few types of light biscuits. In days of old, there would have been black, green, and oolong, plus a tisane specially created from the herbs grown in the gardens, and a host of treats and endless laughter and conversation.

Cady was lucky things weren't worse off.

At that thought, she immediately imagined several ways they could worsen. She might be declared Lady Calder, thus gaining more attention than she was ready for. She might be arrested on a charge of murder, if the magistrate ever decided to actually get around to investigating the rumors that were clattering around the county. She might—

"Have you tried the lemon biscuits, Mrs Mitchell?" Cady asked, mostly to distract herself from the growing feelings of discomfort. She put wide-eyed innocence in her face, though she'd suspected why her guest had not touched any of the treats laid out on the tray.

"Oh, not yet," Mrs Mitchell replied, alarmed to have been caught out. "They look too pretty to eat, do they not?"

"Cook would be devastated to hear it," Cady said. "They are one of her specialties. She uses fruits grown here in the orangerie."

Mrs Mitchell took a tentative bite from one of the pale yellow biscuits, perhaps expecting to drop dead that instant. Pleasure warred with fear for a moment, and then pleasure won. She took another bite. "Delicious," she murmured when it was polite to do so.

"Mrs Prowse is the most accomplished cook in the shire," the vicar's wife declared, probably loudly enough that Cook could hear her all the way in the kitchen. "I'd hire her myself, but I know that she is devoted to the Osbourne family."

Devoted to Father's memory, more likely, Cady thought. *And she's one of the few workers who haven't run away, so stealing her would be rude at this point.*

"My goodness, the hour is later than I thought," the vicar's wife went on. "Mrs Mitchell and I have more calls to make."

"And I must be off as well," Mr Heath said.

Mr Pollack could not very well stay when everyone else was leaving, so he too rose and announced that he looked forward to see Arcadia next week, a wish she did not share.

"Thank you for coming," Cady told them all, leaning hard on the polite formulas her father insisted she use… lest she say something unexpected and therefore unwanted. "I do hope you call again." She did not hope for that at all, but God forbid anyone say what they were truly thinking over tea.

Cady stood politely until they all left. Her body was clamoring at her to run, to get out of the house, to escape into open air. But ladies did not run. And anyone who saw her running would know something was wrong.

"Just walk calmly," Cady told herself as she fetched her cloak. But that wasn't what her feet were doing. Heart pattering, and sweat beading on her forehead, she pushed open the glass doors and bolted into the gardens. She took a breath, and another and another, until she realized that she was gasping for air and sounded like a drowning fish. Her heart thudded against her rib cage. Surely this was what dying felt like? She couldn't take this much longer.

Verging on panic, Cady darted toward the Italian garden, where the high border of boxwoods formed a green wall that would hide her from prying eyes.

But just as she turned on the gravel path, past a massive yew, she ran smack into something solid and fell backward, her palms hitting the gravel hard.

There was not supposed to be anything on this path.

Gasping, she looked up at the figure of a black-haired man she'd never seen before in her life.

"You all right, miss?" he asked, offering a hand to help her to her feet.

Feeling as though the whole world had been knocked off its axis, Cady gazed at him, wondering where he'd come from. Such a big man couldn't have been on the grounds without her noticing…could he?

"Who are you?" she whispered.

♑

CADY'S WHOLE UNIVERSE NARROWED TO take in the figure standing above her. She had to look up, and up, to do so. He was well over six feet, with very broad shoulders to fill out the rough brown leather workman's coat he wore. Above the collar, black-as-soot hair fell in waves around a face that was quite handsome, considering it was a little dirt-smudged and quite unshaven, with a short black beard shadowing his chin and jaw. His eyebrows were just as black as his hair, which made his eyes even more noticeable. They were the blue of a summer lake, that deep, pure blue without any gray to muddy it.

Angels probably had eyes that blue.

"Oh, my lady!" called Mr Rundle, hurrying up to them both. "I thought you were still inside with your guests! I was waiting till you were done to see about hiring this man as a new gardener."

"Gardener?" Cady echoed, looking at the stranger more closely. He wore plain but sturdy clothing, and his boots were certainly muddy enough. "Is that what you're doing here?"

He nodded, explaining, "My name's Gabe Court. Mr Rundle suggested I walk through the grounds a bit while we waited for you. I didn't expect to meet the lady of the house quite like this, though."

Smiling, the man again offered to help her up. Cady lifted her own hand, and felt a deep shock when her skin met his.

Her nerves tingled at every point where he touched her, and her heartbeat trebled in half a second, unsure of how to deal with this overload of sensation. He pulled her to her feet, and she stared up at him, trapped by a blue-eyed gaze that sent waves of embarrassed heat all though her limbs. How could she be so affected by a mere touch?

Cady retracted her hand. Of course! She wasn't wearing gloves, and he apparently didn't own any himself. With a start, she realized that this man might be the first person besides her maid to touch her bare skin in nearly a year.

"Erm, perhaps we should go inside for this interview, my lady?" Rundle suggested, shivering in the brisk wind. The fact that he framed it as a question rather than just herding her in was probably due to a stranger's presence.

Cady nodded quickly. "Yes, of course. Your office, Rundle, if you please."

She trailed after the butler, acutely conscious of the figure following. He must weigh as much as three of her. *He'd* have no trouble managing a pair of wolfhounds, even if they were tearing at their leashes. At that thought, she glanced over her shoulder…and was alarmed to note that he was looking directly back at her, his eyes unapologetic and definitely not deferential. Part of her knew she ought to be offended. Her father had detested servants who didn't know their place (actually, he'd detested anyone who didn't know their place). But another part of Cady was still remembering how it felt when his hand grasped hers. She quickly turned to face the front again.

Rundle's office, in the hallway just off the kitchens, was snug and very warm, and Cady was grateful to be inside.

"His references, my lady," Rundle said, handing a few

sheets of paper to her.

Cady read through them, and noted a distinct lack of detail. "Mrs Hartley here doesn't say much about what you *did* on their property."

"Oh, whatever needed to be done," Mr Court said easily.

She frowned, wondering if she was missing something. His tone was just a little…mocking?

"How long have you worked as a gardener? Did your past positions include work in formal gardens, or more kitchen gardens and herbs and crops for home consumption? Calderwood has both French and Italian gardens, a sunken garden, a rose garden, in addition to the usual. You do know about this estate, yes? Calderwood is famous for its gardens, since the first countess brought in one hundred specimens from the Holy Land and planted them in the first walled garden. The work requires considerable expertise."

He looked annoyed for a second (at himself, Cady thought), then he sighed. "The truth is, miss—"

"Address her as *my lady*," Rundle whispered in alarm, as if Cady might not hear the mistake.

"My lady," the man said, "the truth is that I saw a post for a gardener or groundskeeper, and I need a job."

"But you don't have any actual experience with the special tasks that such a position requires," Cady pointed out, holding up the letters. "Your past employers seem to not have taken much notice of what you actually did all day."

"Lady Arcadia must have confidence in her groundskeepers," Rundle said, looking down his nose at Mr Court. Or rather, he tried to look down his nose, but Court was several inches taller than the butler, which made it a difficult task. Still Rundle radiated disapproval.

"The gardens are the jewel of the whole county."

"I'm sorry, Mr Court," Cady began to say, folding up the letters to hand back to him.

"Wait!" he said, taking a step forward in his urgency. Cady instinctively retreated, alarmed by the prospect of the stranger getting within arm's reach. He stopped short, and said, "I'll work, my lady. I'll do whatever needs to be done, I promise. I'm a quick learner. Tell me how to do a thing once, and you'll never have to tell me twice."

"Her ladyship is not a tutor!" Rundle said, affronted.

"No, that's not what I meant," the man said. He looked at Cady, perhaps trying to gauge how offended she was by the image of her high-born self instructing a mere mortal how to mulch the roses. If he only knew just how involved Cady was!

He cleared his throat, and half raised a hand as if he desperately wanted to scratch at his beard. "All I meant is that I know how to take orders. And orders for how to garden and take care of the grounds can't be any more difficult than the orders I carried out in France and Italy."

She glanced at him, those disconcertingly blue eyes. "You were a soldier?"

He nodded once, his expression tightening. She guessed why—many men who were eager to go off to war were not so eager to discuss their experiences once they returned. *If* they returned.

"And when did you leave the service?" she pressed.

"Not long ago, my lady. And definitely not long enough to have learned a new profession. But I'm not afraid to try. I'm not afraid of anything."

That got her attention. Considering how many of the servants left due to rumors and fearmongering, it would be novel to hire someone who was immune to that.

And an ex-soldier, a man without many options for

employment in a world that no longer needed him to charge mindlessly at a line of enemies. Cady sensed his desperation, and something in her responded to it. Could she really afford to turn away the one applicant she'd had in the last three months? Especially for the gardens, so necessary to her own work.

Rundle caught her gaze, and she read many of the same concerns in his eyes. Though Rundle was a stuffy old man, his own son had been a soldier, and he was not made of stone.

"Let us say…a fortnight, Mr Court," she said slowly. "If you prove yourself to be capable of the role by the end of that time, I will hire you on."

He grinned, looking relieved. "Thank you, my lady."

"It is a trial only," she cautioned him. "Rundle will give you the particulars and show you where everything is. Beyond the kitchen and servants' quarters, the house is strictly forbidden. Several of the gardens are forbidden as well, as are all of the glasshouses."

His brow furrowed. "But…how can I take care of a garden if I'm not allowed in it?"

"Never mind what's not yours to mind. Those restricted gardens belong to me, Mr Court," Cady said firmly. "And if you set one foot on the their soil, you will no longer work at Calderwood. Now, if you'll excuse me, I have other matters to attend to."

Cady swept out, her back straight and her expression set. She hoped that no one noticed how she was practically shaking at the proximity of the stranger. Like the spider in the garden, he was unexpected and unknown, and thus a threat. Her body clamored warnings, and her heartbeat seemed to thump a *get-away, get-away, get-away.*

She didn't like strangers on the estate in the first place, let alone a stranger working among her precious plants, her gardens, her domain. Not that she'd let him! No, he could keep to the outside and work on the broader grounds of Calderwood. A hulk like him wouldn't know how to handle the rare varieties and delicate seedlings so important to Cady's experiments. He'd probably crush tender shoots under his foot, and rip up special plants along with the invasive weeds.

Cady hurried away from the men as fast as she could, retracing her path back outside. Her footsteps led her through the chain of walled gardens that she'd so recently forbidden Mr Court to even think about. Only when she reached the gate in the wall marking the next garden did she pause to catch her breath.

Cady passed through the gate and into the garden. Every square foot of it was constructed according to a rigorous pattern. Tightly pruned hedges of boxwood formed four living, green patterns that resembled knots, one in each quarter. In the spaces between the knots, nearly every well-known Mediterranean herb was grown, all planned to take best advantage of the abundant sunlight, and the fact that the high outer walls prevented the worst of the winter winds from chilling the plants. Two paths separated these knotted quarters and met in the middle, where a small circular bed was planted with twelve different plants, one for each hour, all surrounding a sundial in the very middle. Cady's mother had planned this garden herself, and Cady always felt that it was a place of order and calm where the chaos of the world could be kept at bay.

"At bay," she murmured, reaching out to touch a particular shrub that just happened to be bay. The dry, summery scent came to her nose as she brought her hand back. She smiled. Her mother had always loved such little jokes, silly word games that made everyone laugh. Cady sighed, the weight of the present day returning. It seemed like it had been a very long time since she laughed for real —a belly-deep, soulful laugh that left the body tired but content. Now all she had was worry and fear.

Glancing over her shoulder to ensure she wasn't being followed, Cady continued on to another gate, this one locked. She pulled a key out of her pocket. The gate opened silently, for she was careful to oil the lock and hinges and keep everything in working order.

She locked the door behind her and let her breath out in a deep sigh. Relief. No matter how lovely and peaceful the other gardens were, this particular garden was Cady's secret realm, a place where she could be assured of peace and quiet…and no interruptions. Especially not from dark-haired, light-eyed strangers.

"Time to think," she murmured. Working on her experiments always calmed her mind, and she needed that now. She walked over to one of the brick buildings in the corner of the garden. The moment she got there, she washed her hands, hoping to remove not just the traces of dirt from her stumble in the garden, but also any trace of the stranger's touch. Odd how she could still feel every point of contact on her hands, and she remembered how warm his hands were, despite the cool weather.

"Probably just sweat all over him," she muttered to herself, mostly to demystify a very mysterious sensation. "Men never wash up properly." He didn't shave, that was certain. He had rough stubble or the beginnings of a beard all along his jawline, shadowing his face but not yet obscuring the outline of his lips.

Why was she thinking about the outline of his lips?

"You are losing your mind, Cady," she told herself. "Stop worrying about the gardener. Worry about distilling this batch of flowers."

The stillroom was, as the name implied, set up for the distilling of liquor, aqua vitae, and—under Cady's watchful eye—the essential oils of the many plants in her gardens. Fresh plants were best for eating and for medicines, of course. But plants, once picked, had a distressing habit of not staying fresh. Thus, the determined practitioner needed to find ways to preserve the core parts so that they could be used when needed. Some plants could be dried, hung up in bunches, or with the leaves spread out in the sun. There was the process of cooking plants in oil and wax to emulsify the precious oils in a salve that could last for years. But to really tap the essence of a plant, distillation was key.

Today she had a small amount of jasmine harvested from the conservatory. Cady set up the apparatus, and fired up the little burner below, which would heat the water and create steam. The steam rose up through the plant parts on the tray and took the essence of the plant with it into the next chamber, where the newly infused steam condensed back into water. But the volatile oil of the plants was lighter than water, and thus floated on top, or clung to the glass. Cady carefully skimmed the surface and scraped the glass with a little rubber block, gathering all the precious liquid to store in dark glass bottles, each labeled with the species, the date, and the concentration.

Soon, the issues of the outside world faded, the aroma of jasmine swirled around her, and Cady inhaled deeply, cherishing a rare moment of joy.

But even that joy was fleeting, replaced by the image of the new gardener—foreign, dangerous, unknown. A man who knew nothing about gardens…so what brought him into hers?

♑

SEVERAL DAYS PASSED SINCE GABE first wormed his way into Calderwood. So far, he hadn't done anything impressive. In fact, he regarded his first (and thus far only) meeting with Lady Arcadia to be a harbinger of things to come…intriguing, but ultimately a dead end. He hoped for some information or hint he could use later, because after nearly a week at Calderwood, he wasn't any closer to the lady within, or the secrets she kept.

Gabe was still disgusted with himself for failing to take advantage of his arrival. He'd been walking through the gardens as Rundle suggested he do. He'd kept a close eye on the windows of the drawing room of the house, where he heard the lady would be taking tea with her guests.

Then Gabe had turned away from the house for one damn minute, and of course that's when this woman hurtled into him with the full force of her body. She didn't even cry out as she fell onto the gravel pathway. Only her ragged breathing revealed that not all was well.

"You all right, miss?" he'd asked, remembering just in time to use the lower-class accent he perfected over his career as an agent.

She gazed up at him, alarm spreading across her features. No, more than alarm. She was terrified. Of *him*?

Gabe knelt down, not wanting to frighten her. He couldn't risk scaring a lady of the house. He avoided touching the fabric of her skirt—black silk, with a massive floral pattern dancing across it. Her cloak was a very dark brown, and the overall effect was that of a wounded songbird, a thrush shot out of the sky.

"Who are you?" she'd whispered, her face pale amid all the dark fabric.

The butler had run up then, cutting off any chance Gabe had to charm her—at which point he'd learned that this slip of a thing was none other than Lady Arcadia Beatrice Osbourne herself.

He'd helped her up, trying not to show his reaction when the incredibly soft skin of her hands grazed his. Damn, he should have been wearing gloves, if only to avoid exposing her to sandpaper-rough palms. Yes, he'd begun with an accent that sounded nothing like his usual tone. But that was acting. Same for the dyed hair and hasty beard, because it was usually a good idea for a spy to disguise himself a bit. But the ripped skin on his hands and the ache in his back? That was just the result of doing a very grubby job (espionage) in very grubby conditions (politics). Luckily, she must have assumed it was physical labor.

The interview had gone as well as he could have hoped, though he'd had to beg and plead a bit. From his preliminary scouting around the village, Calderwood was in dire need of help, though the villagers were vague about why they wouldn't work there themselves. It defied all he knew about people's desire for money. *Not* work at the great house where you'd have a position for life? What could be so bad there?

Gabe's false letters of reference, hastily provided by the Zodiac, seemed to do their job…though he had a nasty moment when he realized that the lady was actually reading their contents, and that she actually seemed to care about his qualifications.

A very subtle hint that he'd be happy to do *whatever* the lady told him went nowhere. A woman of over twenty years, wealthy, and the daughter of a lord…still unmarried? Gabe had looked at those facts and concluded that she'd managed to ruin her reputation. But Lady Arcadia hadn't seemed to pick up on it. She was either not that perceptive, or she was more innocent than he assumed, even though she was certainly good-looking enough to attract attention.

He snorted at his own bland description. She had a rare beauty. Those solemn brown eyes and the dark, windblown curls surrounding her lovely face, with its prominent cheekbones and her pretty, almost too-ripe mouth…he'd have no difficulty spouting the usual tripe about how she took his breath away.

Whether the figure matched the face, he couldn't tell yet. It was impossible to know under the loose-fitting, billowy gown and the even more shapeless cloak—which she wore throughout the interview, as though she were the visitor and planned to leave again as soon as her business was done. But she moved with grace. And she was so little, perhaps an inch or two over five feet. He felt like a lumbering giant next to her. No wonder she'd been so apprehensive when she first collided with him.

Apprehensive? No, that wasn't correct. Gabe was used to assessing people's attitudes and emotions. And hers were wrong. It would be normal for a woman to be startled by the appearance of a stranger. Perhaps even nervous.

Arcadia Osbourne was *terrified*. At the conclusion of the interview, she'd darted off before he could say anything else. Of course he followed her—at a distance, after pretending to Rundle that he wanted to get the lay of the land—but his pursuit stopped abruptly when he encountered a locked gate. He could see a formal, walled garden through the bars, and beyond, another door in the far wall. But when he paced the perimeter of the garden, he found only more walls, constructed of unforgiving sandstone blocks that brooked no resistance. He frowned as he looked up at the surprisingly high wall. Ivy grew thick over the very top, and he could see the tops of a few narrow trees within.

He could get a ladder and climb up to peek over, but not until nighttime. Until then, he had to play his part. He returned to the house, but his mind was full of the young lady who'd slammed into him and then just as quickly fled.

Unfortunately, Gabe's choice of cover meant that he had little reason to be in contact with the lady of the house. For days, he received instructions from Rundle (who clearly was just listing off what the mysterious lady told him). His tasks were all simple. Not pointless though —clearly Calderwood's grounds had been neglected over the past year or so. Gabe didn't mind hard work. He dug holes, moved piles of earth and stones, directed the estate's goats and sheep to the appropriate areas to crop the grass, and pulled hardy, tough weeds from the white gravel drive that led to the house.

The next day, Rundle also gave him a short accounting of how fine a job he was doing.

"Good work on digging the holes for the poplar avenue. Remember to not harm the moss on the north walk —there was a scrape from the wheelbarrow yesterday. Excellent job on weeding the drive. You've proven you have the wherewithal to weed the vegetable gardens as well now."

All these observations meant that Lady Arcadia was

watching somehow. But he heard from the other staff that she rarely left the house except to go to the gardens, and since he never saw her, that meant she had to be flitting about at night, or when his back was turned.

Gabe did not like being outspied, and Arcadia's knowledge of his work implied that she might be sneakier than he was…and that she had a reason to be so stealthy.

Patience, he reminded himself. Gabe always considered himself a patient man. Much of his work with the Zodiac featured long stretches of nothing happening, followed by a few frantic hours of action, often ending with a death or two.

Weeding just wasn't the same, though there was something strangely satisfying about seeing the tangible results of his work. Before: the beds choked with random plants and decaying vegetation. After: a tidy arrangement of what was intended to be there, set against the dark, rich earth. It was, in a way, a little like investigation work. Pull away the unnecessary dross hiding the important facts, and then you see the whole picture clearly.

Lord, was he comparing gardening to spying? He must need a break.

But Gabe kept to the tasks he was assigned, all too aware that he was being watched. At the moment, he continued to prune the low hedges, hoping he was doing it correctly. Any of his family or his old school friends would laugh to see him now. Mr Gabriel Albion Maximus Courtenay, son of Lord Hargrave…scrabbling in the dirt like a medieval peasant?

Luckily, no one he knew would ever see him like this. If they did, he'd have to silence them. And Gabe didn't like to do that except when it was absolutely the last option.

When he finished his tasks for the day, he made his

way to the kitchen and the hall where all the servants took their meals. The kitchens of Calderwood provided some of the best food he'd ever tasted. On the first day there, he was impressed with the generous portions. He'd been in situations before that allowed him to see how servants were treated, and in some houses, they were practically starved due to the landlord's stinginess. But at Calderwood, the servants all ate like kings. Granted, there were far fewer servants than just a couple months ago. Gabe found out at his first dinner there that Mr Rundle had actually advertised several positions in the London papers, so Gabe let everyone assume that's what brought him to Calderwood.

That was his first and last stroke of luck on the assignment so far. Despite keeping his eyes open, and questioning the other servants very subtly, he hadn't learned what he needed to know.

After he sat down that evening, Gabe was offered a brothy soup that tasted so good he could have cried. The accompanying bread was crusty and covered in seeds and crushed herbs, and he was fairly sure he devoured a whole loaf on his own.

"You eat up, now," the cook advised him. "The lady is very particular that everyone in the house be well fed."

"She ought to take her own advice," the maid named Martha muttered. "Wasting away, she is. Her father wouldn't have stood for it."

"Hush, now!" The cook, a stout woman of about fifty years old who hailed from Oswestry, would not tolerate any harsh word or complaint about her mistress.

It was odd, Gabe thought, that half the servants fled the house because they thought she might be a murderess, but the ones who remained thought she was a saint.

Mr Rundle walked in. "Where is Vernon? The lady's

dinner will get cold! You there, Mr Court. Can you look outside and find the footman?"

Gabe straightened up, sensing an opening. "I could, but would it not save time if I were to take the tray up myself, sir? I promise I'll not track dirt on the floors."

Mr Rundle narrowed his eyes, then sighed. "Aye, why not. Everything else is topsy-turvy, so why should we not have an gardener serving meals to the mistress! What a time." But giving in, he gave Gabe precise instructions for where to go to deliver the tray.

As he walked past her, Gabe complimented the cook on the meals he'd had so far, and she blushed like a schoolgirl. "Away with ye," she said, waving a hand.

"Just the truth, ma'am. Can't believe the mistress would miss a single dish you make, ma'am."

"Oh, I know all the foods she likes best. The late lord said she was the greatest treasure in the house and ought to be treated as such. But ever since her father passed, she's been a shadow of herself. Can scarce keep down a cup of tea. Take that tray up and leave it at her door. Knock once, and don't linger. She'll pick up the tray after you've gone."

Gabe nodded, and grabbed the tray. It was a good thing he'd made the effort to change into clean clothes for dinner. He'd never had the opportunity to see the main part of the house before. A flaw in the plan of being hired as a gardener was that he had no business inside. But it wasn't as if he exactly had the credentials to get hired as a lady's maid...

As he walked, he took in everything, committing it to memory.

The house was massive, and dead silent. Gabe wasn't a fanciful person, but the phrase "quiet as a tomb" rang through his mind, and he almost looked over his shoulder, expecting a ghost to be hovering there.

The shade of the late Lord Calder, whether real or not, oppressed the whole estate of Calderwood. Gabe had wrangled the story out of the other servants within a day. The lord had come in from riding one afternoon, went to his sitting room in his comfortable leather armchair to enjoy his usual predinner brandy…and never got out of the chair. When he didn't answer the bell for dinner, his daughter, Lady Arcadia, had gone to find him, and discovered him stone dead.

She'd been in deep mourning ever since. And unfortunately, some locals (out of sheer spite, Cook assured him) started a rumor that she killed him, thus creating a cascade of mischance. Servants left the house. Visitors stopped calling. The lady of the house stopped going out to town. The result of her removal from local society meant that more servants left, and even fewer people called, and the lady soon refused to leave the estate.

With her commitment to a wardrobe of somber colors, and her predilection for moping in gardens at midnight, it was perhaps not surprising that some folk were now whispering that she was a witch.

"Have you ever heard such blather?" Mr Rundle had cried during one dinner. "We are at the vanguard of the nineteenth century, and yet people still see witches and goblins around every corner."

Martha declared in response, "Of course the lady's *not* a witch. An Osbourne would never dabble in witchcraft. The old lord wouldn't hear of it."

Gabe did not believe in anything himself. But if the lady wanted to avoid being thought of as a witch, or an eccentric, or a murderess…she might want to light a couple candles in these gloomy halls, or wear a shade lighter than black.

He set the tray down, and knocked once. "Your dinner, my lady!" he called.

There was no response from the other side of the door. He remembered the warning not to linger, but this was too precious a moment to miss out on. Perhaps he could see inside her room, or even speak to her, if the moment seemed right. He retreated several paces and slipped into a room on the opposite side of the hall. From there he could just see the lady's door, with the tray in front of it.

The door creaked open. Gabe couldn't see anyone but he had the sense that someone was looking out. Then a shape emerged—Lady Arcadia, with those big brown eyes darting around as though a mob was about to attack her.

She bent over and picked up the tray, backing up into her room. Then the door was pushed closed and he heard the distinctive scrape of a key in the lock. He hadn't been able to see a single thing. It was as if her room was unlit. Oddly, the scent of witch hazel drifted through the hall.

He frowned. Why did this woman secure herself in her own room as if she were already a prisoner? How the hell was Gabe ever supposed to get close enough to her to win her confidence, let alone discover if she was the notorious poisoner of London's elite?

♑

When Gabe returned to the kitchen, all evidence of the servants' meal was cleaned up, the long table spotless. He glanced over at the scullery, and saw that Martha and Cook were hard at work near the big basin, which was full of sudsy water.

He put a general question out if he could help with anything else. Mr Rundle told him that it would be a great help if he could walk to the front gate and ensure it was closed for the night.

Gabe nodded at the order, guessing it was a way to get him out of the house for a bit. This small band of servants were very clannish. Despite his efforts to ingratiate himself, he'd sensed that they didn't trust him. Maybe they didn't trust anyone who hadn't worked there under the late Lord Calder, who seemed to have a grip on people from beyond the grave.

Heading outside, Gabe made quick work of the errand, running rather than strolling down the long drive to the gate, a massive thing that looked like a medieval portcullis, except that it split vertically down the middle to allow both sides to swing open. Gabe took hold of one of the heavy iron sides and pushed it forward, rewarded with a screeching noise so loud it could wake the dead.

A horse whinnied on the road, startled by the sound.

Gabe called out an apology to the rider.

The rider was a heavy-set man who looked to be about

fifty. By the quality of his clothes, he was either a merchant in the village or perhaps a gentleman farmer.

"Who're you?" the stranger asked, obviously surprised by a new face. How nosy *was* this village? "Work here?"

"I'm a gardener," Gabe replied, to keep him talking. "Just started this week."

"From the city, are you? Well, then, you don't know any better."

"Any better than what?"

"Get out now. Leave Calderwood and work somewhere else. Anywhere else." The man's tone was kind, even though the warning was dire.

"I can't do that," Gabe said with perfect honesty.

"Then you'll come to regret it, my good man. Calderwood is a deadly place."

"Just because the old master died?" Gabe put puzzlement and even a little stupidity in his voice.

"Not *just* the old master," the man said with emphasis. "The old mistress too, years before, bless her heart. And the son—no one's seen him in years, so how do we know he's alive at all? Now it's only the daughter's left, with her potions and whatnot."

That was the first Gabe heard about potions.

"I'm not one to gossip," the man said, apparently believing the words he spoke. "Listen here, though. Don't eat or drink anything in that house, and flee back to London quick as you can."

The man rode off before Gabe could question him further. *Potions?* Had that man just accused Lady Arcadia of killing her entire family over the course of years? What the hell was he getting into?

Gabe finished shutting the gate, pulling the thick chain tight around the bars. He wondered if the gate was meant to keep people out…or in.

Back in the kitchen, the staff had completed all the other work. Even the wash basin was empty and shining. Gabe looked over the small crew of loyal servants. Would they stay on if they thought their employer was a killer?

"Gate's closed and chained," Gabe informed the butler.

"Good.   Don't like the notion of anyone wandering onto the grounds."

"That happen often?"

"Just local children playing pranks," Cook said hastily. "Boys will be boys."

"That's quite enough chatter," Rundle said. "It's late. You'd best get off to bed."

"Aye, sir." Gabe ducked his head and resumed the pose of the humble gardener.

After waiting an hour or so to let the others find their beds and fall asleep, Gabe went back outside. Earlier that day, he had secured the longest ladder he could find and carried it toward the walls of the locked gardens, hiding it from the view of the house behind a long hedge of boxwood. He had severe doubts about its ability to hold his weight, though. It had been stored in a disused shed, possibly not used since the restoration of the monarchy.

The grounds were deserted when he left his warm bed and snuck outside into the gloom, making his way toward the ladder's hiding place. He propped the ladder up against the wall of the locked garden and climbed gingerly, testing each rung as he went. When he could look over the top of the wall, he reached out and used the ivy to hold himself in place—it felt considerably stronger than the ladder. Then the moon came out, and Gabe beheld a fairy-tale landscape below.

The walled garden was perfectly square, and the

plants that grew here were relatively far along thanks to the protection from the weather provided by the wall. White gravel paths intersected at the middle, with an elaborately carved stone sundial as a centerpiece. The moonlight washed away all color, bathing the graceful forms of the plants in an otherworldly glow. Everything looked as if it were coated in silver leaf, or frost, or pure white marble.

Gabe leaned forward. The rung he stood on sagged, then snapped. He gripped the ivy vines hard, dangling for a moment with that twelve-foot drop below. He took a breath then hoisted himself to the top of the wall, scrambling for a steady perch. His heart thudded at the thought of his near fall. He did not fancy the idea of smashing his head on the flagstones below.

He contemplated jumping into the moonlit garden, but then thought better of it. First, if all the gates were locked, he'd be in a silver-gilded cage. Second, from the top of the wall, he could now see that there were more spaces beyond, possibly more gardens walled off from the world, but perhaps something else. Ahead, glass flashed as the moonlight hit it. Some kind of conservatory?

Gabe was no acrobat, but he could crawl easily along the top of the wall, confident that the thick growth of ivy would provide footholds and some extra breadth as he moved.

After the moonlit garden, he saw another rectangular yard, this one featuring small buildings in the corners. One had a sloping glass roof, with gold light emanating from below. The shifting of the light suggested someone was within, moving around.

He paused, wondering if he heard something. After a moment, there it was again.

"Very good, my darling. You're growing so well! So

much faster than the last crop."

It was Arcadia's voice. But there was no fear in the tone now, just a happy cadence like that of a mother talking to her child. Was she talking to her plants? Maybe Lady Arcadia wasn't just a murderer, she was also insane. Something that could change the assignment considerably.

He heard her humming then, a little tune that repeated after a few bars. He didn't know the melody, but there was something haunting about it. He leaned over a few more inches, hoping to get even a glimpse of what was beyond that glass. Then his nose picked up something else.

A scent. Faint but intoxicating, like a recollection of a warmer season. The image of the first woman he'd ever been with flashed across his mind. He hadn't thought about that encounter in *years*, yet now he could count the freckles sprinkled across her chest.

The memory mingled with the strange humming sound, and he felt dizzy for a moment, lost between past and present. He swayed to the right, almost losing his balance. He made a grab for a thicker branch of the ivy, his heart hammering.

He didn't fall, but he also felt much less secure than he had only moments ago.

And the humming had stopped. His movement must have alerted whoever was inside. Instinct told Gabe to drop down to a prone position, stretched on his stomach along the wall.

Not a moment too soon. A door swung open, spilling gold light out in a wedge shape. A wave of the elusive scent spilled out too. Gabe inhaled a second too late and caught a huge whiff of it.

A woman's silhouette filled the doorway. Arcadia,

looking around in a slow, sweeping examination of the walled yard.

Don't move, he thought. Don't even breathe.

Gabe reminded himself that the lady couldn't see as much as he could. She'd just stepped from a well-lit room, so she was night-blind, her eyes not adjusted to the darkness. If he stayed absolutely still, he'd blend in with the other shadows. His body should be hidden within the rough outline of the mass of ivy against the sky.

God, the way she scanned the area, her gaze running over anything and everything. Did she pause when her eyes passed over Gabe? Or was that his imagination?

The air in his lungs seemed heavy with that scent, and he thought he might pass out. He exhaled, hot breath slipping between his lips into cool night air, dangerously close to becoming visible mist.

"Oscar?" she called out, questioning.

No answer, and no hint of whether she'd noticed Gabe's figure. Who the hell was Oscar?

She took one step forward, head swiveling as she did so. He saw how wide her eyes were, and the quick rise and fall of her chest. She was nervous, not angry.

Then she withdrew, pushing the door shut behind her, plunging the garden into darkness. Gabe remained where he was, just in case she emerged again. But when he heard the sound of a bolt sliding home, he knew she was locking herself away once more.

He inhaled, more deeply this time. Now the scent had gone, his head cleared. What was she brewing in there?

Since he was already up here, and he felt steady again, he continued his exploration. Next to that yard was a long, narrow building entirely made of glass. Christ, this place. It was a labyrinth, seemingly constructed to hide secrets within secrets.

No outsider could hope to understand the layout of all the buildings and gardens, let alone know what each one contained. He could wander in this place for years and not find what he was looking for. He needed a key. He needed to coax Arcadia Osbourne to his side.

But that was easier said than done. Seduction was usually the most direct way, and he'd never felt any compunction about it. He was a spy working amid other spies, and it wasn't as if the women moving in those circles were exactly innocents.

However, Arcadia Osbourne defied all his expectations. Reclusive, eccentric, and decidedly not eager to dally with any man who crossed her path. She was a challenge.

Gabe liked challenges.

♑

CADY WOKE EARLY AND SPENT her morning in the glasshouse, harvesting a crop of cola nuts that had finally ripened. In the morning light, the glasshouses were a haven. At night, the reflections on the glass sometimes made her think that someone might be outside, watching.

She tended to several tropical specimens, checking the soils for mold (the moist air of their glasshouse made it a constant threat). And then she checked the Iranian salvia.

"Almost ready," she murmured, examining the dark green glossy leaves and aerial parts of the plant. "Do you know," she said, "you may well be the first example of your species to thrive on the isle of Britain? How do you feel about that? Proud, I should hope. Myself, I'm quite a common example of my type—female human—and I can't say I'm thriving. Half the time, I'm scared to step outside my door. How am I to survive in the world if that's the case? Survive in the biological sense, I mean." She sighed. Cady worried about a lot of things, but she never worried about her habit of talking to plants. They were, if not stimulating conversationalists, then at least polite ones.

Cady tested the soil of one pot and slowly poured more water in. She envisioned a world where there were whole farms under glass, growing not just hothouse fruits, but also medicinal plants that would be harvested and made into medicines that everyone could use.

"Ah, that reminds me," she murmured aloud. "I've got to get that old glasshouse back in working order. The hot walls are a wreck."

She strolled over to her worktable and scrawled out a note to speak to Rundle about it. Now that the gardener, Mr Court, had proved he wasn't a bumbling idiot, Cady felt better about giving him a more complex task. And restoring her mother's old glasshouse would be a monumental effort, even for that bull of a man. It occurred to Cady for half a second that the work would go much faster if she were there to direct him in all the particulars and help out with the less physically demanding tasks. But that would require her to actually be around him and speak with him....

Unbidden, his image flitted across Cady's mind. She bit her lip, trying to stamp it out. But how was she supposed to do that? In fact, she'd found several excuses to "supervise" his work from various vantage points in the house over the past week. She told herself that it was merely curiosity about a new person, after quite a long time without any contact with new people. But somehow she doubted that she'd be so curious about a woman, or a man who wasn't quite so striking.

Which he was. So Cady peeked out of the windows on the upper floors of the house, just "happening" to be there when he was working below, often in just his white shirt, which allowed her to get a glimpse of his muscled form underneath. Dear Lord, what was she going to do if he was still working at Calderwood when the weather got hot?

Ugh, if she was still lurking in the shadows in June, it would mean that all her experiments had failed, and she wouldn't have learned how to treat the affliction that had come upon her. She'd be a recluse to the end of her life, living in the shadows, reviled, abandoned…

Before her imagination could totally run away, she heard footsteps approaching. Turning around, she saw Rundle.

"Apologies for interrupting, my lady, but in case you've forgotten, it's Thursday. And you have said you would at home for tea."

"It's Thursday?" she asked in dismay.

"I'm afraid so, my lady."

Cady sighed, resenting the need to stop speaking to plants and start speaking with people. But she dutifully went back to her rooms so she could change into suitable attire for the afternoon. Martha helped her dress, choosing a green gown so dark it was almost black. The somber hue was appropriate for mourning, and Cady added a wide black velvet sash around the high waist, as well as long black gloves. Martha brushed her hair and put it in a simple knot at the nape of her neck, secured with a black ribbon.

Another afternoon, another gauntlet of sociability. Cady had hoped that no one would call on her today—she was practically mad to get back to her glasshouse and all the newly sprouting plants. But instead, she was here in this cold, dry drawing room, presiding over yet another awkward gathering of neighbors and so-called friends.

This time was worse than last, because while Mr Heath wasn't there, Mr Pollack very much was, and something in his demeanor suggested that he hadn't come for the lemon biscuits.

"You look very lovely today, my lady," he told her after sloshing down a cup of tea.

"How kind of you to say," Cady replied.

Mrs Bowcott was her usual chattering self, speaking of the planned festivities for Easter, and did Arcadia expect to attend?

So they can burn me as a witch? No thank you, Cady thought. Aloud, she murmured that much would depend on the weather.

But Mrs Bowcott could not stay long, and within twenty minutes, she stood and announced that she must be on her way. Cady hoped that Mr Pollack would follow suit, but he did not. Instead, he walked to the French doors. As he did so, a ray of sunlight broke through the clouds, illuminating the rose garden as if God had special intentions there. Cady wished she was out there, rather than inside with Mr Pollack.

But then he said, "Well, my lady. It seems that the sun is finally coming out. Before I leave, may I take you for a turn around the gardens?"

Against all her better judgment, Cady said yes.

* * * *

Gabe hadn't known that it was possible to hate plants. But after a week, he hated crabgrass, and ragweed, and creeping thistle. Though it hadn't been long since the family had lost so many workers, the neglect was evident. The grasses in the meadows were overgrown and straggly. Branches blown down from recent storms still needed to be cleared away. And every square foot of the gardens needed to be weeded.

His hands ached. The skin had been pierced by thorns and nettles. His back felt like it was on fire when he finally lay down on his bed each night. But the work allowed him to keep watch on the house, and speak to the other servants at mealtimes, and note who was coming and going.

He'd sent two short notes back to the Zodiac so far,

irritated by how little he had to report. He knew how many secrets lay just beyond the next wall, or the next locked door, or the next garden gate. But he was constrained by his role, and his nighttime forays were short and always risky. One thing, however, was clear. The lady was a recluse, so the odds that she was darting off to London to poison people were long. But of course, she could still be the *supplier* of the poison.

On this day, he was working in the Italian garden, clearing the ground of last year's detritus. Gabe dug carefully around a little green shoot, giving it a wide berth should the roots have spread wider than the leaves had. He lifted the plant out of the ground, and placed it gently into the pot, taking care to dribble loose dirt all around.

"There you are, a temporary home until I find out what you are and where you belong," he told the plant. Then he shook his head. This place was getting to him. Here he was, talking to the plants when he ought to be cutting them down. But what if this one was important?

He felt a prickling sensation across his back. He casually raised his hand to his neck and rubbed as if he got a sore muscle. But he looked around as he did so, for that feeling was well-known to him, and one he developed during his years as a spy. Someone was watching him.

Gabe twisted his torso, pretending to need to stretch. His movements allowed him to scan the whole garden, and the meadow beyond and the house that loomed up to the east. There were so many windows…any one of them could harbor a pair of unfriendly eyes.

Then he heard voices approaching. The lady! And a man's voice as well. Dear God, she'd left the house. He had to figure out a way to get her attention.

He quickly resumed working on his hands and knees, scraping old brown leaves and twigs into the wheelbarrow, where the lady and her guest wouldn't notice him.

"I believe I shall go to Bath this summer," the man was saying. He had a loud, grating voice. "Have you been, my lady?"

"No, Mr Pollack." Arcadia's voice was much softer, though her words still carried.

"You ought to, you know. The waters and all that."

"It sounds rather too crowded for me," she said coolly, waving away some invisible insect as she spoke. She peered at the garden beds rather than her guest, and Gabe intuited that it was not merely a burning need to see how the flowers were sprouting.

She doesn't like him, Gabe thought. Then he spied the bucket of manure sitting in the pathway and got an idea.

Mr Pollack was strolling as near to her as he politely could. He used a walking stick, though from the big swings and the jaunty way the bottom landed in the gravel each time, he didn't need it for balance. It was an affectation.

She sent a narrowed, sidelong glance at Pollack when the stick hit the ground again. Though the irritation on her face was brief, Gabe could see it. *She doesn't like affectation.*

They got closer and closer and then, just as they rounded the corner where Gabe was working, it happened.

Quite predictably, the man tripped over the bucket and the contents spilled over the path, splashing up onto his shoes and trousers, covering them with foul-smelling manure.

"What the bloody hell...you *idiot*!" the man yelled, glaring at Gabe. "Leaving that where a man is walking. Who are you? Why are you even here? Why is this disgusting stuff here?"

"I'm a gardener. I'm gardening," Gabe said innocently. "The manure fertilizes the plants."

"Come, Mr Pollack," the lady said, trying to assuage him, though there was a flicker of amusement at the corner of her mouth. "There is no need for anger. It was an accident."

But Pollack was enraged beyond all reason. Without warning, he whipped his walking stick toward Gabe. The fact that Gabe was kneeling before him made him an easy target.

Instinctively, Gabe flung up his arms to protect himself, as blows rained down on his head and shoulders. The walking stick's top must have been weighted with lead. He was about to spring up and tackle the man when the attack suddenly stopped.

Arcadia had darted in front of him.

"What are you *doing*, sir?" Arcadia cried out, alarm replacing the appeasement in her tone. "You cannot strike my people! Stop it!"

Pollack stepped back, panting. "*You* punish him, then. Bloody fool, ruining my outfit and my afternoon. He ought to be locked away."

"I think you should leave, Mr Pollack." Lady Arcadia Osbourne was a tiny person, and her voice wavered, but there was no mistaking the bravery she showed in blocking Gabe from another strike.

"I will! Apologies for my harsh language, my lady," he said then, pulling at his waistcoat. Then he stalked off, still muttering angrily. A moment later he left the garden and had turned to the front of the house, where his carriage was no doubt waiting.

She spun about and crouched down in front of Gabe. "Are you all right? Who could have thought a man would be so cruel as to strike someone for no reason? Let me see your face."

Her hands were already pulling at his forearms, examining him for injury. Whatever reserve normally ruled her behavior, the act of violence seemed to have shocked her out of it.

"I'm not hurt, my lady. Well, not much." It would ache in the morning, but he could stand that.

"You *are* hurt. The skin is broken here," she said, touching his cheek, where the first blow had landed. Her fingers barely grazed him, but he felt the touch like fire. "It must be cleaned immediately, or it may fester. Come with me."

In a bit of a daze, he followed her. She was moving with surprising speed and he had no idea where she was heading. Gabe had been hoping for some opportunity to speak with the woman, but he didn't plan to do it through bodily harm. Still, through that odious neighbor's display of violence, Gabe got the lady's attention. Now, he had to make the most of the opportunity.

♑

CADY LED THE MAN THOUGH the gardens to a small gate that would provide quicker access to her workroom than the usual paths. The ferocity of the beating—all the more for its suddenness—had snapped her out of her usual frozen state and propelled her feet forward.

She was so upset about the attack that she didn't think twice about allowing this near stranger to see her most sacred space, the laboratory where she spent so much time and put forth so much effort in her experiments.

"What is this?" the gardener asked, looking around the laboratory with intense interest, despite the clonk to the head that was already sending a trickle of blood down his cheek.

"My…workroom, essentially," she said, not wanting to explain the details at the moment. "Now, if you please, sit down there so I can clean up those cuts."

He dutifully sat. Cady shook her head. "I still can't believe that Mr Pollack did that. It was completely unacceptable."

"Well, at least he apologized to you for the harsh language," the man noted, a hint of humor in his voice.

Cady rolled her eyes. "The lesser offense, I assure you. My goodness, what was that cane made of? You look as if you've been pelted with stones!"

"It felt a little like that."

She soaked a cloth in warm water and then turned to him. It was good that he was sitting down—he was much taller than her. Her arms would grow tired just reaching up to his head. She first cleaned the trail of blood down his face, then dabbed lightly at the wound, careful to not press down and cause him pain.

She leaned over to clean the nastiest cut. His quick intake of breath made her pause.

"I'm sorry, does that hurt, Mr Court?" she asked.

"Only a little," he grunted. "And everyone calls me Gabe."

Cady assumed he was being manly about the pain, and guessed it would require a bit of numbing. She bustled over to her medicine cabinet, unlocked it, and reached for a few bottles that she used for treating the inevitable scrapes and bruises that occurred when people worked for a living.

"What's that?" he asked warily when Cady returned to the worktable and opened a bottle.

"It's very safe, I assure you. I make an ointment that will help stop the bleeding, and also keep the bruising to a minimum."

His eyes widened. "You make it?"

"Yes, using plants I grow here at Calderwood."

He seemed apprehensive, and she supposed that made sense. "What plants?"

"Feverfew, arnica, calendula, and chamomile comprise the bulk of the herbs. And the beeswax and flax oil holds it all together."

"Are those plants that grow in the gardens? I haven't seen them."

"You've not seen a great deal of the Calderwood gardens, Mr Court. Many of them are private."

"But if you need help gardening, shouldn't I know about them?" he asked. "And if there's work to be done, aren't you the best person to tell me how to do it? I know Rundle's just passing on what you say. When I've got questions, I wish I could get answers straightaway."

She paused, not expecting this topic, but considering it all the same. "There's something in that, Mr Court. Perhaps it would be best if I could give the instructions directly." Though that would require her to see him and talk with him every day. But maybe Gabe Court wasn't quite as intimidating as he first seemed?

At the moment, he wasn't intimidating at all, half slumped over and looking with suspicion at the bottle. "You're completely sure it's, um, safe?"

Cady smiled. "Absolutely. I'd never offer one of my concoctions to another unless I know it won't hurt them. I test everything I make on myself first."

He nodded, and let her apply the solution to his cuts. He winced slightly, because of the astringency, but otherwise sat still.

But then he said, "How did you test it? Did you have to wait until you got a bruise?"

She chuckled. "No, I gave myself a small cut."

"With a *knife*?"

"A scalpel," Cady corrected him, then saw the expression on his face. "Oh, don't be so shocked. It's important to be rigorous in all scientific inquiry. Otherwise, it's just alchemy and superstition."

He opened his mouth as if to argue with her, then checked himself. "You're not what I expected of the lady of the house."

"No?" She was so intent on examining his wounds that she wasn't really thinking about what she was saying. "Funny, I spent a lot of time being exactly what everyone expected of me."

"And what was that?" he asked, leaning forward as if he was truly interested.

"Oh, your arm!" Cady exclaimed, noticing that the red

on his sleeve wasn't just a spot where he'd wiped at his head, but was evidence of another wound. "You were hurt there too."

"I didn't notice," he admitted.

"Well, let's see how bad it is. Come, come, don't waste time."

He rolled up the sleeve of his shirt so she could assess the damage. She tried not to notice the shape of him generally—the smooth skin, the musculature beneath it, the faint smells of earth and sweat. He had vitality to him that she found herself responding to. She wanted to be near him, to learn more about him…

Instead, she focused on the wound, an inch or so of broken skin in the center of what was already looking like a vicious bruise. "That's going to ache for a few days," she murmured. "I'll clean it and wrap it, but I can't make all the pain disappear."

"I raised my arm to block the blows," he said. "He must have hit with the top of the stick just there."

"I won't let him back in the house," Cady vowed. "Actually, I should thank you. Mr Pollack was a vexing guest at the best of times. But after this, I'm perfectly justified in never being at home to him again."

"Why let him visit at all, if you don't like him?"

Cady smiled sadly, running a fresh cloth over the wound to remove any dirt. "There are unwritten rules in Society. I'm supposed to be polite and welcoming, and Mr Pollack is a neighbor and a rather important person in the area. He's been…well, the fact of the matter is that he wants to marry me."

Gabe's expression of revulsion almost made her laugh. He said, "You wouldn't."

"He hasn't asked yet, so I don't yet know what I'd say."

"Why hasn't he asked? I mean, you're young and beautiful and kind. What's he waiting for?"

Cady paused, arrested by the compliment so plainly delivered. *Young and beautiful and kind.* This man had only just met her, but this was what he saw? Not *rich and strange and murderous*?

"Begging your pardon, my lady," he muttered, evidently realizing that the remark was a bit too personal.

She held his arm steady and began to wrap gauze around the wound, careful not to pull the cloth too tight. "No, it's fine. And to answer your question, he's waiting till he finds out if I'm to get the title or not."

Gabe blinked and looked at her in surprise. "You don't *know*?"

"No one knows. Papa didn't want my younger brother to inherit, so he tried to change things so that the title and everything goes to the eldest child, rather than the eldest male child. I'm a year older than him, not that you'd know it. But getting a title changed—there's something called letters patent and it's all rather convoluted, but the gist is that there's an office in London where they decide such things, but it takes them a very long time to decide, and Papa died in the meantime, so now nobody knows if it's Lord Calder or Lady Calder they should be trying to marry, and…it's all a bit much," she concluded, her shoulders sagging as the full weight of it settled down upon her again. The bizarre attack against Gabe, no, *Mr Court*, had distracted her from her own problems for a precious quarter hour. But now she could feel the clouds returning.

"I'm sorry to hear that," he said quietly. His voice was practically a rumble in his chest, not unlike that of a great cat.

It sounded so calming, so sympathetic and yet unaffected that Cady wanted to weep. "Why sorry? What did I just say? It's not your fault. And anyway, you're the one who's bleeding."

"I'll be better in no time," he told her, his gaze intent on her face.

Caught by those deep blue eyes, Cady couldn't say anything. *It would be nice*, she thought, *to be better in* any *time*. She envied him.

"Still," she whispered. "It shouldn't have happened at all. If I hadn't encouraged him and let him visit the house —"

"Stop. It's not your fault. He's the one who decided to hit me." Gabe's mouth curved at one corner. "And when it was over, he left and I'm still here. I'd call that a victory."

Cady exhaled in a short little laugh, tying off the gauze so it wouldn't unravel. "That's a very positive way to look at it."

"Oh, I'm good at that. Anyway, whenever I get into a fight, I usually end up on top."

"Do you." It wasn't really a question. Cady was rather lost in his eyes, and she wasn't fully registering the conversation. The only thought that flitted through her mind was that she had told him much more than she intended to, and it felt so natural, even though she hardly knew a thing about him.

Just then, she noticed a lock of that night-black hair had slipped forward. She reached over to tuck the hair back, and beneath her fingertips, his skin was warm.

When was the last time she had been alone with a man?

Does it matter? I'm alone with this man now.

This unusual thought blossomed quickly, into a full and detailed premonition of a world gone terribly wrong. If the man took the wrong message from her unconscious gesture—and why wouldn't he?—Cady would have no recourse or indeed anywhere to run if he did decide to take advantage of having her alone.

Here she was, having unlocked a private room and invited him into it, and then she asked him to remove some of his clothing... Of course he'd think she was offering something else, something she didn't fully understand but a man like him certainly would. And then Cady would be not just ruined, but destroyed. And what would happen to her then? God, why was she eternally foolish? Why had she not foreseen this and taken steps? She could have been smart and careful, instead of acting like someone too pigheaded to live...

Amid the flood of thoughts, Cady recognized the familiar dreadful feeling welling up. It was like being caught at the very edge of a maelstrom, seeing the inevitable doom, and yet not being able to steer free of it. She stood up quickly and stepped back, trying to control her body, if not her mind.

"Please leave," she said.

Gabe half reached for her before abruptly stopping. "I offended you."

"You didn't." Cady found it difficult to speak over the rising sense of panic in her chest, the feeling that her heart was about to shudder to a halt. "But you need to leave. Now. I have to be..." *Safe*, she was about to say, but she couldn't say that to a man she barely knew. "Just leave."

His eyes narrowed in concern. "Are you feeling well?"

"Perfectly well," she lied. "But it's very important that I be undisturbed...starting this minute." She put on a bright, brittle smile, the smile she used in the drawing room. "I advise you get some rest. And don't resume your duties tomorrow if you feel ill."

"Yes, my lady." He went to the door they'd entered from, but hesitated at the threshold, casting a concerned glance over his shoulder. "If there's anything I can do…"

"No. Thank you." Cady kept the smile plastered on her face until he was gone. God how she hated every time the fear took over, rendering her weak and shaky and so certain that she was about to die. This wasn't even the first time that happened in the past week, and yet it still struck with all the force of a sudden thunderclap.

Raising her hands to her face to wipe at the tears already forming, Cady saw something out of place and went still.

Her hands were *covered* in something.

She gasped, in her heightened distress first taking the stain for drying blood.

But no. It wasn't that at all.

Cady's more analytical side asserted itself. She cautiously lifted her hands, examining the stain more closely, then sniffing delicately. The substance was far too dark for blood, and it smelled wrong. How did it get into her laboratory, onto her hand? She tipped her head, confused by this very unexpected thing, like finding a butterfly in a snowstorm. The puzzle was so odd that it actually snapped her away from the spiraling horror she had been falling into.

She rubbed her thumb and forefinger together thoughtfully. The stain on the pads of her fingers was slick and sooty. She frowned. On a hunch, she reached for the cloth that she'd first used to clean the cut on his head. That too was streaked with the black substance.

Cady put the evidence together and arrived at the inevitable, if nonsensical, conclusion. Gabe Court couldn't be over thirty, and he didn't seem like a vain man. Yet, for no discernible reason, he'd dyed his hair.

♑

ONCE OUTSIDE THE HOUSE AGAIN, Gabe took a deep breath. He wasn't prepared for what just happened in that room…or maybe Pollack hit him harder than he thought, knocking him off his game.

When Arcadia had leaned over him at one point during her ministrations, he got an absolutely first-rate, front-row view of her breasts, visible past the neckline of her gown, and he was simultaneously hit with the scent of witch hazel. He wouldn't be able to smell witch hazel for a long while without that memory rushing up.

The woman had mistaken his reaction for one of pain when she touched a wound. In fact, someone could have been amputating Gabe's leg just then, and he wouldn't have cared. But when Arcadia pulled back, it was clear that she had no idea what happened, and that if he even hinted that he'd seen more than he should, she'd be mortified. He scrambled to get an expression on his face that wouldn't offend her, and just in time.

He got his libido under control and managed to ask a few questions that should lead her to give him some more information, and trust him as an ally. He even got her to agree that it would be a much better idea if she gave him instructions in person for the more important gardens.

Inquiry, curiosity, sympathy. All emotions agents used in getting people to trust them. And it had all been so easy for Gabe, almost as if he really did care about her feelings. Which of course he didn't, especially not when she confessed how that shit-sack Pollack actually thought he could *marry* her. As if he was a match for such a lovely woman…

Anyway, everything had been progressing very well indeed, and then she got that strange look on her face and abruptly ordered him out. Gabe tracked back over their conversation. Had she said something she shouldn't have, given him a clue she hadn't meant to drop? Or had *he* said something to alert her?

No, they hadn't been talking about anything of substance then. She'd simply been wrapping his arm with the gauze, showing more openness than at any point before.

Was that it? She'd just been reacting to him? Gabe smiled, thinking that he'd certainly reacted to her. Though his impulse wouldn't have been to leave. He would have much rather stayed to see where things might have gone…

Then he shook his head. Idiot. Arcadia was a lady, and an inexperienced one. Of course she'd recoil from physical desire—she would have been taught to fear it. But he could shape that impulse, and soon have her reacting very differently, as long as he used every opportunity he had to get her alone.

A little part of him didn't like the plan. It was heartless, and even mean to manipulate and seduce her like that.

Gabe shoved that thought back into the place in his mind where he kept everything that wasn't directly related to his assignment. He had a directive: find the poison, find the poisoner. Nothing else mattered. Not even Arcadia Osbourne, with her big, innocent eyes and her soft laugh and the touch of her fingers on his skin.

He gave another shake of the head, annoyed at himself

for allowing the woman to affect him at all. It was just because he'd spent so long trying to figure out how to get close to her that when it happened he needed time to adjust. But the plan would still work. As someone who'd fought real battles, Gabe was used to adjusting the plan. Soldiers who couldn't adjust to new factors tended to die.

Well, even soldiers who did know how to adjust died. He'd lost several good friends thanks to Bonaparte's ambitions—a wiser man would have found another way to occupy his time when it was so clear that the wars in Europe would last a while. But being the youngest son, Gabe didn't have the luxury of choosing another occupation. His eldest brother, Gerald, would inherit nearly everything, his next older brother, Gilbert, had sensibly decided on a career in the church, and that left the army for Gabe.

Not that he'd have preferred the church. Gabe laughed to himself. He didn't have the temperament to shepherd souls toward the next world. He was more interested in this one. He supposed that was what first got the attention of the Zodiac. When Gabe was in the army, he took on missions that few other soldiers would touch. They were dirty, sneaky assignments that required a lot of humility and some bending of the usual rules of gentlemanly warfare. But it was for the right reason—ending the war as quickly as possible.

For one such mission, Gabe had to circle around behind the enemy and deliver a message to a French corporal whose loyalty was a bit suspect. Gabe managed the first part perfectly, but when the corporal decided that he didn't want Gabe to remain alive to report on his conduct...*that* had got messy. Afterward, the French army was down a corporal, and Gabe had to leave his favorite knife behind in the corporal's chest.

He was certain that he'd be disciplined—or worse—

when he reported back. Instead, he found himself offered more assignments like it. He learned fast, and by the time he was shipped back home, he had a formidable collection of skills that he couldn't tell anyone about. That was when he met Julian Neville and the mysterious Miss Chattan. They told him he was perfect for the Zodiac: independent, intelligent, resourceful, and above all, discreet.

For the next several years, Gabe handled countless assignments. Some required him to travel to France, Germany, Portugal…and further. Some were completed without leaving London. Gabe never turned an assignment down, and he never liked the idle time between assignments. He'd found his calling. Anything else felt like a waste.

To be sure, he visited his family and old friends, establishing that he was still around, though not terribly reliable. Gabe liked to spread rumors that he was involved in gambling, loose women, and, most shockingly, trade. It kept questions from his old set to a minimum, and it prevented anyone from trying to match him with an eligible daughter. (Not that it was a big risk, considering that on the marriage mart, third sons were as attractive as three-day-old fish.)

All that left Gabe free to do his real work. He liked the process of the Zodiac's assignments. No matter how unusual the task, the same general procedure applied. Gather information, assess the situation, find the weaknesses, choose the right moment, and strike. Then he could go back to the Zodiac with his victory. Sometimes it was information like a secret letter or a document. Sometimes it was a report of an unfortunate death. Sometimes it was nothing more than Gabe assuring them that he spoke a certain phrase to a certain person.

But here, at Calderwood, Gabe was distinctly uneasy.

He'd arrived at the estate thinking that the lady of the house was directly involved with the poisonings in London. But that was no longer a safe assumption. She never left the estate, and she didn't have any motive for the killings anyway. Plus, if she were some cold-hearted killer, would she have dragged him off to be patched up following a scuffle with an idiot?

He didn't like being so unsure of the situation. He wished he could reexamine the dossier Miss Chattan had compiled for him, but of course he'd burned it after he'd read the contents. And yes, he'd dutifully committed everything in it to memory, but perhaps he'd missed some nuance, some fact that would help him now.

"Or there just wasn't much to find," he muttered, stalking through the gardens and beyond to the broad lawn that swept out over to the west of the main house. Both Chattan and Julian had been close-lipped about exactly what the previous agent, Pisces, had been doing before he'd been killed—maybe they didn't even know. Agents were used to having free rein on assignments. Actually, the fact that Aries insisted on regular reports showed how nervous they were about this, willing to risk discovery of the report just so they'd know if their agent was still alive.

Gabe thought that he could actually send off his next report now. He had some positive news to relate, since he'd actually spoken with Lady Arcadia and gained a measure of trust from her...or had he? She acted very oddly at the end of that encounter, as if something forced her to withdraw from the whole conversation. On second thought, maybe he should hold off on that report for a day or two.

Just then, a low, mournful sound drifted over to him. Gabe went still, listening hard. Then the sound came again, and he relaxed. It was a dog howling.

He spun about and headed toward the sound. When Gabe found the old shed that served as the kennel, he stopped as a huge shape emerged from the shadows, accompanied by a low growl.

Gabe exhaled only after he scanned the fence and saw it was secure. Christ, that was a big dog. He'd never seen a wolfhound that big before. With the shaggy gray coat and the shining eyes, this animal would easily be mistaken for a wild creature.

He approached, speaking quietly and calmly as he did. "Hello there, boy. You a hunting dog? Lord Calder's dog? Getting bored now, I'd guess. I'm Gabe, and I wish I had a treat from the kitchens for you, but I don't. Don't know your name either, and oh, Christ, there's two of you."

Gabe sucked in a breath as another massive form rose up from the straw bedding in the shed, and padded over to join the first. What the hell did the late Lord Calder hunt? Giants?

Gabe put his hand against the fence, half fearing it would be ripped off. But the first dog just sniffed, and then licked his palm.

"That makes us friends now, yes?" Gabe asked hopefully. The dog's shoulder hit against the fence, which sagged a bit. "I hope we're friends."

"Ah, you found the dogs!"

Gabe turned to see the footman Vernon approaching with a pail.

"One was howling a bit," Gabe explained. "I was worried it was hurt."

"Oh, no. Just bored, I'm sure."

"Why not let them out?"

"And who'll mind 'em? We've all got our work and can't be letting these lads wander off."

"I'll take them," Gabe volunteered. "I have to walk the grounds anyway. It's no trouble to take the dogs along."

"No trouble for *you*, maybe," the footman replied with a laugh. "If you want the job, ask Rundle first. But he'll say yes."

"What are their names?"

"That's Romulus with the red collar, and Remus with the blue. The late lord hunted deer in the forest, or he'd take the dogs with him to other places for a hunting party in the fall. Poor things haven't been out for more than a half hour at a time since he passed."

Gabe noticed the pail of kitchen scraps in the footman's hand. "Here, let me feed them. May as well get them on my side."

So Gabe fed them, and soon had both of them staring hopefully at him. Then he spied the leather leashes hanging from a wall and decided that there was no time like the present. He'd get Rundle's approval afterward.

The dogs were ecstatic to be out of the kennel and Gabe strained to keep them from bolting toward the woods. He had to admit that the others were correct. No one at Calderwood that he'd seen so far had the physical strength to control these animals. He pictured the delicate Lady Arcadia doing so, and actually smiled at the image.

Luckily, Gabe was used to wrangling big creatures (though in the war, he'd been more likely to be dealing with a recalcitrant horse or wayward cow—some animals simply did not respect battle lines). He soon got both Romulus and Remus moving in the same direction at a steady pace. The dogs sniffed and yelped happily, but they'd been well trained, and when Gabe tugged lightly at the leads, each dog responded instantly.

With the dogs, his daily task of walking the perimeter

of the grounds was actually fun. They knew where to go, making him think that this was a habit they used to share with the old master, or perhaps a now-departed servant, one of the ones who'd run off when things started going badly at the estate.

Gabe continued along his route, which wrapped around the huge open area centered on the great house, and carried him into the woodland along the north part of the property. The wooded area the dogs were leading him through was just waking up after a long winter. There were as yet no leaves on the branches above, but tufts of grasses and small mounds of flowers poked out amid the brown litter of the forest floor. White star-shaped flowers on nodding stalks swung in the breeze, and little butter-colored blooms peeked out here and there. Even the mosses on the rocks seemed especially green. Gabe grudgingly admitted that it was beautiful. He normally didn't spend much time thinking about landscapes, but compared to the scenes he'd spent so much time in while a soldier…the churned-up fields, the endless mud, the piles of broken and discarded things that any army left in its wake, and always the stench of death…well, this was better.

Suddenly, both dogs went still, their heads high and snouts quivering. Gabe tightened his grip on the leashes, anticipating a wrenching tug if the dogs scented prey.

"Romulus, Remus, stay," he warned in a low voice.

Then he heard a rustling sound a hundred yards ahead. He saw a flash of color across the path, and the shape resolved into a figure, just for a second. Then it vanished once again, and he heard the figure running away.

Romulus howled, eager to chase down something after so long. Remus howled too, and the pair strained to run, their front paws rising into the air.

Part of Gabe wanted to see the dogs in action, and wanted to know who was lurking in the woods. But he feared that any chase would end in blood, so he spoke firmly to the wolfhounds, assuring them that the time for hunting would come later.

Eventually, the dogs calmed, and though Remus cast wistful glances to the woods ahead, he allowed Gabe to turn back toward the meadow and lead the dogs across the wide open space behind the house.

They passed by the formal rectangular building called the orangerie, and continued on, nearing the house. After passing by a rabbit who'd been exploring the young shoots in the vegetable garden, Romulus got so excited he reverted to puppy status, whining and rolling around in the grass. Gabe looked around and decided it was safe enough with walls on two sides. He let the dogs' leashes go and allowed them to romp and wrestle on the soft grass of the lawn.

They yelped playfully as they tumbled over the grass. Gabe realized he was smiling like an idiot as he watched them. It had been a long time since he'd done something like this—there wasn't much call for dog-walking in espionage.

Something flashed in his peripheral vision. He looked up toward the house. A curtain flicked on an upper floor, and the fabric fell in front of the window. But just for a split second, he'd seen the perfect silhouette of a woman in a dark gown.

Arcadia.

* * * *

Cady watched in amazement as the two massive wolfhounds leapt and rolled and played on the green grass, happy as puppies. And so willing to let Gabe be in charge, even though he was an entirely new person in their lives. Some people just had the gift, she supposed. The gift to be accepted by everyone, to simply slide into new lives and new places and fit in like a puzzle piece.

She pulled the curtain closed when Gabe looked up at one point, afraid he'd notice and think she was even stranger than he must already. She'd acted so oddly before, in her workroom. But the panic always shut down her better sense, and she couldn't bear anyone to see her like that—scared and unreasoning in the face of the nameless fear that kept coming back to haunt her, no matter how much she tried to avoid raising its specter again.

Cady had spent nearly an hour enduring the attack and its aftermath, which left her feeling faint and unwell, her breathing weak and her whole body wrung out. God, she hated what the fear did to her, how it turned her into this pathetic caricature of a person.

Oscar's presence had helped. One of the cat's most charming traits was his comfort with being picked up and moved anywhere. He never scratched or struggled when Cady scooped him into her arms. He merely readjusted his body and went back to the important business of dozing. The soft rumble of his purr calmed Cady as she tried to forget the worst of the panicky feelings.

She ought to have known this would happen. She always reacted badly to surprises, or new situations. And having an unknown man within arm's reach certainly counted as new.

And it wasn't just that he was new. It was also disconcerting to look at him and feel so shy and simultaneously so intrigued. Cady rarely got a chance to see such a virile man up close. Some of Trevor's friends had been stunningly handsome, back when Trevor still lived at Calderwood and his friends would come visit. Cady always peeked, even though she really had no business noticing them.

But Gabe Court was different. Big and strong and capable…all things Cady was not. And she couldn't deny that he was attractive. Or at least she was attracted to him. Cady had no female friends to share these sorts of thoughts with, so perhaps other women might not be as drawn to him?

"Nonsense," she told herself. Those blue eyes would melt any heart.

She abruptly turned away from the window, annoyed that she was acting so silly. What did it matter if he had blue eyes or no eyes? Cady would be better off never seeing him again.

Unfortunately, she had agreed to meet with him in the mornings to discuss the necessary tasks for the gardens and grounds. And she couldn't ignore the importance of that, for Calderwood was only a few weeks away from reverting back into a wildwood.

Clearly, he didn't need much instruction from her about most things. He'd apparently charmed the dogs to his side in a matter of minutes, and now they regarded him with total adoration. Cady loved animals herself, and there was a time in the past when she would have been delighted to play with the dogs on the lawn. But after so long when she had ignored them and been scared of them, just because they were big and shaggy and didn't speak human language…well, Cady was sure the dogs hated her now. Why wouldn't they? She could have gone to see them every day since her father's death. But she didn't. Instead she hid inside and was scared of her own shadow. Dogs could sense fear. Her father always warned her of that.

Cady ought to leave the dogs and the whole grounds to this new gardener, if that's what would keep him here. She needed this man to help her keep the place civilized.

When she looked at Gabe Court, however, civilized wasn't how she felt.

♑

THE NEXT MORNING, CADY PUSHED Oscar off her pillow, and pulled the bell cord to summon Martha.

"Help me get dressed, please. I'll need an outfit to stand up to the weather."

"You're going *out*, my lady?" Martha asked incredulously.

"Outside in the main gardens and the meadow, yes. I'm not leaving Calderwood." Cady laughed at the mere idea. The world beyond her gates was a terror to her now.

"Oh." Martha sagged in relief. "The gardens, yes. I suppose that's all right."

"It has occurred to me that I ought to be overseeing the efforts of the new gardener if there's any hope of getting all the necessary work done this spring. Have you spoken to him much?"

"A bit, my lady. He seems quite personable, and he always does what he's asked, so says Mr Rundle."

"Did he mention anything about his past or his family?" Cady asked, realizing she knew almost nothing about him.

Martha replied, "Come to think of it, I can't recall a single thing he's said about himself. He's one of those types that lets others talk."

Once dressed in a sturdy wool gown in a deep coffee shade, and wearing her usual dark cloak over it, Cady proceeded outside to find Mr Court. He was working out-side the main garden shed on the north side, just past the paddock. A wheel had come off one of the carts, and he was busily repairing it.

"Good morning," she said.

He straightened up and gave her a smile, before think-ing better of it and nodding his head once. "My lady."

"Is the cart damaged?"

"Nothing that can't be fixed. I may have to go to the village to see about a part. There's a blacksmith there, I assume."

"Yes, name of Lowell. He's always done very good work. Well, I should hope he does. Perhaps don't mention it's for Calderwood," Cady said, thinking that it was quite possible that no one would do any work for her or her people at all by this point.

Mr Court looked surprised. "Never met a tradesman who didn't like getting paid."

"You've yet to meet the tradespeople of Dorbridge," she said wryly.

Before he could press her on it and bring up all sorts of awkward subjects, Cady gestured toward the small building that held the kennel. "You took the dogs out yes-terday. Was it difficult? Handling them both at once, I mean. Papa never had a problem, but he got them as pups. They adored him."

"They were very good," he assured her. "Tried to bolt just once, but it was understandable. They got the scent of someone in the woods and wanted to chase them down."

Cady stilled. "Someone in the woods? My woods?"

"Yes, my lady. I only glimpsed him. A man or boy wearing a reddish coat. Didn't wonder at the time, but he was probably a poacher."

"But there's fencing all around the property."

Gabe gave her an odd smile. "No fence in the world that can't be climbed, or cut, or dug under, my lady. Your land is prime territory. All those woods and nothing to stop the deer and rabbits and birds from breeding."

"I don't want strangers on the estate," Cady said. If someone was bold enough to be in the woods, they might get bold enough to reach the house, or enter the house. And who knew what damage they'd wreak then…

"My lady? Are you well?" Gabe had stepped closer to her, and half raised a hand to touch her shoulder. His form was large enough to block the sunlight for a moment, and Cady blinked in the unexpected shade.

"What? Yes, I'm perfectly well." She was imagining scenarios of casually cruel youths trooping though the gardens or invading the glasshouses. She shivered. A few minutes ago, she'd been so secure in her belief that at least here she was safe.

"You said that yesterday. But you didn't look well, if you don't mind me saying so."

She pulled herself together. "I do mind, Mr Court," she said, striving for a more formal tone.

"Oh. Well, in that case let's pretend I didn't say anything." He gave her another smile, this one half sweet, half mischievous.

Cady couldn't stop a laugh from bubbling up. He really was rather charming. "Very well, Mr Court. Let's simply go on. I believe you requested that I give your instructions personally."

"It's just that I want to do well," he said, looking earnest now. "If you can tell me what you really need, then I'll be able to help. In the gardens, I mean."

"We have a prodigious amount of work. Spring is the most important season for any garden. The bulbs and roots planted last autumn need to be checked to see that they've made it through the winter. There are seedlings in some of the glasshouses that will soon be moved outside, so you'll have to prepare the beds, and let's see, oh yes, I'll need more mulch at the front for the rose garden, and the woodland garden…"

"How many gardens do you actually have here? It seems like a hundred."

"It's actually only about two dozen, depending on what you call a garden versus, say, a landscape."

"And you manage *all* of it?"

"Of course. Who else?"

"A gardener, maybe? I mean a proper gardener, who knows how to do everything."

"I know how to do everything, Mr Court."

"But you're the lady of the house. Don't you have other tasks?"

Cady bit her lip to hide a smile. "Some ladies might, but I do not. I'm not married, so I've no husband to attend to. I'm not a mother, so I've no children to raise. Since my father's death, I've been quite out of Society, so I've no events to plan for."

"There were people here, though. That Pollack idiot, and the other man, and the ladies."

"A few neighbors do insist on observing the niceties," Cady acknowledged. "Mrs Bowcott—that's the vicar's wife—feels it's her duty to visit. Mr Heath is a gardener himself, so he's all right. And Mr Pollack…well, we've established both his reasons for coming before and why he shall never be welcome here again. But I assure you, that is practically the end of the list."

"Do you mind?"

"Mind what? Being ostracized? I'd mind more if I didn't have Calderwood to care for. And anyway, I don't like leaving the estate now."

"Why not?"

She shuddered. "I just don't care to. Now, let's see how the Italian garden is progressing. The warm spell should promote a lot of growth these next few days…"

Once on the firm ground of garden talk, Cady felt much more comfortable. She pointed out several items for Gabe to do (somehow, though she'd never say it out loud, he seemed much more like a Gabe than a Mr Court). He noted them all and nodded as if he was actually listening, even asking questions to be sure he got things right. When Cady asked him to remind her of what she'd said so far, he recited the entire list from memory.

"How do you do that?" she asked, impressed.

"Just a knack," he said with a shrug. "I'm used to having to keep a lot of int—that is, things in my head."

"A good skill to have, no matter what you do." Cady looked around. Somehow they'd made their way through several of the gardens, and ended up at the gate that eventually led to her own secret garden.

"Where's that go?" he asked, pointing to the gate and beyond. "Looks like more gardens, but I can't see how else to get there."

"You don't get there, Mr Court. It's restricted."

"Why?"

He didn't seem upset about it, only curious. Almost like a puppy with a new scent…except that describing Gabe Court as a puppy made him seem harmless, and no one interested in Cady's private domain was harmless.

"It's where I do my work and conduct my experiments. There are plants and substances that could be very dangerous to someone just wandering in."

"But if you were there to show me around, I wouldn't be wandering," Gabe countered.

"Why are you so interested?"

He shrugged, giving her a lopsided, almost bashful smile. "You make it sound interesting. In fact—"

Before he could go on, Cady heard her name shouted from all the way across the yard, and spun around to see what was going on.

♑

"Who's that?" Gabe muttered, jerking his head toward the main gardens. He was deeply annoyed that someone interrupted him just then. He was breaking down the barriers Arcadia kept all around her, and with a little more effort, he would have got her to agree to take him into the restricted gardens and glasshouses. He'd gleaned that Arcadia—whatever else she might be—was the sort of person who kept her word once she gave it. He was going to use that to get what he needed.

She was heading toward the source of the call, with a look of such delight that Gabe actually felt a stab of envy.

A man strolled up the garden path, gazing left and right at all the greening beds, nodding in approval. He had a walking stick, but he used it only to poke at the soil, testing its depth and dampness. When he got close enough to Arcadia and Gabe to *not* shout, he said, "Good day, little Cady!"

Rather than being offended at the familiarity, Arcadia beamed at him. "Mr Addison, I didn't expect to see you today."

"I ought to have sent word, but as I was already heading in this direction, I thought it would be acceptable."

"Always," she assured him.

While Addison was speaking with Arcadia, he was surveying Gabe with a certain coolness, even skepticism. The man's gaze lingered on Gabe's admittedly muddy boots, and then noted the dirt on his clothes before giving the slightest nod of acceptance. *He's judging me*, Gabe thought. *What right does* he *have to judge me?*

"New people at last, my lady?" he said. "How fortunate."

"Indeed. I couldn't bear the thought of neglecting the grounds. Remember how I mentioned that idea of advertising in the London papers several weeks ago? Well, it's borne fruit…so to speak. Mr Court answered Mr Rundle's advertisement."

"Did he?" Addison gave another, more suspicious glance at Gabe, and again, Gabe didn't know why.

Arcadia was oblivious, already introducing the men just as if they were at some Society function. "Mr Court, this is Mr Addison. He's a longtime friend of my family, and an avid gardener and botanist himself. Mr Court came here from London." She didn't add anything else, for which Gabe was grateful.

Gabe looked at the other man with interest. "You're a botanist? With a laboratory, like Lady Arcadia's?"

Addison chuckled. "*Nobody* has a laboratory quite like hers. Though I do try to be as meticulous as possible, and keep accurate records of all my plants. Breeding, size, growth, and such. It's very important to do that for each species. My goal is to create new hybrids that will change the world."

"Change the world?" Gabe echoed, thinking that he might have found a likely candidate for a megalomaniacal poisoner. "How?"

"Through scent and beauty, of course!"

"Mr Addison's particular interest is roses," Arcadia added helpfully. "His rose garden must be six times the size of mine."

"Ah, but you have a few specimens that I do not,"

Addison protested, though with a smile. "I will not be content until I possess them for myself."

"Then you must bring me a specimen that *I* do not have," Arcadia told him. "That is the agreement."

"Agreement?" Gabe asked.

"You see, Mr Court," Addison said. "Some time ago I made a deal with Lady Arcadia's mother, Lady Calder, may she rest in peace. An even exchange of plants so that both our collections can grow, the only rule being that it cannot be a specimen already in the recipient's garden. But think of it! Our lady here has so many different gardens and varieties of practically everything. Whereas I specialize in roses. Every time I think I've found a plant that will surprise her, she looks it up in her infernal gardening journal, and of course she's got an example tucked away in a plot or a greenhouse or what have you."

"It keeps you on your toes, Mr Addison. Honestly, if you didn't try to find new plants for our exchanges, you'd never look at anything other than a rose again."

"Why should I look beyond the queen of flowers? Although that reminds me. Speaking of which, Cady dear, did you ever make use of that book I gave to you last year? The herbal from the Persian botanist?"

Arcadia brightened further. "Funny you should ask! There's a very interesting formula he describes that makes use of Iranian salvia, which I've been growing in the glasshouse for the past several months. And I've just been able to harvest some of the parts in great enough quantities to try to duplicate the experiment. I'm going to try tonight, in fact."

"Wonderful. I shall hope to hear of your results next time we talk. However, that will have to wait, for I've brought you a gift."

"Indeed?" She smiled wider and Gabe was starting to

want to kick this man off the property. *Cady dear*, indeed.

"The gift that every woman longs for…rose petals!"

Cady chuckled. "I believe that most women expect the petals to still be attached to the stem, but I am happy for the gift."

"Why?" Gabe asked. He sounded surly, but then, people expected servants to be surly.

"Rosewater is a key ingredient for many of my recipes," Arcadia explained, not at all put out by his tone. "But I'll have to process these rose petals as soon as possible, so I'm afraid that you'll be on your own for the rest of the day."

"Can I help move anything? The crates or… whatever?" he offered, hoping it might allow him to see something interesting.

Mr Addison nodded. "No time to waste! The cart is by the main entrance, so your man there can haul it closer to your distillery."

"The sooner the better," Cady agreed. "Mr Court, take that cart to the large stillroom—that's the red brick building by the kitchen gardens. Unload the baskets into the stillroom and then return the cart to the drive."

Gabe hurried to do the task. He wanted her to trust him, and he was very curious about what this cart contained. Could it actually be something as straightforward and harmless as roses? Or perhaps some rare and mysterious tropical plant helpfully labeled *poisonous*? He could only hope.

But once he got to the cart, he was nearly knocked down by the intense, all-encompassing aroma of rose. The cart was loaded with huge baskets all leeching the cloying, sickly sweet odor. He steered the cart to the stillroom, and lifted the first two baskets (they weighed practically nothing) and walked briskly to the stillroom door. He dropped the baskets and returned to get the next.

Oh God, now he stank of rose. He always considered it a pleasant scent…now he was rethinking it. Gabe moved quickly, unloading the baskets so he could then poke around in this stillroom without being observed. Because this shed wasn't behind multiple walls and gates, he assumed there wasn't anything of particular interest here. But he might get a hint of what was going on at Calderwood.

The distilling apparatus appeared normal enough. Gabe had seen similar for whisky up in Scotland, and brandy over in France. Glass tubes and big barrels filled a large part of the shed. But on one wall there was a cabinet. It was locked, but the lock was a simple one and he had it open seconds later.

He opened it and peered in, finding a treasure trove. Dozens and dozens of bottles and jars and little crocks were packed in there. All were labeled in a fine, educated, feminine hand. He picked up one bottle, reading out: "Distillation of Rosa Gallica, 12 September 1810." Another glass jar held a grainy substance: "Powdered willow bark, 16 November 1810." A tiny, slender bottle was labeled: "Tincture of Papaver Somniferum, 30 June 1810." Evidently, these were ingredients that Arcadia made from plants grown here at Calderwood.

Hearing footsteps, Gabe closed the cabinet, snapped the lock back on, and stepped away, bending down to the last basket of rose petals as if he'd just put it down.

When he looked over to the door of the stillroom, however, it wasn't Arcadia who came to see him. It was Mr Addison.

"Just got the last basket, sir," Gabe said, using his most servile tone. "That cart can go now."

"Glad to hear it," Mr Addison responded, looking

around the stillroom almost absently. "Quite an unusual place this is."

"The stillroom?" Gabe asked cautiously, not sure where Addison was leading him with that question, but very sure the man wanted to tell him something. "Don't most estates have such things?"

"Ah, but for very dull reasons. Making spirits to drink, or possibly to preserve some fruits or herbs. Lady Arcadia uses her stillroom for a much higher purpose."

"There's more than one."

"Oh, yes. This is for ordinary crops. She has a smaller one in her private garden for more specialized tasks." Addison seemed to enjoy his greater knowledge of Arcadia's activities. "You know she is responsible for a good number of the medicines and remedies in the county?"

"I didn't, sir."

"She cultivates exotics so rare that the medicine made out of their parts seems like magic. And magic can be feared as well as desired."

"How so? Nothing she makes is venomous, is it?"

Addison raised a finger to stop him. "No, no. That is wrong. Snakes and spiders are venomous. Venom is delivered via a bite or injection of some type. Poisons work though contact…whether by touch, or being eaten or drunk. It's very sloppy to use words imprecisely."

"Forgive me, sir. What I meant was, does she grow poisonous plants?"

"Indeed she does, and guards them well lest some fool stumbles over them and hurts someone. A fool from London, for example." Addison leaned forward, blocking the stillroom door. "From what Lady Arcadia said earlier, you've only just come to Kent."

"Yes, sir."

"Do much gardening before this?"

"No, sir. I was in the army. Not much call for gardening there."

"I suppose the only thing the army uses shovels for is graves."

Gabe only nodded, not liking the grim image, or the memories it stirred up.

"How did you hear about the position again?" Addison asked with more than casual interest.

He shrugged. "Newspaper? Don't remember which one."

"And you came all the way from London to be a gardener, despite having no qualifications or knowledge of the work."

"Her ladyship's given me two weeks to prove I'm useful."

Addison crossed his arms. Though shorter and smaller than Gabe, he didn't seem at all concerned—as the richer, higher-born man, he knew he'd be given every benefit of every doubt, while Gabe would be given nothing at all. "How exactly do you expect to prove useful to her?"

Gabe frowned. "By…gardening? It's a big place. She can't do half of what needs doing. Hell, a dozen men couldn't keep all the grounds under control. Don't know what you want to hear."

"I want to hear that you know your place. Lady Arcadia is a woman of delicate constitution and she's had an extremely trying life, though it may not seem so. If I hear even a hint of impropriety about you, Mr Court, you'll be lucky to get out of Kent alive."

"You're threatening me?"

"I'm protecting Lady Arcadia. She has very few people who are willing to do so. I am one."

Gabe nodded slowly, finally understanding all the antagonism from Mr Addison. "I'm not here to make trouble. I'm here to do a job." Not the job of gardener, but Addison didn't need to know that.

"See that you remember it, Mr Court."

"I will. And by the way, since you're threatening me, tell me if you grow any poisonous plants."

"Not by choice! There are of course some garden specimens that are not wise to eat." Addison reverted to his typical sententious hobbyist tone. "Or touch, in the case of hogweed, though it boasts a rather splendid inflorescence, you know. Every patch of land in England has some plant that is poisonous. Roses on the other hand are completely edible. One just has to mind the thorns." He gave Gabe a chill smile.

"I see. Can you think of anyone else in the area who might have plants like that?"

"Aside from Lady Arcadia…no, I do not. Why do you —" Addison glanced over his shoulder, and stepped aside just as Arcadia walked up.

"There you both are," she said. "What were you talking about just now?"

"Oh, nothing much. Mr Court had a question about the lay of the land, and I was pleased to explain it," Addison said smoothly.

Gabe coughed because he didn't trust himself to speak.

"Too much rose?" she asked Gabe, sympathy in her tone. "Go to the kitchens and ask Cook if you can stick your nose in the coffee beans she keeps in the pantry. That will help counteract the effect."

"I'll do that, my lady, thank you."

Mr Addison glanced at a pocket watch, made a sound of irritation, and gave a little bow to her. "The time has got away from me, and I must return home. I do hope that someday soon you will visit my roses. It's been too long."

He nodded coolly to Gabe and then turned and strolled away toward the drive.

"Roses? Honestly?" Gabe muttered once he was out of earshot.

Arcadia gave a little rueful laugh. "He's a gifted gardener and I can't fault his enthusiasm, but in truth, it's a bit of a waste of talent. I'll never tell him so, but roses are…well, at the end of the day, they're *roses*."

Gabe sighed inwardly. It seemed that Mr Addison was not the devious brewer of poisons he was seeking. Now, if someone were slaying the people of England with perfume, he'd have a lead.

"He's a good man, though," she added loyally. "A few years ago, he offered marriage, I think because he felt sorry for me. I told him that while I appreciated the gesture, I ought to remain as I am. But he's always been a very stalwart friend."

If Cady only knew how stalwart, Gabe thought, recalling Addison's previous words to him. "So he's a longtime gardener. Are there many of you in this area of the country?" Perhaps he could meet others and find a clue that way.

"Several, most of whom are like Mr Addison and choose a particular type of plant or garden style to devote themselves to. I'm rather an odd duck, because I'm truly more interested in the medicinal properties of plants. Mr Addison, for example, couldn't care less about how roses may heal someone. But tell him that you've seen a new shade of pink petal, and he's galloping off to see it for himself!"

"Well, at least he finds plants for you. Where does he procure them?"

"Oh, who knows? Gardeners all talk to each other and we're forever sending off seeds and cuttings to our colleagues. I have specimens from the Americas, Asia, and Africa—mostly the tropical climes, for some reason. Possibly because the less tropical regions don't have as much variety. I've seen pictures that are just desert or plains. Can you imagine all of England being simply a single, unending ocean of grass? Nothing else? I'm told much of the North American continent is like that in the west."

"Would you like to see it for yourself?"

She paused, thinking. "On the one hand, yes. Who wouldn't want to see such a marvel? But on the other, to actually be there, to stand in the midst of an alien landscape with no knowledge of what it contained...." She shivered, and Gabe had the unexpected impulse to embrace her.

But then she said lightly, "Seems a long trip. If I want to see such things, I can visit an art gallery."

"But you'd still have to leave your house to do so."

Something in his tone made her glance at him, and he hoped he'd given nothing away. Gabe certainly wouldn't mind if the lady left her estate for a day or two, allowing him the freedom to investigate more.

"You're done here," she said briskly. "I'll need to distill all these petals to rosewater, and judging from your reaction to the scent, you definitely don't want to hang around for the next step."

"I'm happy to help," he offered. It would be a good opportunity to remain close to her, asking little questions to draw out what she knew. That was the reason he was here after all.

Arcadia shook her head. "No need. It's not a difficult procedure. Not like some of my experiments, which require far more rigor and attention. Anyway, you've much more important work to do."

Gabe blinked, his mind still on the assignment. "I

do?"

"Yes, Mr Court. The mulching."

"Ah, right. The mulching." He really couldn't put *that* in his report to Aries.

"Never disdain to do the small things, Mr Court. The glory of a garden in full bloom hides all the hard work we do earlier, when no one notices except when we get covered in filth."

Thus dismissed, Gabe left the stillroom, trailing the scent of rose in his wake.

* * * *

Late evening brought Cady back to her laboratory. She'd spent the whole afternoon distilling the massive amount of rose petals down to their essence, in the form of rosewater. Then she'd dutifully bottled the results and carefully labeled each bottle.

Hours later, she was still surrounded by the fog of rosewater, which made it difficult to use all her senses to assess what she created in the lab. In hindsight, she would blame this fact for her mistake.

She was eager to get to work on the solution she had read about in the book Mr Addison had given her. Since she was able to finally harvest the sap of the Iranian salvia from the glasshouse, she had everything she needed. Cady was excited about the possibilities for this solution, because the author of the herbal (a Persian doctor) claimed that it had the ability to calm even the most anxious and upset patient. In his words, "*I have used a mere dram of this solution to bring a patient suffering from hallucinations and panic to a sedate and happy demeanor.*"

Well. That was just what Cady needed.

So she measured and mixed, stirred and separated.

Finally, Cady peered at the solution in the glass tube. Viscosity was correct, the color was correct, the smell was correct (she thought). According to the description in the book, she'd followed all the directions and made the solution exactly as she ought. But there was only one way to be certain that her creation would do what it was supposed to.

With a slight grimace, Cady drank down the prescribed dram. The taste was bitter—she'd need to remember to have a strongly flavored drink right after so anyone else using it could keep the initial dose down. She leaned over the table, recording the time she took the dose, the amount, and her impression of the taste. She'd add to the entry every quarter hour, with precise details of the physical effects she experienced.

Was she calmer? Hard to tell. Cady wasn't willing to wait until she was in the throes of one of her attacks to try the first dose, so she'd just have to hope that she'd notice a difference even now.

Oscar the cat meowed at her, having snuck in an open window from the walled garden.

"Oh, Oscar, you shouldn't be in here. There's far too many breakable things." Turning to shoo the cat out, Cady stumbled, lurching to the right. Perhaps the base ingredients were stronger than she thought. She ought to drink some water to dilute the substance.

Before she could pick up the water glass, she fell forward, directly onto the worktable. Glass tubes and dishes shattered, and items went flying. But Cady didn't even notice, because she had crashed, unconscious, onto the cold marble surface.

* * * *

Gabe couldn't wait any longer. Everything he had learned so far pointed to secrets contained within Arcadia's walled and locked garden. So tonight was the night that he'd scale the walls and investigate for himself.

Scaling the wall wasn't Gabe's first choice. He did try to pick the lock on the heavy gate, but without luck. The lock was a strange one. If he were a superstitious man, he might blame magic for his failure to open the lock. But he didn't believe in magic, or witches, or ghosts, or anything else that seemed to be whispered about around here.

So, if he couldn't get in through the gate, he'd just have to go over the top of the wall. He used the same ladder as before (with the broken rung repaired). This time he also attached a rope to it, wound about in such a way that he could pull the ladder up behind him and take it along if needed.

By a combination of climbing and crawling along the wall's ivy-massed top, Gabe reached the same point he'd got to in his last excursion, tantalizingly close to the windows of the lit shed in the walled garden. He was not surprised to see light coming from the windows. Lady Arcadia mentioned something to Mr Addison about working on an experiment from a book. She'd seemed unusually excited about it, which made Gabe curious to see what all the fuss was about.

He moved forward as quietly as he could. Once he nearly lost his balance when a dark shape moved unexpectedly ahead of him, and then turned and gave a huge meow.

The cat Oscar. He'd seen the tabby cat lurking around the house and gardens from time to time. God damn, someone should bell that thing.

The cat leapt from the wall to the ground with no effort, and then darted over to one of the windows, which was cracked open several inches. Gabe heard a murmuring voice from within, but couldn't make out any words.

Then he heard the sound of breaking glass. He held still, listening. Had someone in the house seen him, and broke the glass to raise the alarm? No, that made no sense. Any servant in the house would yell if they saw an intruder.

Oscar darted out again, streaking through the dark garden as if being chased. Whatever happened in there, the cat didn't like it.

Spurred by a sense of unease, Gabe swung over and let himself down feet first to ground level, not far from where the cat had landed. He was a tall man, and by holding on to a particularly fat branch of the ivy, he reduced the drop to about three feet, but it was still not a treat to do in the dark.

Light continued to flicker through the window of the shed, but he heard nothing else. He hurried to the window that cat had used and peeked in though the gap.

For a split second, he saw what appeared to be the gruesome image of a corpse about to be dissected, but then he realized that the body was not on the table but rather bent over it, with feet on the floor. Coldness hit his lungs when he recognized the pattern on the dress—massive lilies on a black background.

Lady Arcadia was the one half flung across that table.

♑

CADY FELT LIKE A TON of granite had been lashed to her body, pulling her down, down, down into fathomless depths. Somewhere above, there was a faint light, but she couldn't reach it. Her thoughts came to her in a dreamy, abstracted way, and one of the thoughts was that perhaps the solution she synthesized worked perfectly…too perfectly. She would never escape this abyss. Cady wanted to move, to open her eyes, to wake up. But she simply couldn't. Her limbs had been replaced with lead, her head was stuffed with wool, and everywhere was the velvety darkness urging her to sleep.

Then a voice broke through the deep haze, and something gripped her and yanked her roughly into consciousness.

"Jesus Christ, you're alive," a deep voice rumbled.

Cady blinked slowly, things coming back into focus. She frowned at the dark-haired man in front of her, trying to put a name to that face. "I know you," she whispered, suddenly frightened by the weakness in her own voice.

"It's Gabe," he said roughly. "Your…gardener. I found you here, unconscious. I thought you were dead…oh, no, you don't! Don't close your eyes. Tell me what happened. There's broken glass everywhere, and something spilled, it smells godawful…"

Ah, yes. The solution that she sampled.

Cady sighed, and with a monumental effort lifted one

arm to point at the worktable. "Green bottle, yellow label. I need to drink some."

He frowned. "A drink? Now?"

"It's an…antidote…" Lord, she was tired.

Gabe put her down gently, warning her to stay awake. He stood up and fetched the bottle from the marble-topped table. He uncapped it and grabbed a small empty glass as well.

"How much?" he asked, returning to her.

"A capful," she said, thinking hard. "No more."

He carefully poured a little into the glass and held it to her lips. Cady opened her mouth and he let the liquid trickle onto her tongue. She swallowed, instinctively licking her lips after tasting the honey-based substance. "All right. Put the lid back on."

"What if you need more?"

"More might kill me. Just give it a few minutes to take effect."

He capped the bottle and then moved a bit to hold her upright, which had the result of her leaning into his chest. She could feel his heartbeat, rapid but deep. In a few moments, her own sluggish heartbeat should match his pace.

"What happened here?" he asked. "Why did you have an antidote handy?"

"It's not an antidote, exactly," she explained, her head already clearing a bit. "It's a heart stimulant. It counteracts the effects of the solution I imbibed earlier, which is a sedative. I think the concentration of the salvia's sap was stronger than expected. I'll have to adjust the proportions next time."

"*Next* time? What are you doing, trying to kill yourself?"

"Don't be absurd." Cady felt a flutter in her chest, a sign that the dose was working. "It was a simple experiment, with an unexpected result."

"A result that could have killed you if I hadn't found you."

She blinked, realizing how odd it was for anyone, let alone this particular person, to be in her private workroom. "How *did* you find me? My laboratory isn't open to anyone."

"I heard glass break," he said.

It was not an answer, but Cady let it go for the moment. She didn't have the mental fortitude to interrogate her handsome but huge gardener about how he *just happened* to get past a locked and walled garden to even hear the sound of breaking glass in a further, also locked laboratory.

She sighed, letting her eyes close.

"Don't," he ordered, laying one hand on her chin and turning her head toward him. "Open your eyes. Don't fall asleep."

"The danger is past," she told him, finding his gaze intent on her face.

"How can you know that?" he asked, his brow furrowed.

Lord, he really was concerned that she might drop dead on him. Cady smiled weakly. "I'm an expert. I have a high degree of confidence that I won't die tonight."

"Do you do this often?"

"Experiment with new plants? As often as I can, yes."

"Jesus," he muttered.

"Look, I can't test new solutions and remedies on anyone else, can I? That's unethical. I try them on myself. And then I can assess the results, and make notes as well."

"Would have been tricky to take notes on tonight's little experiment if you never woke up, wouldn't it? What the hell were you testing anyway?"

"This time? Iranian salvia. It's been reported that the sap may have a therapeutic effect for those with insomnia and general nervousness. Of which I am one."

He stared at her. "Your pupils are dilated. Is that normal?"

"No, but it's interesting. Can you make a note of it, please?" With a trembling finger, she indicated the notebook that had fallen to the floor when she lost consciousness.

Grumbling, Gabe grabbed the notebook and a nearby pencil and scrawled the observation down.

"Now what?" he said then. "I can't leave you here."

"I'll be perfectly all right. I just need a little while to recover."

"You need more than that." Gabe slid one arm under her knees and the other against her back. Standing, he lifted her up, cradling her against him. "I'll take you to your room."

Cady wanted to object. Surely it was not proper to have a man simply scoop a woman up and carry her to a bed. It was…barbaric.

But also impressive.

"You can't possibly carry me all that way," she objected without much force.

"Watch me," he ordered, his voice low in her ear.

With no other reasonable course of action, Cady allowed him to carry her out of the laboratory and through the winding, shadowed halls of Calderwood. He carried her as if she were no more of a burden than a sack of rose petals, and she took a few easier breaths, realizing that she could not have walked all this way on her own.

Only when he nudged the bedroom door open with his foot did Cady realize that she never gave him directions.

"How did you know this is my room?"

"I had to deliver your lunch one day," he returned, not even sounding winded. "Don't know why you can't eat in one of your seven dining rooms. You take being reclusive to an art form."

"I can't eat out among others," she said, slightly annoyed that he brought it up.

"Why not?"

"It scares me."

"Scares you?" By then he'd reached the bed, and he laid her down on it, with a gentleness she wouldn't have guessed he'd have. "What's scary about eating?"

"It's difficult to explain."

"What about an unknown man in your bedroom late at night? Shouldn't that scare you?"

"Yes." She thought about it, then shook her head. "Though at the moment, I believe I'm too tired to be scared. And anyway, you're leaving."

"No, I'm not."

Her eyes widened as she regarded him, standing there with all the confidence of a man who knew she couldn't do a thing to force him out. "Excuse me?"

"I'm staying here to watch over you," he said bluntly. "At least till I can be sure you won't stop breathing."

"That's…completely unacceptable," she sputtered. "I'm an unmarried woman."

"Who drinks strange potions and then falls down half-dead. Sorry, my lady, but this is how it will be tonight."

"You're just going to stare at my sleeping form and hold a mirror to my mouth to see if it fogs up?"

"Hadn't thought about the mirror until now, but it's a good idea." He turned, looking around, then walked over to her vanity, where he picked up the hand mirror without asking.

"That was my grandmother's!" Cady protested.

"Very pretty. Silver? Don't worry, I won't nick it."

"That was not my biggest fear."

"What is your biggest fear?" The way he asked the question made her think of the litany of terrors that haunted her these past months and years (which was extensive, and yet a man in her bedroom was too outlandish to have made the list at all).

Cady frowned. "I couldn't possibly choose."

"Well, list some of them, then." He pulled one of the room's sitting chairs over to her bedside and sat down as if he did it every night.

"Spiders, because they're venomous. Rats, because they convey plague. Thunderstorms, because the lightning might strike a tree and make a limb fall on me. Fire, because it could get out of hand and burn my home to the ground. Falling off a horse…falling off a bridge…falling in general. The dark, because then you can't even see the things you should really be afraid of…"

"That's enough. Sorry I asked."

"Everyone always is sorry," she noted. "The topic is not a pleasant one to discuss."

"Well, this hasn't been a pleasant evening so far, what with you nearly dying," he said, sounding as if it really did matter to him. "So we may as well forge ahead with the unpleasantries. Have you always been so scared of things? Even as a child?"

"Children are innocent," she countered. "They don't know enough to be afraid."

"Nonsense. Children get scared about anything. My older brother thought ghosts lived on the third floor."

"Did you think that?"

"Sometimes," he admitted. "But we're not talking about my fears. I'm more interested in yours. Plus I want to keep you alert."

Cady absentmindedly plumped a pillow behind her head. "I don't know why I'm so scared of everything. I do know it got worse over the past few years. When Mama died, and then when Trevor left."

"Trevor?"

"Trevor's my younger brother," she explained. "But when I was child, I didn't feel frightened, you know. I didn't shriek when a mouse ran though the dining room—they loved the dining room on account of all the crumbs. Papa was always very exacting in his manner, and he'd never tolerate a wailing female in his house."

"What did he tolerate?"

"Very little," Cady admitted with a soft chuckle. "He insisted everything be just so, myself included. He felt that Mama was too lax in my education and upbringing, so after she passed and my upbringing fell to him, he was…intensive."

"How so?"

"Oh, just that I had to present myself to the best of my ability at all times. Which of course is what any father would demand. Impeccable manners, perfect behavior, never speaking of subjects that might annoy or offend. His view was that a lady should be an ornament and a comfort, not an additional burden."

Gabe's calm expression flickered for a moment. But then he just shook his head. "And you agreed?"

"Of course I agreed. He was my father, and the master of the house." Cady usually put more conviction into her statements…but then she wasn't usually recovering from a botched experiment. "He cared for me very much," she added defensively.

"Who wouldn't?" Gabe responded, with a smile that gave her insides reasons to flutter—or was that another side effect of the various compounds she'd ingested?

"Can you make another note?" she asked. "My stomach is possibly a bit upset."

"Left the notebook downstairs. Nauseous?" he asked, immediately looking serious.

"Mmmm, no. Not exactly. Just…odd."

"When did you eat last? Not counting your magic potions?"

She made a face at him. "They're not potions. They're medicine. Or they will be, once I get the proportions correct. And I ate dinner."

"How much? Cook thinks you're wasting away."

"Cook is a busybody," Cady said. "I had soup, and bread, and…well, that's all. Some tea."

"You might feel better if you had something in your gut besides whatever the hell you boiled up out there. There's food in the kitchen."

"Do not ring for Martha!" Cady objected. "It's late, and I don't want to explain myself to anyone else."

He stood up, again reminding her of his sheer size. "I'll go fetch something. Promise not to die while I'm gone."

"I wouldn't dream of it."

By the time Gabe returned several minutes later, Cady was feeling much better in terms of her heart rate and her breathing, though she was undeniably exhausted. He offered her a tray with several roughly cut slices of bread and a chunk of butter, along with an apple. He immediately took the apple and began to slice it with a knife he produced from nowhere. Cady nibbled on the bread, watching him.

"I don't know anything about you," she said finally.

"Don't you?" he asked. "You know I served in the army, and I have an older brother, and I can slice apples very well. Here." He placed a few perfect slices on her tray and then ate the rest of the apple himself.

"What's your brother's name?"

"I have two. Gerald and Gilbert."

"What color is their hair?"

"Blond. Why?"

"Do they have blue eyes like you?"

"Yes. Runs in the family. They're not as good-looking as me." Gabe smiled at her.

"What makes you think you're good-looking? Perhaps I find you hideous and I think you should wear a mask." Cady laughed at the image, and the very idea that anyone would find Gabe Court hideous.

"Happy to if you've got one handy," he agreed, showing not the slightest concern at this supposed fault in his appearance.

"Alas, I do not," she said. "My parents held a masquerade ball one winter for Twelfth Night. That was when Mama was still alive. I wonder what happened to those masks." She was drifting again, her mind losing focus as past and present blurred together.

"I feel as though these past few years I've been wearing a mask," she said, her thoughts running to her mouth before she could stop herself. "But the mask is of my own likeness. I just hold it up in front of my face whenever someone comes near. The mask is wearing a smile, and people don't notice that it's just the mask, it's not me. And I know all the things I should say and all the things people want to hear. So no one ever questions how I really feel."

Gabe leaned forward, his gaze intent. "You mean when you get scared? How do you really feel?"

She paused, then slowly put the feeling into words, words she'd never spoken out loud before. "Like the walls are closing in on me. Like I can't catch a breath no matter how much I want to. My heart pounds and I sweat—you'd think I've been running through a desert at noon, but in fact I've just been sitting in the parlor reading a book."

"What causes an…let's call it an incident."

Cady shook her head helplessly. "Sometimes nothing at all. Or something very mundane. Once I saw a spider spinning a web in the corner of a window. And my first thought was how interesting it would be to know what the web was made out of. How does a spider know how to weave it? Why does the pattern vary? Did you know that not all the strands of a web are sticky? The spider chooses as she weaves it. But then, I thought…what if that spider bites me and I die from the bite? And just a week before you came here, a spider actually did jump on my hand. I was wearing gloves, but I was sure it had bitten me and I was going to die."

"Was the spider the sort that can do that?"

"I don't know. I get crates and things from all over the world. A dangerous spider could easily stow away in one. And even if it looks like a harmless spider, what if I'm wrong? It's the not knowing that's the worst."

"Sound exhausting." He leaned over her, took away the tray, and settled a blanket around her.

"It is. It was. That's why I only stay here. I know what's going to happen here. I just feel so unsettled any-where but here at home. And even then, I prefer to be alone when I can. It's the closest I get to paradise." Cady snugged down under the blanket. She laughed softly. "*Et in Arcadia ego.*"

Gabe went still. "What did you say?"

"Oh, it's Latin. It's a reference to a painting that my mother admired. Very bucolic—though also a bit melan-choly. She always believed that paradise is a garden, and she named me Arcadia because she liked the idea of an earthly paradise. But Papa wouldn't let her name a boy, so Trevor is Trevor because it was Papa's grandfather's name." She laughed again. Perhaps this drug did improve one's mood.

"So that was a phrase your whole family knew about?"

"Hmm, yes. But so do thousands of others. It's quite famous. Someday I'd like to see the original painting, but to do that I'd have to go out among people. So that will never happen."

"Are people so horrible?"

"Depends on the people."

"Let me guess. You're scared of men particularly."

She nodded. "Yes. Not all men. But tall men. Or big men. Or any man who tries to speak with me. That's the worst. Actually, I suppose that means I'm afraid of all the men I know."

Gabe said, "I'm tall. And big. And I'm speaking to you. Are you afraid of me?"

She thought for a moment. Although Gabe had startled her initially, she'd never felt scared around him. Actually it was just the opposite. She was drawn to him.

"My lady?" he prompted when she didn't answer.

"No, I'm not afraid of you," she said quickly. "But one of the promised effects of the solution is to repress fear. So perhaps I'll be afraid of you tomorrow when it wears off."

"I'd prefer it if you simply weren't afraid. Of any-thing. But I'd also prefer it if you didn't have to take a drug to do it. Especially if it renders you unconscious or dead."

"Oh, I'll adjust the dose, silly," she said.

He raised an eyebrow. "Did you just call me *silly*?"

"I did. People afraid of discovering new things are always silly. It's a promising line of inquiry. And logical, considering how salvia sap affects the general energy level in the body….emotions come from the brain, and are malleable…"

Her eyelids slid shut, and she let out a long, slow sigh. "I don't think I can stay awake much longer. Are you really going to stay here all night?"

"That was the intention. But if the idea scares you, I'll leave."

"No, I think I'd like if you could stay," she admitted, surprising both of them. "If you don't mind. I know it's not your job as gardener—"

"I'm not really a gardener, Cady," he said…or she thought he said. But then she was asleep.

♑

THE NEXT MORNING, CADY WOKE up with a headache and a deep sense of embarrassment. She'd lost all sense of propriety last night. She told Gabe—Mr Court—literally everything that popped into her mind, no matter how odd or personal or just agonizingly childish. She hadn't told *anyone* the things she told him. Something in his voice and his eyes encouraged her to confide in him, and suggested that he wouldn't laugh at her or tell her how the things that terrified her were all in her head.

And worst of all, she'd asked him to stay. In her own bedroom! No matter that she was asking him to watch over her, not bed her. If that was ever discovered, Cady would be in serious trouble. Lord, she'd have to hide any evidence of him being there before Martha arrived to see about her breakfast and ask about the day ahead.

Sitting up, Cady looked around her bedroom in surprise. There was no tray of food. The chair Gabe had been sitting in was back by the fireplace. Even her grandmother's silver hand mirror was once again at the vanity where it belonged. Gabe had been very careful to leave no trace of his unsanctioned presence.

Though she appreciated his discretion, Cady was still mortified at everything that had happened last night. It was nearing the end of the two-week trial period. Perhaps she could let him go…though it wouldn't be fair to him. After all, he'd done everything he was supposed to as a gardener, not to mention probably saving her life last night. But she'd crossed several boundaries in talking to him, being alone with him… Yes, she had to let him go. Still, it seemed rather rude to tell a man that he'd be sacked just for being a good listener.

But Cady also couldn't imagine facing him again.

Perhaps she'd just stay in her room forever.

Now there was a solution that she could work with. After all, she'd had lots of practice.

Fully prepared to tell Martha that she intended to hide inside all day, Cady nevertheless felt a pang. Something in her *wanted* to be outside, feeling the wind on her face and working with the soil and waking up her gardens after a long winter. But was that worth the risk of absolutely embarrassing herself when she had to look Gabe straight in the eyes once more? She didn't know.

As it happened, Martha came in with news that made Cady's decision for her.

"Morning, my lady," the maid said, entering the bedroom with a busy air. She walked to the curtains and pulled them open. "Brought you a tray of toast and tea, but you'll want to dress and go downstairs straightaway."

"I will?"

"One of the dogs is ill. Don't know if it's Romulus or Remus. But evidently quite serious."

"Oh, no." While Cady was still afraid to get too near the creatures, they'd been favorites of her father's and she had fond memories of playing with them when she was younger. If she could help in any way, she had to. "Yes, take out the green wool gown with the white trim and I'll dress as soon as I finish my toast."

Twenty minutes later, Cady stood in front of the dog kennel north of the house. Romulus was within, looking out from behind the fence with an expectant, longing expression. Remus was nowhere to be seen.

"Hello?" Cady called out. "Has someone taken Remus?"

The thought occurred to her that perhaps she was already too late, and Remus was…no. Cady shrank from that thought.

"Romulus," she asked softly, raising a hand toward the wolfhound but not getting near enough to touch. "Where's your brother?"

Romulus made a low, whuffing sound, looking behind Cady. She spun on her heel and saw Gabe approaching with Remus on a leash.

"Where did you take Remus? Is he all right?"

"He is." Gabe gave her a half smile. "I thought you might avoid me today, so I had to come up with a reason to entice you outside."

Cady's mouth fell open for a moment. "You…lied? About Remus being sick, just to get me down here?"

"Exactly. I guessed that you'd not let Remus pad off this mortal coil without seeing him. And I do have something very important to say to you."

"He's really fine?" Cady asked worriedly. She realized with a start that Remus had moved closer to her and managed to put his head in prime position to have his ears rubbed. She obliged, and after a moment, it seemed that she'd done this every day, rather than a months-long gap when she didn't even see the dogs.

She asked, "What was so important to tell me that you had to lie about the dog's health to do it?"

"Well, considering what you explained last night, I had a thought," he said. "You're scared of a lot of things. Too many things. And most of them aren't worth being sacred of."

"Easy for you to say."

"I'm not just *saying* it. That's my thought. I bet I can teach you not to be afraid of at least some of those things."

Cady narrowed her eyes. "What are you suggesting? You're offering to be my tutor in bravery?"

"If you like to put it that way."

"How would that work? And why would you even want to do that sort of thing? I hired you as a gardener, not a…whatever you'd be."

"Think of it as natural philosophy, except instead of studying plants as a botanist, you'd be experimenting with your psyche. Testing what scares you to see how you can overcome it."

"But why do you even care?"

He paused, then said, "There was a lot of fear when I was a soldier. I felt plenty, and saw even more. It's not a pretty thing, to be so scared that you can't even move."

"I'm aware of that," Cady said bitterly.

"But it's one thing to be scared in a war. That's supposed to scare you. What you're sacred of, my lady, isn't normal. You shouldn't have to live like this."

Cady considered his words for a long time, and finally said, "You're a very odd gardener."

"Well, I wasn't always a gardener. Just as you weren't always a recluse. Will you let me try?"

"Perhaps, Mr Court. However, no matter what, I must insist that you never trick me like that again. No lies about dogs dying or anything else just to shock me into speaking to you. And you still need to work in the gardens. That's far more important."

He gave her an odd look, but then said, "Yes, my lady. Speaking of, you were going to tell me how to repot seedlings so they'll live after they're transplanted."

"So I was. Let's begin, shall we?"

Thus, Cady ended up spending most of the morning with Gabe, and after a little while, she even forgot to be embarrassed about the intimacies she'd confided last night. Working with him felt very natural. He was quick to learn and he was genuinely interested in the grounds, asking question after question about the plants he saw, the various buildings, and Cady's experience as a botanist.

"Where did you get all these plants?" he asked, while peering into one of the glasshouses where Cady maintained most of her seedlings.

"Often, the seeds are mailed to me by colleagues, or sometimes agents in specific cities, and I propagate them here in the glasshouse. On the east side here, I've got shipments from the west and east coasts of Africa, India, Persia, and China."

"Those places are all hot, aren't they? I don't understand how they can survive in England," he said, sounding baffled. "The winters..."

"That's why they're inside," Cady explained. "The glass traps the heat of the sun and keeps it much warmer in here. Even in December, it might be below freezing outside, but in here I don't even need to wear my shawl. And for the plants that are truly sensitive, we've got the hot walls."

He looked blank. "The *what*?"

"The hot walls. I'm glad you brought the issue up, actually, because one of your tasks will be to help restore them. After my mother's death, some of the hot walls got damaged and I never quite had the time to see them repaired. Come, I'll show you."

Cady led the way through the glasshouse to the other end, where it connected to a brick hallway that turned a sharp ninety-degree angle.

"One of the previous generations planned for a continuous passage through all the glasshouses all the way to the orangerie, which is the building due west of the main house."

"How? That building isn't connected to anything."

She said, "The passageway drops below ground level between the last glasshouse and the orangerie, in order to preserve the symmetry of the view from the house."

"Interesting," he said softly.

"The passageways allow us to take tender plants from place to place without exposing them to inclement weather," Cady went on. "But they also exist to give access to the hot walls." She laid a hand on the wall to her left. "This wall here—it's the north side of one of the glasshouses. That means that in the glasshouse, it faces south, which gives the plants growing there full exposure to sunlight for the longest stretch of time."

"What if it's cloudy?"

She chuckled. "A problem my predecessors acknowledged. To make absolutely sure that the plants in the glasshouse would survive, they designed the hot walls."

She rapped on the wall, which echoed with a distinctly hollow sound. "There's four feet of space between both sides. Within, ceramic pipes can carry hot air through the walls, heating them up day or night."

"Where's the hot air come from?"

"A coal furnace, centrally located. After the ideal temperature is reached, a single worker can maintain the fire easily, just periodically shoveling in more coal."

Gabe put his hands up against the wall, but then looked disappointed. "Doesn't feel hot."

"That's because the system is damaged. That's what I need your help to repair."

"Show me where to start."

"It's not very far," she told him, continuing down the

passage. The air here was faintly musty, but nothing like what one would have expected of a windowless, lightless hall.

"Do you use this route often?" he asked.

"Parts of it," she said. "Other parts…well, you'll see."

Ahead, a whole section of ceiling and wall had crumbled, blocking access to the next part. But the space widened into a squarish room, with a coal stove in one corner, a pile of coal nearby, and a few shovels lying on the floor.

"This is where the heat would be generated if things weren't broken. One worker can keep the heat level up with only a shovelful or two of coal every few hours."

"But they have to run through the house and your workroom and all those passages each time?"

"Oh, no!" Cady laughed. "The best entry point for the coal shoveler is actually beyond that door. There's another passage continuing toward the orangerie that has a door to the outside. It's much more direct than the route we took today."

"Then why not use that?"

"Because it collapsed in several years ago. It's too dangerous to use now. The collapse also damaged the airways that carried the hot air further. We continued to use the stove for the closer glasshouses, but after my father died, I lost so many servants that I couldn't spare anyone for this work. Luckily the winter was mild." She rapped her knuckles on the coal stove, and a dull clang reverberated through the space. "I'm worried there's more damage than I can see. So if you could do anything toward restoring the system, it would be a great help."

"How did you get the coal in here?" Gabe asked, looking around.

"Through a chute above the pile. Above ground,

there's a small brick structure that looks like an odd little Roman ruin."

"I've seen it."

"It's completely fake, of course. There was a passion for false ruins a while ago. But this structure hides a trap door. The coal was carted up to the structure and then just tossed into the chute, and it ends up here."

"Ingenious."

"My grandfather's idea," Cady said proudly.

"How bad is the collapse?" he asked, gesturing to the other door.

"Bad. And it may have got worse. It's been a long time since I've been down there." Walking to the door, Cady put a key into the lock, but it wouldn't even turn.

So Gabe simply grabbed the mostly rotted door. "Step back," he warned.

* * * *

Cady did as he asked, and he put all his strength into pulling the door out from its damaged frame. After a moment of seeming failure, the door came off in a flurry of splinters and a cloud of dust.

Cady darted back, and Gabe stumbled as he worked to maintain his balance. Once stable, he tossed most of the door into a corner. "That was more spectacular than I thought it would be."

She started to step into the dark, dusty space. As she did, she accidentally kicked a piece of the door forward into the shadows.

There was a loud squeak and two rats dashed out of cover toward them, and passed by.

Cady stifled a scream, and Gabe saw her whole demeanor change.

"I can't go in there," she whispered.

"That's where you wanted to go."

"I did want to, but now I can't. I just can't."

"Rats are one of the things you're afraid of," he said.

"Yes! Who wouldn't be?"

"Um…me?"

"*How?*" Cady looked at him as if he were some mystical creature. "How can you just stand there and not mind?"

"They've already run away, my lady. The rats don't want to have anything to do with you."

"These rats didn't. But what if they'd been rabid?"

Oh, that's the real fear, he guessed. It wasn't the animal itself, but the possibility it represented—the slight but real chance of a bite and a subsequent terrible death. She kept looking all around, from one corner to the next to the next. She had taken hold of the loose skirts of her gown, as if prepared to jump to avoid more rats should they appear.

"Had they been rabid, they'd have acted quite differently," Gabe said, hoping to calm her. "You'd notice straightaway and you'd be very careful to not let them close enough to hurt you," he said. "They're gone, my lady. Truly."

"You don't know that." Cady's chest rose and fell in a quick, shallow way.

"I do, but I'm guessing that we're not going to get much done in this room today. Shall we leave? Try again another time?"

Cady looked to the long, shadowed hall and shook her head, eyes wide.

"You just walked down that way," he said.

"That was before the rats did. Lord, this is my fault. I should have known. I could have done it differently, brought a lantern, or made some arrangement…" She twisted around as she spoke, either looking for more rats, or possibly a way to make time run backward to a point where she wasn't yet angry and afraid.

Gabe tried again to offer a reasonable statement she could hold on to. "It will be fine. The rats have already found another hole to dive down."

Cady didn't move.

"You don't want to stay here, do you?"

She looked at him, her expression desperate. "I want to be *anywhere* but here."

"I could carry you," he offered.

"Absolutely not!" The horror on her face was, frankly, a little offensive. Was he such an appalling option?

"Why not? I did last night."

"Last night was different!"

"How? You were incapacitated in your laboratory. And you're incapacitated now, just for a different reason."

"I should be able to walk on my own," she protested. "It's ridiculous that I'm just…standing here!"

That was when he realized that she wasn't angry at him, only at herself.

He moved toward the place that the rats had run out of, but the moment he came past Cady, he turned and scooped her up in his arms.

Unlike last night, she was alert and struggling now. But Gabe was also a lot bigger than her. He held her tight to him, preventing her from falling in her attempts to wiggle free.

"Would you stop that?" he asked, putting irritation in his voice to hide the surge of physical response when the smell of witch hazel hit him again. Unconsciously, he glanced down, catching the curve of her breasts above the edge of her gown.

Too frantic to notice, Cady put one hand against his chest, pushing ineffectually. "I didn't say you could pick me up!"

"No, but you also couldn't walk away on your own. So I'm going to take you back to the first glasshouse. And if you keep twisting around like a stray cat, I might drop you."

Immediately, she went still.

"Let me guess. You're afraid of being dropped on the ground? Does that count as falling?"

"It's not funny," she muttered, hiding her head.

"Sorry. I didn't mean it like that," he said. The distress on her face was real, and something in Gabe responded to it, wanting to make it go away. He never liked to see innocents suffering.

"And you wonder why I hide in my house. Your offer to make me brave was very sweet, Mr Court. But I'm a lost cause."

No one, ever, not even when he was a boy, had described him as *very sweet*. Maneuvering around the sharp corner, he turned sideways and held her closer to him. "Watch your toes," he warned gruffly.

Cady dutifully contracted into an even smaller space, pulling her legs and feet in and tucking her head onto his shoulder.

Now Gabe had to contend with the darkened space and the softness of female flesh pressed against him. Those two things together usually pointed toward imminent pleasure, and his body was reacting in anticipation. It didn't help that Cady's breathing was still quicker than normal, or that he could feel the rapid thump of her heartbeat. Lord, this woman was more tempting every time he saw her.

"I'll be better once we get back to the glasshouse,"

Cady said. "The daylight will keep the rats out. And I'll put out some poison to make sure," she added.

Gabe's grip tightened a little. "Poison? What do you use for that?"

"I have a powered alkaloid that I make from a certain plant. It's a bean, actually, that grows in Asia, and they've used the ground-up powder to kill rodents for ages. A few bites of food that's been coated with it will stop their little hearts. Thank goodness, I don't like them to suffer. And I hardly ever have to use much, which is good, because it's not easy growing beans that came from halfway round the world…"

Cady chattered away. He noticed that as soon as she had something else to focus on besides the thing that frightened her, she calmed down. So he kept asking questions, slipping in ones about poison when he could.

"Well, of course there are many plants here that no one should be near," she said in response to one. "I've said that before, have I not? But you know that rats and mice don't actually like to try new things to eat? They avoid what they don't know. Not unlike me."

The last was uttered with a sort of dark humor that seemed out of character. He glanced down and saw lines at the corners of her eyes and mouth, suggesting prolonged distress.

By then, they reached the glasshouse door, which Gabe couldn't open with her in his arms.

He put her down, but Cady clung to him for a moment, her hands curling around his arms as if she were uncertain her own feet would support her.

She said in a low voice, "We're not going to ever mention this."

"Mention what?"

"Thank you," she breathed. "It's bad enough that you

had to see me. I think I'd die if anyone else knew you had to carry me back."

She turned and opened the door to the glasshouse before he could reply.

Inside the bright, sunny space once more, Cady's shoulders sagged down. He followed her in, closing the door again carefully.

"Where's that poison? Do you keep all your dangerous substances safe?"

"Yes, they're in a locked case in my locked workroom in my locked garden. Why, do you think I'm such a fool that I keep them in the kitchen pantry?"

Now he wanted to see the inside of that case. Aloud he said, "I don't think you're a fool."

"You ought to, considering what you've seen about me. I didn't used to be like this."

Before Gabe could figure out what she meant by that, they heard Mr Rundle shouting from somewhere. Cady immediately straightened up and smoothed out the wrinkles in her gown.

"I'd best see what's the matter," she muttered. She ran the back of her hand across her eyes.

"Shouldn't you rest?" he asked. "After having an… incident?"

"That?" Cady actually laughed. "That was nothing back there, Mr Court. I was doing very well in keeping my panic at bay. When I actually do have an incident, as you so kindly call it, I go completely to pieces, I terrify everyone who sees me, and I can barely sit upright for hours afterward. Now if you'll excuse me, I must see what Mr Rundle needs."

Finally, an opportunity, he thought. *Leave me alone in the glasshouse where you grow your poisonous plants.*

In a rush, Cady turned to the doorway that eventually

headed to the house. Just as she was about to go through, however, she turned back.

"Oh, my Lord, I nearly locked you in here! How terrible would that have been? Some of these plants are dangerous even to touch. Quickly, come with me, Mr Court."

Wordlessly, he did, cursing how careful she was.

"Maybe another time you'll give me a tour."

"Whyever would you want that?" she asked, eyes wide.

And of course, that was one thing he couldn't tell her.

♑

THE NEXT DAY, CADY ENCOUNTERED Gabe working diligently in the rose allée in the front of the great house. He had carted wheelbarrows of mulch to put around the roots, and was carefully moving bits to each plant, just as Cady had instructed.

"How many of these infernal things do you have?" he asked with a rueful grin as he saw her approach.

"Two hundred in the front here," she said with an apologetic shrug. "More in the other gardens, of course."

"Of course. And I've done…thirty so far. Fuck me," he added in a low tone.

Cady happened to have very sharp hearing, and she couldn't quite stop her reaction to that.

"Oh, shi—" he said, realizing she heard him. "I mean, I'm sorry. Still not quite back to civilized standards."

"It's fine," she said. "Just…surprised me."

"Bet that term doesn't come up at your social calls," he said.

"Definitely not. Perhaps the social calls would be more interesting if it did," she suggested.

He laughed, shaking his head. Then they were just staring at each other, smiling. Cady bit her lip, not knowing what to say. Why did she feel so comfortable with this very discomfiting man?

Gabe suddenly stood up.

"Come with me," he said. "I have something to show

you."

Cady followed him to the garden shed, assuming that he had a question about some assignment or needed to confirm which tools to use.

Inside the shed, which was well lit thanks to the large, open doors and the side windows, Gabe told her to stand near one of the worktables. "I just need to get something."

Cady waited, wondering exactly what was going on. Then Gabe reappeared, carrying what looked like a small wooden birdcage. He set it on the table.

"What is going on?" she asked, puzzled.

"Well, I was thinking about how much the rats frightened you."

"And you thought I'd also be scared of birds?"

"Are you?"

"No. I don't think so." She added, "I haven't thought about it much."

"Never mind," he said quickly. "It doesn't matter, because this cage doesn't hold any birds. It's got a mouse."

Cady took a step back…only to walk into Gabe, who'd shifted to prevent her from running out.

"Not so fast," he said. "There's nothing to be scared of."

"Yes, there is. Mice carry disease. How'd you get it in there? Can it get out? What if there are more? What if—"

"No questions. You have to look at the mouse."

He stood right behind her and planted his hands on the edge of the table, effectively trapping her. She stared at the cage, looking for a way the mouse could escape it.

"I don't see any mouse," she said. "This is a waste of time."

"Keep looking." He more or less surrounded her, the bulk of him like a living wall. Cady tried to be upset by it, but in fact part of her wanted to lean back against him.

She remembered how strong and comforting he'd felt when he carried her yesterday.

"I'm looking," she said. She still saw nothing…no, wait, there was movement under the shaved bedding. "Oh, no, it's there."

"I caught it with a bit of cheese last night. I figured a mouse would be less scary than a rat."

At Cady's involuntary hiss, he lifted one hand to her upper arm, and squeezed lightly. "Don't worry. I wouldn't have you make friends with a rat so soon. Mice are less intimidating, right?"

"If it gets out, it'll jump on me."

"It won't, and if it does, it would likely jump on me, because there's more of me to jump on."

"That's true," she couldn't help saying.

He leaned over her shoulder a bit, his breath warm against her neck. Cady felt a jolt through her body, and she was grateful he couldn't see her expression.

"All right," she said to distract herself from how very close he was. "Since you're trying to help me, I'll try to be brave. What do you want me to do?"

There was a beat of silence, then he said, "It's easy. Look into the cage. Try to see the mouse."

"But it's hiding."

"Give it a moment."

A rustling, a squeak, and then there it was—minuscule, trapped, and terribly alert. Cady suddenly felt a kinship with the poor creature. "There it is," she whispered.

"You see it? What color is it?"

"Sort of a tannish brown, I suppose," she said. "And it's so little. They seem bigger when they're running across the floor."

The mouse held completely still while they looked at it. Only its tiny nose twitched.

"It's really rather adorable, for a rodent," she admitted at last.

"I thought so. All right, let's leave." He moved back and took her by the elbow to guide her out of the shed.

"Leave?"

"Yes. That's all you had to do today. Just look a mouse in the eyes."

"I thought you were going to make me open the cage and hold it or something!"

"Let's not get ahead of ourselves. You won't get brave in a day. But you did very well."

"Did I?" she asked, skeptical about his assessment. "I didn't *do* anything."

"Of course you did. You resisted the urge to run, and you remained calm, and you didn't scream or tell me I was out of a job."

Cady glanced over at him. "Did you think that likely, and you risked it anyway?"

He smiled at her, his blue eyes holding laughter. "I can't very well be a tutor in bravery if I'm not brave my-self."

Feeling shy all of a sudden, Cady looked away. "No one can doubt your bravery. You were in a war."

"What does that mean? A coward can wear a uniform just as well. And many did," he added, his expression turning grim. "Not the sort of thing you want to find out too late."

"Did something happen while you were enlisted?"

"I wasn't en—" He checked himself. "I shouldn't say. It's not a very pretty story. And definitely not suitable for a lady to hear."

"Why not? I *am* aware that not all men are saints. And it seems to matter to you—how people deal with fear, that is."

Gabe looked at her with an odd expression, as if he was surprised at her words. "Only when it involves my own safety," he said.

"What happened? I really would like to know," she said softly. "If you would want to tell me, as one friend to another."

He went stock-still, not unlike the mouse earlier, a comparison that was absurd on the surface but nevertheless seemed correct to Cady. It was like Gabe was sensing some sort of threat. From her?

"Maybe someday," he said at last. "But now I've got some roses to deal with. And I don't think the lady of the house is supposed to be friends with her gardener."

Cady flashed back to the feeling of him standing right behind her, surrounding her. It hadn't felt wrong then, but if anyone had walked in…

"Of course. Please excuse me," she said, polite and prim, the way she was supposed to be. "I have…other work…"

She turned and left before he could say anything else that would mortify her.

* * * *

Gabe could have kicked himself. What the hell was he doing? It was the perfect opening to tell her a story that would elicit her sympathy, and deepen her ties to him, the ones he very deliberately set out to build with her so he could get the information he needed.

But her comment about being friends hit him in a way he didn't expect. He wasn't trying to be a friend to this woman. He only wanted her to trust him enough so he could get what he wanted and then get out. He was quite willing to use physical means to do it, hence getting so close to her in the shed before. But his plan misfired when he inhaled that witch hazel scent and whatever else was in the air whenever she appeared. It sent his head spinning, and he lost his concentration. He had meant to kiss her when they were alone in the shed. It was the natural point to do so, pushing their relationship into the next logical phase, preparing her for a seduction.

But that wasn't what happened. Not for lack of interest on his part. While Cady's attention was locked on the mouse, he'd been riveted to that spot where her neck met her shoulder, the skin temptingly exposed when she'd pushed back her cloak. Lean over her, let his lips graze her skin, gauge her reaction.

Instead she'd been disgustingly naive, sweetly telling him that he was helping her. As if he were some kind of altruist.

It was difficult to coldheartedly seduce a woman when she was so sweet and gooey. Gabe did not do well with gooey. He was used to shrewd, worldly players who all knew the game and the stakes.

And then there was Cady, who wanted to be friends.

Gabe didn't have friends. Friends led to openings that could be exploited. Friends had to be protected. And when you failed to protect them, you suffered the consequences of it for the rest of your life.

So no more friends.

He had a task, and he'd complete it. The next time he got Cady alone, he wasn't going to hesitate.

In the afternoon, Gabe made up a reason why he needed to go into the village of Dorbridge.

Rather surprisingly, Rundle not only didn't question his spurious errand, he even told Gabe to saddle the roan in the stable to shorten the journey. "They all need more exercise than we can give them, since Lady Arcadia has no need for travel."

Gabe was delighted to be able to ride, and the roan was equally happy to be trotting through the lanes on such a sunny spring day.

His real errand was mundane. He'd run out of the black dye he was using to change his appearance, and now he needed to cover the lighter roots that were already growing in. Luckily, no one had noticed yet. But he would have to be careful to avoid attracting attention.

Though he was attracting attention of another kind. Without showing it, he noticed the glances from people walking along the streets. Curiosity for a stranger. Veiled interest from some women. One pair of ladies tracked his progress along the high street much in the same way lionesses did on the veldt—except the ladies giggled more.

There was a shop that sold dry goods and sundries where Gabe found a small tin of the black dye he needed. He bought a few other items to hide the fact that he only needed the one.

"You must be traveling through here on the coach route," the proprietor noted with the sort of friendly, false interest that was part of the business. "Where are you bound?"

Gabe could have nodded, lied, and gotten away quickly. But since what he needed more than anything was more information, he did what he usually avoided while on assignment. He told the truth.

"No, I'm actually a gardener at Calderwood," he said.

The conversations between other customers in the shop didn't precisely *stop*. But Gabe was aware of a tightening of attention on him the moment he uttered the word *Calderwood*.

The proprietor's smile slipped for a moment before he recovered with, "Oh, indeed? Quite a big place, Calderwood is. Lots of…gardens."

He nodded. "It would take a dozen men to do everything that needs doing. Surprised that more folks don't take up the positions there. Especially with the pay, and the food," he added, with perfect sincerity. "Do you think there's something wrong there?"

Someone behind him coughed, and the proprietor blinked rapidly as he decided what to say.

"I've never been there myself," he finally got out. "Have you noticed anything, er, odd there since you started working?"

Gabe shrugged. "Just that there's so much work and so few to do it."

"Have you met the lady?" an older man asked from where he stood.

"Yes, she hired me."

"And?" the man prodded.

"And what?" Gabe asked, not feeling particularly obliging.

"How does she seem?"

"She seems like a lady," he replied. "A little sad, but I gather she's lost both parents, so that's expected. How much do I owe?"

The proprietor took his money, though it was clear that he'd rather hear more about the mysterious lady of Calderwood. Gabe left the shop, his mood much darker than before.

His last stop was the local posting inn, where he'd arranged for the Zodiac to send any missives. They would be addressed to Mr Court and held at the inn until he picked them up, for a very reasonable fee.

Today, the young woman at the desk smiled when he gave his name. "Why yes, a letter just came earlier today. Isn't that lucky?"

He could use some luck. Gabe paid her the coin to retrieve the letter and he went outside to read it, hoping that the organization had unearthed something else he could use in his search. The letter was short and to the point, omitting several fascinating points of methodology and ethics:

Local doctor performed novel tests on victims. Identified poison as: clephobine. Very rare. Only one person in England known to have successfully synthesized chemical: A. B. Osbourne.

♑

IT WAS A FEW DAYS after the meeting with the mouse, and Cady was puttering in her laboratory, creating different concentrations of the solution that she'd accidentally overdosed on before. This time, she was taking no chances, and started with a concentration of one percent in an otherwise neutral base. She took a very cautious sip, and recorded her results in the same notebook as before.

She looked at the previous entry for this experiment, which ended in Gabe's note that he'd written down at her rather befuddled insistence.

Subject's eyes extremely dilated. Pale skin, shallow breathing. Unfocused.

She frowned, tracing the words with one finger. He'd been in a hurry, naturally, and there were splotches of ink where they'd dripped from the nib. But the actual penmanship was well done, with clear, consistent lettering. And even the phrasing hinted at an excellent education. Not what one might expect of an ex-soldier turned gardener.

How was it possible that this man hadn't been able to find employment elsewhere, and needed to leave London and come to a house where no one else wanted to work?

There was a knock at the door. Cady frowned, unused to interruptions while she was at work on her botany.

"Who's there?" she called.

"It's Gabe."

Just who she'd been thinking of. She twisted in her seat. "Come in."

He opened the door and leaned in slightly, looking around with sharp, interested eyes. "Am I interrupting?"

"Technically, yes, though I am almost done for the day." She quickly shut the notebook, hiding the entry that puzzled her so much. "Is something the matter outside?"

"No, not at all. I finished with the roses and I cleared out the willow pond."

"Oh, wonderful!" Cady loved the small pond surrounded by a walking path and dotted with huge willow trees. Once, cattails and water lilies grew there in the summer. The pond itself, though, had been in a dire state, more muck than water. She hoped that by removing the dead leaves and rotting vegetation, she could replace the fussy aquatic plants with new hybrids she'd grown in large tubs, and restore the pond to its former beauty. "I can't believe you accomplished all that."

"I do what I'm told to do," he replied, his attention on the various apparatus of the laboratory. But then he looked at her and smiled. "Actually, I'm starting to like it. Gardening, I mean. Once you realize that you have to work at the garden's pace instead of your pace, it gets easier."

Cady blinked, impressed by the insight. "Are you sure you haven't gardened before?"

"Definitely not."

"Have you studied philosophy?"

He paused, surprised by the question. Then he said, a little warily, "A teacher or two tried to shove Plato into my brain at some point. I'm not exactly the scholarly type, though."

No, he wasn't, not with that build. Cady realized she

still didn't know why he'd sought her out.

"Was there something…?"

He nodded. "Yes. But if you're busy—"

"I just need to tidy up." Cady abhorred messiness, particularly in the lab. It didn't take long to clean up her workspace and put aside the various solutions.

"What were you making?" he asked.

"I'm refining that medicine from before," she explained. "A lower concentration is certainly safer." She felt quite calm now, even with the unexpected presence of Gabe. Though on one level he activated all her senses, there was another level where he seemed to serve as bulwark to the other turmoil around her. Her so-called tutor in bravery was actually quite good at offering her reasons not to panic.

"All done?" he asked. "Good. Now, follow me. There's something very important for you to see."

She'd heard *that* before. "What now?" she asked warily.

"Just come along. I promise it's not far."

Cady followed him out of the house and through the south gardens, curious about what Gabe was up to.

He kept going, passing by the now tidy green lawn and further. He led her down a thin dirt path that wound through a patch of woodland. Cady knew it well. She used to chase down it after Trevor, who even though he was younger, had much longer legs and always outpaced her.

"This goes to some outbuildings," she said, remembering all at once. "It was a sort of very small farm. Just the cottage and a little barn and an icehouse for the dairy, I think."

"Exactly." Gabe looked back and gave her a wink.

"It hasn't had a tenant for years! I can't even remember the last time I was here. What's this about?"

"It's part of our agreement."

"Our agreement…" She stopped short. "You haven't found a nest of spiders there, have you?"

"Absolutely not," he promised.

"Then what are you scaring me with?"

"I'm not scaring you, my lady. At least, that's not the goal. Remember, I'm helping you get braver."

"Yes, through terrorizing me!"

"The mouse was adorable, not terrifying. You said so yourself."

"It was terrifying at first," she muttered.

By then, they reached the place she'd been thinking of. Gabe pointed not to the cottage, where she expected he'd go, but to a round, domed building with no windows and a single door. The bottom of the building was stone, rising to about waist height. Above that, gently curving boards rose up to a central point. Though the building seemed quite large, she knew that the walls were at least three feet thick and insulated with straw to keep the interior reliably cold to store the ice that had been cut in winter.

"What's inside the icehouse?" she asked.

"Almost nothing. But it is very dark."

Cady quailed, realizing what he was up to. "Oh, no. I can't, I couldn't possibly."

"You can," he told her. "We're going to walk in there together."

"Or I could just stay outside."

"That won't help you be braver."

"I've decided I don't need to be brave after all. Thank you for everything, but I'll go home now."

As she turned, Gabe reached out and caught her hand in his. "Cady. Please try."

It was the name that got her. Not just the overly familiar use of her given name, but a diminutive he had no right to use or even know. "You can't call me that," she objected, though weakly.

"Mr Addison did when he was here. I heard him say it. Would you walk into the icehouse if he asked you to?"

"He'd have the courtesy not to!" she said. "It's like a tomb in there."

"Have you ever been in a tomb?"

"Well…no."

"Then how would you know? Come, Cady. Impress me."

She took a breath. Part of her very much wanted to impress Gabe. He wasn't scared of anything, and she so wanted to be like that. And it would feel so good to have him look at her and tell her she handled herself well, that she wasn't a disappointment…

"Ten steps," she said. "That's how far I'll go."

"Regular-sized steps," he countered, thwarting any attempt to bend the rules.

"And you won't try to scare me. No pretending to see a ghost or a rat or anything like that."

"Christ, Cady, I'm not doing this as a prank."

She bit her lip. "Fine. Let's get this over with." Thank goodness she'd taken the one percent solution. Otherwise, she might be in a worse state now.

He led her to the door, then told her to keep going, one step at a time.

"You have to do this yourself, Cady. Otherwise it won't mean anything."

Heart hammering as she looked from shadow to shadow, she moved along the narrow slice of light made by the open door. Then all of a sudden, the door slammed shut, plunging everything into…nothing.

Cady let out a low moan, too scared to even set one

foot in front of the other. With the light gone, it was all too easy to imagine anything and everything she feared rushing up to meet her. Rats. Spiders. Ghosts. Her father. Hateful neighbors.

Then Gabe was there. He somehow found her in pitch black and put his arms around her. "Cady, it's fine. You're fine."

"Oh, my God, did you do that on purpose?"

"No! I would never do that to you."

She clung to the sound of his voice as much as she clung to him, her fingers clutching at anything in her near panic. Luckily, his chest seemed as hard as the stone walls around them. She couldn't hurt him.

Gabe kept talking to her, telling her there was nothing to worry about, it was the same emptiness as before, just without light. Cady was appalled to realize that she was crying. But although her breathing was too fast, at least she wasn't gasping for breath.

"You're fine, you're fine," Gabe said, holding her close.

"I am not," she moaned. "I hate this. I hate being like this."

In the darkness, Gabe's fingers brushed away the tears dampening her cheek. Then his thumb dragged along her mouth, and she tasted salt. The touch surprised her, making her gasp.

"I wondered what your lips felt like," he said, a new note in his voice. "They always look so soft."

Cady inhaled, the fear streaming away as something else entirely rushed in. "You can't see my lips now," she said, her heart rate picking up.

"I don't need to. Let me kiss you."

"Is this part of the bravery lessons?"

"No. It's because we're alone in the dark, and I've

been wanting to do this since the day I got here."

"I can't allow that. Besides, I've never kissed a man. Like you, I mean."

"A man like me?"

"Yes. A man who's…the sort women want to kiss."

"You think I'm that sort?" His voice was teasing now, maddeningly so.

"I know it."

"Then let me kiss you. Shouldn't you get some benefit after such an ordeal?"

"I just can't. I shouldn't even be alone with you. And I shouldn't kiss any man until I'm married."

That earned a laugh, low and enticing in her ears. God, it was torture to be so close to him and not be able to see his expression. What was he thinking right now?

He put one finger to her lips. "Tell me that you *don't* expect to make it all the way to the altar before you know what it's like to be kissed."

"Well…perhaps a little before. Perhaps when he proposes? That would be a good time to kiss."

"I imagine so," he murmured. "But that's too late for a *first* kiss."

"When should I have a first kiss, then?"

"Now."

"Now?"

"Am I not your tutor in bravery?" he teased. "You're obviously afraid of kissing, so it's my duty to change that."

"I'm *not* afraid of kissing. Exactly." She inhaled, and then said, "I'm afraid that I'll be terrible at kissing and my husband will be disappointed in me and find a mistress and spend all his time with her and I'll never get any better because my husband is always with his mistress—"

He put a stop to her rush of words. "Your imaginary

husband is an idiot."

Cady went still. "Do you think?"

"Any man would be an idiot to ignore you. And any husband worth the name would be overjoyed to teach you how to kiss, not to mention all the other ways of…well, never mind."

But now she was curious. "What other ways?"

"We'll discuss that later."

"Later when? Gabe—"

Before she could say another word, his mouth was on hers. Cady nearly fainted at the rush of sensation flooding her mind. Smooth, slippery, gentle, then probing. Her mouth fell open and she let it all wash over her.

He then had his hands in her hair, shredding the composed chignon and letting the curls fall around her face, tickling her. He ran one thumb along her jawline, and Cady thrilled at the touch of his skin against hers.

The kiss went on and on, until Gabe completed it by sucking her lower lip to the point that Cady was melting with pleasure and ready to do anything he asked to get more of this divine, shivery feeling through her body.

"Well?" he asked when he pulled away. His tone was knowing, even smug.

"It was a nice kiss," Cady said, not very articulate at the moment.

He only laughed, and that melted her further, causing something in her belly to go warm and heavy.

"I intend to show you all sorts of nice, blossom. There's no need to kiss only the mouth," he said, moving to her cheek, then her jaw, his lips burning across her skin, leaving her heavy-limbed and pliant in his arms.

"And then there's the possibility of a dozen small kisses," he said, demonstrating exactly that in a line down her neck, each spot blooming in his wake.

"I like that possibility," she breathed. "Do it once more?"

"Anything you ask," he said. The second string of followed the neckline of her gown, and she ached to feel his mouth on places currently covered up.

Cady's whole body was alert and awake. Her heart thudded in her chest, and she felt the prickle of sweat on her brow in relation to the sudden flush of heat between them. Her breathing had quickened. Many of the symptoms were the same as when she was struck with terror… but this time she didn't feel scared at all. It wasn't fear surging through her veins now, it was excitement. She wanted to know what came next.

But he instead tipped her face to his. "You need to kiss me," he ordered softly.

"I do?"

"Are you afraid to?"

"A little."

"No time like the present to conquer that fear."

She leaned in to cover his mouth with hers. For a moment, that's all it was—he wasn't going to help her here.

But she remembered what he did, and she mimicked it, brushing her lips against his, and finally running the tip of her tongue along his lips.

He gripped her waist with a little more force than she was expecting and she gasped.

"Sorry," he muttered. "You caught me by surprise."

"You told me to kiss you!"

"I know. But then you did it so well. Do it again."

Cady did, pressing her mouth against his, exquisitely aware of his size and sheer presence, and also that she would be in dire straits if anyone caught her doing this. But one more kiss wouldn't hurt, would it? Especially since it might well be the last she'd ever get.

She didn't know how long it had been when he murmured, "All right, that's enough."

Cady moaned, unhappy with the command. She kissed him once more, hungry for something she couldn't name. It seemed impossible that any part of Gabe was soft. But his lips and tongue felt like velvet against her own, and all she wanted was more of it.

"*Enough*," he said, his voice almost a growl. He held her back from him, as if she were the dangerous one. "Christ, Cady. I don't want to get you in trouble."

Trouble could mean a lot of different things, all of them bad. She sighed, knowing he was correct.

"I'm sorry. Was I any good?"

Unexpectedly, he gave a low laugh. "You have an excellent natural talent."

"Oh, thank you. I don't know if your talent is natural or the result of practice, but it's prodigious."

"You flatter me." He ran the back of his hand along her jaw, a very gentle touch that nevertheless set Cady's nerves into a dance. "But we shouldn't stay here."

"No, I suppose not," she agreed, the disappointment coming out in her tone.

"I'll go first and open the door for you."

"No! I mean, I don't want to be left behind. Let's walk together?"

Gabe answered that by slipping one arm around her waist and leading her toward the razor-thin crack of light where the door didn't quite fit the frame.

Cady liked the feel of his broad hand on her back, the firm pressure that reminded her she wasn't alone in the darkness. How many men would take the time to do that for her, to allay her fears by showing her that she could endure them? Especially since he got nothing out of the bargain. Well, he got her kisses.

She hoped they were fair payment, considering how little she knew about kissing.

When they reached the door, Gabe put one arm out and pushed it open.

Sunlight poured over Cady, and she stepped out into a world of tender gold-green leaves and wildflowers growing at the edges of the scene. The sky arched above her, impossibly blue and infinitely distant, allowing her to inhale and breathe as deeply as she wanted. It was like being reborn.

Smiling, Cady turned back to speak to Gabe, but he wasn't standing by her. Cady retraced her steps to the doorway of the icehouse. For some reason, Gabe hadn't followed her out. He stood there, framed by the blackness of the interior. His expression was strangely lost.

"Gabe?" she asked.

His eyes found hers and they simply stood there a moment. Cady felt his attention like a physical thing, a rope binding them both together. Was it the kiss that had done it? Bound them somehow? Or was it something deeper than that, a chemical interaction ignited whenever they got close? All Cady knew was that she felt a special connection to him, as if she could share his senses. And that he was troubled.

"Gabe? What's wrong?"

"Cady, there's something I ought to tell you."

"Yes?" She started to walk back toward him. But just as she reached him and lifted her hand to touch his face, a booming voice interrupted.

"What exactly is going on here?"

♑

GABE SAW THE FIGURE OF Vernon atop one of the riding horses. He looked furious.

"I've been looking for you all over, my lady!" Vernon said. "And only to find you here, alone with…this man!"

"She had plans for the icehouse," Gabe said smoothly. "She was just giving me instructions for cleaning it out. Right, my lady?" He gave her foot a nudge with his.

"What? Oh, yes! Um, tuber storage!"

Vernon looked as perplexed as Gabe felt. "Tuber storage?"

"Yes!" Cady responded. "I had the idea to grow more potatoes and other nightshades and we'll need storage for that, won't we? So I thought of the icehouse and I wanted to show Mr Court what to do to prepare the building. To store the tubers. Obviously."

Her explanation made a little sense…maybe. But Gabe could sense the animosity rolling off the footman as he took in the sight of her ladyship standing practically in the arms of the gardener.

The old guard of servants were all fanatically loyal to the family, and in particular the late Lord Calder. Naturally they'd be livid at any hint of impropriety that would threaten Cady's reputation.

Gabe moved subtly to put a bit of distance between himself and Cady. Uncharacteristically, he resented that he had to. Who was Vernon to tell him what to do?

He's doing his job of protecting the mistress, Gabe told himself. Just as Gabe should be doing the job of extracting information from the mistress. Not thinking about how incredibly soft and smooth her lips were.

Idiot.

Aloud, he said, "Go back with Vernon, my lady. It sounds like there's an important matter for you to address at the house. I'll get to work here, as you instructed."

Cady nodded, with a hint of uncertainty in her face. But she turned and went to Vernon, who had dismounted and bent to help her up on the horse (never mind that she'd walked here on her own two feet). Why did all the servants treat her like glass? Was it part of the unreasoning fear she dealt with? Or was it just the overprotectiveness for a sheltered lady?

He waited a good twenty minutes before walking slowly back to the main house, putting together a more plausible story should Rundle or the others question him at length about this afternoon.

Tuber storage.

Gabe laughed out loud, and then just kept laughing. It felt good to do that. He couldn't remember the last time he had been so…surprised. And not just surprised, but delighted.

Was Cady always so funny? Was her constant fear stifling that sudden, flashing absurdity? Gabe found himself wanting to see more of that side of Cady. When she smiled it was like sun coming through clouds.

Wait. Did I really just think that? Gabe shook his head. This assignment was getting to him. Not once had Gabe ever fallen for a mark. He couldn't start now.

It was just that Cady was so different from what he expected. Vulnerable in some ways, yes, but also clearly able to think her way through most problems and motivated to pursue what she loved. And someone eager to master new things…as shown by her stunning progress in the icehouse. Given a few more minutes, she'd have Gabe begging for her.

He had to finish his work here before he did something incredibly stupid.

That night, he decided he couldn't wait any longer. After learning about the passageways that were part of the odd heating system in the glasshouses that Cady had called hot walls, Gabe now had a way inside the forbidden space where he knew the deadliest poisons had to be.

He broke into one of the other glasshouses that had a hot wall, smashing a pane in a corner behind a shrub, where the damage wouldn't be seen. Then he picked the lock on the door that led into those dark passageways fronting the hollow walls holding the conduits meant for heating.

Unlike Cady, Gabe long ago conquered his fear of darkness. He loved darkness. It hid him from prying eyes and allowed him to get closer to his enemies. He learned to love the dark while fighting in the army, working as an assassin behind the curtains rather than an ordinary piece on the battlefield. The darkness was his ally. So he didn't need a lantern to navigate the narrow passage. He trailed one hand along the walls to his right, using memory to tell him where to go. He'd carried Cady this same way—he wasn't going to forget that.

As he walked, he sensed he wasn't alone. Little squeaks and rustling noises told him that the rats were there too, alerted by his presence yet not scared. Because they knew their own. At the end of the day, this was where he belonged. Gabe was a rat too.

Finally, he got to the door that led to Cady's forbidden glasshouse. The lock on this door was simple. Why should anyone bother trying to make it complex? It only led to the hidden passages that so few people even knew about.

He picked the lock, and eased the door open, holding it firm against any sudden push thanks to a change in air pressure, or the screech of ungreased hinges.

Nothing.

He stepped inside and was immediately overcome by the difference in the air. First, it was warm as a balmy summer evening. Second, the air in the glasshouse was humid. When he inhaled, there was a weight to the air, and he almost coughed in surprise. His skin prickled at the sensation of the moist environment—like moving through mist, but without the chill that mist and fog always carried. And third, the air was drenched in fragrance. Floral and green and dark earth all mingled, teasing his nose. Despite the flowers, it was nothing like perfume. This was vital and elusive. He realized this was the scent of Arcadia, under that witch hazel sharpness.

He stepped forward, sniffing as he went, trying to match each scent with the plant sending it forth.

There was a deeply rich and sensual, even creamy, aroma coming from a cluster of small white flowers with long petals that grew in a basket covered in moss. Then a bolder, more roselike fragrance from a plant with blooms in a deep pink shade, their petals looking as slick as satin. He wanted to touch them but hesitated, remembering that he was, after all, searching for a poison.

Like any rational person, Cady had carefully labelled practically everything in her work area, but he couldn't read it in the dark. Begrudgingly, Gabe moved to where he knew a candle and fire-starter would be. In the feeble light of the candle, he could bend over and read the labels…but they were primarily in Latin, or simply referred to by the native names from wherever they'd been first grown, making it impossible for Gabe to learn much more than he knew. None of the labels said clephobine or any words vaguely like it. How was Gabe going to ever get to the next step in this investigation if he couldn't find out where the poison was being made?

"What are you doing here?" Arcadia's voice came out of the dark, swirling in with the waves of scent in the air.

He turned quickly. "I didn't mean to intrude."

"You picked a lock. Of course you meant to intrude." She walked closer and out of the gloom he saw that she was wearing that same gown as the night he found her unconscious in the laboratory. Black with huge flowers vining across it. In the shadows, the pattern seemed to writhe, giving the tiny Cady a mystical, menacing air.

"I wondered what was growing here. Why no one else is allowed to see it."

"Well, for the first question, the answer is simple. All the plants that are too tender to survive outdoors in the English winters. A sudden drop in temperature, a storm, or even too much sunlight could be deadly. And as these plants are very rare—unique—I must protect them by putting them under glass."

"And the second question?"

"Some of them are dangerous, too dangerous to allow innocent people to be near them."

"But you're near them. What are you guilty of?"

She gave him a faint, chill smile. "So you think I'm a murderess as well? The local gossip is still going strong, I see."

"That's not what I meant." He had to get her mind off what he was actually doing in there.

Gabe moved to her. "I was just curious."

He bent his head to kiss her before she could say another word.

Cady slapped his hand away. "What do you think you're doing." She didn't make it a question.

"Apologizing?" he ventured.

"No. An apology uses words."

"It doesn't have to."

"When you came here, I asked *one* thing of you. Don't go where you're not allowed. For your own safety, I asked you to obey that single rule."

"Cady—"

"Don't call me that. You have no right to call me that! You've got a gift for ending up in places you shouldn't be, Mr Court. My laboratory, late at night, when I'm the only one there. My bedroom, even later, when you're supposedly watching over my health. Now here, in a locked and walled space that you've been repeatedly warned not to go. And yet here we are, with you touching me and thinking that a kiss will make me biddable and compliant. Was that what the exchange in the icehouse was all about? I must have appeared so very weak and easy to manipulate."

"Cady—I mean, my lady. No." Christ, this was going to shit.

"Oh, yes. Since I've actually caught you sneaking in, at least do me the courtesy of not lying to my face. I don't know why you wanted to get in here, but I assure you that you'll be leaving now."

"My lady, if you'll let me explain—"

She cut him off, pointing imperiously at the door. "Get out."

"Please—"

"Get out! This is my place. This is my *world*, and you're not welcome here! So get OUT!"

♑

FURIOUS AND TERRIFIED AT FINDING Gabe in the glasshouse, Cady had barely closed her eyes since. To think that when she saw a flicker of light in the glasshouse, her first concern was an accidental fire. Instead, she discovered the one new person she'd opened up to, proving that she'd been foolish to think he was different.

She remained in the glasshouse for the rest of the night, with oil lamps burning bright to ward off any return, to let him know that she wasn't going to relax her vigilance now and let him back in to do whatever he'd planned to do. Destroying her carefully cultivated specimens, perhaps, out of a misguided belief that she was some evil creature out to hurt people? Or perhaps just wanting to see what was forbidden, as if myths and fables hadn't warned humanity over and over again that nothing good came of such curiosity. Eden, Pandora, Bluebeard... How many times did the lesson need to be taught before it was learned?

She woke up from a fitful slumber on the floor of the glasshouse. The panes were thick with condensation. Getting up, Cady moved back to her bedroom so as not to alarm the servants. She had to move Oscar, who had made himself quite comfortable on her pillow. He meowed in protest as Cady shooed him off.

As for Gabe Court, she avoided him entirely that day

and the next days, again funneling all instructions for the gardens through Mr Rundle (who didn't like it, but of course didn't complain). She should have sent Gabe away the very next day, but two things held her back. First, she desperately needed the help. And second, the memory of the way he kissed her lingered in the depths of her heart, and the thought of never seeing him again was too painful to contemplate at the moment.

What was certain was how his betrayal sent her emotions into a tumult. She'd found a fragile happiness in his little lessons in bravery, genuinely believing that she was improving in some way. And then there was the thrill she felt every time she saw him, that flutter in her belly and the flush under her skin that was so delicious after months and years of coiled, cold fear ruling her body and mind.

Then he had to go and ruin it by invading the one space she told him not to go.

She should have known. What was in it for him? The lure of discovering deep, dark secrets and finding out if all the worst rumors were true? He seemed like the type of man who would be drawn to that. The type of man who didn't let little things like rules or her attempts to keep other people safe get in the way of his need to know.

Stupid, stupid Cady. Trusting a stranger who showed up at her door, taking his word at face value. She knew he was still watching her, still curious about what she did. No wonder she once again couldn't sleep at night, and the iron bands were tight around her heart again, and the whole world beyond her home felt like a trap.

But she needed to make more medicines.

And spring was advancing, meaning she could finally harvest some different specimens growing outside on Calderwood land.

One day, Cady went to a particular patch of woods in

hopes that she'd find the first crop of the mushrooms she used for making a tea that calmed the mind. It was a good recipe, but it couldn't compete with the more severe attacks. Cady considered it a stepping stone on her way to a more effective solution.

The mushrooms she sought were so tiny and unremarkable that most people would never even see them. They grew only on the rotting logs of birch trees—a fact she found fascinating. Cady had ordered several birches felled and their trunks dragged to this spot in the hopes of encouraging more mushrooms to grow, which they finally had.

She harvested her crop very carefully, selecting only one in every five specimens, leaving plenty to remain and spread throughout the warm months. The final harvest barely filled her handkerchief. She folded it up into a little pillow and tucked it into her pocket, smiling with relief that she'd be able to create a batch of the medicine she needed.

Cady was so intent on her future work in the laboratory that she failed to hear the footsteps on the path behind her. Only when she heard a male voice did she stop in her tracks.

"Hey, isn't that the witch of Calderwood?" someone called out.

Cady's stomach dropped. She turned to see two men, one older than her, one younger. But both much, much bigger than she was. They stared at her and sniggered.

"I think it is," the other man said, sounding smug. "Why are you out in the daytime, witch?"

"This is *my* land," Cady said, wishing her voice sounded stronger.

"Not what I asked," the older man said rudely. "I asked what you're doing out here. Up to no good, I'll bet.”

“What I’m doing on my land is none of your business.”

“Maybe we’ll make it our business. After all, we can’t just let a witch and a murderess walk around free.”

They moved closer, cutting off her access to the foot-path.

“Leave me alone.” Cady looked toward the leather bag she’d left on the side of the path. There was a small knife inside, in case she needed to cut any plants tougher than mushrooms. But it was ten feet away, which was practically the other side of the world. She had no way to defend herself against these men if they got violent.

“Maybe we should tie her up and drag her to the mag-istrate,” the first suggested.

“Maybe there’s a reward,” the other agreed with a nasty grin.

They both lunged toward her, reaching, clutching, putting hands on her skin. Cady let out a cry of panic and tried to twist away, to shrink down into the young under-growth like the prey she was.

But by now the meaty paws of the two poachers gripped her shoulders and arms, their fingers pulling at her cloak. One man casually flipped it back to reveal her gown and her exposed neck underneath. His leer made Cady’s throat close up.

“You can’t do this,” she whimpered, knowing that they could do whatever they wanted.

Then without warning, the older man grunted in sur-prise, and the younger went flying backward.

“Get the hell away from the lady,” a new voice com-manded.

Dazed, Cady looked up to see a dark-haired figure towering over her, facing the two men, who were now somehow five feet further away. Gabe.

"Who're you?" the younger man spat out, glaring at Gabe as he tried to get his footing back.

"I'm the one telling you to get the hell away from the lady," Gabe snapped back.

Not much room for diplomacy from that quarter, Cady noted, still not quite comprehending what was going on, only knowing that the situation changed.

The three men clashed once more, and then Gabe did something to the older man's arm. Cady couldn't see because the arm was twisted behind the man's back. But whatever it was, it must have been painful. The man winced and cried out, begging Gabe to stop.

After a moment, Gabe relented. He strongly suggested that the two men leave Calderwood property by the fastest possible route, and threatened to remove several important body parts if he saw either man again. His warning was quite descriptive. Cady thought she'd heard crude language from him before, but it was nothing compared to what he used toward those men.

They left, at a pace just under a jog, looking back over their shoulders with expressions of mingled fear and hatred.

Gabe waited until they were out of sight. Then he knelt down where Cady had fallen. "You all right?" he asked, his tone gruff.

"Oh, Lord." Cady reached into the slit of her dress to get at the pocket, patting frantically until she felt the little linen packet containing the mushrooms. "I've still got them."

"What?"

"Something I was harvesting," she said evasively, remembering that she didn't trust him. *Even though he just saved me*, she realized.

"Did you know those men? Can you tell me their names?" he asked.

"I've never seen them before, but they guessed who I was. I wish I knew what they were doing here."

"Poachers, most likely," Gabe said. "Like that person I saw before. They were after rabbits or some other game, and saw you by chance. Can you stand? You didn't get hurt when he pushed you down, did you?"

He held out his hands, and Cady puts hers in his. He pulled her up easily, and encouraged her to walk a few steps. Cady was relieved to find that the only damage was to her dress. "I'm fine. I can walk."

"Until we know who those men were and who else might be sneaking onto the estate, you shouldn't go out alone, Cady."

She nodded, too upset to correct him about the familiar term of address. "This is what I get for going out at all. I should have stayed inside. Then I'd have been safe."

"You couldn't have known. It wasn't your fault."

"They called me a witch." Her voice shook. "When they first saw me, one said *Isn't that the witch of Calderwood?*"

Gabe's expression went stormy. "Don't listen to them."

"They hate me."

"They're idiots and they don't know anything."

She shivered. "If they hate me, why would they touch me like they did?"

Gabe reached out one hand to take her by the shoulder, but then stopped abruptly as her words sunk in. He said, in a tone that very much sounded like he could ensure it, "They'll never touch you again."

"But *why*?"

"Men are pigs," he answered. "Whatever we might

say, our minds usually all go to the same place."

She gave one sad little chuckle. "You know, when I was going through all the things I'm scared of today, one thing I forgot to fear was being assaulted by total strangers while I walked in my own woods."

"Maybe that means you can let go of some of that long list of fears. Then you can worry about the bad things that actually do happen."

"Or I'll just never leave my room."

Gabe looked concerned. "But if you do that, you'll lose all the progress you've made. And I won't see you again."

"You might. You seem to show up wherever you want to be anyway." She pulled away and looked at him inquisitively. "Why are you out here? There's no task that would take you to this part of the property."

"What if I said I got a premonition?"

"I wouldn't believe you, particularly not after you broke into my glasshouse. But it was very good of you to rescue me," she added, too grateful to ignore that effort.

"The truth is I saw you walking out this way and I got worried. What were you doing out here?" he asked. "Harvesting what? You could have asked someone else to gather whatever it was."

She looked at him steadily, then sighed. "It's not so simple." From her pocket, she produced the little square of fabric. Opening it, she revealed the cache of minuscule mushrooms, straw colored and fragile, already shriveling up.

"Mushrooms?" he asked. "Are they safe to eat?"

"These aren't for eating. I dry them and then grind them into powder and then steep a little in boiled water and drink it." Why was she even talking to him, after he'd invaded her space?

"Oh, Christ. Like last time?"

"No, nothing like last time. I know how to use these. I've used them many times before. The tea I drink from these calms me down, it stops the shaking and the agitation and the…the endless circle of bad thoughts."

"Will you tell me when you drink it?"

"Why, so you can spy on me?" she asked.

He flinched, but said, "You should have someone with you. After seeing you lying unconscious across the worktable of your laboratory once, I don't want to see it again."

"I feel like such a fool," she said, the words rushing out of her. "I just *never* thought that could happen on my own land. And I couldn't do anything. Couldn't even get to the knife in my bag, not that it would have been much use."

He nodded. "Listen, you need to protect yourself in the future."

"I thought you just said I was protecting myself too much."

"I mean from real threats. Like those men. Whenever you walk the estate, you should take Romulus and Remus with you." He paused. "They still make you nervous, don't they? The dogs, I mean."

"A little. I'm afraid they'll bite me. Or I'll lose control of them and they'll bite someone one else, like a child…"

"One of the imaginary children in the wood." He sighed. "You ought to walk the dogs anyway. Or you can take me along and I'll mind the dogs," he added.

The image of him and the two wolfhounds flanking her every step was surprisingly comforting. Except that she couldn't trust Gabe. Even though part of her still very much wanted to trust him.

"We should return to the house," she said, wishing she

wasn't always fleeing toward it.

"Wait. You're disheveled."

Gabe brushed away some loose debris from her hair. His fingertips grazed her neck and her lips parted in silent surprise. She peeked at him from under her lashes, trying to discern if his gesture was simple courtesy…or something else.

From the way he was looking at her, it was the something else. Tension built between them, like the charge in the air before a storm.

Cady knew he would kiss her. But she wanted him to kiss her again, ever since the encounter in the icehouse, when he showed her just how much she was missing by hiding alone in her tiny world.

So she tipped her head up and allowed it.

She let herself be subsumed by the intimacy of lips sliding on lips, breath that wasn't hers filling her mouth, a voice too low for her to match saying lovely things that were undoubtably lies.

Oh, I remember. I still can't trust him. Cady turned her head to the side, rejecting his admittedly dazzling attention. "This isn't what I need," she said.

"What do you need? Tell me." The invitation was crystal clear, but Cady refused to respond to it.

Instead, she stepped back and said, "I need to go home and work in my laboratory. Without interruption and without intrusion."

"Cady, don't hide away again."

"Mr Court, you do not dictate terms to me." Cady's tone was frosty, mostly because whenever she let him get close to her, she had a tendency to melt into a puddle. "Thank you for rescuing me. I won't forget it. But I also won't forget anything else you did. Now, since you seem to have difficulty following directions, let me be very clear. You will escort me back to the house, then you will work on the ha-ha this afternoon."

"The what?"

"The raised earthworks that separates the lawn by the house from the lower meadow. It's called a ha-ha."

"First tuber storage, and now a ha-ha. Who came up with that name?"

"Probably the person who laughed when they saw people fall off it because they didn't realize the ground went away. Part of the wall's fallen down and it needs to be cleared of dirt and the stones reset. Otherwise the sheep and goats get up to the lawn and gardens and wreak havoc."

"Is this a real task? Or are you making things up to punish me?"

"You can always leave Calderwood, Mr Court. Go find another gardening position somewhere else."

He was silent, which gave Cady something to think about. She could send Gabe away. Or perhaps she could find out exactly why he wanted to stay.

♑

GABE DISCOVERED THAT THE HA-HA was indeed a real thing, and that goats loved to climb across the damaged part to chomp on the tender green grass of the lawn above. He spent the whole rest of the afternoon lifting and moving rocks so he could clear out the damaged area and reassemble the wall. It was hard work, and the spring day warmed as the sun moved west. Gabe was a sweaty mess by the time he was done.

And all he could think about was Cady's expression when she left him at the door to the house. Those deep brown eyes regarding him with a thoughtfulness that unsettled him.

Still, he did his work, and when he was done he washed himself clean, carefully avoiding getting his hair or beard too wet, lest the black dye bleed all over.

Another excellent supper from Cook, but the attitude of the other servants toward him was as chilly as it had been the first day he arrived. Vernon must have shared his suspicions about what he saw at the icehouse the other day. He must have thought Gabe was using his proximity to Lady Arcadia to seduce her. Gabe could only imagine their reactions if Vernon actually knew what happened inside the icehouse just before he arrived. Gabe would likely have been tarred and feathered before being run out of town.

A bell on the wall rang—the laboratory, not Cady's

bedchamber—and Martha stood. "Wonder what she needs. Already pecked at her supper," she commented as she bustled away.

Gabe listened as the others talked. He knew better than to try to work his way into the conversation. He'd have to find another tactic to regain the tentative trust of the old guard.

Then Martha returned to the kitchen, looking a little annoyed. "My lady wants to see you, Mr Court."

He sat up straighter, but frowned. This was exactly the sort of situation he needed to avoid—being alone with Cady. "Now?"

"Aye, in her laboratory. She said something heavy needs to be moved."

"Oh, I can do that." He stood up, and offered a quick goodnight in case any of the others should retire before he got back. He felt the gazes of Rundle and Vernon like daggers in his back. Gabe hurried though the dark halls to Cady's laboratory.

He knocked quietly, mindful of her hatred of intrusion. "My lady? Martha said you have need of me."

"Yes, come in."

The laboratory was dimly lit, with only a couple of lamps burning, both turned down quite low. Cady perched on a stool near her gigantic worktable.

"What am I moving?" he asked, looking around. Nothing looked like it was out of place.

"I told Martha that as an excuse." She gestured to the table, which held a number of glass containers, and—incongruously—two small teapots and cups. One was chipped. "You said that someone ought to be with me while I drank my mushroom tea. Since you're so interested in my doings, I've decided that person will be you."

Gabe looked at the tea things and winced. "Am I part

of this experiment?"

"Don't be ridiculous. First, it's not an experiment. I already know how the mushroom tea works. Second, *your* tea is the same blend that Cook uses for tea at the evening meals. Did you know I make it?"

"Not surprised. It's good," Gabe added, recalling the herbal blend Cook always made in the big ceramic teapot. Heavy on the mint, it was refreshing without keeping a person up all night.

She gestured to a second stool and he sat. It was oddly formal, him and Cady at the table. He felt like he ought to be dressed better, and said so.

She smiled as she poured his tea from the pot closest to him. "It's not a party. It's for information." She poured her own brew from the other pot. It looked and smelled much different. Earthier and dark.

"You took the chipped cup," he noted.

"Oh, I've had it for years and years. I like the chip." When she took the first sip of her tea, she frowned and reached for a jar of honey.

"This crop is more bitter. Interesting." After adding the honey, she made a note in her little book.

Gabe drank his own tea, watching her. "I'm surprised you allowed me in here again."

"I'm surprised you haven't quit on me," she replied, her gaze challenging. "Calderwood can't be the most coveted post."

He shrugged. "I do the job I'm told. And right now, that's working here."

"That sentiment comes from your time as a soldier?" she asked.

"Maybe. I've never liked leaving things undone, even when I was young. I suppose it's ingrained in my personality."

"What were you like as a boy?" she asked, leaning in. The scent of witch hazel wafted toward him, mixing with the steam from the teas. The combination made Gabe a little dizzy. Or was that the proximity of Cady, and her exquisitely full lips?

"Terrible, probably," he said, after a second. "I was ill behaved, wild, rude. Hated school even though I liked reading. Spent time with the dogs and horses whenever I could. No one really wanted me around, so I had a lot of free time."

"No one? But your family must have. You said you have brothers."

"I'm not saying I was abandoned in the streets. I had a very comfortable life. It's just that everyone was always busy with something else. I was an afterthought. I don't even know why I'm telling you this."

"I do." She smiled. "Your tea tonight contained a quarter dram of verocine."

He blinked. "What's that?"

"Its primary effect is mental. It makes the user less able to dissemble or lie."

His stomach lurched as the words sunk in. "*What?*"

"Lying is very complex, you know," Cady said, keeping her eyes on him as she spoke. "One must hold two different versions of the world in one's mind: the world as they know it to be, and the world they wish to present to others. Truth and falsehood. And this substance seems to make a person unable to hold both views of the world at once. They have this urge to pick one—the real one. It's been used for centuries to interrogate prisoners and spies...or so I'm told. Anyway, that's what I just gave you."

"But...I thought I was here to watch you drink your weird mushroom tea."

"And I told you that I had no need to test this particular tea. I've used it many times before. No, Gabe. Tonight's experiment has you for a test subject. Honestly, considering everyone thinks I'm a murderess, I'm astonished you drank anything I offered you."

He stared into bottom of the cup with horror. "I can't believe you did that."

"Well, I can't believe a lot of what you told me," she retorted. "You show up claiming to be an ordinary man just happy to have a position as groundskeeper. That's fine, as far as it goes. But then you turn out to be inordinately curious about my house and gardens, particularly about everything behind a lock. Perhaps you're just a thief?"

"I've stolen nothing from here," he said, grateful that he could say that.

"Nothing a person can hold in their hand, perhaps. I do recall a few stolen kisses. I'd like to think that you simply were bewitched by my perfect appearance and attire, since I'm the model of a young miss. But somehow I doubt that."

"Cady, believe me that I wanted to kiss you."

"Do you mean you enjoyed it?" Her expression changed to one of vulnerability. "You weren't lying when you said I had natural talent?"

The truth came easy this time. "Hell, no."

"That's something at least. But the fact remains that you're not what you say you are." She held up her notebook, open to the page where he'd written the note about Cady's eyes being so dilated. "You speak and write with far more skill than the usual laborer. Your handwriting and language are that of a man who's been well educated."

"Perhaps I'm down on my luck?" he suggested.

"I should also tell you that I wrote to the people who you offered as references when you got yourself hired by Rundle. He records all that information, you know."

Gabe sighed. "You…wrote?"

"Only one replied. They'd never heard of you. Perhaps the others didn't reply because they don't even exist."

"I…um." Yes, the Zodiac had to rush some of the details of his cover, but he hadn't realized it was *that* rushed. Words that usually came so easily to him now hovered beyond reach. He felt idiotic.

"And finally…" She reached over to him and ran her hand through his hair. When she pulled back, he saw the smear of black on her fingers.

Damn.

"What did you use?" she asked, wrinkling her nose. "It's very sticky and honestly I don't see the point. Did you think you wouldn't be hired if we knew you were fair-haired?"

"Perhaps I'm on the run from the law and I had to disguise myself."

"Well? Are you?"

"No," he admitted. God, was this what it was like, telling the truth all the time? "Not at the moment."

"So why did you dye your hair? And is that beard fake? Horsehair or something?"

"It's real, but also dyed. To be truthful"—and he was, like it or not—"I don't care for it that much. And whatever time I save by not shaving I lose in the dyeing."

"Then why do it?"

"Sometimes it's useful to look a little different than usual. You never know who you might meet."

"Gabriel Court, stop dissembling this moment." Her eyes narrowed. "Your hair is fake. Your lower-class accent is fake. Your letters of reference are fake. Is your name fake as well?"

"It's…shortened."

"Oh, Lord have mercy. Who are you really?"

"I shouldn't tell you." But, God, he wanted to.

"You're higher born than you pretend. What are you? The wastrel offspring of a duke or something? A second son?"

"Worse. Third son. That part is true. I can't even claim to be a spare. Thus the entry into the army. My father isn't a duke, of course, but did buy my commission. It simply wouldn't do for me to tramp about like a common enlisted man."

"I imagine room and board is better as an officer."

He snorted a laugh. "You're right about that."

"Tell me why I shouldn't just scream my head off and tell everyone you came in here with evil intent and I had to fight you off. Vernon would certainly believe me, after finding us together before."

"*Don't* do that," he begged. "Christ, Cady, I don't want to hurt you."

She glared at him. "You already have hurt me. You showed up here and wormed your way into my household and my life, and you fought off those men in the woods, and you carried me to my room when I misjudged the dose on my experiment, and you were interested in my work—oh, Lord you were so interested—and you pretended to care about me, and you kissed me, and the whole time you were just planning, I don't know—"

"That's not true," he objected. "I mean, most of it's true, yes, but I wasn't only pretending to care about you. I do care about you. I might even love you."

She backed up a step, her eyes widening. Shock, dismay, disbelief…

He knew exactly what she felt, because all those things were hitting him too. Did he just say *love*?

* * * *

At the word *love*, something inside her body thudded to a halt. Her plan had gone awry. Did she give him the wrong tincture in his tea? Were aphrodisiacs real after all? Cady wanted to run from the room. She asked in a choked voice, "What did you just say?"

"Nothing!" he said quickly. "I'm not…speaking right. I meant that I care that nothing bad happens to you. After all the other bad things."

Gabe looked sick. This was not a man used to spilling his guts, and Cady had just tricked him into doing exactly that. Wait until he learned that there was no such thing as verocine.

"Why don't you just leave Calderwood?" she suggested. "I won't say anything to the law. Whatever you're up to, you can do it somewhere else. Go spy on another botanist."

"That's not possible." He looked a little more in command of himself now.

"Oh, I assure you it is. If you don't quit as my gardener, I'll have you sacked."

"That would be inconvenient. Look, I'm sorry I had to hide some things about myself, but I didn't know what I'd find when I got here. The subterfuge was necessary for my investigation."

"Investigation? You *are* spying on me?"

That word caused something to flit across his face. "Well…yes."

"Why? Are you from the magistrate or something?" A familiar wash of worry flooded through her again. "Mrs

Bowcott told me that it was just gossip, and that it was fading as people got bored with the same old stories."

"It's not that, Cady!" he burst out. "It's something else entirely. Look, there's this substance called clephobine."

She frowned, surprised he even knew of it. "That's a very dangerous drug."

"It's made from a plant."

"I know. The plant is called Actaea Claviscortuum or commonly, scarlet baneberry. It's from North America. I've got some specimens here. Wait... What business do you have with a poison like that?"

He took a breath, and closed his eyes, obviously arranging what he was about to say. "It's been used to kill someone very close to me."

Cady recoiled, the thought of violent death instantly causing her to tense up. "Oh, my God."

"I think the killer got it from here."

"What!" The familiar urge to hide from a threat suddenly got supplanted by pure shock. "Here? Who thinks that?"

His expression twisted. "I can't tell you."

"I think you had better," she said coldly. "Or shall I scream for help after all?"

♑

NO MATTER WHAT CHEMICAL CADY had dropped into his tea, Gabe was too well conditioned to tell her anything about the Zodiac. The rule was too ingrained in him. Don't ever mention his code name, don't mention the name of the group, don't even acknowledge that such a group exists. Gabe had worked as Capricorn for several years and had yet to break that rule. He wasn't starting now.

"Tell me why you're doing this," she insisted. "You were sent here particularly, to follow me particularly."

"I *chose* to come here after I heard about my friend's murder," he explained, picking his way carefully so his words were all technically true. "His name was Lewelleyn Parrish."

"He must have been a *very* good friend," she said, giving him an odd, speculative look.

"It's hard to explain," he said after a second. "We were both in the same…circle. I can tell you that he was the sort of person you'd want on your side." *Just like any agent of the Zodiac*, he thought.

Cady was watching him, trying to make sense of his explanation. "I think I see," she said at last. "And I'm very sorry to hear that he died. Are you *sure* he was murdered?"

"There's no question."

"And you're sure he was given clephobine? It's extremely rare."

"You're the only person in England who's successfully synthesized it," he said.

"That's true…as far as I know anyway. I don't know whether to be flattered that you went through the trouble to find that out, or horrified because you thought I left poison lying around."

"That's why I'm here. Parrish left a note before he died. It was only one word: *Calderwood.*"

Cady's eyes widened. She looked as if she'd just been struck. "How…" was all she got out.

Gabe didn't like how much pain he was causing her now. But she had insisted on the truth.

"Listen, Parrish was actually investigating a few other murders, where the victims were also poisoned with clephobine. Maybe he realized that this estate is the only place where the plant it comes from is growing."

She nodded slowly, uncertainly. "It's a New World species. Mine was sent to me by a colleague in Boston. But I'm sure other botanists in England have their own contacts. Did you check with the royal gardens? They *must* have a specimen. Wait, I remember. They did get a few several years ago, but they died. Anyway, it's a leap from growing baneberry to committing murder." Then she blinked and asked, "Lord, do you think I'm the killer?"

"No…not anymore," he admitted. "Actually, I never thought it was likely, not once I saw you and learned how you've not left your estate for months. But I still think that the poison must have come from here."

"Let's just take a few steps back," Cady said, holding up her hands. "I need to understand what you're saying. What happened to Mr Parrish? I mean, what were the specific symptoms? How did you, or the doctor or whoever, conclude that clephobine was involved?"

Gabe had to be very careful here, so he told the truth but left out everything about the Zodiac. "Well, I have a connection with a certain—let's say—department of the government. They have ways of finding things out. On the surface, it wasn't even considered murder. It just looked like Parrish died in his sleep."

"That makes sense," Cady said, nodding. "Clephobine works by slowing down all the body's processes: breathing, blood, heartbeat. A little acts as a calming agent. Too much sends the victim into a coma and then death."

"Well, some doctor in London has developed some sort of test that shows whether clephobine is present in the body, even after death," Gabe said. "When he tested the suspected victims, he found traces of the chemical in their organs. Don't ask me for more details on the process—I don't know them."

"Interesting. I'd like to speak to him at some point. I wonder how he devised the test."

"You're handling this news very well," Gabe said suddenly.

"That's the mushroom tea. I suspected that I'd be rather distressed when I heard the truth about you, so it was wise to drink something soothing first."

"Wait, if your mushroom tea does that, why make the clephobine at all?"

"The mushroom tea is quite mild. I'd hoped that the clephobine, and then the solution I made from the Iranian salvia, would be more effective. Unfortunately, they both turned out to be far stronger and more dangerous than I'm comfortable with. Hence, the mushroom tea."

"Will it wear off?"

"Undoubtably, and I hope that I'll either be asleep or have some answers from you by that point. I don't look forward to another attack."

"And I don't want to be the cause of one. So if you can prove to me that the clephobine wasn't made here, I can leave tomorrow." *Don't tell me to leave tomorrow*, he thought. For some reason, he wasn't at all ready to leave Calderwood.

"One can't prove a negative," Cady told him with a frown. "That's one of the most basic rules of logic."

"I may have skipped out of my lessons that day. Is there anything you can show me that might help?"

"I could show you the scarlet baneberry," she said. "When you broke in the other night, you actually invaded the wrong glasshouse. Follow me and I'll take you to the correct one."

Not long after that, Gabe was standing in yet another glasshouse, a smaller one that was tucked away in a corner, shielded from most people's attention by a wing of the house and a walled garden on the other side. He never would have found it on his own.

The air here was also humid and warm, and the plants grew with vigor, reaching for the sunlight just past the glass roof. Vines clambered up wooden poles. Deep green, glossy leaves folded like fans in the flickering light of the lantern. And the air was honeyed, with a thickness to it, as if breathing too much might fill up your lungs until you drowned. Part of Gabe was afraid of this place, this slice of the tropics in cold England. A tiny world invading the larger, as out of place as a dagger in a body.

"Now listen closely," Cady said, looking quite collected, those big brown eyes solemn. "*Everything* in here is poisonous. Don't pick anything, don't touch anything, don't eat anything. You may look and ask questions, that's all."

"How do you keep these plants alive if you can't even touch them?"

She gave him a tiny smirk. "Because I know what I'm doing. Now, look here. This one is scarlet baneberry."

He bent over to get eye to eye with the plant. And that's exactly how it felt, because at the end of the long, nodding stalk, a cluster of berries grew. The berries were oval and pure white, with a little nub of deep red at the tip, like a bloody pupil.

It was like staring at some monstrous creature with twenty or thirty eyes staring back at him. Unconsciously, he shivered. "Well. That's…striking."

Cady nodded happily. "It's a fascinating plant, isn't it? The common name among the early settlers was baneberry, because sometimes cattle ate the berries and died. But the natives use other parts of the plant in medicines. The leaves can treat anything from headaches to difficult childbirth. But only in tiny amounts. And the berries are highly poisonous. I'd never even touch a whole berry without gloves, let alone a broken one with the juice exposed. Far too dangerous."

"What would happen if someone did touch the juice?"

"Depends on the person, but mostly likely they'd show signs of lethargy or confusion, a weakened state, and possibly death due their heart simply failing to beat. Clephobine has been suggested to be a potential medicine for those who have too-rapid heartbeats, or those who might suffer from other heart conditions. But only in minuscule amounts. When the juice and sap is purified and rendered into pure clephobine, even one part in ten thousand could have a lethal effect."

"You're very well versed in the details."

She blushed. "I experimented with it. I do that with most of my specimens, and especially any exotics."

"Do you have any clephobine on hand now?"

She shook her head slowly. "No. As I said, it's highly

lethal."

"What did you do with the quantity you made?"

"I disposed of it, of course."

"How?"

"Safely, if that's what you're asking. The last thing I need is people or animals or even insects dropping dead at Calderwood."

"How did you determine that clephobine is so lethal? What did your experiments do, exactly? Oh, God, you tested it on yourself. Just like you did with the new solution you made, that night I found you unconscious."

Cady looked away.

"Jesus *Christ*. How are you not dead?"

"It was an extremely dilute solution."

"What did you hope to learn?"

"I wanted to know if there was medicinal value!" she burst out. "My God, if you felt like I do for just one week, you'd have broken into every chemist's and doctor's office in London. I've been living with this condition for years. I can't sleep through the night, I can barely go an hour without feeling my heart rattling in my rib cage, and I am constantly scared of everything. Do you think I enjoy this? This *excuse* for a life? I hate it!"

Before Gabe could talk himself out of it, he reached for her, pulling her into his embrace, despite her resistance.

"Let me go!" she spat, clawing at his chest with her entrapped hands.

"No. You're the only thing in this whole room I can touch without dying."

"Don't make a joke of me!"

"The joke's not on you, Cady. Please take a few breaths. You're upset."

"I'm more than upset, you idiot. Haven't you been

listening? I'm a wreck and I can't fix myself!"

"You're a person, not a piece of luggage. You can't just fix your mind like it's a broken strap."

"What does that have to do with how you're pinning me down?"

"If I were pinning you down, it would look different, darling. I just thought you might need a hug."

"A…hug?" She sounded stunned.

"Well, when was the last time you got one?"

"Seven years ago, probably."

"What?" Now he was stunned.

"Mama gave me hugs. And Trevor did too. But Mama died, and Trevor wasn't allowed in the house, and I wasn't allowed out of it, so…ooof!"

He'd tightened his arms around her. "Lot of time to make up for."

Cady had stopped struggling against him, which he regarded as a success. She actually leaned her head against his chest, and he once again inhaled the smell of witch hazel, astringent yet springlike.

"You're a very strange gardener," she said at last, her voice meek and muffled.

"Yes, I know."

"The hug is helping."

"Good."

"I'm going to cry in a moment."

"I'll live. Why will you cry?"

"I cry a lot. Sometimes I think it's the only way I can get all the bad feelings out of my body. It's not even sadness, it's just…all the feelings I'm not supposed to have."

"According to who?"

She shrugged, her shoulders pressing against his chest. "What does it matter?" she mumbled. "I am the way I am, and the way I am makes everyone hate me."

He leaned back and tipped her head up to see her expression. The tears were there, not yet falling but all too close.

He kissed her, knowing he shouldn't. This wasn't strategic, this wasn't a way to win her confidence so he could extract information from her. No, he just wanted to feel her, and be close to her, and revel in how soft she was, how alive and tender and altogether unhateable she was.

"Cady, you taste so good."

"That's the mint I put in my tooth powder."

He nearly choked on a laugh. "Now who's joking?"

"I'm trying desperately to not be serious, because if I were serious, then what's happening between us could get serious, and…"

He kissed her again, partly to get her to stop talking. But mostly because he needed her. Her lips were just as soft and warm and yielding as before. After a moment's hesitation, she slid her arms up his chest, and raised herself up on her toes for better access to his mouth. When she flicked her tongue against his, he nearly lost his mind.

Gabe pushed away all the thoughts and worries hounding him, and let his body tell him what it wanted.

And it wanted her, to a degree that was almost painful. But in this place, they were surrounded by poison, and the wrong move could possibly kill them. Not the best choice for what he had in mind.

He held her with one arm and ran his hand along the neckline of her gown, hooking one finger underneath to tease the skin he couldn't see. Cady's inhalation told him she was just as interested in continuing this as he was.

"Cady. Tell me where we can go. Right now. Where we'll be alone and you'll feel safe."

She looked at him, and because she was so much

smaller it meant that she had to peep through her thick lashes to see him. There were courtesans in London and Paris who would pay in gold to learn how to do that so well.

"I'm not sure there's anywhere I'd feel safe," she whispered.

"You'll be safe with me," he promised.

She took a breath, then sighed softly. "Follow me."

♑

REALIZING EXACTLY WHAT HE WAS offering, Cady knew the only correct response for a lady was to swiftly reject the advance and tell him to leave her alone. But Cady didn't feel like being correct, and she felt a pull toward him unlike anything she'd felt before.

So she led him outside into the chill night, and they went to the orangerie. She couldn't take him to her rooms, and not simply because of the other servants in the house. Her bedroom was too important to her peace of mind to allow him in it again. Especially if they were going to do what she guessed they would do. His memory would linger in that room till the end of days. Cady couldn't handle that.

But the orangerie was secluded and warm, and meant nothing to Cady's peace of mind. Her life was in the workroom and the glasshouses.

She opened the door with a key from her ring, and Gabe pulled it shut as soon as they both slipped in. Cady locked it again, and took a breath.

Gabe was looking around in wonder. Well, the orangerie *was* a sort of jewel box: stone columns and leaded glass windows and skylights to let the precious sunlight in. And instead of mere jewels, it contained lovely, slender trees that bore luscious fruits or heavy blossoms with rich scents: lemon, jasmine, neroli. The orangerie was not quite as damp as the glasshouses, but actually a few degrees warmer. It was dim, but the gloaming of the night sky filtered in enough to let them see.

"What do you think?" she asked.

"Fancy," he concluded. Then he reached for her again, a wicked smile spreading across his lips. "Tell me you've got somewhere in this jungle where we can sit down."

Cady walked to a bench placed in the center, with trees at each corner. Some monstrous shrubs with antediluvian leaves blocked the view to the doorways in either direction. The bench itself was more like a bed, wide and covered with a very comfortable cushion.

"In the daytime, I used to come here and read. Or nap," Cady said. "It's a good place for sleeping."

"I can think of other things it's good for," he said. Rather than sitting, he stood facing her. "You certain you're not brewing up aphrodisiacs in your laboratory?"

She chuckled. "Those aren't real."

"No? Not any of them?"

"No. Never take anything that claims to be an aphrodisiac. It's all guesswork or wishful thinking or folktales or outright fraud."

"Fortunately, I don't need any outside influence to know how I feel about you."

"Which is what?" Cady asked.

He smiled. "Hard."

She had just discovered that for herself, and she froze for a second, uncertain how to respond. Her moment of stillness was all it took for him to reconsider.

He moved back, putting her at arm's length. "Sorry," he muttered. "Thought you…never mind."

"No! Don't give up on me!" Cady rose up toward him.

He leaned forward and kissed her with surprising lightness, as if he wasn't sure she wanted this, despite her literally leading him here. So Cady deepened it, putting her hands on his shoulders to draw him closer.

Maybe it was the novelty of it, but Cady's thoughts swirled into pleasurable confusion as the kiss went on. She'd be quite happy to just kiss him all night, and said so.

She felt his smile when he heard her. "If that's what you want, I'd be delighted to oblige."

"You can't mean that."

"Why not? It feels good, and I like to feel good."

"But you'd want more."

"Wanting feels good too." He shifted his attention to her ear, her neck, her shoulder. Cady moaned a little when she felt his teeth nip her skin.

"You always smell like witch hazel," he murmured.

"Do you not like it? I use it after I wash up—"

"I love it. You claim aphrodisiacs aren't real, but that scent on your skin drives me wild every time I get within a few feet of you." He tugged lightly at her gown, in case his meaning wasn't completely clear.

"Gabe! You can't say things like that."

"I just did." He gave her a more serious look. "We don't have to do anything, here or in your bedroom or anywhere else. It's up to you."

"You think I don't know what I'm getting into?"

"Well, you're a virgin, aren't you?"

"Yes, but that's not the same thing as being an idiot. I'm quite familiar with the process of reproduction. I hand-pollinate plants all the time."

He bit back a laugh. "Not quite the same, blossom. But now that you mention it, I'm interested in exactly what hand-pollination entails."

Cady covered her face, feeling the heat in her cheeks. "Stop teasing me," she begged.

"Embarrassed?"

"Ugh, yes."

"Why?"

"Because…it's not proper."

He pulled her hands away from her face. "Fuck proper."

He had her sit down on the bench and knelt in front of her. Then he pressed his mouth to her palm, and she wriggled as heat streamed through her. Something about the way he was kneeling, his bent head…it was almost like worship. But in a *very* profane way. Cady let one hand fall to his head, running her fingers through the night-black hair.

"What color is your hair naturally?" she asked.

"Sort of blond," he responded between kisses. He was working his way up her arm now, and she was realizing that the skin on her inner wrist was incredibly sensitive. "Why?"

"Because it's a bit strange how I'm letting you kiss me senseless and I don't even know what you truly look like."

"I look like this, but blond," he assured her, then grinned. "Do you really feel like I'm kissing you senseless?"

She inhaled as he licked the inside of her elbow. "Yes."

"And you like it?"

She sighed, "Yes."

"Would you let me do something else that I think you'll like?" Gabe half rose, just enough to take a seat on the bench. He slid one leg around so that she was firmly between his thighs.

"Lean back," he murmured, his mouth just by her ear. Unsurprisingly, he took the opportunity to lick her there, sending a shiver up her spine.

Cady leaned back cautiously, her back tensing up the second she felt the heat of his chest.

"Relax, Cady. It's no good for you if you're scared. *Are* you scared?" he asked suddenly.

"No," she said after a moment of assessing. "I should be, shouldn't I? This is out of the ordinary, and that usually makes me hysterical. I suppose it could be the mushroom tea."

"Or it could be that desire is stronger than fear," he countered.

"Is this a lesson in bravery too?" she asked skeptically.

"It could be. Here I was just thinking that we were enjoying each other's company. But how brave are you feeling?"

"Not *that* brave," she whispered.

"Brave enough to let me touch you a little more?"

"Where?"

"Well, I was just thinking that the bodice of your gown is getting in my way. Mind if I loosen it?"

Cady didn't mind. He made quick work of a short row of buttons and a tie at the back, and then he gently pulled the fabric of the gown down, the little sleeves falling at her elbows now. He loosened her stays and removed them, leaving only her chemise to cover her chest.

His hands came up to cup her breasts, a layer of the thinnest fabric between them. Cady squirmed, wanting more. "You can take the rest off," she told him.

"You're sure?"

"Do I have to make it an order?"

He hooked his thumbs around the straps and she shimmied to help him tug the chemise downward. The sound he made when he saw her bare breasts was so pleased and so primal that Cady thought she might faint just due to the intensity of it. And then he laid his hands on her bare skin, and she knew she *was* going to faint.

He gave Cady a moment to get used to the feeling. Then he began to tease her, rolling the pads of his fingers over her nipples until they hardened under his touch. She leaned back, pressing closer, drawn to both his desire and the need arising in her own body. He resumed his barrage of kisses at her neck and shoulder.

Cady's eyes slid shut, and she thought she'd die of pleasure.

"You like this?" he asked then. "Because I do."

"I can't even describe how I feel," she said. "But what does it give you?"

"At the moment, it gives me ideas," he growled. "All the things I'd do to you if I could. All the ways I'd make you sing for me."

"Why?"

"You ask questions when you should be speechless." He tipped her head back and kissed her roughly, and Cady was swept into the sensation of his mouth and his hands and the sweetly scented room and endless night sky above them.

I wish it could always be like this. Feeling joy instead of fear.

She sighed deeply, kissing him back. He continued to tease her breasts. Something about the warmth and the heaviness of his touch, the way he palmed her breasts and played with them…all of it caused her to lose her mind. Heat pooled in her belly and her skin felt tingly all over.

She closed her eyes and reveled in his touch. Her hips began to rock against his inner thighs, and she heard him muffle a groan. She flexed her fingers into the tops of his legs where she was gripping him, far too hard. She needed to tell him something very important if she could only figure out what to say. But Cady just whimpered and gasped until she couldn't stand all the teasing.

Then something inside her just burst, a full bloom of deep, dark pleasure that spread out in a flood through her body. She sagged, and he caught her, holding her close to him, his breathing just as fast as hers.

"My God, did you just come undone from *that*?" he demanded, stunned.

"Felt so wonderful," she moaned, still recovering.

"Just me playing with you. My God, what will you do for me when I'm inside you?"

"That can't happen." Oh, but she wanted it to. More than anything, she wanted Gabe in her bed and in her body. She wanted to be with him in ways that no one else could.

"That *will* happen," he said, unknowingly echoing her desire. "Sometime. Even if I have to give up everything I own to convince you."

She turned her head to try to look at him. "What do you own?"

He went still for a long moment, and she regretted bringing up the difference in their stations. It wasn't fair of her.

"Never mind." Then he captured her mouth, pulling her lower lip until she whimpered with need. Cady was so caught up in the aftermath of her unexpected climax that it took her a moment to realize that he'd moved one hand to her leg, gathering up the fabric of her skirt to the knee, to the thigh.

"Gabe," she said in warning.

"Let me," he begged. "Just for a moment. I need to know how you feel."

His hand slid along her thigh, and Cady slowly let her legs part, allowing him further, inch by inch.

He paused when he reached the curls between her

legs. "Please, Cady?"

"Yes," she breathed.

Then he dipped his fingers into her cleft, lower, where all the heat and dampness gathered.

Gabe gave a low moan, and bit her neck. "Christ, you're wet. When you decide you're ready for me, I want you just like this."

Cady had to admire his confidence. But before she could reply, she was turning into pure heat as he began to stroke her, circling a particular spot when she moaned in pleasure.

He encouraged her to lean back against him and enjoy everything she felt. Cady's world narrowed to just them, with Gabe bringing her to a slow, sensual release amid the verdant, scented nighttime.

After she came undone once more at his touch, he gave her one last, lingering kiss before he pulled her skirts back down.

"Are we done?" she asked, disappointment mingling with the desire raging through her body.

"For tonight. Any more and I think we'll both regret it. You seemed quite happy a moment ago. I'd like to keep it that way."

She wondered how he knew her emotions better than she did. How he'd guessed that pushing her desire too far might easily tip it into panic, tainting the whole encounter with fear and bad memories.

She got her gown back into place, bunching up the stays to bring back to her room with her.

"Where's my shawl?" she asked, looking around. It was black, and the glasshouse was nearly so. How would she find it?

Gabe dropped to his knees and reached under the bench, returning with the shawl a moment later. "My lady," he said.

"Thank you. It was my mother's," she added in explanation.

She and Gabe slipped out the orangerie once more, and they moved like shadows across the lawn, keeping close to each other, their paces matching.

From far away, the bells of the village church tolled once, the sound faint but clear. One in the morning? That was all? She felt like she'd slipped into a fairy hill and been lost for years.

"One o'clock," Gabe murmured. "Seems later."

Cady didn't reply, but she smiled at how his thoughts echoed hers.

He walked her all the way to the gate of the Italian garden, which Cady could unlock and make her way through to her own workroom, where this whole unreal adventure began.

"You'll be all right from here?" he asked.

She nodded, getting her key ring from its pocket. What does one say in such situations?

"Cady, I'll see you tomorrow. When anyone else is around, I'm going to act like all…this…didn't happen."

"That would be best," she agreed, unlocking the gate.

"But we do have more to talk about, so we will need to find time to talk."

"I'll come out to the gardens tomorrow morning. I have to give you your instructions anyway. At least at gardening, you're not an expert."

That earned her a wry smile.

Then Gabe took her hand and raised it to his lips. "Good night, my lady. I hope you'll sleep well."

Cady did indeed sleep well and deeply, dreaming of deep green, sweetly scented worlds.

When she woke in the morning, she could barely believe that it all happened. Her trick in the workroom, Gabe's confession of why he'd come, and the cathartic, sensual exchange in the orangerie.

She was smiling when she stepped outside the next morning, eager to find Gabe, if only to assure herself he was real.

He was in the sunken garden, but he wasn't working. He was just standing there.

"Gabe?" she called when she got close enough.

He turned and looked at her, his blue eyes icy and serious. "My lady."

Her heart chilled a little. Yes, he'd said he was going to act as if nothing happened between them. But only when others were around. Had he changed his mind about her? Did he regret that he'd done what he did? Regret not going further? Did he despise her now? Cady felt a tingling in her arms and legs, a numbness that often preceded an attack.

"What's wrong?" she asked, though it felt difficult to even get the words out.

"Cady, I got a message delivered early this morning. From London."

"What's it about?" He was leaving her. Just after she'd opened herself to him, he was going to abandon her.

"There's been another murder: Malcolm MacCuley III. The victim was given clephobine."

♑

Gabe watched Cady carefully as she absorbed the news. Her eyes went round, and her breathing, already oddly fast, shallowed.

"No, it can't be," she said, shaking her head. "It's not possible." She wavered on her feet, and Gabe lunged forward to catch her arm to steady her.

"I'm sorry, but it's true."

He was getting used to telling Cady the truth. Thanks to her serum or whatever it was, he'd spilled far more than he ever intended and then went and made it worse by indulging in one of the most arousing encounters he'd ever had with his clothes still on. Yes, he'd instigated the seduction as a way to divert her attention and to keep her under his influence. But it had quickly spiraled into outright lust. He couldn't believe how strong his reactions to her got, and how much he wanted her. He actually told her what he was thinking, which was something Gabe never did. With anyone. About anything.

He didn't even want to tell people how he liked his eggs cooked, because an enemy agent might use it against him. And there he was telling Cady how much she aroused him. When he had a moment, he needed to find out more about what she put in his tea.

When the message arrived in the post, Gabe had assumed it was another scrap of information, or possibly just a curt instruction from Aries to stop wasting time at

Calderwood and steal something worth knowing.

Instead, it was a punch to the gut. Another death, another failure by the Zodiac to stop the killings. His failure, because it was his assignment now.

And Cady was involved too, somehow, even if it wasn't the way he'd first assumed.

"The murder took place two days ago," he explained. "My connections sent word as soon as the doctor performed the test that confirmed the poison."

"Who was this man?" she asked. "Another friend of yours?"

"No, but that doesn't matter. This can't continue."

"What are you going to do?"

"I don't know yet."

"Come to my workroom and we'll go over everything you know." Cady suddenly straightened up. "I just remembered something. I subscribe to several journals of botany and chemistry. Perhaps one of them has an article on clephobine, or a mention of who has been experimenting with it. We all correspond with one another, and when someone is successful at synthesizing a tricky chemical, they can't resist bragging about it. All in the name of reporting new advances, of course."

"What will you tell the others? What's the reason for my joining you in your workroom this time?"

Cady just shook her head. "No one will see you at all. You'll be using the passageway to the glasshouse. Here's the key to the door you go in, and I'll make sure the glasshouse door is unlocked."

She hurried off, leaving Gabe to stare at her retreating figure. She was offering to help him? Why?

To clear her own name, you dolt, he told himself. Cady was already ostracized by the locals, who were quite content to spread malicious rumors for their own entertainment. Because Cady was just a woman—though a well-off one—she had very little ability to fight back. If her other world of botanists and gardeners and chemists also decided to shun her, she'd be completely alone.

So she had just as much reason to find the real killer as he did. Possibly more.

Not long after, Gabe made his way to Cady's workroom. She'd already pulled several issues of journals that she declared likely to have information.

"Here's the issue of the *Proceedings of the British Horticultural Society* where I described receiving and planting the specimen, and my plans to use the berries to create clephobine. And here are three letters I got in response. One from a French botanist who wanted to know what process I'd use for synthesizing the chemical, one from a Scottish gardener who asked if I thought she'd have any luck growing it as far north as Glasgow—I replied with my doubts—and then one from someone on the staff of the Royal Gardens, asking me to send any illustrations of it. In retrospect, that was a clue theirs had died."

Gabe made notes of all that, disappointed that none of the interested parties looked very likely as killers. "Very well. Looks like we'll have to comb through more of these."

It took a few hours of steady skimming and back-and-forth questions. Cady proved to have an excellent memory once he nudged it with a name or a phrase from part he was reading. But all the results were negative.

Once, there was a knock at the workroom door, and Gabe had to move fast to get out of the sightline before Martha walked in with a message.

"Mr Pollack has sent a note around, my lady. He says he regrets that he'll not be able to call upon you this

Thursday."

"Good," Cady muttered in response. "I don't recall asking him in the first place. Though I suppose Mrs Bowcott will visit, with one of her flighty friends in tow. Tell Cook to only make the treacle tarts. I am not wasting the last of my citrus."

"Very good, my lady. Oh, Mr Addison sent a note too. He's got some new specimen for you and wants to come round in the next day or two when convenient."

"Oh, that's lovely." Cady's voice warmed, and from his hiding spot, Gabe got vaguely annoyed. "I'll send a reply to him this afternoon. And can you bring a very big tray of food here for lunch? I've got an appetite today."

"Yes, my lady!" Martha sounded so pleased, and Gabe almost felt sorry for her, knowing that Cady only intended to conceal the fact that the tray would be serving two people.

When Martha left, Cady shut the door and groaned. "Ugh, I hate Thursdays. You think that by limiting the gawkers to one day a week, I'd feel better. But I just keeping counting the days till the next Thursday."

"Is it that bad? I mean, the people living here in the village are still coming to you." Gabe moved away from the wall and rejoined her at the marble worktable.

"Ah, but they don't come by choice. They come because the vicar's wife wants to prove that I'm nothing to be afraid of. But I suspect she's only doing that because she's worried that the church and parish will lose the annual donations from the Lords Calder." She sighed. "I hope the issue of the title is resolved soon. I don't care which way they decide, but it's difficult to live with the not knowing."

He had the urge to comfort her, but resisted. One kind of comfort tended to turn into another, and they had work to do.

Hours passed. Lunch was devoured. At one point, as Gabe was leafing through one of the gardening journals, he paused on seeing something familiar. "Ambrose Addison, *New cultivars of wild rose with stronger stems*. Is this your friend? The same Mr Addison?"

"Oh, yes. I remember that article. He was so proud."

"Of being published?"

"Oh, no. He's had lots of little things published over the years, always on his own developments. He was proud of those stems! Said it took him six years to get the right result. I often wished he'd apply his skills to more practical issues."

Gabe sighed and kept scanning the journal's contents. Then something caught his eye. "There's a mention of baneberry in this one!"

Cady leaned over, snatching the journal from him. "Oh, yes, I remember it now. Hmm, longer ago than I thought! Was it really four years ago? The first known specimen, taken to the royal gardens. Mention of the danger of the berries. The story about M. Lalacon, who was the first to synthesize clephobine. The origin of the name: fear-stealer. *Klepto* and *phobia* from the Greek, of course. The 'ine' suffix is used for most chemical solutions. But since Lalacon was French, he changed the K to a C. They don't like k's across the Channel, for some reason. Yes, it was this article that made me ask my colleague in Boston to send me a few specimens." She put down the journal. "But those specimens at the royal gardens died."

"That must have been why Parrish was looking for other places where it was growing. That's where he found the name of your estate."

Cady shook her head, looking puzzled. "That reminds me. I was thinking about your friend's death."

"What about it?"

"I'm not sure," she said, speaking as though picturing something in her mind. "There's something not quite right about it."

"What, exactly?" Gabe was interested in this line of thought. "What bothers you?"

"He wrote a single word."

"Calderwood. He probably didn't have time for more."

"But…that's so roundabout. Why not write the name of the person who gave him the drug?"

"Maybe he didn't know who actually put it in his drink," Gabe said. "It can take a while before the effects start to appear, and any number of people might have been able to do it."

"But if you're dying, and you know you're dying, wouldn't you call for help? Try to save yourself? Not jot down a random fact."

"Perhaps in his mind, it wasn't random. I mean, we can't know the state he was in. From what I understand, the early phases of poisoning look like drunkenness. Maybe people around him just thought he'd had one too many."

Cady frowned. "No. It's just…I can't picture it happening like that. I still think there's something we're not seeing."

"Yes, the identity of the killer." He shoved the stacks of journals to one side. "We need to think of another angle. We'll never know exactly where all the baneberry is growing in England. So let's focus on the product instead. Someone used clephobine to kill. They must have bought it from a supplier. So let's think about who knows how to make the refined chemical. This Frenchman who first did it obviously can."

"No, he passed away last year. There was a mention of it in *The Journal of the International Society of Chemistry.*"

Why did every lead he came up with have to shrivel up and die so fast? "Let's stay closer to home, then. You've successfully made clephobine before. When you got rid of the batch of clephobine made here, exactly how did you do it?"

Cady's eyes were huge, and spots of red appeared high on her cheeks. "I…I'd rather not say."

"I'd rather not have to ask. The fact that you won't tell me doesn't bode well. So let's hear it, with detail."

"Why? I'm quite certain that none of what I produced was used to hurt anyone. I told you, as soon as I recognized the danger, I got it as far away as possible."

"*Got it away*? So you didn't destroy it."

"No! I mean, yes. I mean, you're confusing me."

"I am not," Gabe told her flatly, refusing to let her retreat into that mental shell where she'd spent so much time. "You know exactly what I mean, Cady. Tell me what you did with it."

He could see her pulse fluttering at her neck, and the way she tensed, as if about to run. He lowered his voice. "Did you hide it in a safe place, Cady? You weren't able to destroy it, were you? You must have thought about how valuable it was to science, and how rare. You couldn't just whip up another batch. It would take a year for the plant to bear fruit again. So you tucked it away somewhere on the estate."

"It's not on the estate," she whispered.

Ah, progress. "Then where? I thought you avoided leaving the grounds."

"I haven't left the grounds for months."

He frowned. "Then where did you take the poison?"

"*I* didn't take it anywhere. I gave it to someone with strict instructions to take it to sea and spill the bottle out over the ocean."

"What? I don't believe you. You don't have any servants left who could fulfill such an order, and you don't trust anyone else to do it."

"I trust one person."

"Who, for God's sake?"

She lifted her face to his, revealing terrified eyes. "My brother."

♑

"YOU MADE A DEADLY POISON and then just gave it to your brother?" Gabe asked, obviously trying to control his expression.

"I didn't just *give* it to Trevor," Cady objected, feeling unmoored. "It was only after I decided that it was too dangerous to simply sit around here, particularly considering what people say about me! Don't stand there and tell me what I should have done differently. If I'd kept the bottle and you found it when you started snooping around, you'd have stolen it and disappeared."

He looked caught out, but only for a second. Then he said, "I thought you haven't seen your brother for years."

"Not as much as I'd like." She looked out the window suddenly, and her voice was tight when she said, "And not at all since my father died."

"You two didn't have a falling out, did you?"

"Never!" Cady said. "But my father and he did. Trevor swore that he'd never set foot on the family grounds again."

"So what happened? If he doesn't come here, when did you give him the bottle? How did he get to Calderwood with no one else noticing?"

"The truth is that Trevor did come back a few times. But his visits were secret from everyone but me. There was a little cottage in the woods where, in time past, a gamekeeper lived. When Trevor had to stay overnight, he stayed there. He'd have food readied for him in the village, and he'd eat meals there like he was having a picnic. Anyway, at night, he'd come to the main house and use the passageways of the heating system to get into my private garden."

"When was the last time he came here?"

"My birthday. Last June. He even brought a little cake for me. It got smashed on the way, but it tasted good." She felt tears prickling along her eyelids.

"Is that when you gave him the bottle of clephobine?" Gabe's attitude grew more gentle, as if he knew she was near the breaking point.

"Yes. I gave him precise instructions for disposing of it, and when he wrote to me about a month later, he promised he'd done it just as I asked. Trevor always keeps his promises to me."

"I'll have to talk with him," Gabe said with a frown.

"Why? I just told you what happened."

"No, you told me what you believed happened. Not the same thing."

"Trevor isn't a liar!"

"Lower your voice." He glanced at the door, and Cady realized that if anyone was passing in the hall, they'd hear her arguing despite supposedly being alone.

Quietly, she said, "Please keep Trevor out of this. He has enough on his plate."

"Doing what? Lounging around London instead of taking responsibility for Calderwood, leaving it all to you? Doesn't he know about your attacks?"

"Of course he does! He's asked doctor after doctor about it for me, trying to find someone who can explain my condition. They all say I'm just a hysterical woman. Isn't *that* helpful?"

"If you went to London yourself and saw the doctors,

maybe you'd get a better answer."

"If I could go to London myself, it would mean that I wasn't suffering from whatever is keeping me locked up here!"

"Cady, please. If you let yourself get too emotional, it might trigger another attack."

"Don't you think I know that!" Cady already sensed the dizziness coming on, the iron bands tightening around her ribs. She dragged in a breath, telling herself to calm down, knowing that it wouldn't help.

Then Gabe was embracing her, his arms also going around her like iron bands, but not painful. He held her close to him, one hand on her head, his lips pressing against her forehead. "Forget everything I said, Cady. Just breathe. In and out. Don't worry about anything else. We'll figure that out later. Just breathe for me."

She wanted nothing more than to breathe, even the big gulping breaths that felt like drowning. Gabe didn't let go, and just repeated simple orders to breathe in, out, in, out until the dizziness passed and she calmed, averting the oncoming attack. For now.

"You can let me go now," she said. "I won't collapse on you."

He stepped back and held her at arm's length, surveying her with concern. "You're sure? Can I get you something?"

"Water would be nice."

He poured some from the pitcher on a side table, and Cady drank it gratefully. Her limbs still felt oddly heavy, and she was a bit sick to her stomach. But that was far, far better than an attack.

"Now what?" she asked. "You're going to leave here for London, aren't you? You'll find Trevor no matter what I say, and then you'll keep pursuing this killer until you find him."

"That's the plan," he told her. "But it doesn't feel right to leave you."

"I was alone here before." She shrugged, trying to hide the extent of her disappointment. In a very short time, she'd come to expect Gabe nearby.

Then he said, "Why don't you come to London with me?"

She looked up, trying to see the joke. "You know I can't."

"What if you could?" he asked, his eyes intent. "When was the last time you tried to leave the estate?"

"Just after Papa died. I had an attack in the carriage before we'd even passed through the gates."

"But you haven't tried since?"

"I came up with reasons why I couldn't. And the locals helped, with their gossip. It felt safer to stay."

"What if we went together, you and I? I'd be with you the whole journey."

Cady sat back, nibbling her lip, considering. Her heart was fluttering at the thought, but perhaps it wasn't from fear. "I don't know."

"You could see Trevor."

She inhaled. "That would be...I'd like that very much." Being separated from her brother was the single worst aspect of her life of the past few years, even worse than the panic and the loneliness.

"You can bring Oscar along. I can arrange a place for you to stay, somewhere safe, in a good neighborhood. And I'll be close by, so you don't feel abandoned."

"Oh, no!"

"Cady, please hear me out!"

"No, I mean I have a place to stay," she said to clarify. "We own a house in town. Though it's been years since

I've been there, Trevor tells me he checks in and makes sure it's all kept up."

Gabe frowned. "He doesn't live there?"

"No, he has a place of his own. That's where I write to him."

"Would you feel safe staying at your town house?"

"I…think so? There aren't any regular servants, though."

He smiled suddenly. "Now, that problem is easily solved. Leave it to me."

"I haven't agreed to go yet," she warned him.

"We're just talking about the possibility, blossom," he said, leaning over to brush her lips with his. "It's good to plan for several outcomes. Then you're less likely to be surprised when things don't go as you expect."

"Did you make multiple plans when you first came here?"

"Of course. But no one can plan for Arcadia Osbourne."

* * * *

It didn't take very long for Cady to decide that the need to discover who was using clephobine to kill was far more important than her own trepidation about leaving her home. Gabe assured her several times that he'd be with her as much as social rules would allow (and probably more, she reflected, thinking about how much Gabe flouted the rules so far). He told her that she could return to Calderwood at any time. No one would blame her for not wanting to get involved in the matter. But Cady knew she was already involved. Someone had exploited her work, and possibly stolen her supply of the chemical. She had a duty to help find out what happened.

The announcement that Lady Arcadia was not only leaving Calderwood, but actually going to busy London, was met was stunned disbelief by the remaining servants.

"My lady!" Martha gasped out. "You can't!"

"Excuse me?" Cady gave the maid a sharp look.

"I mean, you're certain that's wise? It's not safe out there in the world, my lady."

"Is staying locked up for the rest of my life wise?" she asked. "I must go to London to address some matters about the letters patent." In their talks, Cady and Gabe had agreed that this issue would make for a very plausible explanation not only for the servants, but for the local gentry and villagers who might learn of Cady's sudden decision.

"For how long, my lady?"

"I am not sure. But my brother will provide anything I may need. And I will need you to help pack everything I might require."

It was indeed a hectic few days. Cady almost forgot that Mr Addison was going to visit her, and thus when he drove up, she was in the herb garden, smeared with mud, thanks to rain the previous night.

If it had been any other neighbor but Mr Addison, she would have been embarrassed to be caught like that. But one gardener understands another. When he took in her appearance, he merely nodded in approval.

"Good morning," he said, kneeling down momentarily to set a large wooden bucket on the ground. "Beautiful day, isn't it? I'm glad to be back in Kent."

"Oh? Were you traveling?"

"Just a short trip to London to secure some specimens I'd ordered for the spring planting. The roses from Germany arrived at last."

"What's in there?" she asked, gesturing to the bucket.

"Doesn't look like a rose to me."

"A surprise for you, little Cady! A species of Nymphaeaceae known as Sleeping Lotus."

She removed the lid and saw two small, green aquatic plants tucked at the bottom of the bucket, half-full of clear water.

"I've been on the hunt for something rare enough to meet your exacting standards, and I found it," Addison explained. "Ship came in from the China route, with six specimens alive from the journey. Four are destined for the pond at Kew Park, but I procured these two for you. Here." He handed her a scroll of paper. "This is an image of the mature plant. I'm told the flower looks almost blue!"

She unrolled the rice paper and regarded the illustration with delight. "This is wonderful, Mr Addison. It's a true beauty."

"Precisely! It is purely ornamental, so none of your plucking and snipping and distilling for this. You simply enjoy its appearance, knowing that nature has created it with no interference from man."

"Can you imagine how the pond would look if it thrives and spreads? Like a fairy garden."

"I knew you would appreciate it, my dear."

"Now I owe you a rose!"

He chuckled. "I am happy to leave it on account for now. The journey from town was awful after that rain, and I'm sure my gardens will be full of weeds. I'll be busy for days!"

"I'll let you know as soon as I've got a specimen ready," she promised. "It may be a little while. I may be rather busy myself over the next week or two." For some reason, she didn't want to tell him about the London trip. It was too overwhelming to even think about, let alone explaining the reasons and her fears about it. Plus Gabe's role…no, she couldn't say anything about him! Lady Arcadia wasn't even supposed to be near plain Mr Court.

"Whenever you like, Cady. I must say, you're looking well. Got a little color in your cheeks. That's spring for you. After a long, dreary winter, it's as if we're all set free again."

Cady bid him goodbye and promised to nurture her new plants with all the care they deserved. She was grateful that some people stood by her no matter what. She'd have to find an especially rare rose to thank him properly.

♑

THE NEXT DAY, THE CARRIAGE containing Lady Arcadia, her cat, Oscar, and a ridiculous number of trunks headed to London. Gabe had sent word to the Zodiac for a discreet person who could act as a driver for the journey, and stay in Arcadia's employ for as long as she remained at her town house.

The Zodiac had a good supply of such useful souls, colloquially known as the Disreputables. These were a collection of people from the country's vast working class, all of whom had a criminal past. But thanks to the efforts of the Zodiac, they had reformed themselves, retrained as servants of all types, and used their less-legal skills to assist agents in their work.

Gabe hadn't used them much in his own assignments. He preferred to work solo, not liking to rely on anyone else for delicate tasks. But this was a perfect role for them: acting as servants for Cady in London, where they could keep an eye on her during all the times that Gabe couldn't. He'd sent word that in addition to the driver, they would need a butler, housekeeper, cook, and assorted maids and footmen—the usual complement of help expected at the home of a titled lady in town.

The young man who arrived with the carriage said his name was Jem Harper. He was on the lanky side, but was very good with the horses, and had sharp eyes that missed very little. For example, he showed absolutely no surprise when Gabe instructed him that when he drove out the gate of Calderwood, he was to stop a quarter mile later, just where a huge oak tree stood to the right of the road, to allow Gabe to board the carriage where no one would see.

"Very good, sir," Jem said. "If someone should be passing, I'll pretend one of the horses needs attention."

Gabe nodded, pleased with the man's acumen, and his lack of questions. The departure from Calderwood went off without a hitch, and when the carriage stopped at the oak, Cady smiled when Gabe opened the door.

"Oh, hello," she said. "Do you need a ride to London?"

Gabe grinned as he took a seat on the padded bench opposite her. He knocked on the roof and Jem resumed driving. "Very good of you to offer," he said. "How are you feeling about this?"

She looked uncertain. "It's been a long time since I've been in London, and it's so different to the country."

"Loud, dirty, smoky, lots of rats in the streets. It will require a lot of bravery from you to endure it."

Cady winced and swallowed hard. "I know. I'm trying not to think of the rats. Or the mice. Or the people."

"Well, Oscar here will surely defend you against the rodents. As for anything else, if you get upset or scared, just tell me."

"What if you're not there?"

"Then breathe slowly until you feel better. You'll be perfectly safe in your town house, I promise."

"And outside of it? While we're looking for a murderer?"

"Less safe, but we'll be careful."

Cady nodded, taking out a notebook and pencil from her reticule. "It's several hours to get to town. I thought we might go over everything you know about your friend's murder, and the one that just happened. Then we'll have a good idea of where to start as we investigate."

"You're very methodical."

"One must be methodical in any branch of natural philosophy, or logic. This is no different. We assemble the facts we know, make our hypothesis, and test it. And repeat the process until we get a useful result."

So Gabe gave her more details of the victims and the circumstances of their deaths, beyond the basics he'd told her before—while he was under the influence of her damn truth tea. But he refrained from telling her much about the earlier killings, the ones Parrish had been investigating in his role as Pisces. Cady didn't need to know how many actually occurred, and it would only make her question Gabe's cover.

"By the way," he said before he forgot. "I want to know exactly what you put in that drink you gave me to make me tell you everything you asked."

Cady glanced up from the cat curled on her lap, surprised at his question. "What?"

"The stuff you put in my tea. Don't pretend you forgot."

"Oh, you mean...the verocine. I didn't forget. But that's hardly the most important topic right now." She brightened. "That reminds me! I'd been working on another chemical—"

"Dear God."

She shot him a withering glance. "It's a sort of antidote to the clephobine."

"Wait, you've got an antidote?"

"No, I've been *working* on an antidote. And it's not specific to the clephobine. It's more of a general antidote—it has stimulant properties to increase heart rate and blood flow. In other words, taken soon enough, it could counter the effects of clephobine. But it's not perfected yet, and I'd be quite hesitant to offer it to another person unless it was a last resort. But I did bring a few vials, just in case."

"That's good information," he said, wondering what else Cady had stashed in her luggage. "Maybe you could tell me these sorts of things a little earlier next time?"

"Next time? How many times do you expect to be chasing down a criminal madman? It's not as if you do this for a living."

"Fair enough," he said. If only Cady knew that such work was his living.

"Now, can we please return to the matter at hand?" She tapped the page with her pencil.

"Fine. Where were we?"

"Who's Baron Murol?" she prompted. "The man whose death your friend was looking into?"

"Married to a very wealthy lady from somewhere in Dorset. No political leanings, unless you consider a distaste for Napoleon a political leaning. For his personal life, it's fairly typical, though he's had more than the usual number of affairs."

"How does his wife feel about that?"

"We'll never know. He had her put away in an asylum."

"What! Did she go mad?"

"Not exactly. He had her committed for..." He coughed. "Er, a particular kind of illness. He claimed she was an adulteress and that was her punishment, though it's nearly certain that he's the one who gave it to her."

Cady's eyes widened in shock as she processed that. "She contracted a venereal disease from him, but he's still walking around free to spread it, and she's stuck in a cell

somewhere? What a horrible man. I'm glad he's dead."
She frowned as she wrote that note down. Annoyed by all
the note-taking, Oscar relocated to a far corner of the
bench seat, and curled up on Cady's wool cape.

When he finished telling her what he could safely dis-
close, they both moved into that quiet space peculiar to
travel—where one could just sit and stare out the window
at the passing scenes, unlinked to any specific location
and thus free to let the mind wander where it will.

Gabe thought about the assignment, about spring,
about London, about his brothers and whether he should
even let them know he would be in town. He started to get
moody, and frequently glanced at Cady, who maintained
her perfect posture, her face composed as she kept her
gaze on the fields passing by. He observed the prettiness
of her profile—strong brow, slightly upturned nose, soft,
pondering mouth, and a narrow chin that sometimes gave
her an elfin appearance.

At the moment, she was so still that it was a little disconcerting. As if sensing his attention, Cady turned to
face him. "Gabe, tell me something. Are we having an
affair?"

He blinked, not expecting *that* question, but had to
admit, "A lot of people would say so. A woman alone
with a man she's not related to tends to raise ideas like
that."

"I ask because if we were having an affair, then that
would mean that you wouldn't mind if we sat together on
the same side in the carriage, and also you might hold me
a little. I've been thinking about London. Everything I'll
have to do and see and deal with. And I'm getting
scared."

She looked to the side as she spoke, and she'd reduced
a handkerchief to a wrinkled ball of cotton and lace. Be-

latedly, Gabe realized that this had been gnawing at her for a while. He was annoyed at himself for not picking up on it sooner.

He moved from the front of the carriage to the back, now sitting next to her and facing the same way. He held out his arm. Cady slid along the bench seat until she was next to him, and he dropped his arm around her shoulders.

She leaned into him and closed her eyes. "Thank you."

"You'll be fine in London," he told her, guessing at the cause of her worry. "I'll be near you and we'll work as fast as we can to find out who's responsible for this. And then you can go home."

"You don't have to reassure me of things. I'm not sure I'd believe you anyway. There's too much we don't know. But if you just hold me like this now, that's more than enough."

He didn't even know how to respond to that, so he said nothing.

Gabe was glad when they finally got to London, not least because having Cady draped across him for miles of bumpy road was doing absolutely nothing for his peace of mind, though his libido was evidently in fine shape. Not long after he sat by her, she'd actually drifted off to sleep, and he wasn't going to disturb her. So he simply enjoyed the pleasure/pain of being in a state of arousal and knowing he couldn't do anything about it. He kept his arm around Cady, enjoying the way her curves pressed against his side, and he used his excellent angle to enjoy her breasts rising softly every time a wheel hit a dip in the road. He decided that people who complained about the state of the highways didn't fully understand the situation.

When the carriage reached London, dusk was falling. Jem had been told the location of Cady's town house, so he continued through the increasingly crowded streets toward the correct neighborhood. Gabe nudged Cady awake.

"Almost there," he told her.

Cady blinked and hid a yawn behind her hand. "Really? So soon?"

"You slept for a while."

"Oh! I'm so sorry."

"Nothing to apologize for, blossom. I enjoyed being your pillow."

That comment caused a little pink to spread across her cheeks, which he liked more than he should.

"I hope the house is in a suitable state," she said, changing the subject. "I sent word that I'd be arriving today."

"Does your brother know as well?"

"I thought I'd make that a surprise," she said. "And I wanted to get settled before I saw anyone, even Trevor."

Just then, Jem brought the carriage to a halt. Gabe glanced out his window, and was surprised at the sight before him. Cady's family had their home in Wimpole Street, an excellent part of the city. But he hadn't realized just how excellent.

The town house was large, at least four stories tall. Unsurprisingly, there was a garden in the front, the trees and flowers just coming into spring bloom. Light spilled out of the windows of the house, giving it a welcoming air.

"This is yours?" he asked, just to be sure.

"Yes, indeed." Cady was smiling, but she gripped Gabe's hand tightly.

"Then you ought to go in."

She looked at him with alarm. "Alone?"

He nodded. "It would be better if we weren't seen

getting out of the same carriage, at least not at the moment. But I'm certain that everything will be ready for you. And I'll call on you as soon as I can tomorrow. Then the world can know that we know each other, and it won't cause any comment when I visit in the future."

"But…won't it be odd if my gardener keeps calling on me?"

"Cady, the next time you see me, I won't be your gardener."

"What will you be?"

"A surprise, little blossom. Now go."

"I'm scared."

"No you're not. You are Lady Arcadia Osbourne, and you're delighted to be in London." He raised her hand to his mouth and kissed the tops of her fingers. "As your tutor in bravery, I strongly suggest you believe that."

"You promise you'll return here tomorrow?" she asked anxiously.

"Of course. When have I ever lied to you?"

"Um, frequently?"

"But never about seeing you again. Good night, Cady. Welcome home."

He opened the door for her but remained in the shadows of the carriage. He watched as she made her way slowly up the path to the front door, which was already swinging open, the interior gleaming in contrast to the blue twilight.

Cady vanished inside. Gabe waited patiently as Jem drove the carriage around the back to the alley-side entrance of the property where the trunks would be unloaded. He got out and helped Jem with the heaviest trunk. In his ordinary groundskeeper attire, he fit right in.

Jem shot him a look. "Assume I'll be seeing you about the house again, sir. Anything we ought to know for tonight?"

"Keep her safe. Tell the other Disreputables to keep her calm if she should experience any distress at all. Don't let anyone else in, and for God's sake don't let her out."

"Aye, sir."

Gabe strolled away. It was late, but he had plenty of work ahead of him tonight. Report to the Zodiac, plan his next moves, and most importantly: make Gabe Court disappear.

♑

"WELCOME HOME, MY LADY," SAID the boy who held open the door for Cady.

"Thank you. Who are you?"

"Name's Rook, my lady."

Rook was a skinny thing, but quick with a smile. A maid appeared next to him and offered to take Cady's hat, cloak, and gloves. "When would you like dinner, my lady? Cook has everything ready for your arrival, but if you'd like to freshen up first, she'll keep things warm."

Cady was so used to Martha bringing a tray to her room that she was momentarily not sure what she wanted. "Ah, I'll freshen up, thank you. Who are you?"

"I'm Judith, my lady. And Bond, your lady's maid, is waiting upstairs in your room."

Judith directed her up the staircase with a gentle shooing motion, as if Cady were a small duckling instead of the lady of the house. Upstairs, she was startled to learn that "her" room was the master suite, though of course she couldn't use the nursery that she slept in as a child.

She could count the number of times she'd been in this room on one hand, but when she stepped inside, the faint aroma of jasmine—a perfume last used here over a decade ago—wafted over her. She had a vague memory of kissing her mother goodnight before being sent off for bed. Her mother had been dressed in a sumptuous gown for some glittering party, the old-fashioned kind with the tightly laced long bodice and the huge, wide skirts. Cady remembered it as being almost entirely gold lace and jewels, which was surely a little girl's vivid imagination, making her mother into a fairy queen. Her mother had leaned over, smelling of jasmine, and kissed her cheek.

"Sleep well, my darling girl. In your dreams, you can always be in Arcadia." That was her line, the ritual they went through each night.

"Welcome home, my lady!" a very real voice said.

Cady blinked, seeing a young woman walking toward her from the direction of the dressing room.

"I'm Lucy Bond, and I'm to be your lady's maid while you're in town. I've just drawn a bath for you. Why don't you have a soak while I unpack your things and find you something to wear down to dinner."

"I usually just eat in my room," Cady said.

"Surely not in town, my lady," Bond said, easily countermanding her suggestion without seeming to. Martha had done that too, but Bond was much more lighthearted when she did it. "Now you get in that bath before the water gets cold. Travel is dirty, no matter how nice the carriage."

So Cady soaked in the bath, and then was dressed in an evening gown, and her hair put up in a simple style, then sent down to the dining room, where she discovered that she was famished.

Her meal was served by Judith and Rook, who worked with that magical efficiency unique to well-trained servants. As Cady ate her delicious meal, she found herself wishing that she had someone to share it with. The only people she really knew in the whole city were Trevor and Gabe. Her brother, and a man who had lied himself into a job on her estate. Had she isolated herself so much that she had no friends at all?

All at once, halfway through the creamed spinach, Cady wanted to cry. The panic crashed into her: the urge to flee, the tightening of her throat, the struggle to breathe. As she pushed away from the table, she dropped her fork with a clatter.

"Ready for the next course, my la—" Judith said as she walked in, but then stopped on seeing Cady. "My lady, what's wrong?"

"Nothing. I need to go to my room. Now." Cady tried to push past her, but Judith pivoted to walk beside her, placing one arm about Cady's shoulders when she stumbled.

"There now, my lady. Just one step at a time. Very good, up the stairs. One at time."

"I'm…I'm…" Cady wanted to say that she was fine, that she didn't need help, except that she clearly did need help, since she was clutching at the banister and felt so dizzy and light-headed that getting to the top of the steps seemed impossible. "I get like this," she gasped out.

"No need to explain, my lady. Certainly not now. Just keep walking, and we'll get you into bed."

"I need to be alone. Alone where no one can get to me…can see me like this."

"Poor lamb, we'll do just that," Judith said in a soothing tone. "Up a few more steps, there you are." She seemed remarkably calm about Cady's weird behavior.

Cady wasn't sure how she managed to get to the bedroom, though Judith probably half lifted her along. Oscar arched his back and darted out, alarmed by the sudden entry of humans. Amid heaving breaths and bouts of crying where she felt like she was about to die, she was degowned and bundled into the huge four-poster bed, then tucked under a fluffy down blanket.

"Have Cook make a tisane," Bond told Judith as she

reached the last side of the bed. Then she bent down to Cady's level. "My lady?"

Cady, now curled on her side like a baby, peeked at her from under the mass of down. "What?" she asked miserably, tears running freely.

"What do you need?" Bond asked.

"To never leave my bed or my room again as long as I live."

"How about for the rest of the evening?" Bond offered. "Why don't you nestle in there for a while, and when you're ready, come out and there will be tea and biscuits."

"I'm never coming out. I never should have come to London." Cady had been at the town house for less than two hours and already managed to suffer an attack of nerves and humiliate herself in front of servants she didn't even know.

"You should come out eventually. They're quite good biscuits. Ring when you're ready." Bond pulled the last curtain closed, enveloping Cady in a blessed darkness.

She huddled there for a long while, shaking. She wished she could flee back to Calderwood but she was paralyzed, unable to even consider the feat of getting up, standing, and walking across the room. The notion of facing people and telling them she was going right back from where she'd come was impossible.

How did she get to this point? She was physically weak and afraid of everything, even things that weren't there. She couldn't perform the simplest acts, like eating dinner in her own home. If word got around the city about just how strange she was, Cady would be shunned by everyone. And word *always* got out. Especially when one's servants were recent hires, with no connection to the family and no sense of loyalty. Why should they have?

Cady would be gone by next month. She might be gone by tomorrow. She might be dead by tomorrow.

The thought was a familiar one, because it always hovered during her attacks. When her heart was leaping out of her chest and she was doubled over clutching her torso, it was easy to think that her body was about to give out. But somehow, Cady kept on living.

She swallowed, coughing due to her parched throat. Remembering what Bond said about the tea, she pulled the down duvet around her body and slowly crawled out of bed and shuffled to the chaise by the fire.

She sat down, wrapped up like a wild sheep. Oscar reappeared, looking at her curiously before he decided to jump up and join her, his purr rumbling as he pushed his paws into the thick blanket.

Cady picked up the teapot, but her arms were still shaking and she put it down again immediately, afraid she'd drop it and shatter it. Tears pricked at her eyes again, and she let out one sobbing breath.

She couldn't even pour her own tea. Pathetic.

The door squeaked open, and a different girl in a maid's outfit peeked in. "Oh!" she said, on seeing Cady awake and sitting up on the chaise. "Excuse me, my lady. I was just coming to bank the fire and blow out the candles. But as you're still up…"

"Wait," Cady said. "Could you come here and pour me some tea?"

The chambermaid stepped forward hesitantly.

"What's your name?" Cady asked, hoping to calm her.

"Minnie," the girl replied after a short hesitation. "Actually, Minerva. But everyone calls me Minnie."

"I'm Arcadia. Some people call me Cady."

Minnie gave her a look, as if she might be joking. Then, reaching for the teapot, she poured a cup.

"I'm not strong enough right now," Cady explained. "I was afraid I'd drop it."

"Are you ill, my lady?"

"Not with anything you might catch," Cady assured her. "But yes, there's something wrong with me."

"Do you need anything? Medicine?"

Cady looked over toward the dressing room, wondering if Bond had a chance to unpack all her things. Cady had brought along several of her most useful medicines. "If you don't mind, have a look over there for a small wooden chest that's about as long as your forearm and half as wide."

The maid did so, and after only a moment returned bearing the case, setting it on the carpet by Cady's seat.

Cady opened it and pulled out a bottle. She uncapped it and allowed two drops into the tea, then carefully closed it again.

"What's that?" Minnie asked curiously.

"A sedative to calm me down enough so I won't be awake all night." Cady sipped her tea, already feeling a bit better. "How did you get hired? There can't have been much time to hear about the position."

"Ah, I know Cook very well. She recommended me." Minnie gestured to the teapot. "More?"

"Yes, please. How are the biscuits?"

"Very good, you should eat them. Cook always makes more." Minnie smiled. "Will you want a tray up here for your breakfast tomorrow, my lady? Cook was wondering."

"I'm sure everyone's wondering about me," Cady said dryly.

"No, ma'am. We just want to make you comfortable."

"A tray, yes. Obviously, I'm not normal enough to eat in a dining room," she added bitterly.

"What good is normal, ma'am? Ring if you need anything else. And sleep well."

After nibbling her way through three crumbly, nutty biscuits, Cady made her way back to bed, blowing out candles along the way. She once again pulled the curtain shut, enveloping herself in darkness. But this time it felt more like a cocoon than a trap.

She nestled beneath the covers. In a way, her attack wasn't surprising. New surroundings, new people. She probably pushed too far, pretending she was well enough to eat downstairs the very evening she arrived. But it was still mortifying to go to pieces in front of an entirely new staff who didn't know a thing about her.

Cady had terrible trouble getting anyone to work at Calderwood, but at her London town house suddenly there were people falling all over themselves to do every type of job. On the one hand, she was suspicious of her sudden luck, but on the other, she could barely manage things as they were. She knew that Gabe had pulled some strings to get all these people at the town house in time for her arrival. Cady just wished she knew which strings he'd pulled.

♑

BY THE TIME CADY AWOKE, her mantel clock was chiming ten. She groaned and pulled aside the curtains blinking in the morning light.

She wasn't alone in her room. Bond was there as well. Cady saw she'd brought up the breakfast tray, which had replaced the tea tray from last night. Now, however, the lady's maid was poking through Cady's things in the dressing room area. Her medicine chest had been moved to a side table.

"What are you doing?" Cady asked Bond.

"Oh, just checking for moths," she replied. "You have a number of silk gowns and wraps, and if moths get into the clothespress, they're done for. To say nothing of the woolens!"

"I always make up fresh lavender sachets each year. The smell discourages them."

"As you say, my lady," Lucy agreed, piling heaps of gowns on her arms. "But I've found that sunlight is even better, which is why I'll air these in the back. You know, it works for people as well as clothing. A ride in the park later would do your complexion a world of good."

"Am I too pale for your liking, Bond?"

"Just hate to see the day wasted," the maid said, neatly avoiding the question. "Jem could take you. He's an excellent driver. He was driver to Lady Cordelia, Countess of Thornbury. That's where we met, when I was hired as her lady's maid."

"If you've worked for a countess, why lower yourself by working for me?"

"Oh she wasn't a countess when I started," Bond explained. "She married Lord Thorne. And as for me, well, I'll go wherever my Jem goes."

"Ah. You're married?"

Bond blushed prettily. "Not yet, ma'am. We have an understanding, though. We're saving up."

"Very prudent. You've been a lady's maid for a while, then."

"Years and years. I can do hair, and mend, and I've a good eye for fashion. You won't regret taking me on."

"You may regret being associated with me," Cady returned in a low voice. "And I cannot guarantee that your skills will be in much demand. I do not go out, and I do not entertain."

"Still get dressed every day, I wager," Bond replied, not at all daunted. "And you'll have callers."

She ate toast and tea, and then Bond dressed her in a softly draped day gown in a dark green cotton lawn. Then she did Cady's hair, pinning it in such a way that waves and curls spilled down without actually getting in Cady's way when she turned her head. "Very nice, Bond."

"Thank you, my lady. You've got a jet necklace. Mourning?"

"My father passed away some months ago."

Bond gave a small nod, and put the jet necklace on. It looked well with the green, but Cady still made a face in the mirror. The mourning attire *was* getting dreary.

Downstairs, she'd got a quick tour from the housekeeper, who pointed out where they'd cleaned and what still needed attention. Cady was impressed by how sparkling everything was. For a house that had been all but unlived in for years, it was in fine shape. Like a bulb that had been merely waiting for the right time to push up and bloom.

In the parlor, she'd hardly sat down when Rook leaned in. "My lady, a Mr Gabriel Courtenay is here to see you. Are you at home?"

"Well, I should hope so, considering all the work that's been done to make me presentable. Show him in." She stood up, feeling nervous all of a sudden.

Half a minute later, Rook reappeared, stepping aside to allow the guest to enter. "Mr Courtenay for Lady Arcadia."

Cady turned to face Gabe, but her smile faltered as she took in the appearance of the man who entered.

A gentleman, in every sense. No more the rough groundskeeper with muddy boots and canvas work clothes. *This* man was dressed in an excellently cut jacket of rich brown wool. Underneath, his shirt was snowy white, and clearly of the finest linen. The pantaloons were a darker brown to complement the jacket, and so well-fitted that she could see the shape of his muscles.

And he was blond. The black-as-night hair was gone, replaced by waves of dark blond, trimmed but still on the long side compared to the average man on the street. He'd shaved off the rough beard too—he never should have attempted a beard in the first place with the jawline he'd been blessed with. Only the blue eyes were the same, now surveying her intently.

"Surprise," Gabe said, holding out his hands as if to ask her opinion.

Was this even the same man? With the dye washed out of his hair, and in proper clothing, he looked completely different. He even seemed to have changed his body shape slightly. He still had broad shoulders and he was still an unquestionably big figure, but he looked so much more refined.

Cady gave a little helpless shrug. "My God. You look…I could swear that you're even walking differently," she said, managing to put a few words together as he moved to the fireplace.

"I am. Those boots I wore for the groundskeeping made me move in a different way to how it is with these." He wiggled his foot, now shod in expensive, well-tanned dark brown leather. "Also, I was slouching when I was Gabe Court. Mr Courtenay never slouches."

"Hard to imagine you being even taller."

"Well, to be fair, you're quite little, my lady."

"Ah, still *my lady*, is it? Mr Courtenay is very proper, isn't he?"

"Most of the time," he said, and she was fairly sure his eyes twinkled.

Lord, he was even more attractive now. That wasn't helpful at all, considering that Cady was already being quite silly about him.

"What do we say if someone recognizes you as my old gardener?" she asked.

"Who ever saw me, outside of your servants who are still at Calderwood? Would you have, if you didn't know?"

Cady shook her head slowly, saying, "I don't think so. It's just too farfetched to think of a lord's son grubbing around in the cabbages."

"There's your answer, then. Though you're a lord's daughter who grubs in cabbages."

"But there's still the problem of you being an unmarried man hanging about the house. What will people say to that?" Then she winced. "I mean, I'm not sure what they *could* say. After all, they're already calling me a murderess."

"Rumors are easily dealt with. You just look the gossips dead in the eye and dare them to repeat it to you. They won't, but if by some chance someone is so bold, you just blink like a newborn fawn and tell them you've got no idea what they're talking about. Come, let's see your innocent face."

Cady widened her eyes and gave a little gasp. "My innocent face? What are you implying, sir? Are you saying that I possess a guilty face? How impertinent!"

He laughed. "That's perfect. You are a force to be reckoned with."

"So what do we say about your presence? It may well come up if more visitors arrive."

"If anyone asks, I'm a very close friend of the family, here to help you navigate your first Season in London. I'm a son of Lord Hargrave, so it's plausible. Let people think your father suggested it in his last days, and they'll fall into line quick enough."

"I can do that," she said with a nod. "Papa loved telling me what to do. He *would* have a plan to continue doing it from beyond the grave. If we can get Trevor to say he knows you, then that will help too."

"Soon enough he will know me. I'm going to call on him later today at that location you mentioned to me. I thought we'd go together."

"I don't think that's a good idea."

He frowned. "But it's your brother."

"It's just that I had…um, I had another attack last night."

In an instant, he had her in his arms. "When?"

"Didn't they tell you?"

"Who?"

"Any of the servants. You're the one who got them

hired."

"What's that got to do with anything? The Disrep—that is, your servants are good at what they do, and that means not carrying tales about their employer. So you'll have to tell me what happened."

She moved to the couch and he sat next to her as she related the incident.

"Damn. Too much, too soon," he said afterward. "I should have known. But you'd done so well the whole day." He brushed a curl away from her forehead, his fingertips lingering in a tiny caress. "You must have just been through more than you could take."

"It was supper. A supper party of one. And I simply… lost it." Cady shook her head in disgust, and the curl bounced back.

He patiently brushed it away again. "You have to take things slowly, blossom. I'm sorry I pushed you to come here and then left you at the door. But now that I'm a little more presentable, that won't be an issue. I'm going to be here when you need me."

"Gabe, you're not my nursemaid. You have far more important work to do."

"*We* do," he corrected. "But for now, you'll stay here. I'll return later today with more information about the most recent poisoning of MacCuley, and we'll figure it out from there."

♑

GABE WAS DRESSED IN HIS normal kit for the city—normal, that was, for his identity as Mr Gabriel Courtenay, the son of a lord. That meant the well-tailored jacket, the crisp white shirt, the leather shoes that pinched his right pinky toe, and all the rest. Gabe strove to wear the most average attire possible for a man of his rank. He wasn't a dandy and he wasn't a slob. His newly cut hair and shaven face actually left him feeling a bit exposed. He preferred to be forgettable.

In the neighborhood just next to St James, Gabe rang at the address Cady had given him for Trevor. The door was opened by a footman (a very formidable footman) and he stepped inside…only to find himself in a sort of glass cage. The foyer had been altered so it was not more than ten feet on a side. A wall had been erected to separate the immediate entry from the rest of the house. Panes of frosted glass allowed some light to pass through, but obscured the details of who or what might lie beyond.

"You are not a member," the footman said.

"No," Gabe admitted. "I didn't realize this was a club. I'm hoping to find Trevor Osbourne, Lord Calder, that is. Is he here?"

"I could find out, sir," the footman said, not committing to anything. "Your name?"

Gabe told him.

"Very good, sir."

He then left Gabe standing in the strange glassed-in room while he went in search of Trevor. The room was deceptive—it didn't look like a prison, but the doors were heavy and bolted, and even the glass panes were all quite small. If Gabe broke one, he still couldn't get through the wooden frame. Odd.

A few moments later, the footman returned. "Follow me, sir."

Gabe was led by the footman (guard?) to a room just off the main foyer, which was conspicuously quiet and unpopulated for a club.

"In here, sir," he said, holding the door open. "His lordship will join you shortly."

He closed the door firmly after Gabe entered, and the point was made. Wandering around would not be tolerated.

With nothing else to do, Gabe examined his new surroundings. The walls were beige, the ceiling was beige, the drapes were beige, the carpet was beige. He sat down on a beige divan, and ran his hand along the edge of a table made of a beige-toned wood.

The walls were free of distracting art (actually, any art at all). Only a few sconces held candles (of beige wax). There wasn't even a mirror. The shelves on either side of the fireplace contained only a small number of books, bound in beige cloth. Curious, Gabe got up and walked over to the books. He pulled one from the shelf and flipped through it. Blank.

He snorted. Someone went to a lot of trouble to achieve an effect of total plainness.

Behind him, the door squeaked open. A man walked in, wearing an outfit that would make Brummell jealous, especially since this man had the height and build to carry it well. He possessed the same chestnut hair and the same deep brown eyes as Cady, but his expression was world-weary. Even the flicker of curiosity seemed antagonistic.

"Lord Calder?" Gabe asked politely.

"For now. Who the hell are you?"

"My name is Gabriel Courtenay. I'm a friend to Cady," he said, using her pet name to make it clear that he really did know her. "I hope that makes us allies."

"Cady has a new friend? What an unexpected surprise," Trevor said, stepping all the way in and closing the door carefully. Then he made a face. "Stupid turn of phrase, isn't it? Surprises are always unexpected, or they wouldn't be surprising."

"Thank you for seeing me," Gabe replied, noting Trevor's fast speech. Was it nervousness, or just a normal trait? "Cady's come to the family's town house, but she told me this is where her letters go. I had no idea this club existed. Thought it was a private resistance."

"It *is* a private residence…for the club members. Top floor is all bedrooms. Most of us have reasons for not wanting to stay with family when in London."

"What are the requirements for membership?"

"Ah, I don't think you'd qualify," Trevor said with a tiny smirk. "Especially if you're the sort of *friend* to Cady that I'm guessing you are."

Gabe guessed the requirements for club membership. He wouldn't meet them, seeing as he generally preferred women in bed. "Unlikely. Let's just say that given the choice between the Osbourne sister and the Osbourne brother, I'd choose the sister. But no choices have been made by anyone. Particularly Cady."

"So you really are just her friend?"

"It's complicated."

"Ha, how well I know. Welcome to my world." Trevor took a seat in the beige chair across from Gabe. The vivid burgundy tone of his jacket jumped out in contrast.

"Your world is an interesting place," Gabe said. "Though this particular room could use a bit of life."

"The choice is deliberate. The Beige Room is the one space where nonmembers are allowed, and in deference to the often bland taste of the general Englishman, we spare them all hints of beauty, art, or personality."

"Harsh."

"Petty, I admit." Trevor flicked at his cravat. "But sometimes when one can indulge in pettiness, one can avoid worse reactions."

Gabe nodded, then said, "Have you seen your sister since—"

"Since the old man pushed off? No. She felt that it would be best for me to avoid the pile of bricks we call home, even after our father departed this vale of tears to go despoil another vale...I hope a very hot one."

"I take it this means I don't have to express my condolences."

Trevor laughed. "Don't bother to even say the words. You mentioned Cady. I assume that's what you're here to talk about? My God, you're not asking me permission to court her, are you? Or her hand in marriage or any of that frightfully old-fashioned stuff? I suppose some people think I'm in charge of her now. Not that Cady needs anyone in charge of her. She barely leaves the house. What were we talking about?"

"I've been working with her regarding some of her botanical experiments," Gabe said, not yet ready to reveal all the details. While Cady trusted her brother unconditionally, Gabe had his doubts.

"Oh! You should have said that right off!" Trevor's face cleared of any lingering suspicion. "Of course that makes sense. You're one of those types, the ones who dig in the dirt all day."

"A lot of digging lately, certainly," Gabe agreed. "The collection at Calderwood is remarkable."

"So I've heard. I don't know a thing about it, obviously. But Mama was a great one for the gardens and Cady followed in her muddy footsteps. There were always people bringing pots to and fro."

"I met one. Mr Addison."

"Ha, yes! The old crew still at it, are they? I remember Addison—he smelled constantly of rose. Little much after a while, but no one can doubt his devotion. Wait a moment! Cady's *here* in London?" Trevor, having finally processed the earlier fact, looked like the world had just shifted beneath his feet.

"At the town house, yes. I said that."

"Sometimes I don't listen to people. Most people are boring. But you, Mr…what's your name?"

"Gabriel Courtenay."

"Mr Courtenay, you just got interesting. You managed to get poor Cady out of that tomb? Are you magic?"

"I persuaded her that it would be helpful."

"My God, do you think she'd actually go see a doctor? She needs help, you know. She thinks she can figure out everything all on her own, and she's forever brewing up this or that as if she's lecturing on chemistry at Cambridge. But she's really just so helpless sometimes. I hate it, but she's unwilling to let me in on her troubles. She says I've got my own, and I understand what she means, sweet girl. I *had* troubles. But living here in London is far better than being stuck at Calderwood like I was before. You can't live in two worlds, Mr Courtenay. You can't be two things. If you try to do that for too long, it will rip you apart. I tried, oh I tried. Mostly for Cady's sake, and Mama's, when she was still alive. That meant playing the part of the heir. Learning all the most dull stuff to keep the estate in good condition and then there's rents to collect and everyone wants you to give them money for this or that. But Papa insisted, and didn't we all try to please him." Trevor rolled his eyes in disgust.

"Until you didn't?"

Trevor's lip curled into a sardonic smile. "It was the courting that undid me. Got a little difficult to hide my inclinations when I kept ignoring the young ladies he tossed toward me and I kept getting caught with the stable boy or an old schoolfriend down for the week, or the blacksmith's son…oh, Lord, *he* was worth getting caught for. Those arms. Anyway, Papa got the message eventually and I was soon on my merry way to merry old London and I've never looked back. Why are you here again?" Trevor gave him a puzzled glance. "Did Cady send you for something?"

"I actually have a question for you. Cady has a minor problem, which I volunteered to help her with."

"Oh, that's very decent of you. What's the problem?"

"She's been accused of murder."

"What?" Trevor jumped to his feet. "Who? Why? Don't they know her? Who's dead?"

"Your father. His unexpected demise left the locals with a lot of questions. It's been suggested that perhaps Cady poisoned him."

"Oh, Lord, tell me a doctor didn't go poking around in his body like some ghoul."

"There was no autopsy. And the inquest found nothing either. But the rumors happened anyway."

"They would," Trevor muttered. "I need a drink. Do you need a drink? I'll make you a drink."

He beelined to a cabinet that hid several bottles of liquor and the various accoutrements to mix any cocktail imaginable. When he walked back he offered Gabe a glass of amber liquid that smelled like it could start a fire. Gabe gently placed it on the table.

"What I need to ask you, my lord—"

"Christ, call me Trevor. You're calling Cady Cady, aren't you? That practically makes you family. Can I call you Gabriel?"

"I usually go by Gabe."

"Even better. I love short names, they're easier to remember. What's the question, Gabe?"

"Do you remember Cady giving you a bottle of a chemical she asked you to dispose of? She may have called it clephobine."

Trevor frowned. "Of course I remember. I'm not a simpleton. Cady told me it had to be dumped at sea, because it was some deadly stuff that she couldn't allow to get loose. I'd already booked passage across the Channel anyway, so I chucked it overboard when the ship got about halfway. Then I spent a very pleasant few days in Paris with a gentleman I was quite enamored of at the time."

"Leaving no proof that you did what she asked."

"My darling man, what proof could there be? The whole point was to have nothing left."

"God damn it," Gabe muttered.

"Cady makes things difficult sometimes," Trevor said sympathetically. "But she's very brilliant, you know. And I'm sure she knows the right way to do these sorts of things. I mean, no one wants to leave poison lying about, do they?"

Gabe leveled a look at Trevor. "I hope you're telling the truth about this, for her sake. Because someone has a supply of that poison, and they're using every drop. Maybe not on your father, but possibly him too."

"I swear on my mother's grave that I dumped that bottle overboard. I watched the stuff spill into the water, and I hope it didn't take too many fish to the grave." His eyes widened. "God, do you think I'm a fish murderer?"

"Even if you are, you won't go to prison for it. You swear on your mother's grave, yes?"

"Indeed. I mean, I swear on my father's grave too, but a very different sort of swearing."

"You're not sad at all?"

"Sad? The sun has shone brighter every day since he departed. He was a terrible father, and of course it was a thousand times worse for Cady, stuck there with him all alone. He did his best to knock all the spirit out of her, make her into a proper young lady, whatever *that's* supposed to look like." He shuddered. "Not that I'm any judge. But by the time he was done making Cady into what he thought she ought to be, there wasn't much of Cady left."

"Sounds like a reason for murder."

Trevor's easygoing demeanor evaporated. "Don't ever say that. Cady would never even *dream* of that."

"You might."

Trevor held his gaze, then said, "Oh, now *I* dreamed of a hundred ways to hurt him. But every time, I remembered that I was already having the best revenge I could have—living the way I want, with him not able to do a thing about it. That's why he petitioned to get the letters patent altered. If Cady could inherit, then he wouldn't have to pass it all on to his disgusting excuse for a son... plus there was a chance for another generation of Osbournes. Because I'm sure as hell not sowing wild oats anywhere they'll actually take root."

"So you knew about the petition?"

"Of course! He announced his plan like it was some

coup de grâce. But then I laughed in his face, and that took the piss out of him. Because I'm not just indecent and perverted in the bedroom. It turns out that I *also* don't care about some moldering title given by a long-dead king in exchange for mindless loyalty. Cady can have it, and she'll wear it better than I ever will. At least she cares about the land we call ours."

"Her becoming the heiress would bring even more suitors out, especially if the estate is worth what it's rumored to be."

"Yes, not even the rumor of her murderous ways will stop a fortune hunter," Trevor said, nodding. "For what it's worth, I've told her to turn all offers down. She doesn't need a husband. She's got a house, she's got an income, and she's got her gardens. And she's got control of her life. Marriage will strip her of the one thing that matters: the ability to tell anyone else to go to the Devil."

"Would that all brothers were so mindful of their sisters' happiness."

"I'd die for Cady, if I had to. But I'm more fun to be around when I'm alive, don't you think?"

"You're certainly unexpected."

Trevor held up his glass. "To unexpected friendships."

Gabe could toast to that. But as he was drinking, Trevor added, in a lower tone, "Why are you taking note of Cady's suitors? Something I should know?"

"Not at all. I'm simply trying to help her."

Trevor shook his head, leaning forward, all traces of merriment gone. "Oh, no, Mr Gabriel Courtenay. I don't believe you. No one in this world just wants to help a beautiful young heiress. How about you tell me what you *really* want from her?"

♑

BY AFTERNOON, CADY FELT A bit more settled in the town house, and she had put aside her intention to flee homeward, at least for a day or two. Gabe had, among other things, suggested that she could speak with a few doctors now that she was available to consult personally. And she could visit the gardens at Kew Park, which she very much wanted to do. And Trevor was here. And as Gabe said, she wasn't an invalid. Yes, she had attacks, but they were intermittent and once she'd endured one, she was more or less fine again.

The house in Wimpole Street had only a small amount of land attached to it. The front yard had been designed to appear formal and gracious, welcoming the residents and guests inside. Thus it featured heavily shaped and trimmed boxwoods and beds of flowers and other plantings that would change over the seasons. It was not intended as a space to linger. However, there was also a narrow side yard on the south side of the house, behind the fencing that cut off access to the street. Here, Cady's grandfather, and then her mother, had worked to create a secluded oasis in the city. Slender poplars bordered the house, their silvery-green leaves coming out in the warm air. Oscar had discovered that butterflies loved the side yard, and he was trying (without success) to catch one.

The trees didn't shade the ground too oppressively, so there were several curving beds of spring blooms amid the narrow lawn that was moss rather than grass, grass being ill-suited to the city. At one end of this garden was a small arbor that accommodated a bench and table, perfect for reading on a pleasant day. Toward the other end was a pebbled area large enough to hold a wrought iron table and four chairs, in case an afternoon tea absolutely needed to occur out-of-doors. In all it was a pretty, private space, as quiet as one could hope for in the otherwise busy metropolis.

Naturally, Cady was drawn to it, and she'd made a comfortable little bower under the arbor. The space was sunny since the leaves of the vining plants over the arbor were still tiny and jade green. This was where she was when Rook walked out to find her.

"Lord Calder to see you, my lady," he announced.

Cady experienced one moment of pure horror, thinking of her father coming through the doors. But no, it was her brother who stepped into the garden, his smile lighting up the world.

"Cady, you're awful!" he accused. "You came to London and didn't tell me straight off?"

"Oh, Trevor!" Cady put aside all propriety and ran to her brother, flinging her arms around him. He hugged her so tight she thought she couldn't breathe, and she didn't mind at all.

Trevor was laughing as he half spun her around, lifting her off her feet. "My big sister is still little Cady," he told her, looking pleased about it.

"I was going to write to you today, but how did you hear about my arrival?"

"That was me." Gabe was leaning against the door jamb, watching the reunion. "It seemed cruel to call on your brother and not mention that you were here."

"Oh, so you did find Trevor at home."

"Not exactly. That address you offered me was actually a club."

"A club?" Cady looked at her brother in surprise. "I didn't know you were a member of any club. You hate joining things."

Trevor gave her a lopsided grin. "It's an exclusive club for…let's say like-minded gentlemen."

Cady's mouth rounded into a little O of surprise. "That's reckless of you."

"In fact, it's quite discreet," Gabe said. "You'd never know what you were looking at from the street. Trevor probably didn't mention it to you in his letters because he is also discreet."

"I see. Well, I am glad you're here now." She squeezed her brother's hands. "Both of you. Please let's sit. We have some matters to discuss."

"Let's get to the matter of the poison first," Trevor said. "That can't have been a casual inquiry."

Between them, Cady and Gabe explained a little of what happened. Gabe steered the conversation to focus on the death of Lord Calder. Cady wasn't sure why he was avoiding the mention of the other deaths, unless it was just because he didn't trust Trevor to not pass the information on (a wise precaution, knowing Trevor).

Trevor was suitably horrified at the rumors and the rudeness of their neighbors in Kent, and he showed a flash of family pride that came out as wounded offense. "I can't believe they'd think the Osbournes could be so grubby as to get involved with murder. Papa would have died before he allowed himself to get killed and thus get mentioned in the papers and the town gossip."

"He *did* die," Cady pointed out.

"And left you to deal with the mess. How typical of Father. Is that the other reason why you're here? To escape his memory?"

"No. But I do recognize that I can't be a recluse at Calderwood my whole life. And while in London, I can take some steps to see about the progress of the letters patent. It annoys me to have it unresolved."

"Oh, that's boring," Trevor said. "What you ought to do is get yourself invited to some parties and such. Or for luncheon or tea or whatever ladies do all day."

"I don't go to parties, Trevor. And even if I did, I don't know anyone who might invite me."

"You know me," Trevor said. "My set have parties all the time, and our parties are actually fun. And Mr Courtenay here must be able to exert some of his considerable muscle in the usual social circles."

"I avoid the usual social circles," said Gabe. "But I can certainly reach out to a few friends who'd be delighted to have Lady Arcadia grace their homes. Also, Cady, you probably ought to think about Almack's. Undergoing the ordeal to get the patronesses to approve you. That may be helpful in smoothing your way into Society here."

"That's not why I'm here, though," Cady objected. "I'm only trying to help find the person who's using the clephobine so we can stop the supply and make sure no one else dies."

"But we'd rather not let everyone know that's why you're in town, if only to avoid tipping off the killer," Gabe said. "So I think you ought to make a few genuflections in the direction of social traditions. Appeasing the patronesses at Almack's will take only a few hours, it will make you appear as though you're simply preparing yourself for the marriage mart, and you won't attract attention from the wrong sort of people."

"All the people at Almack's *are* the wrong sort." Trevor sighed. "Have you ever been? The food's atrocious and the conversation worse. I'd be able to put on a better display in the dining room here."

"We could do that as well," Gabe suggested.

"What!" Cady sat up. "You're not seriously suggesting to invite strangers into *this* house."

"Not strangers. A few people in town who at least one of us knows. A small dinner party, just to allay suspicions by the killer, if he's watching."

Trevor raised his eyebrows. "You think he's watching Cady?"

"Maybe not personally. But he's using a poison that only she knows how to make, so we should assume he's aware of a lot things about her life and her movements, beyond her work in botany and chemistry that she's published in journals. Maybe he knows she's come to London, but if we can make him think it's just a whim or her desire to get married, then he won't bother too much about it."

"I *don't* want to get married," Cady grumbled.

"Pretend you do," said Gabe. "Just for a little while."

"It would help," Trevor added. "The ladies of London are obsessed with marriage. Theirs, and everybody else's. My God, there are still some chasing me, and you'd think they'd know better."

"As long as you might be the heir, they'll chase you."

"I wish Father had tried to disinherit me years ago. It would have made everything so much simpler."

"Did he know years ago?" Gabe asked curiously.

"Oh, he knew."

"But he denied it," Cady explained. "Even to himself. They fought tooth and nail, always at each other's throats. Trevor just wouldn't back down. Ever. I admired him for it, but in the moment I confess I simply wanted the yelling to stop."

"Oh, Cady, I'm sorry." Trevor leaned over and

squeezed her hand. "That's why I had to leave, you know."

"Even after Trevor left the house, Father couldn't leave it alone," Cady told Gabe. "That was why he started the process of amending the letters patent so that the title would come to me instead of Trevor. But with his death, it's unclear whether that process concluded, or if it did, what changes were made. So Trevor might very well remain the heir after all."

"Possibly. I don't want to be."

"Yes, you said that," Gabe said. "And I should point out that while your father's reasons for the change were vindictive, they're also practical. You have no intention of marrying and continuing the family line."

"Ew, no," Trevor agreed. "Not to mention would be very heartless to any woman expecting a proper marriage."

"I suppose we'll just have to wait until the office provides *some* sort of reply," Cady said. "From what I understand, most of the time a change is impossible. There's a reason why things are set up as they are, and Calder's not an important enough title to get the Crown Office to change centuries of tradition. I suppose that as long as the issue is unresolved, it means I'm far less desirable as a catch."

Trevor gave a little snort. "You can keep telling yourself that, dear Cady. But some fortune hunter will try to trick you into marriage, title or no. Father set aside a very tidy dowry for you."

"He did?"

"Of course! He wanted you to scale the social ladder, and that meant enticing those men who were title-rich but cash-poor."

Cady grimaced. "Sold off like a head of cattle."

"Good thing he keeled over," her brother said.

"Trevor! Honestly." Cade glanced anxiously at Gabe.

He just shook his head, dismissing the comment. "It's not as if your brother has concealed his opinion before. And he's right. You should be wary of any man who suddenly shows up at your door."

"Like you did?" she asked.

"Frankly…yes."

"Oh, I don't know." Trevor grinned. "Sometimes it's fun when a strange man shows up at one's door."

"Trevor! *Honestly.*"

"That was honest." He stood up. "Well, this has been lovely, but I do have another engagement in an hour. Cady, ask me to dinner sometime this week."

"This is your house too, you dolt. You can come over anytime you like."

"Perhaps I will. Not tonight, I've got dinner plans. But soon. We could make it a party. My dear Mr Courtenay, do you happen to have any friends in town who might want to drop by as well?"

"Let's take things slow for Cady," Gabe cautioned. "A dinner is a fine idea, but she must first acclimate to London."

After Trevor had left, Gabe suggested that they go to Hyde Park. "Just a short outing, and one of the few activities where you won't have to meet a lot of people or chatter on about stupid nonsense."

"Your prejudices are showing," she teased.

"Sorry, but it's true. Anyway, my point is that it's a good way to dip your toe in. And whenever you're ready, I'll escort you directly back."

So they went to the park. The housemaid Judith trailed behind them in order to maintain the standards of propriety for Cady's unmarried state. It was lovely, as all parks in spring tend to be. It was certainly busy, with single riders on horseback trotting down the paths, families strolling along together, maids pushing prams and minding children, and elegant carriages making their slow and stately way down the promenade so that the ladies and gentlemen of Society could see and be seen.

However, it was the sort of busyness that could be observed, and required nothing more. It was rather like watching performers parade across a stage, Cady thought. She could watch them, but she didn't have to go through troublesome conversations.

Gabe knew a few people, mostly men with whom he exchanged a brief greeting or just a nod. There were also some women who seemed interested, but he was able to avoid acknowledging them without being offensive.

"Are you feeling so unsocial?" Cady asked after a carriage went by them, with a pair of ladies inside (probably mother and daughter) who both leaned toward Gabe as it passed.

"Oh, I don't care much one way or the other," he said. "But if anyone stops to talk, they'll think it odd if I don't introduce them to you, and I assumed *you* were feeling unsocial."

"You're correct about that," she admitted. "Simply being among others is enough for me today."

"It will only grow more crowded as spring marches on," he said. "Funny that it all happens in a park, where everyone is looking at each other, not the trees or flowers."

"Well, the flowers are not terribly interesting," Cady said, looking around. "Though my neighbor Mr Heath would love the water features."

"You are perhaps more exacting in your standards than most—"

"Gabriel? Is that *you*?" a voice called out, interrupting him.

Gabe looked up and toward a man approaching. Cady noticed a slight tightening of his mouth.

"Who's that?" Cady whispered.

"Viscount Nyle. My eldest brother. We seem to be awash in brothers today," he muttered back.

"Gabriel, I had no idea you were in town," the man said with a smile as he reached them. "You are truly terrible at keeping the family apprised of things, you know that."

"Just arrived, and haven't had the chance to look you up yet," Gabe said. There was an awkwardness between the men, and Gabe was so rarely awkward with anyone that it stood out. Then Gabe looked back to Cady. "My lady, have I permission to introduce my brother?"

"Certainly," Cady said, too surprised to say no.

"Then may I present Lord Gerald Courtenay, Viscount Nyle." He then turned as he said, "This is Lady Arcadia Osbourne, daughter of the late Lord Calder."

"How do you do," Nyle said, bowing very precisely. "I never know what surprises my brother has in store, but to keep a lovely lady like you secret in the middle of London truly raises the stakes."

"In truth, I spend most of my time in Kent," she said. "But eventually, a lady must go to London for one reason or another."

The man chuckled. "Very true. There's no place like London. And are you staying in town long?"

"I haven't decided," she said, which was perfectly true.

"Well, say it will be at least a week. I'm having a little party for my birthday at our home in town, Summersby House. The appearance of a mysterious young lady will add so much luster. I'll have an invitation sent round." He then nodded to Gabe. "And you'll be there, of course, since you're in town after all. I expect no less from my little brother."

"Honored to be considered," Gabe said dryly.

Nyle raised his fingers to the brim of his hat and gave another little bow to Cady, then continued on through the park.

"So that's my brother," Gabe muttered once they were alone again. "We're not as close as you and Trevor."

"I gathered as much. He does seem to have the air of heir about him, doesn't he?"

"Gerald's been groomed for it since the day he was born, and he can't wait for the day he steps into the even greater title of Lord Hargrave. Not that our father shows the slightest sign of vacating the post anytime soon."

"Will you go to his party?"

Gabe closed his eyes as if in pain. "I suppose I have to. My invitation was more of an order."

"Would it be more tolerable if I attended? If I ever actually receive an invitation myself." The thought of a party was intimidating, but on the other hand, it might be a chance to meet Gabe's friends and family.

"You'd actually go?" he asked.

"Well, you're right that I need to pretend to be doing silly feminine things while in London. A party qualifies. And then I can help distract you that evening. After all, you've helped me. I should return the favor."

"Cady, you don't have to do this. *His* 'little parties' are anything but. It will be loud and crowded and full of people you've never met and never want to meet."

"If I need to leave, then I'll leave. And you'll be there to protect me, won't you?"

He nodded. "Count on it."

♑

GABE RETURNED TO HIS OWN home in the city. It was a collection of rooms on the second floor of a house near St James which he'd purchased shortly after leaving the army. He never thought much about the space, since he was so often gone. But now when he walked in, he was struck by the barrenness of the whole apartment. Yes, there was furniture and all the usual trappings—curtains and pictures on the wall. But everything had come with the place. Gabe thought it all looked fine at the time, and saw no reason to replace it.

But none of the things had anything to do with *him*. That landscape of the seaside done in pastels? He had no idea where it was done, or if it was accurate. The wooden chair at the small dining table? He couldn't say who the etched initials on the chair belonged to. Was it a previous owner? Children who once lived there? Was is to mark an heirloom that should have stayed with a family instead of being sold off to a stranger?

He'd been living in the wake of other people's lives for years. Even when he wasn't pretending to be someone else for an assignment, he wasn't being himself either. At Calderwood, he'd seen how Cady's laboratory was filled with her life's work, as well as small reminders of her everyday life—a chipped teacup, the shawl that once belonged to her mother, the stack of books and journals she constantly referenced.

Gabe had none of that. He had a chair with someone else's initials carved onto it.

He nudged the chair with his foot just as he heard a knock at the door. He went to open it, wondering who even knew he was in town.

A young girl stood there, dressed in plain but tidy clothes. She could have been anywhere from eight to twelve years old.

"Yes?" Gabe asked, puzzled.

Wordlessly, she handed him a folded note. It said:

My messenger's name is Sally, and she assists me in my work. I've identified another victim. Please follow Sally to my office where I will provide details.

Dr Cutter

Another victim? What the hell was going on? Gabe looked at the young girl. "You're going to lead me to Dr Cutter?"

The girl gave him an emphatic nod.

"Do you not speak?"

She shook her head, then beckoned him to follow her.

"Yes, just let me get my coat and hat," he told her. He locked the door behind him, then followed the girl out to the street and where she pointed to a hired cab. She gave Gabe another scrap of paper, and Gabe read out the street corners written on it. He yelled the instruction to the driver and helped Sally into the carriage. She looked quite pleased to be riding.

"Did you walk all the way here?" he asked, after the carriage had been moving for a while.

She gave a little shrug as she nodded, as if to say, *Yes, I'm used to it.*

When the carriage jolted to a stop, she was outside faster than Gabe could blink, and waited impatiently while he dismounted and paid the driver. She took him by the hand and led him down a narrow side street to a door than she opened without knocking.

Up a flight of stairs, and then down a longish hallway, with Sally peeking in rooms until she found the one she wanted. She pointed to Gabe to enter.

Gabe turned into the room and saw a thin man stitching up a wound on an unconscious patient. Sally rapped on the door to announce them.

The doctor glanced over, saw Gabe, and said, "Good, you're here. I'm Dr Cutter. Hope you don't mind blood. I need to finish this before he wakes up and starts screaming."

"I've seen worse," Gabe said.

"Sally, will you clean and prepare the room at the end of the hall for the next patient, please. It's a young lady experiencing obstructed menses. You know all the instruments I need for that, yes? There's a good girl." For one instant, his expression softened as he gave the instructions. But the moment Sally left, he returned to the business at hand.

"Did they tell you I'm the one who's been testing victims for this poison?" Cutter asked as he stitched away.

"They said a doctor was working on it, but didn't give a name."

"No, they wouldn't. I think they keep secrets for the fun of it." Cutter tied off the end of the thread he was using, and wiped the now sewn-up wound with a cloth that stank of alcohol. "Anyway, for the last several months, whenever someone's been found dead and it might be poison, Aries has arranged for me to get some of the blood and tissue and sample it for a range of possible substances. Some are easy. Arsenic leaves signs, for example. But this new chemical, the clephobine, is quite tricky. Took me a lot of time and effort to find out how to reveal the traces. Awful stuff."

"I know the person who first synthesized it here in England. She agrees."

"I'd like to meet her sometime," Cutter said. "Unfortunately, my work keeps me busy. If people would just stop stabbing and shooting each other… Sally's a great help, and she'll make a fine doctor someday. Anyway, there's another victim. Found early this morning. I just got the results from the test. And it's undoubtedly clephobine, just like that of the MacCuley gentleman a few days ago."

"Damn it. What's the victim's name?"

"Lyndon Huxley, of Jermyn Street. Not older than thirty, otherwise a healthy man from what I could see."

"Any other marks on the body? Did he struggle?"

"Not at all. Looked quite peaceful, other than being dead."

Gabe asked a few more questions, and then took his leave when the patient on the table began to wake up, moaning. He left Dr Cutter's office with the intention of investigating Huxley's life and death as soon as possible. It was a rare opportunity for Gabe to do it before all the evidence was gone and the people involved forgot key details.

It was easy enough to gain access to the dead man's house, since servants were coming and going, along with other people who appeared to be neighbors or family. Gabe, dressed in his respectable but unremarkable outfit, moved among several of them, listening to snippets of conversations without appearing to do so.

"I still don't believe it! Such a vigorous gentleman.

Why only last week we chatted and he was in the bloom of health…"

"What of the house and estate now? Some second cousin will inherit, but they live in America, and surely won't keep the property…"

"The master dismissed nearly everyone but his valet, Watkins, and said he intended to stay in for the evening, which wasn't surprising. But in the morning when Watkins entered the bedroom to wake the master, he was stone dead…"

Gabe leaned back a little to catch sight of who was sharing that last bit of information. It was a nervous-looking housemaid speaking to a constable, who was jotting down notes in a little leather book.

"And the valet, miss—er, Watson."

"Watkins."

"Just so. Had he quarreled with the master at all? Or complained of ill treatment, or thought he ought to be paid more?"

"No! Watkins has been in this house for years and years. Cut himself up in little pieces for the master, sir."

"Hmmmm, well then." The constable looked disappointed at this intelligence. No doubt he was hoping for an easy case to make against a disgruntled employee who finally snapped, resulting in a quick trial and a quick hanging. "Well, if you think of anything else, my name's Phillips, from the parish office in Lion Street."

"Aye, sir."

Gabe took note of the maid's face so he could find her and speak to her later, then continued on through the house. He didn't care about the unprofessional legal system's attempt to solve the crime fast enough to prevent the newspapers from picking it up or for the wealthy of London to worry about a madman on the loose. What

Gabe needed was information about this victim—why he'd been chosen, and what evidence the killer might have left behind.

While standing the foyer, he looked down. There amid the calling cards on the side table, a card that had the familiar illustrations of nightshade, foxglove, and oleander. He picked it up and slid it into his pocket.

"You there!"

Gabe didn't even turn his head at the call. He'd long since learned not to react to every little thing.

The man who'd shouted walked toward Gabe. It was the constable, his expression stormy. "You there, excuse me. Are you a family member? You can't simply walk around, you know. There are rules!"

"Indeed there are," Gabe returned in the most supercilious tone he could muster. "So you're Phillips, eh? Miller sent me down. I think he's not quite pleased with how Lion Street have been handling things lately."

The constable was taken aback. "Excuse me, sir?"

"Who've you interviewed so far? Come on, man, speak up."

"Er, just finished with the housemaid, and before that the butler and housekeeper, and the valet. The valet did it, if you ask me."

"I did not. Your notes, if you please." Gabe held his hand out, palm up.

"My notes?"

"Dear God, tell me you're not so dull as to think you can remember it all. How long have you been in this position?"

"Er, eight months, sir. And I do take notes." He produced the little leather notebook from before.

Gabe took it before he could put it away again. "Well, that's a relief. Let's see what you've got so far." He flipped through the last few pages that had been used. Phillips's notes were actually quite good, tidy and easy to read.

"Did you ask about what the victim ate and drank the full day before, not just the evening meal?"

"Yes, the cook gave me a full accounting, whether I wanted it or not. Ham, eggs, and toasted bread, plus coffee, for breakfast just after ten. Then he went out to make a few calls…"

"To whom? Did he say?"

"Uh, no."

"Did he walk or was he driven?"

"Driven. He owns a carriage that's kept at the nearby mews. Coachman took it round and drove him out and back again."

"Very good, that's helpful. Continue as you were, and I'll let Miller know that not everyone ought to be sacked." Gabe returned the notebook with a little slap and strolled away, leaving a confused constable behind.

He lost no time in moving toward the servants' area by the kitchen, and then through the back to the yard. He found the coachman exactly where he ought to be, patching a corner of the leather seat on the carriage. The coachman was a surly type, though he warmed considerably when Gabe pressed a few coins into his palm as he asked what he wanted to know.

"You want me to tell you where Huxley went that day? Aye, nothing very interesting about it. Stopped at the haberdasher to pick something up. Then went to the Hotel Napier for about an hour—"

"Hotel? Was he meeting someone there? Did he mention a name?"

"Not to the likes of me, he wouldn't."

"What was his mood going in, and then coming out?"

"Ah, he was about the same. I doubt he was meeting a woman, if that's your question," the coachman said, with more shrewdness than one might expect. "And anyway, the hotel isn't the sort that would stand for such meetings."

Gabe nodded. "After the hotel, did you take him home?"

"No, I drove him to White's, but only so he could retrieve a particular walking stick he'd left there. He scarcely got in the door before he was coming back. Then we returned to the house."

"And the master didn't go out again for the rest of the day?"

"He didn't use the carriage or any of his horses, that's all I know."

Gabe thanked him and walked out to the mews, thinking hard. Huxley went on several errands, which would seem to make it impossible to know when he might have been given the poison, or by whom. However, nearly all of those errands had been quick ones, or were not places where he would have eaten or drunk anything. The only exception was the hotel, where he'd remained at least an hour and easily could have ingested the poison during that time.

So Gabe would go to the hotel. But before he did, he decided a little help would be in order. He sent a message to Cady's house, but it was directed to the Disreputables—specifically Jem.

The lanky servant met Gabe an hour later at the location specified, not far from the hotel. As Gabe had requested, Jem was outfitted in the manner of a valet rather than his usual wear as a driver and hostler.

"Aye, sir?" Jem asked. "What's going on?"

"There's been another killing. I believe that the latest

victim may have been given the fatal dose of poison while he visited someone at the Hotel Napier. I'm going to ask the hotel staff about him and find out if any of them remember seeing him and which guest he visited—"

"Could have been a worker," Jem said.

"What?"

"Didn't have to be a guest. Maybe he had a relationship with one of the people who work at the hotel."

"Possible, but I doubt it. The coachman said it wasn't a destination Huxley usually stopped at. But what I want you to do is walk into the lobby, looking as if you're expecting to meet your employer. Wander around, take note of all the doors and windows and how many people are working there. Do it as if you're planning to rob the place, because that's what you'll be doing later."

"And what's so valuable?"

"The guest book. If I don't get an answer today, I'll need to comb through the names of everyone staying there on the day Huxley died. With luck, you'll be able to use a few of your comrades to sneak in and copy out the content of the book tonight, or within a few nights. We don't have much time."

Jem gave him a sly grin. "And here we thought that guarding Lady Arcadia would be dull. All right, sir. Let me go in first, and then in a quarter hour you come along. That's enough time that no one will connect us, though no one will anyway. People generally never notice anything that doesn't involve themselves."

Gabe nodded, and held up the newspaper he'd purchased as a prop. He could easily while away fifteen minutes or so.

Jem strolled off, and Gabe dutifully remained. That day's issue of the paper he'd purchased was not particularly thrilling, though he did note that a reporter had already written about the death of Huxley in an article on the front page headlined with "Untimely Death of London Gentleman Raises Questions." Gabe had to agree. There was a column on upcoming events in the city. There would be a parade to commemorate May Day that would be attended by the royal family. There was going to be a charity tea at Kew Park to pay for the education of some of those orphaned by the war, so for the price of three shillings you got tea and cakes, a rose to plant at the grave of a soldier (or elsewhere, for those not directly affected), and the warm feeling that surely your good works negated all the evils of the war. Finally, the opening of a new art gallery promised to be the talk of London, thanks to the display of "tasteful" nudes depicting several ancient goddesses "painted with every detail in glowing color." Gabe was about to flip the page when he saw a name that leapt out at him.

> *AROUND TOWN: Lady A——— O——— of Kent has been seen in the city in the company of her brother, Lord C——. Does this recent arrival herald a new entrant to the fray on the field of glory known as the marriage mart? The daughter of the late Lord Calder is not yet known to be engaged to any gentleman.*

He grimaced. That didn't take long. He half wondered if reporters hid in the shrubbery along the roads into town, waiting to pounce on newcomers. More likely, though, someone simply noticed that the Osbourne town house was now open and in use. He could only imagine what the papers would print if the gossip from Kent made its way to the city.

That was just one more reason to solve this case as

quickly as possible, so Cady could return to Calderwood and live without being the subject of scrutiny. Just as he was about to get up and walk toward the hotel himself, he saw Jem returning.

"What happened?" Gabe asked, concerned.

"Nothing much. I got your guest book." Jem pulled a cloth-bound book from under his jacket.

Gabe grabbed it and tucked it between folds of the newspaper. "The whole thing? What the hell did you do?"

"Barely anything! Shouldn't even count as a theft if you ask me. The clerk at the desk was helping a lady—a very attractive lady—and he couldn't tear his eyes from her. So while he was distracted I just leaned a little further over the desk and nipped it."

"They'll know someone took it!"

"So? They won't know who, or why. The manager will probably assume a rival hotel stole it to see who their customers are so they can poach them. If you like, the book can be returned when you're done with it," Jem finished kindly. "No work at all."

"I do want it returned. The less anyone questions any aspect of this mess, the better. But I do thank you. It's going to help me sort through and find the likely murderer."

"Maybe it's a case where there's a different murderer every time, sir. A sort of gentlemen's agreement, where they pass around this bottle of poison from person to person. Once you've killed your chosen victim, you give the bottle to the next on the list."

"Christ, Jem. I don't know whether to be impressed or horrified at that notion. It's ingenious. And absolutely morally bankrupt."

"You're too kind, sir. But honestly, I just think about what a man would do if there were no laws standing in his way, and that usually tells me how dangerous a person I've got to deal with."

"How'd you develop that practice?"

"Working among the aristocracy," Jem said bluntly. "Until I met Lady Cordelia, I thought they were all monstrous. If you don't mind me saying so, sir, the problem with those at the top is that there aren't enough people to tell 'em no."

"You may have something there," Gabe conceded, thinking of all his superiors in the army who issued some of the most absurd orders, knowing that they'd have to be obeyed.

"I mean, it's probably the same person," Jem conceded. "Can't picture a half-dozen madmen who all like to serve their victims the same poison. But think about the victims, not the killer."

"Focus on the motives, not the means?"

"Oh, that sounds very professional, sir," Jem said with a nod. "Let's start with the lady's father. He's the only one who wasn't killed in London. That's interesting, isn't it? Do you know who might have wanted to do him in?"

"I wish I did. I've been asking around. There doesn't seem to be anybody else besides Lady Arcadia herself who had access to poison and who wanted to kill Lord Calder. And I'm sure she didn't do it, even if she had a reason."

"Her brother, Trevor, had reason. And access." Clearly the Disreputables had been taking notes.

Gabe shook his head. "He's told me he hasn't been back to the estate in years. And he left as soon as Arcadia gave him the bottle to dispose of."

"So he says."

"You think he's lying?"

"Well, I'd lie if I were sneaking back to procure a

deadly poison to murder my own father!" Jem crossed his arms. "Far as I'm concerned, he's the most likely suspect. Cast out and disowned, probably stewing about it for years. So the wound festers until he just can't stand it anymore."

"And he lets his sister take the fall for it? The one person who loved him and supported him without question?"

Jem frowned, but still argued his point. "Look, these things aren't always logical. I've seen it over and over. A man works on the docks, say, and he's sacked. He's furious at his employer, but he goes home and strikes his wife. Why? She's completely innocent, of course. But she's there, and she can't fight back. Rage is about lashing out. It's not about fairness."

"You've seen Trevor Osbourne when he came to the house. Do you really think of him as a killer?"

"No," Jem admitted. "But it would have fit pretty well."

"We need the answer to fit *exactly*."

"Where are you going next? Can I help?"

"I don't think so, Jem. You get back. I'll call there later to discuss what I've learned with Cady."

After Jem left, Gabe walked to his next destination, the offices of the Royal Society of Chemistry, where he put in a few specific inquiries and was told it would take several days to get answers to any of them.

Thinking of Jem's words, he decided to return to Trevor's unnamed club and see if the man was there to question. At the door, he told the footman, "Here to see Trevor Osbourne. It's important, so if you could just send me to the Beige Room and tell him I'm here, it would be appreciated."

The footman obviously remembered Gabe from the last time, and nodded. Gabe waited impatiently in the oppressively dull room until Trevor breezed in.

"Gabe! Are you sure you wouldn't like a membership? You do seem a frequent guest."

He refused to match Trevor's cheerful tone. "I've got a few more questions. Do you happen to know a Lyndon Huxley?"

"Hux?" Trevor smiled. "Of course I know him! He's a member here."

"Was he," Gabe said softly. That was interesting. Was blackmail an element of the murderer's plans? Was Huxley perhaps killed if he refused to pay it? Gabe shook his head. There was no evidence of blackmail in the other deaths, so he shouldn't look for it in Huxley's.

"Why are you asking?" Trevor prompted when Gabe didn't speak for a moment.

"He's dead."

"No." Trevor shook his head emphatically. "Absolutely not. You're thinking of another man who must have the same name. The Huxley I know is young."

"The Huxley who just died is young. His home was in Jermyn Street."

"That's him!" Trevor said, his forehead wrinkling in distress. "I don't understand. Just last week I saw him ride a horse and shoot at a target and then drink everyone else under the table, and he woke up the next day fresh as a daisy! How could such a man just *die*?"

Gabe said nothing, but Trevor must have caught something in his face, because he said, "What is it? What don't I know?"

"He was poisoned…with clephobine."

Trevor's face blanched, and his eyes got a glazed look. "Oh, God," he whispered. "Poor Hux…oh, *God*, why?"

"I'm sorry you have to hear this," Gabe said gently.

"Why is that stuff still around?" Trevor demanded. "I

got rid of it, and yet it's still killing people. How is that possible?"

"That's what I want to find out. There must be another supply out there."

"Whatever you're doing, Gabe, I want to help." Trevor still looked upset and pale, but he stood resolute. "Hux was a good man. I'm not just saying that because he was a friend. He was one of those people you just…knew you could trust. And he did not deserve to die like that. I want his killer to be caught."

Gabe nodded. "Then it's important that we learn everything we can about Huxley's last few days. Where he went, who he was with, everything you can remember."

Trevor nodded. "I can do that. And I'll get a few others to speak to you as well. I'll send word as soon as I've found anything."

WHILE GABE WAS TRACKING DOWN clues to the killer, Cady was forced to deal with a different challenge. Since it seemed to be expected that young, unmarried ladies went to Almack's to be approved by the patronesses, Cady went. She hadn't suffered an attack since that first night, and she told herself that nothing at Almack's was likely to trigger one. Cady feared spiders, rats, disease, and darkness—none of which was to be found there.

She wore one of her new gowns, one in a deep green silk that was dark enough for half-mourning, but blessedly not black or gray. She did wear the jet jewelry, and her headdress incorporated dyed black feathers. Bond had done up her hair in a very elegant chignon, and judiciously added *just* a touch of rouge to combat Cady's pallor.

"No one will know," Bond promised. "It looks like you've just got a bit of healthy glow."

At Almack's, she waited with a bevy of other women, mostly young ladies in their coming out season, with their mothers hovering close by. Cady felt quite old, even though she was probably only two or three years beyond them. And of course, she had no older woman to shepherd her, only the maid Judith, who acted as a sort of guard dog.

When it came time to step forward and present herself to the patronesses, Cady was grateful for the rouge. She felt deadly cold under their watchful gaze.

The man at the door announced, "Lady Arcadia Osbourne, daughter of the late Lord Calder."

Cady walked forward, and gave a properly deep curtesy. But unlike every other girl there, she then took a silver tray from Judith, who had shadowed her, and stepped forward to the four women in turn, handing them a single stem from the orchids she'd procured. Each cream-colored flower was perfect and exquisite. No one else had these—some people here never would have seen them.

"What are these?" one patroness asked.

"Flowers," Cady replied.

"Well, I can see that."

"Specifically, they are the blossoms of an orchid that grows only on mountain slopes above the clouds in the Hengduan Range. I have always thought them especially gracious in their form and fragrance."

"And you brought them to us," another patroness said, eyeing her carefully.

"I was told of the procedure today, and I thought how very inequitable it was for you." She nodded to indicate all of them. "Here you sit, and lady after lady approaches and you give your judgments, over and over. Young women clamor for your approval, and you must decide. But no one gives anything to *you* for your troubles. So here is a token of appreciation for all the consideration you offer to us."

"How thoughtful. You have not yet had your coming out, though?"

"My mother's passing, and then my father's needs prevented it from occurring before. I know that he would have been so pleased that I am here today. He desired above all else that I uphold our name and lineage by observing all of Society's most important customs." (Trevor had written down what she ought to say, and she repeated every word, though without the sarcasm.)

The patronesses all preened at Cady's speech, and after a few more questions—none of which touched on the rumors surrounding her at home—granted her request to be approved. It was a milestone that she need not have attempted, but she did get an unexpected thrill of triumph that she'd conquered the challenge.

Back at home, she kept the gown on for a lonely dinner. But just as she was about to go into the dining room, there was a knock at the door, and moments later Gabe walked in.

"I was hoping I'd make it in time," he said. "Can I invite myself to dinner?"

"Certainly, though I should inform you that my cook has been given free rein to prepare whatever she likes when no guests are expected."

"An element of uncertainty? Cady, I'm impressed," he said, offering to escort her into the dining room.

A place was quickly laid for Gabe and soon they were dining on a meal that involved spring vegetables, a type of cabbage that Cady had never encountered before but decided to cultivate immediately, and little cuts of tender pork. Cady congratulated herself on trusting Cook, rather than requesting the same few items she relied on at Calderwood.

"Oh," said Gabe. "Speaking of dinners, I have a particular lady who should be on your guest list. She's quite influential in town and it would be good to make her acquaintance."

"Who is it?"

"Lady Sophia, the Viscountess Forester. She's French and very charming. She hosts her own salon. And if she hears that you're in town for family reasons, such as the letters patent, she'll pass that information on."

Ah, so the lady would help maintain the illusion of Cady's visit to London, giving her and Gabe more time to track down whoever had the poison. "I can certainly send an invitation over, but she doesn't know me at all. Wouldn't she ignore it?"

"As it happens, I already sent her a note mentioning the possibility. I know her well, and she'll be happy to accept."

"Very well. I'll have it sent tomorrow morning."

"By the way, I heard about your coup at Almack's," he said.

"My what?"

"It was a brilliant move to offer the flowers to the patronesses. Very few have the guts to withstand the searing gaze of those dragons, let alone speak with them at length! It made you memorable."

"Do you think?"

"Well, I heard about it, and I never hear about what goes on at Almack's because nothing of interest goes on there."

She said, "The idea of those harpies staring down at me was more than I could take. So I thought, if I bring them flowers, at least I can talk about flowers. And Trevor helped me by writing the speech."

"It was perfect. And the chosen gift was perfect too. Flowers could never be called a bribe, and yet these particular ones were rarer than gold in their way, and obviously flattered the women who received them."

"Not to mention that it would be very rude to accuse a lady of murder after you accept such a gift," she added, slyly.

Gabe lifted his glass in tribute. "Well played, indeed."

"I hope you had as much luck," Cady said. "Did you

learn anything about this new victim?"

"Not sure," Gabe admitted. "I've been researching a number of names in connection with my investigation. This Huxley gentleman, though, I'm not sure how he fits in, other than that there's a connection to that club of Trevor's. But beyond that…nothing. Do you have any ideas?"

"Not at the moment," she admitted. "I'm afraid that all this is getting quite beyond me. I'm not good at understanding people. Just plants."

"That's nonsense, Cady. You're very astute. You noticed that I wasn't quite what I said I was straight off."

"Well, you were searching for your friend's killer. You were bound to act a little differently than the typical gardener."

Gabe looked away, an odd expression on his face. "You acted differently than the typical lady."

Cady warmed at the memory of him appearing, promising to become her tutor in bravery. How could she ever have guessed that the rough stranger would turn into such an ally? And not just an ally, an instructor in pleasures she'd never dreamed existed before she met him.

She leaned toward him. "Do you know something, Mr Courtenay?"

"Yes?" He looked at her with a raised eyebrow.

"After dinner, I think you should leave."

"Oh."

The disappointment on his face was hidden quickly, but Cady saw it. And it made her want to laugh. "I want you to leave, Gabe, so anyone keeping an eye on the house will see you leave. And then, I want you to come back. I trust you know how to do that with no one noticing?"

His expression changed to veiled excitement. "I can

definitely do that."

She pressed a key into his palm, whispering, "It unlocks the glass doors to the library. Please use it tonight. I'll be waiting in my bedroom. Top of the stairs, to the left. Midnight?"

"And here I thought I was being sent away." He leaned forward and kissed her once, a kiss that promised so much more. "Midnight."

* * * *

Later, up in her bedroom, Cady was nervous, but it was the thrumming, excited sort of nervous that she associated with Gabe particularly. She kept glancing at her clock, which seemed to slow as the hands approached midnight. Clad in a filmy, ethereal excuse for a nightgown, she perched on the edge of the bed, uncertain what to do.

There was the softest scratching at the door to warn her, and then Gabe slipped inside, turning the key in the lock the moment he had the door closed.

"If I'd known you had such an interesting wardrobe, I'd have arrived sooner," he said, taking in her outfit with an almost hungry expression.

"A year or so ago, I'd ordered a few items from a London modiste," she explained. "I didn't quite understand what I was ordering at the time, but I'm glad they turned out to be useful at last."

"If by 'useful' you mean 'able to drive a man to distraction,' then this one is doing a fine job." He shucked off his jacket, let it fall to the floor, and then took a seat in the large, comfortable chair by the fireplace.

He beckoned her to where he sat, and Cady walked to him, feeling a little like a marionette, with invisible strings tied to her hands and feet…and him in control of all of them.

"Not the bed?" she asked hesitantly.

"Not the bed." He was clearly enjoying her confusion, keeping her off balance but intensely curious.

"Sit," he commanded.

"The chair appears to be already occupied," she joked.

Gabe reached out, his hands level with her bottom. He roughly gathered up her thin gown until her bare thighs were exposed, and then pulled her forward until she was straddled over his lap. But unlike in the glasshouse, she was now facing him, and she could look directly into his eyes.

He smiled lazily. "Well, now that we're here, what do you want me to do?"

"Kiss me," she said instantly.

He did, though he took his time. He kept one hand very firmly on her bottom, holding her in place. The other drifted up her body then began to stroke the bare skin on the back of her neck. Cady gave a little sigh as he leaned forward and brushed his mouth against hers.

He laughed, but it sounded more like a groan. "Cady, you have no idea how much I want you. If it were up to me, I'd have you naked in my bed, possibly chained so you couldn't get away. Not that you'd want to get away, because you'd be begging for me the moment I stepped inside. You'd tell me all the ways you want me to take you and I would be very happy to oblige."

"You've had some time to think about this," Cady noted breathlessly.

"It keeps me up nights," he confessed. "But fantasy is one thing, reality is another. And while I want nothing more than to bed you, it would not be very kind to com-promise you and possibly risk a child when you've been quite clear that you have no desire to marry."

Ah, that was why he'd chosen the chair. He wanted to have this out with her. It was really very sweet of him.

Cady took a breath. "Gabe, do you realize that I know how to synthesize several different medicines that will ensure that an unexpected pregnancy will never be a problem?"

Surprise stilled him. "You do?"

"Of course. Botany is hundreds of years old, and women have practiced with plants forever. It just used to be called something else. In fact—"

"Lecture later," he told her with a low laugh. "Now I've got other plans."

His next kiss was as deep as the first was light. He cupped his hand around the back of her neck as he plundered her mouth, his tongue doing wicked things that made Cady whimper with need. She accepted everything he offered and still wanted more. Her hands curled around his shoulders, and she felt the rippling of his muscles under her fingers, the heat of his flesh beneath his clothing.

"Take your shirt off," she whispered. "I've haven't seen all of you yet."

He seemed to hesitate for a moment, then said in a warning tone, "It's not all very nice to look at."

"I will decide that for myself," she retorted.

"Then you take the shirt off," he said.

Cady tugged the fabric up and over his head. At first, she couldn't see anything wrong with him at all. He was pure muscle and broad shoulders and long, powerful arms, and a flat stomach with just a trail of tightly curled hair to interrupt the expanse of skin. Then she noticed that what she'd first taken for shadows were actually bluish marks all over his left side. She touched him and felt the unevenness of the skin, like pockmarks.

"What did this?" she asked.

"Lead shot from a shell. My back is worse. Some of the metal is still in there. There are nights I can't sleep."

"Pain?" she asked softly, retracting her hand.

"Comes and goes."

"You should have told me. I could give you something for it."

"No thank you. I've seen other men who were 'given something' for it. Now they're like ghosts of themselves, addicted to laudanum, and when they don't get it, there's just more pain on top of pain they had already."

"Oh, Gabe, it doesn't have to be like that," she murmured. "I wish you could trust me. I'd find what you needed."

"What I need is you," he said in a rough tone. He kissed her hard. Then his mouth was on her breast, and he was sucking at her nipples, his tongue curling and pressing. Cady let out a desperate plea for more.

"I remember how sensitive you are there," he growled.

"Yes." She felt faint with need.

"But not just there." He slid one hand between her legs, and let it rest just at the top of her thigh. She realized he was waiting for her approval.

"Gabe, please," she moaned.

With a sigh of relief, he moved his hand to cover her sex, and slipped one finger inside her, stroking gently, even as he kept his mouth at her breast.

How was she supposed to keep thinking straight when so many sensations were surging through her body? Cady thought she might fly apart.

She peaked before she could warn him that it was too much, too fast. She clung to him, wishing she were better at this. "Oh, I wanted it to last longer," she whispered. "It was so nice and now it's over."

"Blossom, we have hours. Tell me how many times you want to feel like that, and that's how many times you will."

She loved how he cut through the many layers of her that were so familiar that she forgot they were there—the enforced propriety, the protective shield, the uncertainty. *Of course* she shouldn't be alone with a man. *Of course* she shouldn't let pleasure decide her actions. *Of course* she shouldn't choose to live for the moment.

He sliced through all that, leaving Cady with nothing but her raw self to respond to him. And because there were no more rules, she could be honest about what she wanted and what made her excited and pleased and interested. It was like discovering a new continent…except that she didn't go anywhere. She just discovered it in herself.

Climbing off him and then kneeling down in front of the chair, she reached forward unbuttoned his falls, releasing his erection from the confines of the fabric. He let out a groan of relief, which turned into a very different sound when she circled her hand around him.

Inspired by his reaction, Cady slithered forward until her chest was even with his cock. It slid perfectly into the valley between her breasts, and the sound Gabe made confirmed her guess that he'd like the feeling of the hard flesh surrounded by her softness.

He put his hands on her shoulders and pressed her closer, his breathing gone harsh and desperate. A string of phrases passed his lips—all profane, all graphic, all utterly inappropriate for a lady's ears and all yet all wildly exciting to her. Cady looked up and smiled to see the raw ecstasy on his face. *She* was doing this to him, she who never did anything to anyone.

Gabe's rhythm increased, and he quickly moved one

hand to tip her head away.

He came abruptly. But then his mouth was on hers and she melted at his kisses, each deeper yet softer than the last. He was still swearing under his breath, a blasphemous litany that she felt was quite flattering, actually.

"Cady," he said at last. "You undid me."

She smiled. "Yes, I know."

"*How* did you know how to do that?"

"I just thought you might like it. You seemed to enjoy my breasts before."

"Before, now, and always." He smiled. "You took all my fantasies and threw them out the window and I don't even care because I can remember this night until I die."

"Oh, Gabe, you can still have your fantasies. But I do think one thing about them is wrong."

He frowned. "What's that?"

"You wouldn't need to chain me up."

His eyes widened. "Are you real?"

"Would you lie down with me now?" she asked a little shyly, which was ridiculous at this point in the evening. "On the bed?"

He stood up from the chair, picking her up along with him. He brought her to the bed and lay her down, stretching beside her, running his hands along her body.

"How are we still wearing clothes?" he muttered.

"Impatience," she said.

"Oversight." He quickly moved to shuck off his already-half-off clothing, and then very gently removed the delicate gown she still had on, careful not to rip anything. Then he told her to lie next to him, half on him. He turned his head to kiss her lingeringly. Cady smiled, feeling delightfully warm and hazy and safe.

He seemed to like tracing circles on her skin, and then occasionally finding a specific place on her body that just had to be kissed slowly. Cady used her fingers to follow the contours of muscles very foreign to her.

He let her play, but eventually his expression sharpened into lust again.

"Give me your hand," he said.

Cady did, and he pulled it down to his cock, once again hard. She didn't need more clues—she began to stroke him, loving the way his breathing changed with every touch.

"I want to feel you inside me," she murmured.

"Are you ready?" he asked. It was both a challenge and a subtle plea for permission.

She answered him by pulling away the sheet covering her.

With a growl of approval, he flipped her onto her back and pressed his knee between her legs, parting them. He bent down and laid kisses all along her stomach, up and down. His hands slid beneath her bottom and squeezed and massaged and petted her until she was gasping into her pillow.

Then he slid one hand between her legs and eased his fingers into the wetness there. Cady bucked and heard him chuckle, delighted with the effect he was having on her. She moaned when his fingers plunged into her center, stirring up so much dark pleasure that she had no words to tell him how good it felt.

He quickened his pace, his fingers seeking some place within her that made her moan with ecstasy every time they touched it. She rolled her hips, helping him hit that place, begging him to bring her to completion.

But he didn't, stopping just short of her peak. He shifted on the bed, his thighs against hers, his shaft pressing into her cleft.

"You want this?" he asked, his expression serious.

"More than anything."

Gabe exhaled as he slid into her. Cady inhaled, not anticipating the fullness she felt, almost too much pressure. But he moved slowly, letting her get used to him. And she was already so aroused that the sensation of his cock nearly tipped her over the edge.

And then he thrust.

Pleasure burst all through her body. How had she lived her whole life without knowing this feeling existed?

Gabe seemed to know exactly what she needed, and within moments she was crying out, the sound muffled in her pillow. Then he pressed his body hard against hers and thrust three, four times, his breathing fast.

She felt the sticky warmth on her thigh as he withdrew, but then he pulled her close to him as he rolled onto his side, keeping her within his embrace.

"I told you I know how to prevent a pregnancy," she murmured.

"And I told you I don't want to risk it." He kissed her ear. "But at this point, you should be rendered senseless with bliss, so I'm not sure why you're talking at all."

She bit her lip to stop a laugh. "Am I? I'm sorry, I'm not familiar with the conventions."

"I like that you're unconventional. It's wildly tempting. The first time I saw you, I wanted you."

"I'm no temptress," she objected. "I was a miserable little wreck, afraid of my own shadow."

"Don't believe that. You have a spark. Buried, true. But I could see it. And I don't just mean I wanted to bed you. It was more than that. Though I'm going to do that again before I leave here."

Lust welled up in her supposedly satiated body. "I'm listening."

It was twice more by the time she finally fell asleep,

completely exhausted in the most pleasurable, hedonistic way. Cady never knew she was so susceptible to the lure of the flesh, but Gabe awakened a side of her that seemed ravenous with need.

Cady still wasn't sure what he saw in her, but then she reasoned that it didn't matter. After all, she had gotten to be with him. The sort of man she had no hope of meeting in her bizarre, unhappy circumstances—yet there he was, and he was surprising and exciting and wonderfully gentle with her strangeness, and he tried to help her, and he definitely broadened her horizons. Cady knew it wouldn't last. Gabe was too good to be true, but at least for now, she would believe in the dream.

* * * *

The next morning, after he'd slipped out of Cady's bedroom, Gabe was still stunned by what happened between them. Here he was being so noble and self-sacrificing by telling Cady that he wouldn't perform the act that would ruin her completely…. And then she just turned around and ruined *him* for life by telling him none of his sacrifice was necessary, and would he please take her virginity. And she was so *sweet* about it, smiling at him while he was losing his mind and probably cursing in six different languages because one language could not contain all he had to say.

Oh, Lord, he was lost. He needed her and what was worse, he was starting to lose all perspective around her too. It was one thing to seduce a woman to further the goals of the assignment, which he assumed he might do at the beginning of all this. It was quite another to succumb to her just because she was so gloriously soft and sensual and made him feel like the only man in the world when she looked at him.

Not good. Not when he needed to find out who was behind the killings all over London. Not when he'd be assigned to something else, somewhere else once this was over, and Cady would learn just how much he'd hidden from her. She'd never forgive him for lying to her about that. And he wouldn't deserve her forgiveness.

♑

CADY AWOKE ALONE. GABE HAD left while it was still dark and she only got a short, cryptic note delivered to the house, telling her that he had something to investigate but that he would be at her dinner party as planned. The note arrived on her breakfast tray, since Cady reverted to her more hermit-like state and requested it to be served to her in bed. She was feeling far too lazy to get moving, especially after her rather busy night.

She frowned, reading over the note as she nibbled at her toast. She didn't expect anything revealing or personal, but some hint that he was thinking of her would be nice.

Perhaps the existence of the note *was* the hint, she decided. And after all, Gabe was tracking down his friend's killer, not courting her. Why be surprised that he wasn't showering her with attention? Really, it was her fault that she was letting her heart run wild. Which it was —Cady found herself thinking and dreaming about not just Gabe, but a *life* with Gabe. However, she'd resolved to not bring up the matter until he had found out the truth about the poisonings. By then, they'd be able to talk freely to each other without this hanging over them.

Later that morning, Cady fulfilled a promise to her brother by at last visiting a doctor, the first on Trevor's list of specialists. Judith accompanied her as a chaperone, though she remained in the waiting room during the actual consultation. The doctor was not inspiring, recommending only that she lic down whenever she felt any sense of excitement coming on, and that she not worry so much.

Oh, thank you, Cady refrained from saying out loud. *It had never* occurred *to me to simply worry less!*

He prescribed laudanum, which he said was the cure-all for nearly all women's problems. Cady paid him his fee and crossed his name off her list.

She went back out into the street, with Judith trailing behind.

"What a waste of time," Cady said with a sigh.

"Well, my lady, there are a lot of other doctors in London," Judith told her.

"I suppose, not that I want to visit them all," she said. Cady was just about to ask Judith to signal for a hired carriage when she heard a familiar voice.

"My goodness, is that you, little Cady?"

Cady whirled around. "Mr Addison!"

"Darling Cady. Excuse me!" he said, stopping when he reached her. "I should say my Lady Arcadia, now that we are in the city with all its manners and customs. I had no idea you had left Calderwood."

"It was a rather sudden decision," she admitted.

"A wise one," he told her, smiling. "Far be it from me to offer any chastisement, but I am glad you have transplanted yourself here. London is brighter for it, and I daresay the new surroundings will do a world of good. You are not meant to be hidden away."

"You are too kind, sir. And what brings you to London this time?"

He smiled. "I was asked to assess the specimens for a rose garden at Kew Park and make recommendations for new roses. Isn't that wonderful? I'm sure they only asked me because someone else couldn't oblige, but it's an hon-

or all the same."

"Mr Addison, clearly what happened is that your expertise has been recognized. Who else would know better in all of England?" She was delighted to see him, and got an idea. "I'm hosting a very small dinner later tonight. If you have no other plans, would you come? It would be like a little bit of home here in London."

"It would be my pleasure," he told her.

After that, Judith nudged Cady to remind her that they should continue on the rest of the errands, which would occupy most of the afternoon. When she finally got home, Cady found the town house gleaming and already prepared for guests. Fresh candles stood ready to be lit in all the rooms, and she could smell something divine wafting from the kitchen.

Cady had been perfectly willing to host a dinner party in the abstract, but she grew increasingly nervous as the hour drew near. In a departure from the morning wear, Bond had dressed her in a stunning pink gown, and added delicate pink roses from the gardens to Cady's headdress, which was otherwise a few simple twists of ribbon serving as a headband. She gave Cady long white lace gloves to wear.

"Oh, Lord, I'll stain these immediately," Cady fretted.

"You own more," Bond told her, while selecting the jewels Cady would wear. "Coral, my lady? Or is that too young?"

Cady considered the necklace Bond presented, which was beads of coral carved to look like little flowers. Cady had received the necklace and the matching bracelet on her twelfth birthday, coral generally being considered a girl's stone.

"I'll wear the coral," she said. "My mother gave me those. Well, I suppose Papa paid for them. But Mama picked them out."

When Cady went downstairs, she found that Trevor had (astonishingly) arrived early, and was now talking to Gabe in the parlor, not quite spilling his drink as he gesticulated, but coming near to it. Gabe did not have a drink in hand, and he moved very slightly back whenever Trevor made a particularly grand gesture.

Gabe was resplendent in his evening attire and his newly golden hair. He looked like the lord of the manor, in fact, and Cady got an odd chill. What if that was his real plan? To take Calderwood from her through all this subterfuge?

That's a ridiculous thought, she told herself. But her mind had a way of reacting badly to even less rational ideas, and once a thought needled its way into her brain, it would stay there and fester.

"Good evening," she said quickly, to distract from the feeling.

Trevor lifted his glass to her. "Cady, you're so darling in that pinky stuff! Doesn't she look darling, Gabe?"

"Darling," Gabe agreed with a little quirk of his lips. His appreciative eyes scanned her top to toe. Cady felt a warmth spreading through her, though it didn't quite cut the chill of her previous, absurd thought.

And then the other guests began to arrive. Cady put on her best, most polite smile and went to greet them. Then Mr Addison came through the door, and all at once, Cady remembered that not only had she failed to tell Gabe she invited Mr Addison, she'd also completely forgotten that Mr Addison already met Gabe…as her gardener!

She looked at Gabe with wide eyes, alarm coursing through her. How could they possibly handle this?

* * * *

Gabe had about two seconds to register Cady's distraught face when the next guest walked through the door. *Addison.*

Well, this was an unpleasant surprise. Fortunately, Gabe spent half his life lying to people. The man gave him a strange look when they were "introduced" by Trevor.

"Have we met before, sir?" Addison asked. "There's something about you that seems so familiar."

"I've heard that from others before," Gabe returned easily. He reminded himself that when he was working at Calderwood as a gardener, he'd had the black hair and the scraggly beard, not to mention his laborer's wardrobe. "I must have quite a common face."

Trevor snorted, but rather unexpectedly offered, "Gabe here is the younger brother of Viscount Nyle, but he's much more diverting. Have you ever met Nyle? Dreadfully dull man." The casual comment worked to establish Gabe firmly in the upper ranks of Society…far above a garden bed. Trevor was really a very clever person. *He'd make a good agent*, Gabe thought.

"Are you at all involved in gardening?" Addison pressed.

"Couldn't tell one end of a shovel from the other," Gabe said with a laugh. "Though Trevor tells me that his sister is quite taken with the hobby."

"Hobby?" Addison murmured with disapproval in his tone.

Good, Gabe thought. Hopefully, Addison would focus on Mr Courtenay's dismissive tone, and not think about his resemblance to a surly dark-haired gardener he met last month.

Having passed the test with Mr Addison, Gabe could relax and enjoy the rest of the evening.

It helped immensely that Cady knew everyone with the exception of Lady Sophia, who was so charming and adept at social situations that she could make friends with a turtle in short order. The other female guest, Mrs Jennings, was a friend of Cady's mother, and seemed quite pleased that the now-grown-up Cady had renewed the acquaintance.

After the dessert course, the ladies moved through to the drawing room.

Gabe took a moment to step into the foyer, where the air was a bit cooler. Rook had opened the front doors to encourage the breeze for a few minutes.

As was his habit, Gabe glanced at the few papers and cards scattered over the front table. It was typical to leave the calling cards of previous visitors displayed, a sort of running tally to prove one's social worth. Cady probably didn't know that, but the Disreputables certainly did, and they would perform all the usual functions exactly. Gabe saw his brother's card, and his lip curled. So Gerald had called on her already? He only hoped Cady had been unavailable when Viscount Nyle stopped by. There were several others as well. Cady was no longer an unknown in London.

Before he could think further on it, Trevor called his name from the dining room and he went back in for the obligatory smoking and drinking that the ladies had escaped.

Trevor tried to interest Gabe in a drink he'd made himself during his brief absence, but Gabe remembered how strong Trevor's drinks tended to be, and begged off. Trevor looked a little wounded.

Rook silently handed him a glass of brandy, the liquor coming up to a blessedly low level. "What were we talking about?" Gabe asked after a sip.

Trevor said, "The mystical coincidence that although London is home to hundreds of thousands of people, we tend to continually run into the same ones over and over, even when there is no reason it should happen. Addison was mentioning how he saw Cady on a street that neither of them normally frequent. Why should that be?"

"I don't know," Gabe said. "But it does seem to be a truism. Not just the meeting of people you already know, but also the fact that total strangers can have so many friends in common. For example…Mr Addison, you seem to have a broad range of acquaintances. Did you know Lyndon Huxley?"

Trevor nearly choked on his drink, but Addison merely raised his eyebrows.

"Huxley? Why yes, I do know him, as a matter of fact! He cultivated a very fine tea rose, you know. Absolutely lovely double bloom, nearly pure white, and bloomed all the way until frost… Why are you asking about Huxley?"

"He just died," Gabe said bluntly.

"Oh, my Lord! But he was so young. Was it an accident?"

"That's not clear yet, but it's possible there was foul play involved. It would be helpful to the authorities if we could know more about his final days. By the way, did you happen to meet him while in London recently? Perhaps to exchange cuttings, for example?"

"We'd often write back and forth, but no…I hadn't actually seen him since last fall when there was a tour of Kew Park we both attended. How terrible." Addison shook his head.

Gabe finished his brandy. "Ah, well, I suppose that his gardening couldn't have had anything to do with the matter. He was much involved in politics, so that is more likely."

"Was he?" Addison asked. "I never read those columns in my papers, I'm afraid."

"You are probably right not to do so," Trevor said, staring into his empty glass. "Usually depressing, and always boring."

"Shall we rejoin the ladies?" Addison suggested. "I find that Lady Arcadia is always able to cheer a person with her presence. In that way, she has always been an ideal friend."

"Yes, let's." Trevor stood up, carelessly sliding his empty glass across the table, until it hit the still-untouched drink he'd made for Gabe earlier.

Gabe put his own empty snifter down, and followed the other two men across the foyer to the drawing room, where Cady sat with the other two ladies. From the sound of it, their conversation was much livelier than the men's had been.

Trevor somehow secured another drink already. As Judith passed by Gabe, she murmured, "I watered it down."

He gave her a tiny nod, then glanced around the room. Cady was nodding along to something Sophie was saying. She was lovely as always, but there was a tightness to her smile, a sense that she was not fully there in the room with the others, and in fact hadn't been so since the beginning.

Gabe approached her and said, "My lady, may I take you for a turn around the garden?"

"Ah, you will want some fresh air, cherie," Sophie said with a little smile that suggested she hoped the "turn" turned into a more romantic interlude.

Cady nodded, slightly less enthusiastic. But she stood and allowed Gabe to walk her to the side doors and out to the narrow garden, now lit with several lanterns for the party.

They walked silently for a moment, then Gabe said, "Cady, what is it? You've been distracted all evening. You've got your mask on," he added, tipping her chin up so she had to look at him. "Did someone say something to you?"

"No," she replied shortly. "It's nothing."

"Like hell it's nothing. Tell me."

"I can't. It's stupid."

"Let me decide that, blossom. After all, how stupid could it be if you've been stewing over it all night?"

"I'd rather not."

"Am I going to have to insist?"

"That sounds like a threat."

"It's a bit of threat, though I'd much prefer not to make any." He gentled his tone. "Please tell me, Cady. Is this about last night? Regrets? I don't like seeing you so miserable."

"You'll laugh."

"And that scares you," he guessed.

"Of course," she retorted. "Everything scares me."

"You sound more angry than scared. So go ahead and tell me."

"I had a bad thought earlier. It just jumped into my head. And I think I've told you before that once a bad thought gets into there, it just sets up shop and stays forever."

"Tell me the thought, Cady."

"I thought you looked so in command earlier, like you owned this house instead of me, that I thought…"

"That I intend to steal it from you, the town house and Calderwood and everything? That this story about the poison and the murders is just an elaborate ruse to gain your confidence and take advantage of you?"

Cady dropped her eyes, too embarrassed to look at him. "Yes. That was exactly the thought I had."

"Would it help if I told you that's not true?"

"I told myself that, and it didn't help at all." Instead she'd just felt that the bad thought got truer and truer the more she tried to deny it. Just like all her thoughts about things that scared her—the terror came from the mere possibility of them being true, not the overwhelming likelihood that they were false.

Gabe took her hands in his. "It's actually a quite normal thought to have."

"It is?" she asked skeptically.

"Well, yes. You're a woman without much in the way of security, but enough wealth and land—not to mention beauty—that a man might easily want to seize all that for himself. And I come along with a frankly mad story about how I'm hunting down a murderer whose weapon of choice is an exotic poison and I need your total trust to do it. Honestly, I'm still sort of surprised you do believe me."

"So..." Cady said, "*Are* you after my land and my income?"

"I wish I were, love. Because then I wouldn't be up to my neck in theories about a poisoner and getting a bit nervous every time I take a sip of a new drink. But consider this. If I just wanted to compromise you and force you into a hasty marriage so I could control all your wealth, I could have done that several times by now."

"Perhaps you're toying with me." But she said it with no heat, letting Gabe know she already recognized the truth of his words.

"I'd never toy with you," he swore. "Tease, yes. Tempt, yes. But I never ever wanted to play with your heart or trick you into anything that would hurt you."

"I'm sorry I acted like I did this evening."

"You have a lot on your mind," he excused her, "and this is a very strange situation. But I do hope you'll tell me the next time you have one of your bad thoughts."

"Part of the problem is that I'm afraid to say any of the bad thoughts out loud. It might make them real."

"But more likely, it will show how unreal they are." He cupped her face in his hands. "Cady, you've got such an intelligent mind. You shouldn't be surprised when it decides to work against you, it's more intelligent than the average person's. But it's also clear that your mind has been working against you for a while."

"Well, thank you for that diagnosis, but what am I supposed to do about it?" she asked.

"You need to step outside your own head and let other people help you. Like me. Just because you have a thought, it doesn't mean it's a true thought. It's just a thought. I think of untrue things all the time."

"You do?"

"Of course. Minds are like that. The difference is that you've been stuck in such a dark place for such a long time, so your mind isn't working the way it used to. But you're not stuck where you are. You can leave. You just need a little help to get started."

Cady's eyes looked a little glassy. She took a breath, and said, "That's just what a man hellbent on stealing my fortune *would* say."

He smiled. "There's my Cady. Now, are you ready to face the people again? Just for a little while."

"Yes, I think so. But after they all have one more glass of sherry, they have to go."

"Is that true for me as well?" he asked.

"You certainly have to leave." Cady shot him a different look then, one that immediately got his attention. "But if you would like to come back later, that would be quite acceptable."

"Mmm. I've always dreamed of having a woman tell me she finds me *quite acceptable*." He gave her a kiss, one that promised more to come. Then he put one hand on her lower back, steering her toward the door. "All right then, let's go face the hordes."

They returned to the group, but Gabe couldn't wait for that dinner party to end. He left out the front door, climbing into a hired carriage. But he had the carriage stop after only about ten minutes, and he walked back to Cady's house, slipping in the back door with the key she'd gifted him. He waited until all the servants returned to the ground floor to take care of clearing up. Then he knocked softly on Cady's door.

She opened it, wearing something so sheer that it hardly qualified as clothing at all.

"What do you think?" she asked.

"Fancy," he concluded.

"Do you like it?" she asked. "I think it was designed to be enticing."

"I'll like taking it off you." He locked the door, and proceeded to show her just how unnecessary it was to entice him. The mere thought of Cady aroused him, and the sight of her drove him over the edge.

Luckily, the bed was a soft place to land.

♑

AFTER A FEW MORE DAY of fruitless investigation and tantalizing half clues, the evening of Viscount Nyle's party arrived. Gabe was in a sour mood, thinking that he ought to be chasing the person poisoning half of London, not dancing attendance on his brother.

Gabe was uneasy about the killer, who seemed to be killing more frequently now, with Huxley's death following so soon on MacCuley's. As an agent of the Zodiac, he was used to working alone, and without being noticed. Hanging about Cady was noticeable. He'd allowed himself to do it too often, lured by her company and, yes, her bed.

The ballroom was already getting quite full, and Gabe did his best to appear polite to the other guests without getting too ensnared in conversations. His brother's set were not exactly the most fascinating people. However, as he strolled past a table where drinks were being served, he happened to start talking with an older gentleman who looked slightly scholarly.

Gabe guessed aloud that he might be a doctor.

"Why, yes, sir. I studied medicine at Oxford."

"Are you familiar with mental conditions?"

"Naturally. What are you curious about?"

"Let's say there's a person who suffers from paralyzing fear."

"You mean a phobia, such as a fear of snakes, for example?" the man asked.

"Well, not exactly. She gets afraid even when there's no actual threat."

"Ah. I know what you're referring to."

Gabe was surprised. "You do?"

"I knew as soon as you said *she*. Women are very susceptible to hysteria."

"I don't think it's that simple."

"Certainly it is. Why be afraid when there's nothing to be afraid of? When a man has a fear of spiders and sees a spider, his reaction is logical even if it may be extreme. When a woman is afraid of heights, and you walk her to a cliff, her panic is understandable even though she ought to trust you. But fear for no reason, just out of the clear sky? That's hysteria."

"But then what *is* hysteria?" Gabe pressed.

"Oh, it's a common female complaint that used to be considered the result of a wandering womb. Which is nonsense, of course. The Greeks were geniuses in many ways, but their understanding of anatomy was woefully underdeveloped. Still, the condition is undoubtably linked to the female sex, and in a sexual way. There's no question that women who suffer from hysteria are also usually unable to conceive and are also frigid."

"Hmm" was Gabe's response. Cady definitely didn't fit the last parameter.

"Happily, the treatment suggests itself."

Gabe couldn't see how there was any obvious treatment for undefined terror. "It does?"

"Yes. Hysteria inhibits a woman's natural capacity to become a mother, or to act as a woman should. Hence, regular sexual engagement between a husband and wife, hopefully resulting in pregnancy, will cure her. Or at least give her something else to think about. In a lot of cases a woman thinks she's hysterical, but in fact she's merely bored."

"I see. Excuse me, won't you?" Gabe removed himself from the conversation. As he walked away, he realized he should have asked which of the colleges in Oxford the man had attended, so he could make sure to never go to a doctor with a degree from there for the rest of his life.

The party was so densely packed with guests that it was difficult to move quickly through the crowd, or to keep track of any one person if you happened to see them across the room. This meant the event was actually well suited for discreet meetings—for example, with one's spymaster and his factotum.

Gabe found Julian Neville and Miss Chattan standing at the edge of the side gallery of the ballroom. Since the gallery was raised by about three feet from the main floor, it provided an excellent view of the dancing and general carousing.

"Aries," Gabe muttered on joining them.

"Capricorn," Julian returned.

Chattan frequently appeared just this side of unkempt at the Zodiac offices (*slovenly* was too strong a term, but she often sported a rather messy hairstyle and had ink stains on her fingers). Now, however, she was the picture of feminine grace. Her ash-blond hair was bound in a high twist, and she wore a pale blue satin gown with an empire waist than made her look quite tall and slender. Gabe said, "Miss Chattan, you look lovely tonight."

"Why, thank you." She smiled winsomely. "Isn't it gratifying to see how many good friends have come to wish your brother felicitations of the day?"

Gabe rolled his eyes. "It's certainly gratifying for him. Now, would you like to hear what I've learned?"

Julian glanced around just long enough to assure himself that no one was close enough to overhear. "Go ahead."

So Gabe reported the most recent developments. He explained about meeting Trevor Osbourne, and the confirmation that he'd disposed of the only bottle of clephobine known to exist in England. He related how he investigated the home of the last victim, Huxley, and the tenuous but tantalizing connections of a few of the victims to the Osbournes.

"But you have not yet identified the killer?"

"I've got a few theories, but nothing I'd offer with certainty. What's clear is that there must be another source of the chemical beyond what was made at Calderwood. When I can find that, I think it will lead me directly to the kill—"

Just then, he saw Cady enter the room. She wore a green gown. This was a perfectly accurate statement which conveyed nothing of the actual impression she made. The top of the gown was pale green silk, with tiny cap sleeves that just covered her shoulders. As the fabric descended, the color deepened. At the high waist, it was a true green, but then darkened to a deep emerald and then to near black at the lower hem, so that when she walked the tips of her black leather slippers couldn't even be differentiated. She was wearing the de rigueur long gloves, but instead of the usual white, hers had been dyed the same shade of brown as tree bark. Her dark hair was curled, but little sprigs of pale pink flowers had been tucked in here and there. The effect was to make her appear as if she'd just stepped from a forest glade, perhaps after seven years trapped in a faerie realm.

"Not exactly following the rules of fashion, is she," Julian murmured. "If there was any question about whether she's half-plant, she's put it to rest."

"Most women wouldn't be able to carry that look off," Chattan noted. "In a field of cultivated blossoms all striving to look the same, she's willing to be different. And of course, it helps to be beautiful. Don't you think, Gabe?"

"She looks very nice," he allowed. The words sounded grudging and ungracious. But the truth was he was lucky he could talk at all. Cady wasn't beautiful, she was bewitching.

Chattan shot him a disgusted glance. "*Very nice?* You've got all the soul of a discarded sock."

"I wasn't asked to join the Circle for my poetry."

"Thank God for that. You'd better go to her and secure a dance before everyone else does. She may be a botanist, but she can't make herself a wallflower. Men will be fighting for the opportunity to say they've danced with the most beautiful new face in London."

Gabe took a last slug from his glass. "Excuse me."

Gabe strode up to Cady just as a dance ended. A young man who'd dutifully filled out his name on her card for the next one took one look at Gabe and conceded the field, retreating back into the crowd. Gabe felt pity for him for one moment, but then the music started again, and Gabe took her in his arms, and no one else mattered.

"And it just happens to be a waltz," he murmured. "Good thing you endured the patronesses, hmm? I was hoping you'd be allowed to dance this."

"Their approval only matters for dances *at* Almack's, as you must know," she said. "I'm surprised you like dancing."

"I like the waltz. I believe it was only invented as a way to allow people to say they're dancing when in fact they're flirting."

"My goodness, do you think people will consider me a flirt?" She glanced around the crowd.

"They will consider you beautiful," he replied smooth-ly.

As the waltz ended, Gabe was unpleasantly surprised to find his brother lurking at the edge of the floor, clearly waiting for Cady.

"He's claimed the next dance," she whispered. "I was surprised by how many men signed my card."

Gabe wasn't. Cady was the most beautiful woman there.

Gerald approached and bowed over Cady's hand. "My lady," he said with far too much fervor. "How lovely to see you again."

"Thank you for the invitation, my lord."

"You know, I forgot to ask earlier. How *do* you know my little brother?"

"We met in Kent," Cady replied with a side glance at Gabe.

"At a house party?"

Gabe saw her expression change to amused. "Something like that, yes. I don't recall the specifics."

"And even here in London, you seem to see a lot of each other."

"I suppose." Cady gave a little shrug.

"I hope he isn't importuning. I am happy to give him a talking-to if he is."

She gave him her most innocent, wide-eyed look. "Importuning? What do you mean?"

"Taking advantage of your good nature, or extracting promises of any type."

Lord, he was talking around the matter. The man couldn't bring himself to ask directly whether Gabe had offered marriage or tried to compromise her into mar-riage.

Cady looked like she wanted to laugh, but she merely

said, "I can't imagine." It was a vague reply that effectively ended the interrogation.

Then Gerald swept her back onto the floor for the next dance.

And the one after.

Gabe's patience was wearing thin. This was the aspect of being a younger son that he hated most: the expectation that he'd attend all the events, show respect for the family name, and bow and scrape to his eldest brother's whims just because he was the eldest. If it had been Gabe's birthday party, Gerald wouldn't have bothered to show up at all, let alone stay this long.

Not that Gabe ever had a birthday party, or any party. Gabe was an agent of the Zodiac. His work was too important for parties. Yet here he was.

When the second dance finally ground to a halt, Gabe swiftly moved to intercept Gerald from dragging Cady along to yet another dance or whatever destination he had in mind.

"You look a little flushed, my lady," Gabe said to Cady. "Perhaps you want to step outside where it's cooler. I want to speak to my brother for a moment."

No fool, Cady read his mood and graciously agreed. "Yes, a moment out on the terrace would be very restorative. How thoughtful, Mr Courtenay." She moved off toward the glass doors to the outside.

Gabe leaned toward his brother. "What are you doing?" he said in a low voice.

"What do you mean? And you haven't said a word about it being my birthday." He seemed slightly tipsy.

"Many happy returns," Gabe said. "What are you doing with Lady Arcadia?"

"Dancing, mostly. Though I think I'll go after her and see if she'll give me a birthday kiss."

"You're drunk," Gabe snapped, and stalked off to find Cady first.

Gabe found her—where else?—deeper in the gardens, having skipped the crowded terrace entirely. "How are you?" he asked, half hoping she'd tell him that she needed to leave straightway to avoid an attack.

But she looked perfectly composed. "I'm fine. You were right, though. It's loud and hot and not my crowd. What did you discuss with your brother?"

"You, actually."

"Me?"

"He's rather taken with you."

Cady laughed. "What?"

"I'm not joking."

"But…no." She made a face. "I mean, I'm sure he's a very nice person…"

"He's not," Gabe said flatly.

"Did I say something to make him think I was interested in him?"

"You're an unmarried lady of quality with some money. That's enough."

"Does he know people say I killed my own father?"

"You could mention that when he calls," Gabe suggested.

Cady laughed again, but it came out too strident. "Oh, my Lord. What I am going to do?"

"You don't have to do anything. You don't have to receive him at all."

"Gabe, can't you talk to him? Tell him not to bother?"

"That would not be taken well. Viscount Nyle doesn't like to be told that he can't have something when he wants it. Plus he thinks I'm after you myself, so he'll just discount it as jealousy."

"I expect he'd very upset if he ever found out that we

misbehaved in his own house, at his own party."

"Misbehaved? How so?"

She rose up on tiptoes and whispered her suggestion in his ear.

Well. Gabe was nothing if not accommodating when it came to obeying a lady's wish. He said, "Come with me."

He knew his way around the house, of course, and he led Cady around the side and into a part of the building much quieter than where they'd just left.

A flight of steps, some judicious listening at a few doors to ensure they wouldn't be interrupting anyone else with similar ideas, and then at last, a small sitting room with a key thoughtfully in the lock on the inside of the door.

Then she was in his arms, her mouth hot on his. "Is it safe?" she whispered.

"Hell, no. You're being very brave." He opened his mouth and quickly trapped her finger between his teeth, sucking on it.

Cady's eyes flared and her expression turned lustful. "Please, Gabe," she breathed.

Turning the key in the lock and then yanking it out, he turned around only to see Cady already sinking to her knees, her hands going to unbutton his falls, and tug his cock free.

She smiled when she ran her hand up and down the length of him. "I always seem to forget how big you are. May I?"

Like he'd ever tell her no. After a few minutes of intense, blinding bliss, Gabe put his hand to her head. "Stop, please. I've got other plans for you."

She gave one last flick of her tongue against the tip of him, but then stood up. "Tell me how you want me."

God, the way she said it.

He grabbed her and lifted her, loving how she clung to him, wrapping her legs around his waist. He pressed her hard against the wall, kissing the exposed skin of her chest, then dragging his teeth across her neck, then sucking on her earlobe. Cady leaned her head back, her eyes closed and her face rapt with pleasure.

Gabe glanced down. There was something about seeing a woman's silk stockings still on, the gentle curve of her calves beneath the fabric looking so perfect, and then feeling so smooth beneath his hands.

She put her arms around his shoulders, her hand curling around the back of his neck. "Don't wait, Gabe. I want to be everything for you."

Sliding into her slick heat felt so good he nearly came right then. Cady started to cry out as he entered her, and he put the heel of his hand into her mouth to give her something to bite down on.

She made a little muffled sound that had him thrusting deep within her, aroused to the point of pain.

Cady released his hand from her mouth, only to whisper in a ragged tone, "How do you know just what I love? I've never needed anything like this before."

"Will you tell me when you come?"

"Watch me and I won't have to," she whispered.

He did love watching her, seeing how her mouth opened and her chest heaved, how her eyes grew big and soft, hazed with passion.

Against his inclination, he moved slower and slower, enjoying Cady's soundless protests and the way her nails raked across his back.

"Ready, love?" he whispered.

"Gabe. Please." Her mouth was hot on his shoulder when he changed his rhythm, suddenly harder, faster.

She tightened around him, convulsing as she reached

her orgasm. There was no way he was stopping now. His balls tightened up, and he rode the crest of her orgasm to his own.

When he came, Cady held him close and kept him from shouting everything he needed for the whole world to hear. Instead, he bit her shoulder as she clung to him, murmuring a string of wonderful nonsense about how she was so happy and she adored him and she would never forget how special he made her feel. He wanted to believe it, but he spent too many years saying much the same things to women he was seducing as part of an assignment. He'd trained himself not to believe anything.

But God, he wanted those things to be true. As he came down from his peak, he laid his forehead in the curve of her neck and shoulder, eyes closed.

She kissed him softly, then whispered, "You could put me down now. Just a suggestion."

A laugh broke free, keeping Gabe from getting too serious, or saying something he shouldn't. "Only because I have to."

Moments later, Cady was standing in front of a mirror, restoring her hair and outfit to their pre-tryst state. The heightened color in her cheeks was all that suggested her recent activity.

"How did you know this room would be empty?" she asked, shooting him a curious glance via the mirror.

"I didn't," he admitted.

Her brown eyes widened. "What was the excuse going to be if someone was in here and saw us together?"

"I'd have thought of something."

"Mr Courtenay, you are being very cavalier with my reputation. And in your brother's own home, how shocking." Her teasing tone warmed him, because he loved how open and confident she'd become. But there was a cold fog underneath it—he was playing very dangerously. Telling himself that he'd solve any problems that came up, rather than doing the right thing and simply walking away from her. As an agent, Gabe got what he needed from Cady regarding the poison. Yet here he was, finding reasons to keep her close, to be with her, risking her reputation.

Christ, no wonder he was alone. He was a terrible person.

$\mathrm{V\!\!\!\!\!_{o}}$

CADY NODDED WHEN GABE TOLD her that he'd leave the room first. She was to wait ten minutes and then leave on her own. If anyone questioned her, she was to explain that she had lost her way while in search of the ladies' retiring room.

"With the amount of alcohol flowing at this party, no one will question it," Gabe assured her. "I'll see you to-morrow."

"You're leaving entirely?" Cady asked.

"There's something I need to look into," he said, sounding slightly distracted. "And it's not something you can help with, so don't ask. Besides, I'm not the sort you should be seen with."

He gave her a swift kiss and then unlocked the door. He slipped through it before she could say anything. Cady locked it behind him, just in case, and then looked at the clock.

Ten minutes.

Ten minutes, when one has nothing to occupy their hands and too much to occupy their mind, is a long time.

Cady paced the room, and checked her hair three times, smoothed her dress, and wondered how she'd got to this point. A month ago, she could not have dreamed that she'd be here in London, having just completed an assignation with a man who made her heart and body sing. A month ago, she was still lurking like a shadow amid the walls of Calderwood, not speaking to anyone she hadn't known her whole life, and fearful that literally anything might suddenly strike her down.

Gabe's arrival at the estate upended her whole existence. He'd barely stepped onto the soil of the property before he'd drawn her out of her shell, tamed her dogs, and awakened a passion she hadn't known she possessed.

And it was all due to a little bottle of poison that she'd mistakenly brewed up in an attempt to cure herself. How many people died because of her fears and her unusual skills in botany and chemistry? Had Gabe guessed what he'd find when he arrived? No, he'd told her that she was a surprise.

But was she the sort of surprise that he liked enough to pursue? Or was their affair just the result of emotions running high, and the fact that they'd been thrown together as Gabe tracked down the person who killed his friend?

Her mood growing tangled and dark, Cady decided that it was time to leave. She unlocked the door, peeked out to see an empty hallway, and then moved out and walked purposefully toward the sounds of laughter and music.

She'd turned a few corners by the time she met anyone, so Cady didn't have to feign being confused.

"Excuse me, but *where* is the retiring room?" she asked a blue-gowned woman with ash-blonde hair who was approaching from the opposite end of the hall.

The other lady gave her an understanding smile. "Just down the hall and to the left," she said. "I don't know why Nyle feels the need to put them so far from the party."

Cady thanked her and went on, breathing a sigh of relief that no one seemed to care that she was wandering around unattended. When she got back to the more crowded part of the house, she went directly to the foyer and told a footman to call for her coach.

"Already outside for you, my lady," the footman said with a little bow.

Bemused, Cady followed him to the street, where Jem looked down from his high perch and tipped his hat.

"Evening, my lady. Ready to go home?"

"Yes, please." Cady looked up at Jem.

"How did you happen to be there even before I called?"

"Mr Courtenay passed by and he mentioned you'd be going soon," Jem said.

Ah. That made sense. The footman helped her in and Cady was soon speeding away from the party and toward the haven of her townhome. When Jem finally pulled the coach to a halt in front of her door, Rook hurried outside to help her out.

The hour was late, but even after Bond had helped her out of her gown and taken down her hair, Cady wasn't sleepy. Minnie brought up a tray with chamomile tea, and Cady sat in bed, sipping slowly while she tried to read herself to sleep by going over the more recent edition of the *Proceedings of the Royal Society for Chemistry*, which was not known for gripping prose.

She finally blew out the candle and lay down. She hoped against hope that Gabe might surprise her with a visit, mostly just so she could see him and hold him. But the clock ticked away and no one appeared. She lay wakeful in her bed, staring at nothing, her thoughts a maelstrom. Gabe. The poison. All the deaths. Everything somehow connected, but not in any way she could see.

Sighing, Cady sat up and flipped her covers back. She'd go down to the kitchen and find something to eat. That would give her something to think about and perhaps afterward sleep could come. Oscar snoozed away on a chair by the fireplace, and she cast a wistful glance at the cat. If only she could sleep as easily as he did!

Putting on her slippers and pulling on a silk wrap over her chemise, Cady left her bedroom and moved silently down the stairs. The house was dark and quiet. Perhaps too quiet. Cady felt a little nervous, as though she were an intruder rather than the owner.

On the ground floor, Cady walked to the back of the house, and saw a thin line of light at the bottom of the closed kitchen door. Lord, was someone still up, or up so early, already at work?

Cady intended to march in and tell whoever it was that they needed more rest. No task was so important as to work through the night. She'd turned the knob and got the door open one inch when something stopped her cold.

"I don't need more people mucking about. This is a delicate situation."

Gabe's voice.

Gabe's voice?

What would he be doing in her kitchen, at four in the morning, talking to her servants?

"Mucking about?" It was Jem who responded. "We're just keeping house, sir. You can do the mucking. You're the one who pretended to be a gardener after all."

"I did what I had to do," Gabe said.

"Wait!" Bond broke in. "Did anyone hear something?"

Cady held her breath, keeping absolutely still. Had Bond heard the door creak as the knob turned? Would anyone notice it was now open an inch, allowing Cady to listen?

"Nah, there's nothing," said Rook. "I locked all the doors, and even walked up to the lady's room about twenty minutes ago. Not a peep."

Cady exhaled silently.

"Good," said Gabe. "It's difficult arranging a safe place and time for all of us to meet anyway. Jem, you start."

"I picked the locks for any room in this house that wasn't already unlocked. There's nothing in most of them, and definitely not any bottle that could be this poison."

"Well, it was worth it to check," Gabe grumbled. "This house is owned by the family, so the poison *could* have been moved here."

At the door, Cady frowned. What on earth was Gabe talking about? She *told* him that the bottle was long gone!

"And what about the cards? Any luck there?"

"No," said Judith. "I found several papers and items that have the word *Arcadia,* but nothing that has the whole phrase *et in Arcadia ego.* Why do we want to find such a thing?"

Gabe explained, "Because the killer left a card with that phrase at the scene of every murder."

Cards? *Every murder?* How many were there? The memory of Gabe's reaction to her saying that phrase came back to her. Was he suspicious of her even then? In her distress, she missed a bit of the conversation and had to put her ear closer to the gap.

"…perhaps if we get her out of the way?" Rook was saying.

Bond sighed. "I suppose I could give her something to make her sleep…"

"No," Gabe said immediately. "She's familiar with sedatives and she'd know when she woke up that she was drugged. We absolutely can't risk her getting suspicious."

"Can't we?" Jem asked.

"I've just got to a level of trust with her," Gabe said. "And I know she's extremely sensitive to the slightest changes. If she suspected anyone in the house of putting something in her food or drink, she'd sack everyone, then lock herself in the bedroom and not come out for years. That won't help us."

"You sure about this, sir?" Rook asked suddenly. "Not that I'm objecting, it's just…it seems dangerous."

"What's dangerous is letting someone keep murdering people with impunity," Gabe snapped back. "When the Zodiac assigned this matter to me, it was because I have a reputation for getting results."

The Zodiac? What is that? Cady closed her eyes, feeling shaky, as if the floor beneath her was no longer steady. And what did Gabe mean about being *assigned*?

"The Disreputables are with you, sir," Jem said in a tone of reassurance. "Tell us what you need, and we'll see it done. We can always work around Lady Arcadia. We're trained to do that."

Cady suppressed a gasp. *Trained? By who? For what?!*

"The person I'm actually most concerned about is Trevor," Gabe said then, and her heart contracted. He could *not* be implying what she thought he was. "Huxley's death suggests a connection to that club, and that's not a good sign. I'd prefer it if he stayed away from the house, but it might be tricky. If he—"

Cady put all the little things together: the poison, the town house, Trevor, Huxley. Did Gabe think her *brother* was the killer? She didn't wait any longer. Cady threw open the door and stormed in, finding a half circle of people all looking over in dismay.

"What's going on? What are you doing here? It's four in the morning!" she announced.

Gabe was standing in the middle of the group, and he took a step forward, those blue eyes locked on her. "Cady, if you give me a moment, I can explain everything."

"Wonderful! Start with whatever the Zodiac is. And then explain what a Disreputable is."

Bond and Jem exchanged looks, and without saying a word, both started to move to flank Cady.

"Stop that," Gabe ordered them. "It's her house, and she has every right to be in the kitchen or wherever else she wants. Besides, where would she go?"

Cady was too furious to notice how her heart was thudding in her chest. "Yes, it is my house! Oh, and perhaps you'd explain what *level of trust* you think I have in you now!"

Rook groaned, shaking his head.

"My lady," Judith said, putting her hands out in a placating way. "This isn't what it looks like."

"It looks like a man I trusted has been lying to me and that everyone else in the house is aware of it," she said, the words bitter on her tongue.

Judith closed her mouth, and raised her hands wider in a gesture of giving up.

Gabe walked toward Cady, moving fast. He got his hands on her shoulders just as she started to turn away, aiming for the door. "Cady, you've got nothing to be afraid of, not from me. Or anyone here."

"Then tell me what you are!" she demanded, feeling her chest contract. "And why you're talking about Trevor!"

"I work for a…a group of… Look, we're on the right side."

"The right side of what?"

"Of…everything. We keep the country safe from threats. Usually that means people, foreign agents, and plots to destroy this or that utterly vital thing. This time it's a person who's using poison…"

"You said Trevor's name!"

"I didn't mean he's the killer," Gabe said tightly.

"Oh, really? Because that's what it sounded like!"

"You need to breathe, sweetheart. You'll feel better if you can calm down."

"Don't *tell* me that! Everyone says I'm too worried and I get excited over nothing, but this isn't nothing! It's *real*."

"Yes, it's real. But you fighting us now isn't going to help anyone."

A high keening sound burst out of Cady. She wasn't even aware of making it—it was just as if the ball of pain that was always sitting in her chest suddenly burst.

Gabe stepped back, as if the mere sound had driven him away. "Cady, stop and breathe. Don't you want to know what's happening?"

"I don't care! I don't c—" She choked on the word, her breathing uneven, no longer in time with her heart. "I —"

She tried to inhale, and couldn't. Black spots started to edge into her vision, and the voices around her became a babble. Gabe was saying something to her, but she couldn't make it out, and didn't want to.

Her heart was pounding, and she could hear nothing but the blood rushing through her body. Something was very, very wrong and it was all his fault. Cady was going to die at last. After all this, all the days and weeks and months of hiding from everything that might get her, she finally went out into the world, and the world was going to kill her.

As she thrashed against the arms attempting to grab her, Cady saw Judith clearly. She was holding something in her hand—a cloth? It was soaked in something pungent. Judith mouthed the word *sorry* and clapped it over

Cady's face.

She gasped, choking, and the black spots in her vision expanded, each dot growing and growing into a great dark flower. They covered everything and the rushing sound of blood became a wind that swept her away to nowhere, nowhere at all.

♑

GABE HELD CADY TIGHT. JUDITH'S quick thinking with the sedative-soaked cloth sent Cady into unconsciousness, interrupting the spiral of her irregular breathing and her panic-induced violent reactions.

"Jesus, Mary, and Joseph," Judith said softly, once he'd lowered Cady's limp body to the floor of the kitchen. "I've never seen anything like that before."

"Her attacks ain't always like that, are they?" Jem asked.

"No. This was worse." Gabe pushed the dark hair out of Cady's face. The color in her cheeks was too hectically red, and he didn't like the sound in her throat as she wheezed in and out. But at least she was breathing.

Judith picked up Cady's wrist and laid her fingers over the pulse point for a long moment, when everyone seemed to hold still.

"Very fast," Judith said at last. "But steadying. We should get her into bed."

"I'll take her," Gabe said. He bent to pick her up, fighting off the disturbing feeling of repetition. Was he destined to always gather a helpless Cady in his arms?

Judith and Bond cleared the way to Cady's room, lighting enough candles and opening doors along the way. Gabe put her into the rumpled bed, where she flinched and twisted as if having nightmares. It killed him to see her like that.

The maids set about making Cady more comfortable, adjusting her blankets and washing her forehead with cool water.

Then Cady said something.

Judith leaned forward eagerly. "My lady? Are you awake?"

"Get him out of here," Cady whispered, her eyes on Gabe.

Bond looked over her shoulder. "Might be best, sir. She needs to be calm, and you don't make her calm."

Gabe wanted to object. He should be near Cady, especially now when she was so weak. But her eyes held so much anger that he knew any attempt to go closer could result in another attack.

"I'm going," he said. "Take care of her."

Downstairs, he took his frustration out on Rook. "You checked and she was fast asleep, huh."

"I checked and there was no sound from her room and it was half three," the boy noted. "What should I have thought?"

Gabe bit back a retort. This whole mess was his fault. Gathering everyone, knowing Cady was close by. He told Rook that he would go and get some sleep and return later to help set things right with Cady.

"You going to sleep in a church, sir? 'Cause you're going to need a miracle to carry that off."

With those heartening words, Gabe walked out into the darkness.

* * * *

Cady had never suffered such bad dreams as the night before. She dreamed she'd walked downstairs and directly into a strange party, except that her new servants were the guests and Gabe was the host and the party was in the kitchen and they were all plotting against her...

She opened her eyes to see Bond sitting on a chair not far away from the bed, not watching Cady but obviously watching *over* Cady.

"What time is it?" Cady asked.

Bond looked over, her expression wary and concerned. "About half past eight, my lady."

"Where is he?" She didn't bother to say who. She didn't have to.

"He left, but he'll come back."

"If he does, then don't let him in."

Bond's eyes dropped. "As you say."

"I'm serious, Bond. I know you all take orders from him, but not this time. Oh, and he needs to surrender the key I gave him."

"Yes, my lady."

Oscar chose this moment to jump up onto the bed, giving Cady a little jolt of surprise. But the cat then nuzzled her and curled up in the hollow made by her torso and her tucked up legs.

"I don't know why I bother," Cady said then, petting the cat. "It's not as if I was ever in control while he's around. He planned every step of this, didn't he? Coming to Calderwood, getting me to London, place all of you here to keep an eye on me..."

"He's worried about you, my lady. He doesn't want you to be hurt."

"Oh? Then he should stay away himself." Cady flipped over to her other side, denying Bond the view of her face, which was going to be streaked with tears in a moment. "There's not even any point in firing all of you, is there?"

"No, my lady. We're here for a reason, and we're not

leaving."

"Because you're—what was the word?—disreputable?"

"That's what we call ourselves," she said.

"What does it mean?"

"Well, several years ago, in another house in this city, a lady discovered that one of her servants had a friend with an unfortunate past—a criminal record that would have made it impossible to find work in a respectable house, or really anywhere. But this lady was rather unusual, and she decided to take the chance on this person. And a while later, another opening came up and she hired someone they knew who was in a similar bad way. After a few years, nearly every servant in her house was a person of disreputable background. But because they were also trusted by their companions and had the will to do right, the lady never suffered by it. And in time, her servants' skills often turned out quite helpful to her."

"You worked for this lady?"

"I did, after escaping a charge of theft and probable transportation to Australia."

"Were you guilty?"

"Of course, not just of that theft but a hundred more. I've got an eye for jewels, and a gift for climbing."

Cady turned back over, looking at Bond with new eyes. "Really?"

"Indeed, my lady. But I'm *also* good at sewing and hair, so when I got the chance to be a lady's maid, I took it."

"And Jem?"

"Pickpocketing, mostly."

"Judith?"

"Petty theft, counterfeiting coins, and inciting riot."

"Inciting riot? Really?"

"She works with the abolitionists and sometimes the demonstrations grow lively. The law calls it a riot, and who's to stop them from saying so?"

"Minnie?"

"Ah, she ran a fortune-telling scam with a partner where she kept the mark's attention on her whilst her partner robbed them blind."

"And Cook?"

"Oh, she's actually clean. Just a cook."

"I see." Cady thought about it, and decided that she was either too tired to be alarmed, or that the moment for alarm was long since past. "And what's the Zodiac?"

"Er, best that Mr Courtenay explains that, my lady."

"Well, Mr Courtenay isn't getting within hundred paces of me again, so why don't you do it."

Bond swallowed nervously. "It's…um…restricted."

Cady gave her a disgusted look. "Is it some criminal gang attempting to gather all the poison in England for some nefarious purpose?"

"Of course not! It's part of the govern—" Bond stopped, then sighed. "Yes, fine, I'll tell you."

So that was how Cady learned of the Zodiac, and how Gabe was an agent of it, complete with a code name and a mission and host of lies to tell Cady to gain her confidence.

"How many deaths?" Cady asked at one point, when Bond was explaining the details.

"Up to eight now, I believe."

"Oh, my Lord. And his friend was just one of them."

"Well, Parrish wasn't a friend. He was another agent who died as he was also tracking down the killer."

"Wait, Gabe *said* he was a friend."

"He said what he thought would make you sympathetic. I don't think Mr Courtenay has many friends."

"Can't imagine why. And what else did he lie about in terms of this whole matter?"

Bond shrugged. "I wasn't there for the first half, at your estate. But when dealing with spies, it's best to assume they're lying about everything unless they have to tell the truth because they'll get caught otherwise. Even when they do tell the truth, it's because they think it will be useful. I'm sorry you had to find out this way, my lady. He would have preferred you never knew, of course."

"Oh, I'm sure of *that*. He really thought I was the killer, didn't he?"

"At first…possibly," Bond said. "When he gave us our instructions, however, he'd decided you couldn't have done it, not least because you were never in London. But he knows you're involved, so we're to keep you safe."

"Safe from what?"

"The real killer?"

"He talked about Trevor. He thinks Trevor did it. He thinks Trevor still has the poison with him and he's running about London like a madman, randomly poisoning people."

"Not randomly."

"Is that supposed to make me feel better?" Cady snapped. "My brother isn't evil!"

"As you say, my lady."

There was a soft knock at the door, and Minnie stepped in. "Pardon me, but Mr Courtenay is here, my lady."

"I am not at home."

"He's very anxious to talk to you."

"I expect so, but I remain not at home. In fact, you can tell him that I will not be at home for the next thousand years. He can take his stupid spying and secret investigations and do whatever he likes on his own."

Minnie nodded uncertainly. "Er, yes, my lady."

"Use those exact words! And tell him he's a bad gardener."

"*Ohhh.* Yes, my lady." Minnie closed the door, looking as if she'd been the one insulted.

Bond stood up. "Shall I fetch your breakfast?"

"I don't care." Cady rolled back onto her side, hiding from the world. The pain of Gabe's deception was still raw, and even with Bond filling in some details, she didn't know how she'd been so silly and naive. She'd given her whole heart to Gabe, and he'd just been playing a part.

But she was the one who had to live with herself now.

* * * *

Downstairs, Gabe did not take the news well.

"She said what?"

"Don't make me repeat it, sir." Minnie had tried to deliver the message in a flat, impersonal tone, but he heard all of Cady's rage in the words.

"Look, she's obviously distraught. I'll go up there and explain everything."

"You won't, sir. She's not ready to see anyone, and she's quite clear that she doesn't want to see you." For such a slender and sweet-looking woman, Minnie could be intimidating when she chose—plus, Gabe knew she usually had several small knives on her person and could do a lot of damage with them.

"She needs to be aware of certain things."

"Bond has already told her most of them. Why don't you work on your own and come back later?"

Gabe did that. He came back in the afternoon. Cady still wasn't at home.

He came back in the evening. Cady wasn't at home.

He stopped by Trevor's club, only to be told that his name was not on the list. He hadn't even known there *was* a list.

He came back to the town house the next morning. The same message awaited him.

That next night, when he decided to let himself in, Jem and Bond were waiting for him. Jem very politely relieved him of the key Cady had previously given, and Bond told him that there was a message for him…but it wasn't from Cady.

"Aries would like a word, sir. Tomorrow at four in the afternoon, at the usual location."

Gabe did not like the Disreputables knowing more than he did about his appointments, but he was too frustrated to object. All he wanted was to see Cady, to know she was physically recovering from her attack. And to hold her and tell her everything on his mind, so that she knew the whole truth, not the outdated facts and the smatterings of half-truths she's been given so far.

Denied the one thing he needed, Gabe was forced to work on his own, turning the clues he'd gathered over and over in his mind, trying to find the thing that was missing, the thing that didn't fit. He read over all his notes, from the very first moment Aries handed him the assignment.

Nothing. The words he wrote had been read over so many times that they didn't even look like words anymore. His brain refused to process them.

Frustrated, Gabe threw the journal across the room. It fluttered open and landed softly in the middle of the rug. He decided that he needed to get out and breathe some fresh air. Dressing in one of his usual, unremarkable outfits, he walked the streets, hoping that the movement would clear his head.

He walked for hours, his mood foul. The sky matched

his mood, but when rain started pelting down, it drove Gabe into a nearby tavern to wait it out.

He sat at a table facing the long counter. Since few men were drinking in the middle of the day, the counter was mostly clear and he could watch the barman working on the other side. When he wasn't drawing a beer for a customer, he either dried off glasses or performed other little tasks all necessary to the smooth operation of the tavern when the rush would come later as men left their work. Gabe sipped his drink slowly, brooding over the maddening aspects of his assignment, all the little details that refused to fit into a neat and tidy pattern pointing to the end.

The barman had started to decant some ruby-colored liquid from a large glass jug into a few smaller containers. He did it all expertly, without fuss or stress or a drop spilled, just a stream of claret falling, falling, falling. It was very graceful in a way, this transfer from one container to another, thanks to endless practice on the part of the barman. If only Gabe's job allowed for such a clean and simple process.

One of the tavern's workers replaced Gabe's empty glass with a full one. Gabe was so focused on his brooding that he didn't even see who it was, he just grunted an acknowledgment and seized on the new glass. God bless a barkeep who kept the drinks coming.

He took a sip, the alcohol setting up a warm burn in his throat. Did the victims know they were drinking poison when they sipped from the tainted glass? Did they taste even a hint of the death that was waiting for them?

At least they wouldn't have suffered. Cady had explained that a fatal dose of the "fear-stealer" would have been like falling asleep. At worst, some of the victims, like Parrish, might have been aware of an unnatural sluggishness, an inability to rise and take action which might have been torture in its own way. But mostly all fell to sleep, and then to a gentle death. There were worse ways to go. On a battlefield, or in hospital afterward, for those who weren't lucky enough to die quickly in the fight.

Had Parrish fought? Gabe never asked Aries about the man's background. He should have. It seemed like the thing one ought to know. Had Parrish known he was dying before the lassitude took him and it was too late to do anything about it, other than to write one word on one piece of paper?

Gabe frowned, remembering Cady's disquiet about that. Her questions. Why that word? Why write *any* word when you could have instead called for help? Why stop there, with "Calderwood"? Gabe would have kept writing until his hand went numb or his face slammed down on the desk, too tired to go on…

He frowned, thinking back. He'd read all about Pisces's death, how he was found with the note beside him on the floor of the study. His jaw twitched. Little things, out of place.

Across the way, the barman was decanting another liquor, this one a pale amber.

Suddenly, Gabe sat up straight, dizzy with the revelation. He swore under his breath.

Could it be so simple?

What if a few clues had been read wrong? A few things they had all known to be facts were not facts, but falsehoods.

It could fit. It could all fit, and he just needed to answer one question before he'd have the only answer he needed.

The name of the killer.

With a burst of energy, Gabe grabbed his hat and left

the tavern almost at a run.

He stumbled a bit, feeling suddenly clumsy and strange. He looked down, but there was nothing there he could have tripped on.

He kept walking, but fell again, this time all the way to the street, spinning so he saw street, sky, street, sky, the halves of the world whirling into a single striped ball he was trapped inside.

"Help—" he got out, and then someone seized him by the arm.

"I've got you."

♑

CADY FELT LIKE SHE WAS in hell since hearing the damning words from Gabe's own mouth when she found him holding court in her own kitchen. Everything he'd told her was a lie, and he'd withheld crucial facts about the poisonings to get her to trust his version of events so she'd give him information.

Naturally, she refused to speak to him again. She sensed that her disreputable servants would have preferred it otherwise, but they said nothing. Days passed, and though she knew he called more than once, the order stood. Then he stopped calling, and she tried not to mind.

Trevor visited once or twice as well; she kept the full news of Gabe's betrayal from him, only informing him that it would be best not to receive him for a while. With his characteristic flair for the dramatic, Trevor declared that he'd bar every door to Gabe and never see him again.

"As far as I'm concerned, he can live at the bottom of a well from now on." Trevor laughed. "Ugh, how damp and slimy would that be? Where do you keep the wine, Cady dear? I feel the need for a drink."

Mr Addison also called at the house, bringing a bouquet of gorgeous white roses and the news that he'd be returning to Kent shortly.

"These are lovely," Cady said sincerely, smelling the flowers.

"I hoped you'd like them. A rare variety—Cecily

White. Very old, though I don't know the origin of it. I find the hue to be particularly pure. So many whites can be yellowish in tone, or fade too quickly. But this one seems to shine from within. I thought of you, my lady."

"That's very sweet," she said. "I do wish you weren't leaving London. I'll miss your company."

He looked pleased. "When you return to Calderwood, please send word and we shall arrange a small gathering to celebrate."

"That sounds like just what I need."

"Are you quite happy, dear Cady? Forgive my boldness, but you appear a little sad."

"A little, yes. But no feeling lasts forever. I will be fine, Mr Addison."

He nodded, though the answer still seemed to trouble him. "Well, I must be off. Much to do before I ride home. I hope to see you very soon. Good day, my lady."

After he left, Cady put the roses in a crystal vase and placed it in the parlor. That's where she was in the evening, quietly reading a journal, when a knock came at the front door.

She frowned, looking up at the clock. In no circumstances could it be considered a visiting hour. Was it Gabe? Perhaps she could see him again. Part of her needed to. "Rook?" she called, seeing the boy cross the foyer. "If that's Mr Courtenay…"

"It's not," he said, sounding upset.

He opened the door, and Cady heard two unfamiliar voices. Then Rook showed a couple to the parlor door.

"My lady, this gentleman and lady must speak with you. It's very important."

Cady had stood up by then, curiosity unfurling in her belly. "Have a seat, I suppose?"

The lady walked to her first. "It's very good of you to

see us. I am Miss Chattan, and this is Mr Neville."

"How do you do?" Cady spoke the phrase far more hesitantly than usual. The woman looked familiar… "You were at Viscount Nyle's party! In the hallway."

"Good memory, my lady," she said with a smile.

"Lady Arcadia…is it still Lady Arcadia, or has the Crown Office rendered its opinion?" the man asked. He didn't sit until Cady and Miss Chattan both did.

"It hasn't…how do you know about that? Who are you?"

"For simplicity, let's say that we are the Zodiac," he replied. "I'm annoyed that you are aware of that name, my lady, but we can't very well just wish it otherwise."

"Are you here because I learned that Gabe works for you? I can't possibly see what it matters. He already got everything he could have wanted out of me." She couldn't hide the bitterness in her voice, nor did she miss a flash of something in Miss Chattan's eyes. Sympathy?

"No, it's not that. Not exactly," Chattan said. "Do you remember the last things he said regarding the poison, or his theories about who had it?"

Cady rolled her eyes. "No! I don't understand what this is about. Does he think I still have the clephobine I synthesized before? Or was he staying close to me in case I made more, and that's why he's upset I won't see him?"

"I'm not sure," the man said. "He didn't tell us everything either."

"Is that why you're here? To get me to tell you because Gabe won't talk?"

"We're here because Gabe is missing."

"What does that mean?" Cady asked, not sure she could handle much more news related to Gabe's activities.

Chattan leaned forward. "It means we can't locate him."

"I am very sorry to hear that you've misplaced your spy. But the last time I saw Gabe, I told him that I never wanted to see him again. So I doubt you'll find him around here."

The man shook his head. "No, we don't think you know where he is. Rather, we were hoping you might help us track him…or who took him."

"Took him?" Cady shook her head. "*Now* what are you saying? Gabe is not the type to be taken anywhere. Are you implying he was kidnapped?"

"Yes." The lady looked steadily at Cady. "That's exactly what we think. In his rooms, we found this." She slid a card along the low table.

Cady picked it up and read it. "*Et in Arcadia ego.*" She looked up angrily. "This is a joke. A very poor joke. I overheard what Gabe was saying about the poisoning, that a card like this was left at each one. That would mean… he's dead."

Her heart stuttered once as she said the words, and she looked away, dropping the card back on the polished wooden surface.

"Not dead," Miss Chattan said. "Not yet. There's no body. If he were just killed like all the others, why would the body be missing?"

"I don't know! I'm not the insane killer, despite what you all think!"

"Gabe realized straightaway that you couldn't be a killer. He told us in one of his first reports that our initial assumption was wrong."

"Only because I hadn't left the estate in months."

"Well, he mentioned that. But he also said it would be out of character for you. That you'd never countenance any violence, let alone murder. And he's an excellent judge of character. He has to be."

"But if he trusted me, then why didn't he tell me the truth of what he was doing?"

"He's a very cautious man—he doesn't say all of what he's really thinking to anyone. He's very slow to trust. I don't think he trusts *us* and we've worked together for years."

"He's not dead," Cady whispered. "He can't be dead."

"Then help us find him before it's too late."

* * * *

Gabe woke up in darkness, with a sick taste in his mouth. His tongue was thick with dryness, and he could barely swallow.

He was sitting in a chair. Why was he sitting? Gabe moved to stand up, and abruptly found himself snapped back to his original position. He was stuck to the chair somehow.

Puzzled, he lifted his arm and got about as far as shoulder height before he felt resistance and heard a clinking sound.

He was *chained* to the chair.

Gabe thrashed out, and his limbs all jerked to a stop when the chains extended to their complete length of a foot or so.

Both arms, both feet were secured to the chair, which itself seemed to be bolted down. Gabe groaned. What the hell was going on? He tried to shake out the fog in his brain. How long had he been unconscious? And what happened just before? His memories were cracked and hazy—more like a dream than a recollection of real events.

"Hello?" he called out. "Where am I?"

Silence. Gabe peered around, trying to get some clue

of where he was. The air was cool and clammy. Was he underground? The idea of being entombed came to him, and he couldn't stop a shudder. How big was this space he was trapped in? It felt very narrow. Was he going to suffocate before someone came back to deal with him?

"Hello? Who's here? Answer me, damn it!"

"Such language, Mr Courtenay," a soft voice chided.

Gabe went still. Someone was here. But he could see nothing in the darkness. "Where are you? Where are we?"

"We're in a very safe place. So safe you'll never be found."

"Why?" he asked.

"You know why. You were getting too close to the truth, and toying with things you had no business being near. I find that inconvenient."

"Who are you?" he demanded, his voice cracking as he spoke.

"You know who I am. *Et in Arcadia ego*."

"You're Death?"

"Sometimes." The shadowed figure stepped forward, but even so Gabe couldn't discern anything about the face or form. The figure reached out and placed a glass bottle on the floor, several feet away.

"I can't reach that," Gabe said, hating the pleading tone in his voice.

"Want me to move it closer? Then answer a few simple questions. Every correct answer brings the water nearer."

"Fine. Anything. What do you want to know?"

"Why are you looking for the person using the clephobine?"

"Because they're a murderer."

The bottle was dragged few inches further away. "No, no, Mr Courtenay. That's not the right answer. But perhaps you didn't understand the question. Why are *you* looking? Something started you on the trail. Tell me who or what it was."

Gabe took a few breaths, trying not to the think about the water when it was the only thing he could think about. "A friend died. Killed. I wanted to know why."

The bottle was replaced in the original position. "Which friend?"

"Lewelleyn Parrish."

"Ah. Yes."

"Did you kill him?" Gabe asked.

"I'm asking the questions. You're answering them. Now, you learned about Calderwood and Arcadia Osbourne. What did you tell her about your search?"

"At first, nothing. I didn't want to risk her knowing that I knew."

The bottle moved closer. "Go on."

"She must have got suspicious. One day she tricked me, gave me some tea that was drugged with something that made me tell the truth. I couldn't lie, I didn't even want to lie. That was the worst part."

"Indeed?" The voice sounded intrigued, alert. "What did she call it?"

Gabe shook his head. "I don't remember. I wasn't myself that night. Don't punish me for that one, I truly don't remember."

The bottle was moved a few inches toward him, and the voice said sympathetically, "I understand, Mr Courtenay. Lady Arcadia is a very determined woman at times."

"How did you get me here?" Gabe asked. "Drugged me?"

"Naturally. A benefit of being close to Arcadia is that one is also close to a vast selection of medicines and other chemicals. I used a strong sedative to knock you out so that I could relocate you."

His captor was disguising his voice, so Gabe was careful not to hint that he'd guessed his identity. The only thing keeping Gabe alive—for now—was that he was supposedly unaware of who he was speaking to.

"Where are we?" Gabe tried again. "London?"

"We're far from London. I believe I said I'd be asking the questions, Mr Court. In your interactions with Arcadia, did she mention any other sources of clephobine? Anyone else who knows how to make it?"

"No. She's the only one in England. There must be someone in America who can, but she had no names."

"Good. I certainly wouldn't like others to be dabbling with it. A pleasure speaking with you. You've earned a drink. But don't move a muscle—or I'll take it with me when I leave."

Gabe held still, not sure what move to make.

His captor moved closer to push the bottle within range. As he did so, Gabe caught a whiff of a different scent, something so far from the musty dank air of this dark place. Something full and fresh…even voluptuous.

The bottle was tantalizingly close.

"Is this drugged?" Gabe asked suddenly as the figure withdrew a few steps, out of any possible attack range. Not that Gabe was in any state to do something physical.

"Perhaps. You'll drink it all the same. Men are predictable in the end. They have primal needs: sleep, shelter, food…water. Like any living thing, the body shrivels and dies without water."

"Why are you doing this to me?"

"None of this would be happening if you'd simply minded your own business and never come to Arcadia."

The figure left, and Gabe was alone once more. He told himself that he wouldn't drink the water. He was stronger than that. He could resist.

He reached for the bottle, just to know that he could get it. His fingers grazed the glass. No. He would outwait this monster. Gabe was a trained agent, a soldier who'd been through far worse. He had to keep his mind clear.

Time passed. An hour? Two hours? Maybe only a few minutes. There was only a sliver of light coming from far above him. Daylight? Fire? He had no idea. God, he was thirsty.

Soon enough the Zodiac would come for him. The Disreputables would figure out what happened, they were all smart, they'd know what to do. Cady would help…

Cady hates me now. Why would she help? Did she even know he was gone? Why would she know? After all, she never wanted to see him again and now she never would.

A drop of condensation ran down the side of the bottle and hit the floor, turning the rough stone a darker, truer shade. Gabe wanted that drop back. He wanted everything back.

"Christ help me." It wasn't a prayer, or maybe it was. Gabe was past caring. He seized the bottle and raised it to his lips.

* * * *

"*Et in Arcadia ego.*" Cady repeated the phrase over and over, looking at the card found in Gabe's rooms and, as she'd only recently learned, at all the previous murders. "Ugh! What can it mean?"

"Perhaps it's a code?" Bond asked from where she sat. She, along with the rest of the newly revealed Disreputables, had joined Cady in the parlor after her strange guests left, and it was now very late.

Whatever their background, they appeared eager to help locate Gabriel Courtenay, and Cady would take help from any quarter. It wasn't about being with him again—she told herself that she didn't want that—but merely about preventing another death.

"No, no," Cady replied to Bond. "It's Latin. It's a very famous line from a piece of art by Poussin. It means *I am even in Arcadia*."

"Oh, so you do know what it means."

"I know what it means *usually*, when we're talking about the painting it comes from."

"What's the painting? Maybe there's a clue there."

"It's a pastoral scene, with a few shepherds and shepherdesses of Arcadia—which is like an earthly paradise, where everything is lovely and simple and happy. They're gathered around a tomb, and on the tomb this line is carved, and they're all marveling at it, because what it means is that even in this wonderful place, this eternal summer land, Death is there. No one can escape death. The whole painting exists to remind the viewer that they are mortal."

"How does that help us?" Bond asked, frowning at Jem, who just shrugged helplessly.

Trevor walked in, dressed in his usual impeccable manner, though his face had a tired appearance and there were lines around his eyes. "Sorry, I had some business that took far too long today. I got your message, Cady. What's going on?"

She quickly filled him in on the most relevant facts, leaving him wide-eyed. "I say, that's incredible. And the phrase from that painting Mama liked is all we've got for a clue?"

"If you can call it a clue," Cady replied. "It's the most unfair type of word puzzle. There's nothing to go on."

"I could find a reproduction of the Poussin painting," Trevor offered. "Maybe there's an image in it that might help."

"I know the painting by heart," Cady said. "I think the significant thing is the phrase, and the fact that I was named for it."

"But why is it the same phrase as all the men who were killed...I mean, we're assuming Gabe is still alive, aren't we?" Trevor looked anxious until Cady nodded.

Jem stood up and started walking around the room. "Right, let's all think about what we do know. Courtenay was here in London on Tuesday. Lady Arcadia last saw him Friday night, but he called the next two days, and I spoke to him late Tuesday. Anyone see him after that? Or received a message from him, or something?"

Cady looked around the room, and saw only shaking heads. She offered, "The couple that came here and told me he was missing said he didn't arrive at a meeting they'd scheduled. That's what first alerted them. He'd never miss such a meeting without sending word."

"So sometime between morning and four in the afternoon on that day, he went missing." Jem frowned. "And all the hospitals and morgues and such have been checked?"

"Aye," said Rook. "Me and the other Disreputables who could be spared moved through the city starting that evening. None of the magistrates have anything to share, and Bow Street's the same. No unknown patients matching his description at hospitals. No bodies matching his description at the morgues or medical schools."

"Ugh," Trevor muttered at the image of dissection.

"Sorry, sir," Rook added politely. "But it happens."

"We'll keep asking around," Jem told Cady. "We're good at that. Someone will pick up his trail and we'll learn more."

"What I don't understand is how it could happen in the first place," Cady said. "Gabe—I mean Mr Courtenay is some sort of agent trained in espionage and investigation and all those sorts of things. And yet he's kidnapped out of the blue?"

Jem sighed, looking rather ragged. "Not out of the blue—the killer must have realized that he was getting close and moved to stop him from reporting what he knew."

"But Gabe is so smart!" she objected.

"Smart men can still make mistakes," Trevor pointed out. "Especially if he was distracted or not thinking straight."

Cady winced. Their spectacular fight and her reaction to learning the truth would certainly affect his thinking.

"Look, we can't do much more now," Bond said. "We need to gather more information outside of this house. I suggest we all get some rest and start early. Everyone on their own initiative. Go out, use your contacts, pick up what you can. We'll meet back here and put what we've learned together. Someone will have a success, and that will point us in the right direction."

"Well said, love," Jem agreed.

The Disreputables filtered out of the room, leaving only Cady and Trevor.

"It's not your fault, Cady," Trevor said quietly. He was watching her, his eyes intent.

"It feels like it is. A poison I synthesized. My name on all the cards."

"That's just a coincidence."

Cady shot him a look. "Oh, really? A coincidence that the killer used a quote with the word *Arcadia*? They wanted to make me look like I'm responsible for everything."

Trevor approached her, his face serious. "My poor, poor Cady. That man broke your heart, and I won't stand for it. Come sit by me and we'll have it all out. You can tell me every last thing he told you, and I'll listen and I won't interrupt once."

Cady gave him a tremulous smile. "Not once?"

"Maybe once. Or twice. But that's the limit. Now come and sit."

She did so, and he offered her a teacup already filled with a golden-hued tea smelling of sweet florals.

"Now drink up," he said warmly, placing the cup and saucer in her hands. "It's exactly what you need."

* * * *

Gabe didn't know how many days had passed since he took the drink offered to him. He'd drifted in and out of dreams and nightmares. He'd been back in France, battling soldiers who turned into long, whipping vines of dark green that curled around his wrists and ankles until he couldn't run. He tripped and fell on his face, only to hear his older brother Gerald laughing. *Bad penny, Gabe. But you're not even worth that much.*

He spun about, finding Cady standing there, smiling at him. She held a glass in her hands and offered it to him. *Drink it down. I made it just for you.*

So he drank it down, and it burned. And Cady's voice changed, lowering into another. *What were you thinking, getting close to her? You don't deserve her.*

"You don't deserve to even look at her, understand?"

"Just a job," Gabe mumbled, his words malformed by the thickness of his tongue.

"She's family, you miserable bastard. What did you do

to her? Why are you hounding her?"

"Not…hounding…" Gabe got no further before losing his voice to a dry cough.

"Drink," his captor ordered, grabbing Gabe's hair to tip his head up enough to pour some liquid into his mouth. Gabe tried to spit it out, but the survival instinct was too strong. His stomach was clenching with the need to have something, anything, and his thirst was even stronger.

"You're pathetic." The voice sounded like Gerald.

Gabe could barely open his eyes. "Happy birthday," he got out, before losing consciousness.

The next round of dreams were worse, twisting him into a dead tree with no bark and only crows for company. Gabe kept calling out for help but the crows drowned his calls in raucous squawking. Then a man walked toward him, a stranger.

You learned nothing, did you, the man said. *I gave my life and all the clues I gathered and you just left it all to rot. Because you forgot what you were. A Sign.*

Gabe realized this was Lewellyn Parrish, the previous agent. The man looked at him and shook his head. *Pathetic*, he muttered. *A failure. The Zodiac is well rid of you.*

Parrish began piling up loose twigs and branches near what remained of Gabe's feet. Gabe pleaded for release, but Parrish only sighed in disappointment. It was then that Gabe noticed Parrish's hands were bones.

Parrish lit the pyre, and flames leapt around Gabe, growing higher and hotter. Gabe screamed in pain, but there was no relief. Just heat and more heat, him burning in hell, forever.

♑

DESPITE RACKING HER BRAINS FOR hours and hours, Cady was no closer to learning what happened to Gabe, but she was much closer to losing her mind, because whenever she dozed or tried to sleep, she had dreams of Gabe trapped somewhere, calling for her, his voice full of pain.

By late in the afternoon on Thursday, the Disreputables had split up and regathered, bearing a few more pieces of information each time, chief of which was on the day of Gabe's disappearance, a man of Gabe's description had been seen leaving a tavern close to his own home. Though the barmaid swore he'd been nursing one drink for an hour, he moved like a dead drunk in the street, only to be picked up by a well-dressed gentleman who hauled him into a waiting carriage.

"What does well-dressed mean?" Trevor demanded.

"A gentleman," Jem clarified. "Not one of the working class but also not higher."

"Perfect—he could be anyone." Trevor slumped back in his seat.

"So we've got our kidnapper, who's probably also the killer," Jem said. "My lady, any further thoughts on that phrase, or what it might mean as a message on the card?"

"No. I'm sorry. I've tried to think, but I'm barely sleeping and it's all just unreal."

There was a knock at the door. Rook stood, but Trevor put a hand out. "I'll answer it. I need to stretch my legs."

Her brother left the room, but returned a few minutes later, his expression excited. "That was a messenger, but he couldn't say who paid for the message. He just got a name and street direction, plus the fee. Cady, this is for you."

She took the folded message and opened it. "It's unsigned, but I think…I think it's the kidnapper."

"What's it say?" Jem asked.

"*Close to your heart, burning in hell.*"

"Now that's a clue! What's close to your heart, my lady?"

"My ribs. My lungs. This bodice. This necklace." Cady pulled the chain out to reveal the necklace's pendant. "But I've owned this for years and years. What's that got to do with anything?"

"I don't think it means your actual heart, my lady," Lucy said. "What do you care about? What do you love?"

"I…I don't know. I love plants and gardens."

The maid rolled her eyes. "No, no, no. That's not what I meant, and you know it. Name something really dear to you."

"Um…Trevor."

"Why thank you," her brother said from where he sat. "But I doubt that's what the killer means. Though perhaps it is. I will certainly burn in hell, if such a place exists."

Bond sighed. "My lady, you must take a moment and *think*. Tell us what you care about most in the world."

"I love Calderwood," Cady admitted. "It's my home and I can't imagine living anywhere else."

"That's a good start. Could it be a hint that you need to return to Calderwood?"

"Do you suppose whoever it is plans to set it on fire?" Trevor asked nervously.

"They had better *not*," Cady snapped. "But anyway,

even if they did, the walls of the house are pure stone at least a foot thick. Even if they tried to set the gardens ablaze, they'd have to start again with each wall. They're natural firebreaks."

"Anyway, it's not exactly burning in hell, is it?" Trevor noted. "It would be burning in Kent, which just hasn't got the same ring to it."

"So not the house or grounds," Bond mused. "What then? Think, my lady. What would break your heart if you lost it?"

Cady swallowed against the sudden lump in her throat, and tears pricked at her eyes. "I've already lost the one thing I thought I loved."

Minnie stood up. "It's time for a meal. My mother always says that empty stomachs stop all thought."

Cady was unwilling to interrupt the discussions, so they all went to the kitchens and sat at the big, rough-hewn table for the servants. Trevor looked around, amazed at this part of the house he hadn't seen since he was a little boy. As they ate the food, Cady kept prodding everyone to say what was on their mind, in the hopes of inspiration.

I am also in Arcadia...

What was close to Cady's heart? Not Gabe, not any longer, not since she learned the truth about him. Trevor, her brother, was of course close to her heart...but Trevor was with her, alive and well, so that didn't make sense as a clue. And who had sent the clue? Was it even meant to help her, or was it merely a taunt?

"This is delicious," Trevor said at one point, holding up a morsel of food. "What's this sauce?"

"My mother adapted it from an old family recipe," Minnie said. "It's a reduction of plums with a little wine. We can find plums in the city markets, but I imagine it would be difficult in the country, except when they're in season."

"They were always in season at Calderwood," Cady said absently. "Thanks to the glasshouse with the hot walls."

Trevor wrinkled his nose. "I never liked that part of the gardens. I mean, I loved getting plums and currants in midwinter, but I just never felt good about the way that room heated up. You'd walk in and be sweltering like you were roasting in the sixth circle of hell, with the sun beaming in from the glass top to those bricks radiating heat from the inside. Never understood how that worked anyway. Seemed like magic."

"There are flues running through the walls, and they pull hot air in from the coal furnace in the…center…" Cady trailed off, a new thought striking her like a thunderbolt. "Did you say hell?"

Trevor looked over. "The sixth circle of hell, yes. That's the hot one, according to Dante."

Close to your heart, burning in hell. Cady jumped up from her seat. "Trev, it's the hot walls!"

"The what?" he asked blankly. They were all staring at her.

"I'm not going crazy! Think about it! He's taken something close to my heart, who also happens to be the person investigating his crimes—Gabe. And he's hidden him somewhere that's like burning in hell—the walled-off space where the workers used to shovel coal into the furnace to heat all those glasshouses. Part of the building collapsed and it went unused for years, but the space is still there, like a secret set of passages and rooms right in the middle of Calderwood!"

"You mean to say that this killer is luring you back to your very own home?" Trevor asked skeptically.

"Where else would be less suspected? It's genius, actually."

"Cady, you can't possibly be serious. If someone was skulking around Calderwood, the servants there would know!"

"The few we've got left?" Cady countered. "They're working day to night on their own tasks and barely have time to glance outside. No, I think that the killer would be perfectly safe so long as he didn't move in broad daylight. Remember, he doesn't have to go into the main house at all. He can access that area through the gardens."

"But the walled gardens all have locked gates."

"I suspect those locks have been broken." She turned to Bond. "Pack some things for me, just what I'll need in the carriage back to Kent."

"You're not going alone," Trevor said, standing up. "I'm coming too. Be absolutely embarrassing if my sister had all the fun."

"Aye, and you'll have Jem and me and Rook as well," Bond announced.

"Bring only what we need," Cady said, already moving. "I'm not waiting for *anyone*."

* * * *

"Ah, I see that you're in need of a wash," his captor said. "Rather disgusting, the minutiae of human existence."

"Feeling fine, all the time," Gabe responded, his voice slurring. His mind was not operating well, and that line seemed awfully funny. Though he hung his head, too tired to look up, he laughed at his own absurdity.

"Solitude is getting to you already, is it? After only a few days. I always thought this place would make a splendid oubliette, but I must say I'm impressed by how quickly it's broken you."

"I'm not broken."

His captor sighed. "Says the man who's tied to a chair, covered in soot, and slowly starving to death. No food or sunlight or hope of rescue. If you're not broken yet, you will be soon."

"I'll outlast you."

"Poor man, last to see the truth. I even encouraged some of your allies, offering help to find you. Alas, I think it will come too late."

"Too late, too late, will be the cry…" Gabe wasn't sure if he was awake or dreaming.

"I may have to adjust the dosage if I ever need to do this again," his captor said. "I'll come back to check on you later, see if you're sane or dead or somewhere in between. Good day."

"Don't leave me!" Gabe yelled suddenly, the reality of being left alone in the near dark hitting him again. "Where are you going? Don't leave me here!"

"Don't yell, Mr Court. It's unbecoming of a gentleman."

Gabe winced as the door was slammed shut, and he was alone again.

♑

THEY REACHED CALDERWOOD WHEN THE sun was just setting. Jem had driven a small, light carriage with a team of four horses, instead of the usual two (Cady didn't ask how he'd procured it). And the weight was lightened further by having no luggage at all—it was just Cady, Trevor, and Bond squeezed into the single seat, while Jem sat up front to drive, Rook next to him. The result was like flying across the fields and forests, everything moving too fast to properly see. Other drivers cursed them loudly, and Jem narrowly avoided a few collisions. Cady clamped her jaw shut to prevent her teeth from clattering together, and Trevor moaned that he'd never recover from the jarring in his bones.

But they got there, and that's what mattered.

Cady didn't want to wait a moment, but Bond and Martha joined forces to sit her down to drink some water and eat a few bites before she charged off into the gardens.

"We'll need lanterns," Cady told the flabbergasted Mr Rundle between bites. "Everyone should have one or two, so that we can leave a few at certain points."

"Where are we taking the lanterns?" he asked, still trying very hard to keep up with the information that kept pouring onto him.

"The passageway that accesses the hot walls and the furnace has two entry points: the far end of my glasshouses, and then another by the false ruin that's actually the trap door for the coal. A team ought to take shovels or picks and break apart the structure to widen the opening. Rook is probably skinny enough to drop down then and see what's below."

"And you, my lady?"

"I'll take Trevor and Bond and we'll go through the passage from the glasshouse to light the way."

However, when Cady and the others reached the doorway, they could get only a short way down the passage before it was blocked by rubble.

"This is strange. It wasn't like this before I left," Cady said.

Bond nudged the rubble with her foot, setting off a small avalanche. "That means you're right—someone has caused this to happen. My lord, go find Rundle and ask him for more shovels. We need to clear this enough to crawl through."

"Crawl?" he asked, looking down at his outfit.

"Trevor! Go!" Cady shouted. Her brother fled.

While they waited for his return, Cady remembered that she had a shovel and trowel in her little work shed and the women quickly retrieved them. Trevor returned soon afterward with additional tools and added to the army. They set to work, kicking up clouds of dust and sending pebbles flying in all directions. At one point, Trevor sacrificed his cravat, tying it over his mouth and nose as a mask.

No matter how hard they worked, the wall of debris didn't seem to give way.

Cady took a breather, setting down her shovel as she gulped in air. She looked around, and realized her party had dwindled.

"Where is Trevor?"

"I don't know, my lady," Bond said. "He was here and then when I turned around he was gone. Maybe he got ill from all this noxious air and had to get back outside."

Cady frowned, disquieted by her brother's disappearance. She needed all the help she could get right now, and her allies were dropping like flies.

"Will you go out and around to check on Jem and his team? Maybe they've got through by now."

Bond nodded, promising to be back as soon as she knew what was happening.

But she did not come back.

Cady continued to claw at the rocks and dirt until she was able to clamber up to near the ceiling, where a faint push of air suggested a clearing. She held the lantern up and looked over. Cady saw some shadows moving against the light, and knew there were rats all through the passage.

"I can't, I can't," she whispered.

But if she didn't go now, and if Gabe was trapped down there, then he'd die.

She called out both ahead and behind, hoping someone, anyone would answer. Nothing.

She climbed over and pushed at the loose dirt, forcing her way through. On the other side, she crouched down, holding the lantern as if it were as precious as gold.

"I can't, I can't, I can't."

But there was no one else to do it.

Cady gripped the lantern tight in one hand, then stooped to grab a chunk of old masonry in the other. She took a breath, and stepped forward.

One step. Another. Another.

A rat burst out from cover and ran across the passageway, squeaking. Cady hurled the chunk at the rat. Naturally, she missed completely, but there was something helpful about taking action. And here she was, still alive. She picked up another rock and continued on, holding the lantern as far out in front of her as she could manage.

Cady kept going, sneaking around piles of rubble and once hitching up her skirts to climb over a spill of dirt from a wall collapsing in. She ran into a cobweb that covered her whole face like a veil. She swiped it away angrily before she even registered what it was. When she paused afterward to look for spiders, she realized she didn't care. Spiders, no matter how venomous or disgusting they might be, were not important right now. Only one thing mattered, and that was finding Gabe.

She turned a corner and almost ran into another rockfall, leaving only a narrow gap at the left side. Cady couldn't possibly get through the narrow gap while holding the lantern. She put it down on the floor of the passage and squeezed through the gap.

Darkness. Light oozed from the gap, but only fitfully, and after several paces, the gloom took over.

Biting back tears, Cady put her hand on the cold, damp wall and stepped forward. What had Trevor said back in London? *He can live down at the bottom of a well for all I care.* A cold, damp well.

And here she was.

Just as Cady had that thought, she felt something move ahead of her. She stopped, inhaling as she did.

The other thing stopped too, waiting, watchful. A rat? Something worse?

Or perhaps her only chance to find what she was looking for. Cady held her breath, and strained her ears as much as she could.

Yes, there was the warmth of a body, and the hiss of breathing too long contained.

Cady reached forward and grabbed the figure before

they could move away.

"Who's—" the person hissed in surprise.

She shouted back, "*Arcadia ego!*"

Cady's breath was ragged as she clung to the figure, afraid to let go lest she be lost, wandering in the darkness.

The figure wrested itself away from her grip, and there was a bright flare of sparks as they dragged a flint against the walls. A tiny flame leapt and danced, and a moment later it resolved into the steady glow of an oil-burning lamp, blocked by the silhouette Cady just accosted.

She didn't have time to let whoever it was recover. She launched herself at the figure, with no skill but more rage than she'd ever felt in her life. The figure pushed at her, but Cady clung to it, clamping her arms around the body and letting a scream rip though her.

The figure grunted, and made a different move, lifting Cady up and pushing hard to unlock her arms from his neck. Then in the lantern light, she saw a silvery flash. A knife.

Propelled by pure instinct, Cady darted backward into the shadows.

"Come here, I won't hurt you," the figure lied.

Cady saw the flash again, but as she took another step back, her foot struck a rock and made her fall with a cry and a clattering of stones.

The disturbance sent several rats dashing outward into the open space. Cady covered her head with her arms, shaking as one rat actually ran onto her and over.

The figure reacted with similar disgust, nervously slashing at the creatures with the hand that held the knife. His movements were wild, too wild, and as one particularly big rat danced around his feet, he tripped and went down. He yelled in pain, more pain than a mere fall should do.

"Cady, what happened?" he said, sounding uncertain. "Cady, come here."

"Why should I?" she asked, sure it was a trick.

"Cady, I need you. After all I've done for you, will you just stand there?"

"Turn around," Cady ordered.

The figure turned slowly on his side, and features became clear. A very familiar face indeed.

"Mr Addison," she whispered. With horror, she saw something dark at his front. Blood?

"Dear little Cady. What are you doing down here? I thought you were afraid of the dark."

"I am. But I was more afraid to fail."

"Fail? But there's nothing to fail at. Let's go back into the open air. There's nothing for you here. Come, Cady. I'm in trouble."

Yes he was. The more Cady looked, the more she saw how his face was creased in pain, how he held one hand tight to his torso. When he tripped, the knife must have twisted in, and he fell on top of the blade.

"I won't help you out till you tell me what I need to know. You took Gabe down here. Where is he?"

"Look for him yourself. Though by the time you find him, it will be too late."

Her heart seemed to stop beating. "What?"

"Fear-stealer, life-stealer, doesn't matter what you call it. I gave it to him, because he deserved it."

"You didn't." It wasn't possible! She was so close!

"I did, and since you're more concerned with him than me…" He took something from his pocket and brought to his mouth, then flung it away. Glass clinked in the darkness.

"Mr Addison, did you just take clephobine?" she gasped.

"Wound in my side…why wait to die horribly?"

"That wound can be treated! Listen, you don't have to die." Cady reached for her bag. "I have something that may work as an antidote!"

"I won't. And you try to force it down my throat, I'll spit it out." Addison gave her a little smile, and she saw blood at the corner of his mouth. Not a good sign. "Look at you, Arcadia. You've discovered a murderer, and your instinct is to save my life, when I've taken so many."

"It's wrong to take your own life!"

He shrugged. "A matter of debate, and let us be honest. I would be destined for a death sentence anyway."

"You don't know that! You might be…"

"Imprisoned for the rest of my life? Behind walls, with no gardens and no sunshine? That's not a life, Cady. And I am selfish enough to wish to choose my own exit. Though I do hope to make it back to the surface before I go. It's one thing to rest underground after you die, but you don't want to start there."

"*Where is Gabe?* Tell me and I'll make sure you get back above ground."

He sighed. "There's a small chamber about forty feet ahead. The door is locked, but I have the key." He used his free hand to wrest it out of a pocket and flung it weakly to the center of the space.

Cady snatched it up and hurried in the direction he pointed.

This passage was practically clear of debris, perhaps because it had never been used, or perhaps Addison cleaned it in preparation for his final act. Cady marched down it, holding the lantern in one hand.

The door loomed up suddenly on her right, and she put the key in the lock. It turned smoothly, and the door opened.

"Gabe?" she called softly, not sure if he'd be able to see her in the doorway, or be aware enough to know she was a friend and not an enemy.

Silence. Oh, God, was she too late? Cady stepped inside the room, glancing behind her down the passage to make sure Addison wasn't following.

"Gabe, where are—" She stopped talking, because she saw the prone figure of Gabe lying in front of a plain wooden chair, a few chains loose about the legs of it. His clothing was filthy and his shoes were completely gone.

She placed the lantern down gently and knelt beside him. "Gabe?"

He was so still, but she could see his chest moving ever so slightly. She reached out to touch his bare forearm.

He twitched at the contact, and his eyes flew open as he tried to push himself away from her. "Get back," he choked out.

"Gabe, it's me! Cady. Oh, my God, I never thought I'd find you. Gabe, look at me. It's Cady. I'm here."

"Cady?" he echoed. "What are you doing?"

"I'm rescuing you."

"He said I'd hallucinate more." Gabe turned his head away from her. "That's all you are."

"No, I'm real." She squeezed his shoulder, and he winced. "See? Hallucinations don't feel like anything. Can you stand? Let's get you out of here."

"I'm chained."

She looked at the chains, which were not connected to him at all, only the chair. "I think you used to be, but Addison must have undone them at some point, maybe because you were drugged and couldn't move much anymore."

"Cady, I'm dying."

Her heart went cold.

"He kept adding things to the water, but I had to drink it or I'd die. The last time I drank it, he said he put the fear-stealer in."

Cady put her hands on his face to force him to look at her. "You won't die, Gabe. Remember what I told you on the way to London? I have an antidote now."

"It's too late."

"If you're alive, it's not too late!" Cady wasn't certain her still-untested chemical would work. But she had to try.

She reached in and uncapped the bottle. "Here, Gabe. Drink this."

He pushed her hand away, his eyes unfocused. "No. It's a trick."

"It's not! Gabe, it's Cady! I'm here, and you need to drink it, before it's too late."

"No more. It was all tricks before. Sleep and dreams and forgetting. I'll never forget the things I did. But he tried to make me."

"Gabe, please." Cady held the bottle closer, but she was afraid he'd knock it out of her hand and send the liquid inside spilling out on the floor. "For me. Won't you please do it for me?" She felt like crying. Here she was, and it didn't matter?

"Just a sip," she begged. "Just a drop."

"No."

Then she got an idea. She poured the contents into her own mouth, then knelt down and kissed him.

He responded to that, probably out of pure instinct. Cady opened her mouth and let the liquid flow into his, bit by bit, hidden in the kiss.

He started to resist her, but she grabbed him, hands on each side of his face, and kept him there until she'd emptied all of herself to him.

"You tricked me again," he moaned as she pulled away.

"I'm returning the favor," she said.

"Let me die down here, Cady. I deserve it."

"Gabe, don't say that. In a moment, you'll have enough strength to get up and I will help you out of here."

But Gabe closed his eyes, and didn't answer. With a cry, Cady flung herself over him and tried to shake him back to consciousness.

That was how the others found her, shaking and crying over the still figure stretched on the ground.

♑

THE DISREPUTABLES GOT BOTH MEN and Cady safely out of the dank hallways of the heating shaft and the coal room, and back into the main house. Cady suffered another attack when it seemed that Gabe wouldn't wake up even after the dose of antidote, and Bond had to drag her away from his prone form.

After a while, Cady came out of the worst of it, only to find two huge dogs flanking the chair where she sat. With a shock, she realized she was sitting in the very armchair her father loved, and where he'd passed away. Now she was there, and Romulus and Remus were looking at her with the sort of devotion they'd always given him.

She reached out to scratch Romulus's ear. Deciding that he looked worried, she said, "It's all right, boy. I'm fine. I'll be just fine."

Bond walked into the room. "My lady, both Mr Addison and Mr Courtenay are awake. But I'm not sure that Mr Addison has very long. If you wanted to speak to him, now would be the time."

Cady rose on shaky feet, the dogs rising up too so she could lean against one of them if needed.

"Let me speak to Gabe first," she said.

Gabe had been helped to bed in one of the guest rooms. He looked like hell—pale and dirty, his cheeks hollowed out. But he was alive.

He sat up when Cady entered, but didn't smile. All he

said was "Addison?"

"Here. Still alive. The Disreputables have him under guard, but he told me he took a dose of clephobine as well, so he may not have long. Assuming he *did* take a dose and it's not some trick."

"You can find that out easily enough," Gabe said. "Just give him a dose of that stuff you gave me."

"What?"

"Whatever you put in my tea that night."

"Ohhhhh, you mean the verocine."

"Yes. Do you have more?"

"Well, there's a slight problem with the verocine."

"What's that?"

"It's not real."

Gabe blinked rapidly. "What?"

"I made it up. Like aphrodisiacs, truth serums don't really exist. But since most people believe they do, I thought that if I told you a chemical was loosening your inhibitions to speak, you'd be more open to saying the truth."

"Wait. You're telling me that that night, I wasn't under the influence of anything at all?"

"No. Whatever you told me, you told me because you wanted to. I just made a few suggestions to, er, encourage you."

His expression was one of disbelief. "Cady, that's the most devious thing I've ever heard of."

"I doubt that."

He sighed. "Fine. Well, you can still pull the same trick on him. He'll probably want to tell you the truth about everything anyway. I know that type. He wants you to know everything he did."

"I need you there," she said. "You know much more than I do about all the crimes he committed. And this might be your only chance to find out the details."

"Start your interrogation," Gabe advised. "I'll join you in a little bit."

She didn't like how weak and distant he sounded, but he was right that she should take advantage of the time she had.

Accompanied closely by the pair of wolfhounds, Cady followed Bond to the room where Mr Addison was being held. Jem was keeping watch on him. He leaned against one wall and never took his eyes off the prisoner.

"I've brought you something to drink," Cady told Mr Addison, holding up a glass of wine.

"Don't need it," he said in a thin, helpless voice.

"You're parched, and I have questions. Indulge me, Mr Addison. As a favor."

He looked up at her. Cady kept her expression as open and earnest as possible.

After a moment, he drank the wine down. "Thank you."

"No, thank you. I've been wanting to know how my verocine works on a subject other than myself. Can you imagine how frustrating it is test a truth serum when you know all the answers?" Cady quickly spun a new version of her imaginary chemical, and discovered that Addison seemed even more susceptible to the idea than Gabe had been.

"Why did you kidnap Gabe?" Cady asked, thinking she'd begin at the end, where memories were freshest.

"So it's Gabe, is it?" Addison asked, sounding put out.

"Yes, not that it's any of your business."

"Oh, Cady. Your family is very much my business. Your mother asked me to look after you, should anything happen to her and your father."

"Look after me? How exactly?"

"However I saw fit. Remember when I proposed to you?"

"I assumed it was a formality."

"Certainly not. And if you'd accepted, then none of this would have been necessary."

"Wait, you're saying that all of these deaths are *my* fault just because I didn't marry you?" Cady could hardly believe this man was the friend she'd always known.

"I did what I had to do to protect you, Cady. As your husband, I could have shielded you from all the cruel things life threw your way. I hoped that your father's removal would have made things easier, but alas, I was unable to anticipate the local reaction. Idiots."

"My father's removal?" she echoed.

"Yes. I was at the house the morning he died. Don't you remember? Anyway, it was during a round of drinks that I slipped him the clephobine."

"You killed my father? Why?"

Addison looked annoyed. "You know why, little Cady. That man was a beast. The things he said to you, the way he was starving your spirit. You forget that I knew you as a little girl. I watched you grow up while I worked alongside your mother. You were such a darling creature, all smiles and curiosity. A joy to know. But after Lady Calder died, I watched all the light drain from that house. He drove the boy away, but what he did to you was worse. Kept you shut up inside those walls with him all the time, pruning you into his vision of the perfect daughter so he could marry you off to just the right titled gentleman... with no care at all for what you might want. A breeding program of one."

"He was my father! And anyway, you breed roses!"

"Breeding plants is one thing. Breeding humans is disgusting, and no less so because it's been done for centuries. You know what happens when breeding stock doesn't expand? Disease, derangement, death."

Cady hated to admit that the man had a point. Still… "It's not an excuse for murder."

"It wasn't murder. It was *justice.* You have a brilliant mind. You're a botanist and a chemist without parallel. I wish my own experiments were half so successful."

"Oh, my Lord. You were there the whole time, watching me. And you never hinted that you cared for a thing beyond roses."

"Any idiot can grow a rose," he snarled. "Collecting new specimens was hardly more than a game to pass the time while I watched over you. If everyone thought of me as a harmless rose-head, then no one looked to me when it came to the cultivation of poisonous plants. I followed every breakthrough you made, Cady. I admired you for it. But when you synthesized the clephobine, I knew that I needed it. To take care of the people who were in my way. When you mentioned in passing that you'd made a dangerous chemical and you were giving it to Trevor to dispose of, I knew I didn't have much time to secure it for myself."

"But wait a moment. How *did* you get it?"

"My dear girl, you were not always as watchful as you got in the past several months. During one of those interminable teatimes with Pollack and the vicar's wife, I excused myself. And I used that time to go to your laboratory and open your cabinet of wonders. There was the clephobine, nicely labeled. I poured all of it into another bottle and refilled the original with a bit of water mixed with spirits to mimic the smell. I didn't think you'd use it again before you handed it off to your brother, and of course he wouldn't know it was a different substance altogether."

"And you killed people with what you stole!"

"Just the ones who needed to be removed."

"Tell me how," a new voice said.

Cady looked over her shoulder to see Gabe leaning against the doorway. He seemed as if he'd collapse at any moment, except for a certain hard glint in his eye.

"Mr Addison, you've caused a lot of trouble," he said. "When did you realize I was searching for the killer and the poison?"

"Not until you both left for London," Addison replied. "At first, I thought you were merely another shiftless worker, and that you'd be gone in a few weeks. While you were employed as a gardener at Calderwood, Lady Arcadia seemed to keep her distance, at least as far as I could tell. But Vernon did mention to me that he saw both of you alone together one afternoon. I didn't like that at all. But I had no proof that something untoward had happened, so I let you live."

"Why, thank you," Gabe said. "I suppose that it was the dinner party at Cady's London home that sealed my fate."

"I recognized you, of course! You did look very different with the dark hair and beard and your rough attire. Perhaps if your names hadn't been so close—Court, Courtenay—I might not have matched your old appearance with your new look as the son of a lord. But once I realized that you were the same person, using a disguise, it was quite logical to guess that you were at Calderwood to learn about the poison."

"Which you had procured long before." Gabe sighed. "Let's make this easy. I'll say the name of the victim, and you tell me why he died. The first death besides Lord Calder was Sir Michael Montgomery."

"He was a friend of Lord Calder. He's always wanted

the property of Calderwood, and he mentioned the idea of marrying Cady to her father. This was even before Calder requested the change in the letters patent. I didn't trust Montgomery a bit. He didn't have Cady's best interests at heart. He had to go. I arranged to call upon him on some pretext—I can't even remember what I said. We had drinks at White's and I dropped a little clephobine in his glass. He was found dead the next day, seemingly in the night, of natural causes. It was marvelous."

"If you'd stopped then," Gabe said, "it was likely that death from natural causes would have remained. But then there was John Worthham a month later."

"Ah yes, he worked with the Crown Office, did you know that? He learned about the letters patent request from Calder, and he grew interested in the idea of a young and marriageable Lady Calder. He's a member of White's too, and we happened to be chatting one evening and the subject came up since I'm a neighbor of the Osbourne family. Well, he was easy to dispatch and I saw no reason to let him linger."

"How efficient. Now, Baron Murol. What did he do?"

"He's a cousin to Mr Heath, and he met Cady at tea once, several months ago."

"My goodness, I didn't remember meeting him until now," Cady breathed. "He was visiting Mr Heath for a month and did come to tea once or twice."

"Well, he made some very crude remarks about your appearance, Cady," Mr Addison told her. "So when he casually mentioned that he might visit again with the goal of pursuing you, I decided to nip that in the bud. Gave him the poison in a bottle of whiskey I offered as a parting gift when he left for home. The man liked his whiskey. He died within the week."

"If you were killing all my potential suitors, why

didn't you kill Mr Pollack?"

Addison chuckled. "As if you'd ever accept him! I had no fear of that."

Cady nodded, though she was still stunned by the depth of Addison's obsession with "protecting" her.

"Charles Tompsett?" Gabe went on.

"Much the same. He went to school with Trevor Osbourne years ago. He visited Calderwood many times. Once I caught him ogling Cady when she didn't notice. She was so young and innocent then. This past year he came to the village of Dorbridge and we struck up a conversation. He asked if Cady was still unmarried. I didn't need to hear more. I asked him for dinner that evening, and did what I had to do. He traveled back to London the next day and had the excellent timing to die there.

"And as for Lewelleyn Parrish, you can guess. He was poking around London, asking a few too many questions about Arcadia Osbourne and the plants she grew and the nature of poisons. I couldn't have him spouting absurd suspicions about her being a killer, so I pretended to have some information he'd find helpful and arranged a meeting. When his back was turned, I doctored his coffee. Honestly, why people weren't more careful about things, I'll never know."

"I picked up where Parrish left off," Gabe told him. "Did you never think that you were taking too many chances? Why did you kill Malcolm MacCuley? I never found the connection to Cady there."

"Oh, that. Well, to be completely truthful, that was a more…personal issue. I owed him some money and he was pressing me to pay. He was very rude when we spoke at the hotel where I was staying…"

"The Hotel Napier," Jem said, from his post at the wall.

"Indeed. He came as I requested. And the bottle was right there, so…" He shrugged.

"Jesus. What about Huxley?"

"I overheard him speaking to someone at Kew Park. Kept talking about 'darling Osbourne' and 'precious Osbourne.' And I'd previously seen him hanging about with Cady's brother, so I assumed he intended to propose to Cady very soon. I also invited him for a chat at the hotel. He was a second son with no reliable income, not a good match for her at all. I couldn't risk it."

"He was talking about *me*, you idiot," Trevor spat. "For someone so obsessed with Cady, you've missed some rather large hints. He was a member of my club, and I was very fond of him…and his income or family lineage never came into play."

"Oh." Addison looked surprised, then slightly abashed. "Well, then that was a mistake."

"A *mistake*?" Cady echoed, appalled. "You didn't bother to confirm which Osbourne he was talking about before you killed him? That's more than a mistake."

"You don't sound very grateful, Cady."

"I'm not, Mr Addison. You did terrible things in my name, and caused me more pain than I can possibly convey. I lived in terror, not even knowing what exactly was going on. But I trusted you as a friend when I should not have. If I'm grateful for anything, it's the lesson you taught me—not to trust anyone purporting to have my best interests at heart."

"Sweet Cady, you have to forgive me."

"I certainly don't. Did you actually take any clephobine, or was that merely a feint to distract me when I found you in the tunnel?"

Addison sighed. "I may have…exaggerated a bit."

"But you did give a dose to Gabe." She glanced over

at Gabe's figure, remembering the terrifying moment when she thought she'd found him too late.

"Only when I saw the carriage approaching, and I knew you'd finally figured out my clue."

"*Close to your heart, burning in hell*," she quoted. "But why did you even send a clue? Why not just kill Gabe in London immediately?"

Addison shook his head sadly, saying, "Darling Cady, do you still not understand? It all starts and ends here at Calderwood. This is your home. I wanted to bring you back home, and this man was the way to do it. But I also wanted to prove my devotion to you."

Cady gasped. "By killing the man I fell in love with?"

"That's not love," he objected. "You're young, you don't understand love yet. Your infatuation with him would have faded with time."

"I don't think you're the appropriate person to explain love, considering that you've killed a lot of men to justify your version of it."

"Nonsense. Cady, you would have come to love me, as I've come to love you."

She shuddered at Addison's idea of love. "No. I'd have hated you forever. What you did wasn't done for love. You just wanted to put me in another box. Controlling me in a different way, deciding who was good enough for me, what I would be allowed to do."

Mr Addison just looked away, shaking his head, still not willing to accept that Cady couldn't ever love him.

"I need to rest now," Cady murmured. Romulus and Remus stood up the moment she shifted in her chair, providing her protection as she stood up.

"Cady, don't leave me!" Addison protested, only to earn growls from the dogs.

Jem muttered something rude under his breath, then

moved forward. "Let's get you somewhere all safe and sound, Mr Addison. Wouldn't want anything permanent to happen to you before we hand you off to the law."

"Is that his destination?" Cady asked.

"Should be, my lady," Jem said. "I'll see that he doesn't have a chance to take anything before the Zodiac chats with him and then hands him off to the usual authorities. All right, Mr Courtenay?"

But there was no answer. When Cady looked back, the doorway was empty. Gabe had gone.

$\mathrm{\mathsf{\eta_o}}$

GABE LOVED SUNSHINE. HE LOVED air. He loved water. He loved not starving. He loved not being fed poison.

A week had passed since Cady and the Disreputables had found him. After rallying for the brief interrogation, he spent two days in a bedroom at Calderwood, weak and delirious from all the drugs Addison had made him take with the water. He dreamed of Cady, but the dreams always turned into nightmares, and the few times Cady actually did visit him, he kept warning her away.

On the third day, Jem drove the carriage slowly back to London. He half lay on one seat, and Cady sat on the other side, looking nervous and worried—just as she had the first few times he saw her. It seemed all the progress she made toward facing her fears was now lost. He blamed himself for getting her too involved.

In London, he was brought to his impersonal, depressing home. Cady left with the carriage, telling him that she planned to remain in town for two weeks because they expected to hear back from the Crown Office soon, and it might require several visits to solicitors if matters changed.

He felt physically better a few days later, only to receive a note from Aries, requesting a debriefing and then hinting at another assignment. He crumpled the note up. The zeal that used to propel him from one mission to the next and the next was absent, and Gabe didn't know when it would return.

Worse, he wasn't sure he wanted it to. The long, deep silence of his entrapment gave him plenty of time to think, and he thought that the agent known as Capricorn wasn't a particularly good person to be. Yes, he'd been effective. Yes, he'd done exactly what was asked of him, and he did it uncomplainingly and often enthusiastically.

But to do it, he'd hurt a lot of people. Some had deserved it. But others had not.

People like Cady. He absolutely took advantage of her and manipulated her in ways that anyone would call reprehensible. And the fact that he'd come to love her didn't excuse his actions.

God. He loved her. Gabe was not good at loving people, and perhaps he ought to vanish into the murky underworld of espionage just to avoid the consequences of knowing that he'd—after years of avoiding it for personal and professional reasons—fallen in love. And not just a little. It physically hurt to think of a life without her.

But that's what he faced, because not only did he love Cady, he'd also lied to her and betrayed her. And now he was here to apologize for it, so that he could take on his next assignment with a clear head.

Ha.

He raised his hand to the door knocker of the town house, and let it fall again.

He was afraid.

Afraid of what Cady would say, how she'd look at him. No matter how he felt about her, Gabe had treated her terribly, and she had every right to never want to see him again.

He summoned his courage, or tried. Before he could knock, the door opened. Rook stood there, dressed in his livery as footman. "What are you doing…sir?" he asked with less than the usual deference.

"I'm here to see Lady Arcadia. If she's at home. I mean, I know she's at home. I mean, at home to me."

"You'd better step inside," Rook said, rolling his eyes. "Her ladyship and Mr Osbourne are at breakfast, but I'll go see if she's at home. Wait in the parlor."

Gabe paced in the parlor, half thinking he should just leave before he made things even worse. Mr Osbourne! Rook's use of the name meant that the Crown Office had indeed granted the old lord's request, and the letters patent had been amended to allow the title and estate to pass to Cady, making her into Lady Calder and Trevor into plain Mr Osbourne. Which was probably for the best—Trevor didn't want the title, and Cady was much better suited to act as caretaker of Calderwood anyway. And her elevation to heiress would of course make her all the more desirable on the marriage mart. No third sons for her, not now that she could have her pick of first sons.

And then Cady came through the doorway. She wasn't wearing mourning any longer. Now she was resplendent in a pastel gown that made her look light on her feet, and illuminated her face in a way that the dark outfits never did.

He straightened up as she approached. "My lady."

"Stop with the false formality," Cady said irritably, taking a seat on one of the tufted chairs by the window. "Sit down if you want to talk. It hurts my neck to look up that much."

Well, that more or less told him how delighted she was to see him. Nevertheless, Gabe sat on the chair across from her and leaned forward. "You decided to stay at the town house?"

"For a while," she said. "I've spent more than enough time at Calderwood after all. This is a change of scenery for me. And I've found a doctor who actually exhibits an interest in treating my condition, rather than dismissing it. Naturally, she is a woman. She's German and calls herself a…what's the word…psychiatrist."

"Oh, that's good."

"Yes, it is." She added nothing more.

It was time to get to the point. "Cady, I need to apologize."

"Then do it," she said calmly, her eyes locked on his.

"Er…may I?"

"It wouldn't make much sense to come all the way here and not say what's on your mind. So proceed, Mr Courtney."

"Cady, you didn't deserve to be used the way I used you. I could try to justify it as necessary to fulfill my assignment to locate the poison and the killer behind it all, but the fact is that I could have been honest with you much earlier, and I don't have any good reason for why I didn't, except that I'm not used to…" He groped for the right words.

"Trusting people?"

"Yes," he agreed in a rush. "I didn't trust you. Worse, I made it so you could never trust me. And I am sorry for that, Cady. I can't expect you to forgive me for it, but I want you to know that I regret what I did."

"What, specifically, do you regret?"

Gabe paused. Was this a trick question? "Everything?"

"You regret everything you did to me?"

He wasn't sure what she meant. Cady was giving him nothing to work with. Her expression was so cool and unrevealing, like a stranger's. He settled for, "I regret the things that hurt you."

"Ah." Cady leaned back in her chair, and looked out the window. "And do you regret anything else?"

He sighed. "More than you'll ever know. But that's not really the point. I just wanted to come and let you know that I am sorry. It doesn't change anything, but I couldn't bear you thinking that I..." God, this was difficult. "After what I did, and how you found out the truth of my reasons for coming to Calderwood...no one would have blamed you for forgetting about me entirely."

Cady's brow furrowed. "Did you think everyone had abandoned you? While you were trapped there, did you think no one was trying to find you? That *I* wasn't trying?"

"Hope's a difficult thing to hold on to in situations like that," he confessed. "Sometimes I thought you were—or someone was. And other times I was sure I was the last person on the whole earth."

He saw her jaw clench and the ripple of her throat as she swallowed. Then she said, "I suppose I can't fully understand what you felt. Who could, if they didn't experience it? And it's true that just for a little while, right at the beginning, before we knew you'd been taken, I really did wish I'd never met you."

Gabe closed his eyes. "I'm sorry. If it's any consolation, you'll never see me again."

"I have no intention of hiding for the rest of my life," said Cady, mistaking his meaning. "All this horribleness has had one good effect. I've learned that I'm not necessarily safe behind a locked door, and that it is possible to be hurt but still survive."

"Good," he said. "I'm glad to hear that, I truly am. You're going to thrive, Cady. And you'll find someone who makes you happy and that you deserve..."

"Yes, I already have."

He blinked. How long had he been underground? "You have?"

"Yes." She gave him a tiny smile.

"When? Who?"

Cady inhaled, opened her mouth to speak, then shook her head. "Oh, my Lord."

"Never mind. You don't have to tell me. I've got nothing to do with it."

She raised her chin, looking more determined. "Yes, you do."

"How?" he asked, puzzled.

"It's you, you dolt."

"What's me?"

She pinched the bridge of her nose, murmuring something under her breath. Then she stood up. "Gabe, I want *you*. I'll be marrying *you*, whenever you get around to actually asking. And I'll be spending my life with *you*."

"But you can do better. You're Lady Calder now. You're the heiress, and you'll have so many suitors."

"Boring ones, who are only interested in my title and wealth. At least I know you're interested in my bed as well."

"Your bed," he echoed. Hell yes, that was a fact.

"I suppose I should say our bed…or it will be, after we're married."

He nodded slowly, his mind working around the boulders he'd placed in his own path. "Yes. Yes, that's…yes."

Cady was still speaking, being very practical in her tone. "And when we're not acting out all our most deeply held desires, because we'll need to occasionally do other things, I know that we'll get along. You're the right kind of funny, and you're gentle and kind and always willing to listen to me. Plus you're good with dogs."

He laughed, not believing his luck. "Oh, Christ. Cady, will you actually marry me?"

"That depends. Why should I?" She asked that with a

raised eyebrow, challenging him even after what she'd just said.

There was only one correct answer, and Gabe finally knew what it was.

"Because I love you."

"Then, yes," Cady said, smiling wider. "I'll marry you."

She rose up on her toes to kiss him and he made it easier by picking her up and holding her close. The kiss went on and on, with Cady murmuring a waterfall of words that didn't make much sense but were all very flattering and sweet and made Gabe think he had a future after all. The best part was when she said *I love you* over and over.

He put her down only when Trevor strolled in, still holding his morning coffee, and insisted on hearing what had happened, though the outcome must have been quite obvious.

Gabe set Cady on her feet again, whispering, "Are you certain about this, blossom? Once your brother knows, the world knows."

"I'm not scared to go through with it." There was a challenge in her eyes. "Are you?"

"Never." He kissed her once more to seal the bargain.

"This is how it was always supposed to go," she whispered. "Besides, I *really* need a gardener."

ABOUT THE AUTHOR

Elizabeth Cole is a romance writer with a penchant for history. Her stories draw upon her deep affection for the British Isles, action movies, medieval fantasies, and even science fiction. She now lives in a small house in a big city with a cat, a snake, and a rather charming gentleman. When not writing, she is usually curled in a corner reading...or watching costume dramas or things that explode. And yes, she believes in love at first sight.